LIZ

Liz Allen isn't going to take it anymore. Men have been trying to victimize her all her young life. But that ends when the fat local sheriff strips her and whips her alone in a cell. It ends with a dead sheriff and Liz on the run. She soon finds Gunson, a pretty-boy hood, and together they create their own little crime spree. But you don't turn your back on Liz for long, and Gunson soon discovers that he's as expendable as the next guy—who turns out to be a hood named Lew Barker. Trouble is, they all figure they know more than Liz. They all figure they're more ruthless than a woman. They know the score. But they all learn the hard way—Liz makes it on her terms, and she's got nothing to lose.

SYNDICATE GIRL

Jackson City is owned by the syndicate. Everyone knows it. Step out of line, you get a bullet your way, courtesy of Zito's men. It's Captain Marcy Lewis's job to keep it that way. But now District Attorney Mal Waters has decided to step in and do something about it. And he's got the city's only respectable newspaper behind him. But Waters is up against the men who put him in office, the men in Zito's pocket. He's also up against his fiancé, who has her own plans and doesn't want him rocking the boat. Zito and the Syndicate have got all the aces in this game, and all Waters has got is his determination. They've framed him, and they've humiliated him. Then he meets Mary Lister, the Syndicate's girl, and he sees a way out….

Liz

Syndicate Girl

Frank Kane

STARK
HOUSE

Stark House Press • Eureka California

LIZ / SYNDICATE GIRL

Published by Stark House Press
1315 H Street
Eureka, CA 95501
griffinskye3@sbcglobal.net
www.starkhousepress.com

ISBN: 1-933586-59-1
ISBN-13: 978-1-933586-59-5

Book design by Mark Shepard, shepgraphics.com
Proofreading by Rick Ollerman

First Stark House Press Edition: April 2015
FIRST EDITION

Frank Kane
An Introduction by Robert J. Randisi

It starts with the name.

Frank Kane.

Frank.

Kane.

Two syllables.

Tough and lean, like the man's writing.

No nonsense.

Plus, I think Frank Kane came along at the right time.

The private eye may have been born in the pages of the pulps. But he was formed, fine-tuned and perfected in the pages of the paperbacks (both original and reprint) of the 40's, 50's and 60's. Kane's contemporaries were Brett Halliday, Mickey Spillane, Harry Whittington, Lionel White, Gil Brewer, Fredric Brown, William Ard, and many others, including the other Kane, Henry. Of course, Spillane was at the head of the class, but all of these authors made their contributions to the genre, and certainly Frank Kane's contribution was significant.

My own personal introduction to Frank Kane was a novel called *BULLET PROOF*, a 1961 reprint of one of his Johnny Liddell books. Liddell was a New York private eye who appeared in 29 novels from 1947 to 1967. Liddell is drawn in the quintessential P.I. mode—smart, tough, clever, good with the ladies and while Kane has been criticized for being formulaic, I find him to be at the top of the P.I. food chain. Yes, the P.I. genre is largely formulaic, but that formula was invented in the paperbacks of the 50's (forgive me for repeating myself, but I believe in this point). It can be looked back on as—to use another word— "cliché," but it wasn't so at the time. Kane was right in there with the best of them, putting his stamp on the genre.

For me, the series had much in common with Brett Halliday's Mike Shayne novels—beyond the fact that they were both reprinted in paper by Dell Books with great covers by the Roberts McGinnis, McGuire and Stanley, Ron Lesser and Harry Bennett, among others—in that New York was as much a character in the Liddell books as Miami was in the Shayne novels.

Also similar in style, tone and substance, was Henry Kane's Peter Chambers series, which was also set in New York. Frank Kane, however, came to writing

New York based P.I. novels armed with a wealth of experience and knowledge. He wrote for New York newspapers, eventually penning a column called "New York from Dusk to Dawn," which followed Hollywood movie stars visiting Broadway. The column later led to a radio show. He also spent some time working in Washington, D.C. on the efforts to end prohibition, and spent much time writing radio scripts for *THE SHADOW, GANGBUSTERS, MR. KEEN, TRACER OF LOST PERSONS*, and many more popular programs of the time.

Kane also had a brother who was a New York City cop, which meant that his cops—unlike those in many private eye novels—smacked of more realism than most, rather than just being the private eye's "chum." In '47 he quit his radio job to start writing his Johnny Liddell novels. Johnny also appeared in countless short stories that appeared in pulp magazine and paperback collection such as *JOHNNY LIDDELL'S MORGUE* (Dell, 1956). Later still, he went on to write for TV.

CBS had approached him about a Johnny Liddell TV series, but they could not come to an agreement on terms. They did, however, form a working relationship and Kane wrote for Mike Hammer's Mickey Spillane series starring Darren McGavin—many of the scripts being adapted from Kane's own short stories. He also wrote for shows such as *Special Agent 7* and *The Investigators*.

The other similarity between the Mike Shayne and Johnny Liddell books is that they were both written in the smart alecky, almost arrogant vein that many of the 50's and 60's private eye series adopted—and fiddled with—and Richard Prather perfected with his Shell Scott series. Kane, however, had more than that to offer, and that is what is represented herein with these two novels, *LIZ* and *SYNDICATE GIRL*.

SYNDICATE GIRL is a hard-edged crime novel that is significantly darker than the Johnny Liddell books. With this tale Kane shows his dexterity with the truly hardboiled form. No smart aleck wise cracks, no over the top gunsels or babes. It's not forced, and the light touch of the Liddell novels is not missed. The cops, gangsters, the lawyers and politicians ring true, all drawn from Kane's past experiences. He draws a successful, realistic picture of a city being crushed beneath the fist—not just the thumb—of a powerful syndicate, and not a private eye in sight to save the day. Instead, that task falls to a young district attorney.

With *LIZ*, still another side of Kane's talent is shown. The main character is not a P.I., not a cop, lawyer, gangster or politician. It's a beautiful young girl, fending for herself in a word of brutal men and venal women. Once again Kane illustrates the scope of his skill, telling most of the story from the point of view of the girl, Liz, who adapts to her surroundings, and becomes a girl who almost always gets her way.

And so the appeal of Frank Kane—to me, anyway, and perhaps to you—is that he is not a one-trick pony, as many of the others of his time were. Oh, they were all very good at that one trick, but Kane was facile with all of his. He proves this with *LIZ* and *SYNDICATE GIRL*, as you will see as you move forward.

My advice is to read and enjoy these two books, then go out and keep reading Frank Kane.

Frank.

Kane.

Good name.

Great writer.

Clarkesville, MO
January 2015

Liz

by Frank Kane

ONE
The Kill

The girl stood on the iron cot in her cell, pressed her face against the barred window. The jail was a low adobe building set back in a clump of trees. From her window, she looked out into matted underbrush and shrubs. She tried to remember how many days she had spent in the hot, foul-smelling cell; couldn't separate the days and the nights.

She got down from the cot, paced the rough floor of the cell. A cheap blue cotton dress made an ineffectual attempt to disguise the shapeliness of her body. As she walked, her full hips worked smoothly against the shoddy fabric, her high breasts almost burst through the cloth. Her hair was black, thick and gleaming, as it cascaded down over her shoulders.

Somewhere from up front came the sound of a metal door grating open. The girl stopped pacing, faced the cell door apprehensively. Shuffling footsteps scuffed down the short corridor toward her cell. Involuntarily, the girl backed away, flattened herself against the far wall. She stared at the cell door with black eyes smouldering, her bared teeth white against the redness of her lips. Her breasts rose and fell in increased agitation.

The shuffling feet came to a halt in front of her cell. They belonged to a short, fat old man. He wore a Stetson perched on the back of his head; an untidy thatch of yellow-white hair stuck out from under the brim. His gray shirt was stained under the arms with half-moons of dried sweat, his jeans were sun-bleached and clumsily patched. On his left breast-pocket he wore a star.

"How's my boarder?" He leered through the bars. In the half light, silver bristles glistened on his chin and upper lip.

"Let me alone."

The old man swung a heavy key on a massive old-fashioned iron ring. "That wouldn't be hospitable, would it, Liz? Ain't right not to pay a little visit to my guest."

"You have no right to keep me locked in here, Sheriff. I haven't done anything. You let me out of here."

The sheriff fitted the key into the big lock. "You act like you don't understand, Liz. It's my duty. You're a bad 'un. It's my sworn duty to reform you."

"I haven't done anything. You got no right to lock me up."

The fat man pushed the door open, stepped through, kicked the door shut behind him. He reached through the bars, turned the key in the lock. "Now don't start acting up, Liz. I ain't aiming to hurt you."

"I'm warning you, Sheriff. You better not lay a hand on me. I'm warning you."

The sheriff shrugged, unbuckled the heavy leather belt around his waist. "You got too much high spirit, Liz. You gotta be broke. A woman's like a horse. No dang good unless she's broke."

The girl's dark eyes followed the belt as he swirled it in front of him. "You lay a hand on me again, and I'll kill you. I swear it."

The fat man swung the belt over his head, lashed out at the girl. She let out a low animal scream as it cut into the flesh of her back. She ran to the far corner of the cell, huddled there. He continued to whip her. The belt found her rounded flesh, brought strangled moans, left large welts.

A stream of saliva glistened from the corner of the sheriff's mouth. He wiped it with the back of his hand, stood straddle-legged over the girl. He was breathing heavily, his shirt was plastered to his back.

"Get on your feet, girl," he told her huskily.

The girl sat huddled in the corner, her elbows shielding her face. She didn't move, gave no sign that she had heard.

The sheriff raised the belt, lashed down at her. His arm continued to rise and fall, the belt snapped monotonously at her flesh. Finally, he stopped. "Ready to do like you're told?" he panted.

The girl nodded, pulled herself to her feet. She stood before him, her chest heaving, her eyes bright with hate. "I'll kill you for this," she spat at him through clenched teeth. "You'll see. I'll kill you for what you're doing to me."

"Take that rag off," the fat man told her. His eyes had almost receded behind the discolored triangles of flesh that buttressed them.

She stood motionless, her dark eyes defying him.

The fat man reached out a pudgy hand, caught the top of the dress, pulled. It ripped open down the front, spilled her breasts free. They were startlingly white in contrast to the sun-tanned darkness of her throat and neck. She made no effort to resist, stood there contemptuously as the old man pawed at her only covering.

"You'll do damn well like I say," his voice was hoarse. "There's no one knows you're here. No one but me. And you'll do what I tell you." He tore the dress free, threw it across the cell.

She was long-legged, full-hipped. Her breasts were round, firm and pink-tipped, her stomach flat. The whiteness of her thighs and buttocks was marred by the angry red welts left by the strap.

The sheriff wiped the beads of perspiration from his face with the crook of his arm, licked at his lips with a thick, red tongue.

"Come here to me," he ordered.

The girl didn't move.

He took a step toward her, caught her by the back of the neck, pulled her to him. He could feel the soft firmness of her breasts against his chest, the pressure of her thighs against him. He covered her mouth with his. His lips were wet, loose. The girl offered no resistance as he scooped her breast into his hand, fondled it.

"Now you're being smart, Liz. Be nice to me and you won't get hurt." He kissed her again, then pushed her away. "Walk around a bit, girl," he told her.

Liz stood like a statue, only her hate-filled eyes giving any indication that she lived.

The sheriff bared his discolored teeth in a humorless grin. "You must like the belt. Every so often you run across a woman that does." He lashed out at her, grinned as she winced when the leather cut into her skin. He lashed at her again, she fell back. "Got enough?"

"Got enough," she gasped.

"Now do like I told you. Walk around. Walk nice and slow."

She walked flat-footed across the cell. Her hips worked slow and easy, the muscles in her buttocks quivering. At the far end she turned, started back, her breasts swaying with each step. As she passed where he stood, the fat man reached out, caught her by the arm. He pulled her to him. Her body went limp, unresisting.

"That's more like it, maybe you are learning something." He pressed his wet lips against hers, pulled her body close to him, arched her back with his knee between hers.

Suddenly, the girl's muscles tensed. She brought her knee up sharply, sank it into the old man's groin. His eyes watering with pain, he released his hold on the girl, sank moaning to his knees. He drew gasping lungsfuls of air.

The girl stood over him, spit down at him.

He looked up at her with pain-reddened eyes. "You'll pay for that trick, you devil." He reached out for her, and when she stepped out of his reach, he sprawled flat on his face.

The girl backed up to the cell door, reached through, caught the iron key ring, drew it through the bars. She waited while the sheriff pulled himself painfully to his feet, stood swaying in front of her. His chin was wet with saliva, his eyes bloodshot as he weaved toward her, reached out with clenched hands.

The girl grasped the key, raised it over her head, brought the heavy iron ring down on his head. It knocked him to his knees. A thin stream of blood started down the side of his cheek. He stared at her, his mouth agape, his eyes clouded with disbelief. She brought the key ring down again, knocked him to the floor.

Then she reached through the bars, unlocked the cell door. She stepped out into the corridor, walked back to the little cubicle he used as an office.

When she reappeared at the cell door, the sheriff was sitting on the edge of her cot, his face in his hands. He wiped the blood from the side of his head with the palm of his hand, stared at it stupidly. When he became aware of the girl in the doorway, he pulled himself to his feet wobbily. "You should have gotten away when you had the chance. Now I'm going to—" His eyes froze on the .45 she held in her hand.

"I borrowed your gun, Sheriff." She pointed its muzzle at the spot where his belt buckle would have been. "I didn't think you'd mind."

The sheriff's face turned a murky white. His loose lips worked hard at a smile, missed it by a mile. They seemed to have difficulty framing words. "What you doin' with that gun, girl? You'll just get in trouble." He held out his hand, couldn't control its shake. "Give it here and we'll just forget what happened."

The girl bared her white teeth in a taunting grin. "How would I get in trouble? Nobody knows I'm here. You said so yourself. I could just pull the trigger and nobody'd ever know who did it."

The sheriff wiped the wet smear of his lips with the back of his hand. "I didn't mean you no harm. I did it for your good. This way there's no record. You won't have a record, and—"

"You're a liar. You didn't book me because you didn't want anybody to know I was here. You wanted to keep me here for your own fun. Okay, you've had your fun. Now it's my turn."

The fat man shook his head weakly. His lower lip drooped, he couldn't control the twitch under his left eye. He backed away. "Don't be a fool, Liz. They'd get you. You don't have to stay here any more. You can walk out now. I won't try to stop you."

The girl laughed humorlessly. "What's the matter, Sheriff? Am I losing my appeal?" She cupped a breast in her hand, taunted him. "I thought you liked me like this." She wet her lips with the tip of her tongue, half closed her eyes. "Come on and take me."

The fat man nodded eagerly. "I knew you weren't mad at old Tom. You're not, are you?" He took a wobbly step toward her. "See, some women like to be treated rough and—"

The .45 boomed like a cannon in the confined space. The heavy slug caught the fat man just below the breast bone, slammed him back against the wall. He slid to the floor, his hands clawing at his midsection, trying futilely to stem the flow of red. As his eyes rolled up to her, she squeezed the trigger twice more.

Two puffs of dust came from the shirt, the old man sighed softly, the clawing hands relaxed. He continued to stare up at her, but the eyes were lifeless.

"I warned you, Sheriff. I warned you that I'm through getting pushed around by men. From now on it's my turn to do the pushing."

TWO
B-Girl

Mickey's Place, a sprawling, peeled-log cabin set back about fifty feet from the dirt road, had plenty of customers. A flickering neon that muttered ceaselessly to itself spilled a red pool out toward the road, dyed the drooping branches of the pines that sheltered it. In front, there was a clustered collection of parked cars, late model and jalopy, gleaming and mud-stained.

The girl stopped down the road, melted back into the shadows, watched the entrance for a moment. She was exhausted by the four hours of steady walking since she'd slipped out the back door of the jail fifteen or more miles behind her.

She wore a man's shirt that hung loosely from her shoulders, the sleeves rolled up above her elbows. The pants were lapped and overlapped at the waist where she had draped them around her. She was grateful for the reassuring weight of the .45 rolled up in the jacket under her arm.

She stood in the shadows indecisively for a moment, then she took a long breath, cut across the road toward the entrance.

In the doorway she waited until her eyes had accustomed themselves to the dimness. To the left she made out a long bar presided over by a gaunt, cadaverous man wearing a vest and no tie. Beyond was a postagestamp dance floor ringed by tables set so closely to pass among them bargirls had to rub thighs and buttocks against the shoulders of the male patrons.

Forty or fifty youngsters had their heads together over the tables and a steady hum of conversation, spiced by shrill laugher, spilled out into the bar room. On the floor another dozen couples were glued together, swaying slowly and suggestively—to the rhythms of a garish jukebox against the back wall. A thick pall of dirty smoke stirred uneasily in the liquor-polluted air.

The man behind the bar looked up from a glass he was polishing, stared at Liz. "Want something, sister?"

She sidled across to the bar, leaned against it. "A beer."

The bartender put the glass on the backbar, shuffled over. "What were you figuring on using for money, sister?" The toothpick in the corner of his mouth wobbled as he spoke.

"I can pay my way." Liz pulled a couple of crumpled bills from the pants pocket, held them out to him.

The bartender shrugged, selected a glass from the backbar, made a production of holding it under the tap. He slopped the glass half beer, half foam in front of her. "Ain't seen you hereabouts before now. Stranger?"

The girl nodded, sipped at her beer, grimaced. "Call that beer?"

The bartender nodded amiably, bared his yellowed teeth in a grin. "That's what we call it." He picked up one of the bills, rang up 15¢ on the cash register, dropped three quarters and a dime on the bar in front of her. "Planning on staying long?"

"Depends. Who would I see around here for a job?"

The man behind the bar chewed on his toothpick, pulled it from between his teeth, studied the yellowed end. "What can you do?"

"Hustle drinks. Anything the rest of them can do."

The bartender pursed his lips, pinched at his nostrils with thumb and forefinger. He leaned over the bar, shook his head at the bunched in trousers, the baggy shirt. "Them the only clothes you got?"

The girl nodded. "Maybe you can help me out until I get some."

"Could be." He squinted at the shapeless clothes, tried to visualize her without them, shook his head. "Only I got to see what I'm buying first."

The girl hesitated a moment, then nodded. "Okay." She picked up the glass in front of her, took a deep swallow.

"What's your name, sister?"

"Liz Allen." She drained the glass set it back on the bar. "Where do I go?"

He nodded at a door at the end of the bar. "There's some cabins around back. Use Cabin One, the first one off the back door. I'll be back soon's I get someone to watch the bar."

The back door opened onto a small overgrown path that meandered among four mean, unpainted prefabricated shacks. A muffled rumble of conversation and an occasional shrill giggle rose from the darkness.

As she stood outside Cabin One, the door to the end cabin opened. A boy and a girl came out, the girl adjusting her dress, her make-up smeared in the dim light. The boy staggered as she guided him back toward the bar. As they passed Liz, they both stared, giggled, then disappeared through the back door.

Liz pushed open the door to the cabin, fumbled until she found the light switch on the wall. A pale, ineffectual yellow light spilled from the single bracket in the ceiling, revealing a huge, badly made double bed, a mirror hanging askew on the wall, a half-open door leading to a lavatory.

She walked wearily to the bed, sat on the side of it. After a moment she unrolled the .45 from the jacket, tucked it under the pillow. Then she settled down to wait.

It wasn't a long wait. Less than five minutes later the door opened. The bartender came in, kicked the door shut with his heel. He carried a yellow dress over his arm, tossed it toward the bed. He glared at the fully dressed girl angrily. "What's the matter? Change your mind?"

"No, but—"

"But nothing, sister. I told you I don't buy anything sight unseen," he growled at her. "If you don't want the job, say so."

"I want the job."

"Then get those things off. You're covered up like a circus tent."

Liz nodded. She stood up, opened the buttons on the shirt, slid it back from her shoulders. The man's eyes narrowed at the clean line of her shoulders, the trimness of her waist, the round firmness of her breasts. He puckered his lips in a soundless whistle. "The rest of it."

She loosened the belt, let the plants slide down her legs to form a puddle on the floor, stepped out of them, kicked them aside with her toe.

She stood there, gave no sign of annoyance at the inventory he took of her obvious assets.

"You sure been hiding some stuff, sister," he nodded. "Some stuff." He shuffled toward her. "I'll buy it."

"That's not the deal. It ain't for sale. All I want's a job."

The bartender grinned at her crookedly. "Now that ain't the way to talk to the guy who can give it to you. How's about being nice so maybe I'll get big-hearted and hire you." He reached out, tried to grab her, scowled when she evaded him, slipped under his arms.

"Forget about the job. I'm getting out of here," Liz told him. "Go away and let me get dressed."

"A teaser, huh? You don't think you can get away with that with old Sam, do you?" he growled. "You'll get out of here when I'm ready to let you go."

"I'm warning you, mister. I don't want any trouble with you, but if you lay a hand on me you'll be sorry."

The thin man grinned obscenely at her. "What'll you do, yell? This is my joint. I'll have you tossed in the brig and throw the key away." His voice dropped to a wheedle. "Why don't you be nice? Old Sam's not the kind of guy forgets a friend. All's I want's a friendly little kiss. That ain't going to hurt no-body."

He moved suddenly, with a speed surprising in a man his age, caught her around the waist. She could smell the foulness of his breath as he pulled her to him. He seemed surprised as she backed toward the bed, grinned knowingly as she sank back on it.

He couldn't see her hand as it slid under the pillow, closed over the butt of the .45. She offered little resistance as he forced her back onto the bed. He leaned over her, pressed wet, slack lips against the side of her neck.

"Cut it out, Sam," a deep brassy voice rasped.

The thin man stiffened, pulled away from the girl, looked toward the door fearfully.

The woman standing there was tall, big-boned, deep-chested. A shapeless brown dress was tied sloppily around her middle, emphasizing her bigness. Her eyes were hard, heavily underlined with make-up, while the rest of her face was blotchy with old, caked powder. Her lipstick was a red, uneven smear across her face, and a mop of yellow, coarse hair was piled untidily on top of her head.

"I wasn't fixing to do anything, Mickey. She got me in here, and—"

"Get out." The big woman's eyes were narrowed, angry. She stood aside contemptuously as the thin man scuttled past her, through the door, slamming it after him. "Who are you and what are you doing here, sister?" She turned back to Liz.

"Looking for a job. He said it was his place, and—"

"It's my place. I'm Mickey. I give out the jobs here."

"I didn't know." Liz slid her hand from under the pillow, reached over for the pants.

"Where you going?" the yellow-haired woman wanted to know.

Liz stopped with one foot in the pants, looked up. "You don't want me around here, do you?"

"You said you wanted a job, didn't you?" Mickey pursed her heavy lips, looked the girl over. "Stand up and let's take a good look at you."

The girl dropped the pants, straightened up. The older woman walked around her, nodded. "Not bad. What you been doing up to now?"

"On the road."

"How old are you?"

"Nineteen."

Mickey rubbed the heel of her hand along the side of her jaw. "You ain't in any jam?"

The girl shook her head.

"How about them marks? How'd you get 'em?"

"My old man. He took a strap to me. That's why I ran away," Liz told her. "Look, lady, I want that job awful bad. Do I get it?"

The yellow-haired woman considered, nodded. "Okay. You get it." She walked over to the crumpled pants on the floor, stirred them with her toe. "These the only rags you got?"

Liz nodded. "He brought me that." She pointed to the yellow dress on the bed. "He was going to let me wear it until I could get my own stuff."

Mickey nodded, walked over to the bed, sank onto it with a sigh. "Put it on." She watched critically while Liz slid the dress over her shoulders, smoothed it down against her thighs, nodded her satisfaction. "Fits real good."

"This all I get to wear?"

Mickey's laugh was a deep rumble in her throat. "That's all any of the girls wear. You got to give the boys a little run for their money. They get real peeved when they set out to cop a feel and find a pair of pants. After all, they're paying for it. Or maybe you got some objections?"

"I got no objections."

"Good," the older woman nodded. She studied the girl critically. "Got any powder or lipstick?"

Liz shook her head.

"You'll need some. And that mop of yours. Pile it on top of your head like mine. Them kids out there got an idea that's how the movie stars wear theirs and that's what they want."

Liz caught her thick, black hair, piled it on top of her head, turned to the big woman. "Like this?" The girl got a nod of approval.

"You'll do." She pulled herself to her feet with a grunt. "You can start tonight. We're short-handed anyway."

"How do I get paid?"

"The same as any bar girl. Percentage. Keep pushing the drinks and don't let no empty glasses set. If you can make them buy you one that's all to the good. You get ginger ale and he pays for scotch. Don't let no slow drinkers take up space at your tables." She patted the girl on the hip. "Stacked like you are, you ought to do all right."

Liz nodded. "What about the cabins? That part of the job?"

The big woman shrugged. "That's up to you. You want to hustle a couple of bucks on the side, I got no objection. The cabin costs you a buck every time you use it. Only, dearie, I wouldn't count too much on it. There's too much free amateur stuff out there for a girl to make a decent buck."

Liz nodded. "Okay. Just so I know what I'm letting myself in for." She pulled the dress down tight over her hips, approved the effect. "I'll get a dress as soon as I can, and—"

"Don't bother, dearie. I take care of all that. The dress'll cost you fifteen. You get all your dresses through me. Shoes are ten and make-up five. It'll come out of your cut the end of the week. Okay?"

"Okay."

"Smart girl," the yellow-haired woman chuckled. "Any other questions?"

"Just one. What about that guy Sam?"

"Him? You don't owe him nothing. He makes another pass at you, cut it off for him. You don't have to take nothing from nobody but the customers."

THREE
Flesh Peddler

Nights at Mickey's Place soon fell into a familiar routine. The same gang of slack-lipped kids showed up night after night to whirl frenetically to the beat of recorded music, then stumble back to their tables and booths where they petted openly. Liz got used to the drunken fumbling of immature hands as she squeezed between customers at the tightly packed tables.

The murder of the sheriff in the adjoining county created a week's sensation. Often during that time Liz fancied she caught Mickey's appraising eye on her, but the big woman never brought up the subject. There was much speculation, much whispering, but it all seemed to die down with the naming of a new sheriff. Liz began to breathe easier, feel more secure. But with security came boredom, the old familiar yearning to hit the road.

It all came to a head on a Saturday night.

Liz was leaning against the bar when they came in. The taller one was dark, curly-headed, his good looks marred only by the weakness of his chin. He stood in the doorway, looked around arrogantly, enjoying the attention his appearance evoked. His companion was a year or two older, hair cut in crew style, heavy horn-rimmed glasses perched on the bridge of a ski nose. His jaw was full, his lips well shaped. He wore a perpetual half grin.

"Who's the hot shot, Sam?" Liz asked the man behind the bar.

Sam stopped polishing a glass long enough to look up. "The Gunson brat. I didn't know he was out." He reached down under the bar, pressed a button. "Mickey ain't going to like this. She didn't like Gunson hanging around. Makes trouble."

"Serve time?"

Sam nodded, breathed on the glass, resumed polishing it. "Drew a five to ten a couple of years back. He must still owe some of it."

"I thought places like this were off limits to guys on parole?"

"They are," Sam agreed placidly. "Gunson don't pay no mind to rules like that."

Liz watched the newcomer as he strutted toward an empty booth. He stopped on the way at a couple of tables, pounded an acquaintance on the back or leaned over a particularly attractive girl. Liz noticed that the girls willingly turned their stickily rouged lips up to him. Their escorts pretended indifference or looked away as the newcomer kissed their girls, fumbled at their flesh.

"Got them all bulldozed, hasn't he?" Liz commented.

"They're scared of him all right. Got a right to be, too. Thing he got sent up for was cutting another fellow's face to hamburger with a broken beer bottle. Them little tramps ain't worth getting cut for."

The rear door opened. Mickey shuffled in. "What was the buzz for, Sam? Trouble?"

Sam picked up another glass, held it up to the light, started polishing it. "Going to be, maybe. You got some company. Gunson and a pal of his just came in." He nodded toward the booth. "Over there."

Mickey swore under her breath, scowled at the booth. "I told you I don't want trouble makers like that getting in here."

"You told me," Sam nodded amiably. "Only you didn't tell me who was going to keep them out. It ain't going to be me. My face ain't no bargain but I like it just the way it is, with my nose in the middle."

The big woman dug at her scalp irritably. "That kid's mean clean through, and we can't stand no trouble in here. You got to handle him some way, Sam."

"Not me," Sam shook his head firmly.

"Let me take his booth, Mickey," Liz suggested. "He doesn't look so tough to me."

Mickey stared at her, considered. Finally, she shrugged. "Okay. Just take care. Don't get fooled by that baby face of his. He's a bad actor."

"I can take care of myself. Ask Sam."

The bartender scowled at her, muttered under his breath, shuffled to the other end of the bar.

Mickey grinned at his discomfiture, chuckled deep in her throat. "Don't forget Gunson ain't Sam, kid."

Liz nodded, pushed her hair into place with the flat of her hand, smoothed down her skirt over her thighs. "He doesn't worry me any." She headed across the floor to Gunson's booth, eluded outstretched hands with the ease of weeks' experience.

The curly-headed tough in the booth looked up as she approached. At close range it was quite apparent that he'd been drinking. His eyes were bloodshot, his hair rumpled as though he had been raking his fingers through it. He gave her an appraising grin as she stopped at the table.

"Well, well. Fresh meat. Hey, Doc, take a look."

The man with the horn-rimmed glasses looked up, gave her an empty smile, stared past her around the floor.

"Friendly, ain't he?" Liz grunted.

"He ain't, but I am," Gunson grinned loosely. "How long you been in this crow's nest, chicken?" He slid his hand under the hem of her skirt, ran his palm along her leg.

"Long enough," she smiled amiably. She brought the side of her hand down in a short chop that caught him on the wrist. He pulled his hand back with a grunt, tried to scramble to his feet. She pushed him back into his seat. "Don't get up for me. I'm just one of the help."

The bloodshot eyes were narrowed, mean. "You little tramp. Who do you think you're playing games with? You know who I am?"

"Never saw you before. But when I want a massage, I'll pick the time and place. You drinking, or did you just come in to see how the other half lives?"

Thus challenged, the man in the booth snarled at her, tried to pull himself to his feet, got his legs mixed up with the table. He let his companion pull him back down.

"Cut it out, Gun," ski-nose told him. "She's not worth it."

"Nobody clips me, Doc. I'll—"

Doc pulled a pack of cigarettes from his jacket pocket, dumped one out, stuck it between Gunson's lips. "Don't start anything here or they'll slap you back to working out the rest of your time." He scratched a match, held it to the cigarette, waited until Gunson had filled his lungs full of smoke, snorted it in twin streams from his nostrils.

"You oughtn't to get gay with my friend, sister. He's had a bad day," Doc told her, the half smile still plastered on his lips.

"He'll have a worse night if he tries to push me around. The only thing I'm peddling comes in bottles. Get that through his skull if you can."

Gunson glared up at her, then the glare watered down into a weak, drunken grin. "Hey, you're a pretty smart broad at that. Get it, Doc?" He hit his companion's chest with the back of his hand. "She ain't selling and all the time I thought it came with the table."

"You haven't even got the table yet. Mickey doesn't like people who take up space without paying the freight."

Gunson nodded his head heavily, grinned. "Okay. Make it a couple of scotches. One for you, too. Unless you're used to champagne."

"I can drink it as easy as you can pay for it."

The look of drunken good-nature clouded into a scowl. "What kind of a crack is that? You trying to make out that I'm a piker?" He jammed his hand into his pocket, brought out a thick wad of bills. "That look like I can't pay for it?"

Doc caught his arm, pulled the hand down under the table. "Gun, stop waving that dough around. First thing you know, these yokels will start talking about the roll you're flashing. We better get out of here." He pushed out the table, stood up. "Coming?"

Gunson glared at him. "Not until I have that drink."

"Okay, pal. Then you're on your own. I warned you I was out if you started acting stupid."

Gunson scowled, dropped his eyes, shrugged. "Okay, Doc, you win." He pulled himself heavily to his feet, pushed Liz aside. "Don't you go away, sister. You and me got some talking to do next time." He shoved past Doc, swaggered through the tables to the bar, and out. Neither he nor Doc looked back.

Liz ambled back to the bar, winked at Mickey. "They decided not to hang around."

"Nice work, Liz," the yellow-haired woman grinned back. "I feel a lot better with him out of here."

"Who's his friend?" Liz asked.

Mickey shrugged her heavy shoulders. "Never seen him before. You, Sam?"

The bartender shook his head sulkily.

"They had an awful big roll on them," Liz dropped her voice. "The other guy got sore at Gunson for flashing it. Sounded like he was the boss."

"A big roll?"

"Big enough to choke a horse."

Mickey looked thoughtful. "It's a cinch they didn't come by it honest. Gunson would never think of working for it."

"Been a lot of stickups in the papers lately," Sam grumbled. "Wouldn't put it past him, none."

"If it's him, they'll catch up with him. He never had the brains God gave a louse."

"Maybe he didn't, but that friend of his is no fool." Liz shook her head. "And Gunson jumps when he snaps his fingers." She dug into her bag, brought up a pack of cigarettes, held them out to the older woman. Mickey shook her head, watched Liz stick one in her mouth, light it.

"Your tables very busy, Liz?" Mickey asked.

Liz shook her head. "Pretty slow for a Saturday."

"Sam, put somebody else on Liz's tables. I want to have a talk with her," she called back over her shoulder. "Come on to my place and rest your feet, Liz."

Liz looked surprised, nodded. She took a deep drag out of her cigarette, blew a feathery tendril of dirty white smoke at the ceiling, dropped the butt to the floor, crushed it out.

Mickey led the way along the path past the four cabins to a small white frame house. Liz followed her into the kitchen, took one of the chairs at the older woman's invitation. Mickey rummaged through a closet, came up with a bottle and two glasses. She tipped the bottle over each glass, shoved one in front of Liz.

"I been watching you operate, Liz," she told her. "I like your style. You got too much class for this joint." She pushed a chair closer to the table, straddled it facing Liz. "Got any plans?"

Liz shook her head.

"That ain't good. You'll end up selling yourself out for pennies when with what you got you should be wearing furs and diamonds." She ran her eyes over Liz's torso. "These yokels don't appreciate stuff like you got. All they want's some little tramp that'll roll in the hay with them. Don't matter what they look like." She picked up her glass, motioned for Liz to do the same.

Liz sniffed at her glass. "What is it?"

The woman's laugh rumbled deep in her throat. "You don't have to worry about it. That's not the popskull we serve to the paying customers. This is private stock." She lifted her glass to her lips, drained it without a grimace. "What do you say? Interested in my proposition?"

"I haven't heard it yet."

Mickey spilled some more liquor in her glass, swirled it around the sides. "I got a business connection up north. A real big shot. He's always on the look-out for smart girls like you. He'd do all right for you—nice clothes, good times, real high-class men, not a bunch of little puppies sniffing around you all the time." She took a sip out of her glass, wiped her mouth with the back of her hand. "I make the connections for you, I get ten percent of what you make. What do you say?"

Liz shook her head. "Not interested."

Mickey shrugged, the corners of her mouth tilted upwards in a caricature of a smile that failed to reach her eyes. "You're making a mistake, Liz. You'll end up giving it away here for pennies. Besides, I don't know how much longer I can cover for you—"

"What do you mean?"

"I don't want to worry you about it, but they've been around asking questions. I been stalling them, of course, best I could."

"Asking questions about what?"

"That sheriff in the next county. The one that got himself gunned in the jailhouse. They figured the one that did it is still around. They think it was a girl, a pretty girl."

"Why?"

Mickey shrugged, pursed her lips. "It figures. The old sheriff liked to pick up girls on the bum, lock 'em up for a few weeks and use a strap on them. Got his kicks that way, mostly. When they found his body, the belt was off. They figure he was strapping some girl who got hold of his gun and shot him."

Liz took a drink out of her glass, gagged.

"New sheriff's been around asking if I seen any strange girls in these parts with strap marks on 'em. Like I said, I haven't told him anything yet but I think maybe he's getting wise."

"I get it," Liz nodded. "This friend of yours. Who is he?"

Mickey grinned broadly, emptied her glass, set it down on the table. "I knew you were a smart girl. He's real class, you'll go for him. They call him Nicky Gee. He books only the best girls in and around New York." She leaned forward, dropped her voice confidentially. "With Nicky looking after you, you wouldn't have to worry about no hick sheriff."

"When do I go?"

"Couple of weeks. Nicky'll want to take a look at you himself. He don't take nobody else's word for it." She winked obscenely. "He gets down this way every so often looking for new stuff. Meantime, take it easy. I wouldn't want you to be getting yourself all tired out before he gets here."

FOUR
Big Deal

The following night Gunson was back. He scowled at Sam on the way in, swaggered to the same booth he'd had the night before.

"I wish he'd stay out of here," Sam grumbled. "Anything happens, Mickey'll blame me."

"Where is Mickey?" Liz asked.

"Won't be back for a couple hours, she said. She didn't tell me where she was going. What are we going to do about him?"

"I'll handle him," Liz promised.

She walked over to the booth, ignored Gunson's scowl. "Break open your piggy bank?" she greeted him.

"Don't give me any of your lip, baby. And don't worry about my piggy bank. I got more money than you ever saw and when that's gone I know where to get more."

Liz sniffed, smoothed her skirt over her thighs. "What are you drinking?"

"Scotch. And get one for yourself. You're keeping me company tonight." He caught her wrist as she started away. "And I said scotch. Don't pull that stuff of drinking ginger ale. You can't get heated on that, and tonight you and me are going places."

Liz shook her wrist free. "I'll drink with you, but I'll decide when I'm going places and who with."

Gunson jeered at her. "Maybe you got someone better? In this burg?"

"If it's such a dump how come you're still hanging around?"

"Maybe it's only temporary. Maybe I got a lot of plans."

Liz sniffed. "Maybe." She spun on her heel, headed for the bar.

When she returned with the two drinks, she set them on the table, slid into the booth alongside him.

"How come a dish like you ended up in a joint like this?" he asked.

"Maybe I'm like you. Maybe I'm just waiting for the right time to move on." She pushed her drink in front of him. "Want to check it?"

He sniffed at the glass, grinned at her over the rim. "So you did take scotch?"

She took her glass back, set it down in front of her. "Maybe I feel like getting warmed up, like you said."

"Now you're talking." Gunson slid closer to her until he could feel the roundness of her thigh against his. "You keep acting nice and maybe I'll break down and take you with me when I blow."

Liz sipped at her drink. "You talk a big deal."

"I'm not just talking, baby. I got plans. Real big plans."

"Like for instance?"

Gunson's eyes narrowed craftily. "Why should I tell you?"

"Don't, if you don't want to. I was just thinking that maybe I might take you up on your proposition." She made concentric circles on the table-top with the wet bottom of her glass. "But I don't tie in with any small-timer. It's got to be big-time or I'm out."

"It's big, all right. We're not pitching for pennies." He drained his glass, set it down. "Get another round and maybe I'll tell you about it."

Liz stared at him, shrugged. She emptied her glass, held out her hand. "No credit. Rule of the house."

Gunson pulled out a small roll, peeled off two singles, tossed them onto the table.

"That roll sure has shrunk since last night," Liz commented.

"Easy come, easy go. It's only money. I can get more any time I want. As much as I want."

Liz picked up the empty glasses, brought them back to the bar. When she came back, there were four glasses on the tray. "One round's on me," she explained. She slid into the booth, sat close beside him. "You know, maybe I did have you wrong last night."

"Sure you did. What made you change your mind?"

She shrugged, reached across for a glass, appeared oblivious to his stare as her neckline plunged. "You've got 'em all so scared. Even Mickey. And I don't think she scares easy."

Gunson laughed, raked his fingers through his hair. "That's because they know me better than you do. They know I'd bust the joint into toothpicks if they even looked cross-eyed at me."

Liz pushed a glass at him, watched him toss it off. "I guess I figured everybody around here was small potatoes like them. I can see now that you're not."

"You're damn right I'm not." He dropped his hand from the edge of the table into her lap.

Liz reached down, caught his hand, held it. "Not here."

"You starting that again?" he growled. "I thought we understood each other?"

Liz shook her head. "I am beginning to like you, Gun. But not here. That's for jerks like them. Not me." She lifted his hand to the table.

"Where, then?"

She picked up her glass. "Have a drink."

An ugly note crept into his voice. "You're not pulling that on me, baby. Nobody teases me and walks away from it." He caught her wrist. "Where?"

She winced as his fingers cut into her flesh. "There are cabins out back. I can get to use one of them."

He let her wrist go, watched her massage it. "You're pretty particular."

She glared at him. "I get nervous with an audience. Besides, we do it the way I want or not at all."

He tried to outstare her, dropped his eyes, shrugged. "Don't get sore. I thought you were pulling a routine on me. No guy'd stand still for that." He picked up a glass, clinked it against hers. "When?"

"Soon's I can get away." She looked in the direction of the bar. "Then, fifteen minutes maybe."

"You wouldn't be pulling a stall, would you, baby?"

"Why should I? I'm the one that suggested it. There's nothing to make me stay here if I don't want to." She finished her drink. Set the glass back on the table. "You want to call the whole thing off, it's okay by me."

"Don't get huffy. Nobody said anything about calling it off." He indicated the last drink. "That's yours. Want it?"

She shook her head, watched him take it. "You sure like the stuff."

"Just catching up, baby. Where they had me for the last couple years we didn't get much." He took a deep slug out of the glass, wiped his mouth. "How about one for the road?"

Liz grinned at him, "I wouldn't want you to get too drunk."

"I'm never too drunk. One more."

The girl nodded. "Okay. I'll bring you one. Then I'll check out my station and go to the cabin. It's the first one off the back door. You take your time about finishing your drink, leave by the front door and meet me there. Okay?"

"Sure."

She picked up the glasses, dropped them at the bar, returned with a drink. "Give me about ten minutes, then come on," she whispered to him.

At the bar, she waited until Sam had finished with an order, signaled him over. "I'll be using Cabin One, Sam," she told him in a low voice. "Mickey said it was okay."

Sam winked obscenely. "Who's the lucky stiff?" he leered.

"You just wish it was you." She slid a folded bill across the bar. "Just see we ain't disturbed."

Sam nodded, watched the play of her hips under the thin fabric of her dress longingly, sighed as she disappeared through the back doors. He flattened out the bill she'd given him, rang it up, went back to polishing his glasses.

Outside the back door, Liz felt her way to the back of Cabin One. She reached down, pulled the old jacket from under the flooring where she'd cached it the first night. She unrolled the .45 from it, shoved the coat back under the end of the cabin, walked around front.

Inside the cabin, she slid the .45 under the pillow, walked over to the mirror, studied herself critically in the flyspecked depths. She wasn't completely satisfied with what she saw; tucked in a stray tendril of hair with the tips of her fingers, studied the effect with pursed lips. Then she reached up, pulled out a few pins, let the hair cascade down over her shoulders. She was standing there when the door opened and Gunson walked in.

"Getting impatient, baby?" He closed the door behind him, leaned back against it.

Liz turned around slowly, turned the full power of her gorgeous eyes on him. "Not very. I knew you couldn't wait too long."

"Pretty sure of yourself, aren't you?" he grumbled.

"Sure enough." She wet her lips with the tip of her tongue, walked over to him, stood close for a moment, then slid her arms around his neck, pulled his mouth against hers. They stood there, glued together for a moment, then she put her palms against his chest, pushed him away. "Don't wear it out all at once."

Gunson pushed his hair back with an impatient gesture, reached for her, growled when she eluded his grasp.

She walked to the bed, sat down on the side of it. From the rough night-table near the head of the bed, she took two cigarettes, lit both, held one out to him.

Sulkily he shuffled over, took the cigarette, stuck it in the corner of his mouth where it wobbled when he talked. "Look, baby, I don't like playing games. Let's quit stalling."

"Stop rushing things, Gun. Finish your cigarette."

He slammed the cigarette to the floor. "Look, baby, I can smoke a cigarette any time. If you think you can bring me out here and—"

"Not very sure of yourself, are you, Gun? Ever occur to you that I wouldn't have made the pass if I didn't want you as much as you want me?"

The sulky look dissolved into a smug smile. "Then why stall?"

Liz shrugged. "I don't know. I guess it's because I don't like one-night stands." She looked around the place with a grimace of distaste. "In a dump like this, especially."

Gunson slid his arm around her waist, pulled her close. "Who said it was a one-night stand? I'll be around."

"You and a hundred other guys." She slid out of his arm, walked over to the door, opened it, started out into the darkness.

He came up behind her, reached over her shoulder, pushed the door shut. "What's that supposed to mean—me and a hundred other guys?"

"Just what is sounds like. Long as I work in a dive like this, every creep with the price of a beer thinks he has a right to pat me on the fanny. I didn't think a guy like you would want to share with others." She turned around, faced him. "I thought you'd like your girl exclusive."

"She better be." He sank his fingers into her arm. "You haven't been messing around with anybody else?"

Liz shook her head. "No, but Mickey's beginning to hint. There are a couple of good customers getting sore because I won't let them make time, she says."

"Forget about her. I'll make a strike and take you out of here. If she gets tough—"

"Why not now, Gun?"

"Why not now what?"

"Take me out of here."

Gunson ran his fingers through his hair, took the cigarette from between her fingers, took a long drag. "That takes money." He pulled out the small roll of bills, held it under her face. "You can't do nothing with chicken-feed."

"But you can get more. Lots more. You said so yourself," Liz lowered her voice. "Get enough so's we can shake this place and we'll be on our way to the big wheel."

Indecision blurred the man's features. He shook his head. "It takes time. I'm not ready yet."

"Not ready?" she spat at him. "Then I was right the first time. You're just talk. Not ready!" she sneered. "When are you going to be ready? When you're ninety?"

Gun tried to take her in his arms, but she pushed him away. "Let me alone. The only reason I went for you in the first place was because I thought you were different from the rest out there. I believed you when you said you were going places. All you'll ever do is hang around and scare kids who believe you when you tell them how tough you are."

Gunson lashed out with his right hand, the palm smacked sharply across the side of her face, knocking her off balance.

"That's right," she taunted. "Hit me again. It'll make you feel like a big man. Go on, hit me again."

He stepped up to her, slashed at her face with a slap and back hand. His face was dull red with anger. "I told you not to get fresh with me, baby."

She stood in front of him, her eyes shining, her lips soft and wet. Before he could lash out again, she was in his arms, pressing against him, her teeth sunk into his lower lip.

"You will do it, Gun? Now?" Her voice was husky, low.

"I—I can't, baby," he shook his head. "It takes time to set a caper up. We've been working on one, but we're not ready." He disentangled her arms from around his neck, walked over to the night table, picked up a cigarette, lit it.

"You're not afraid, are you, Gun?" she insinuated softly.

"Of course I'm not afraid. But what do you think I'm going to do the job with? My fingers? That's the big trouble right now. You don't pick up a rod off a tree."

"I've got a gun," she told him.

His jaw sagged, he eyed her with new respect. "Where?"

She walked over to the bed, pulled the .45 from under the pillow, handed it to him. He hefted it in his palm, whistled tonelessly. "What a cannon. Where'd you get it?"

"What's the difference? I've got it. Do we do the job?"

"We need a car and someone to drive."

Liz tossed her head impatiently. "Who's stalling now? There's twenty cars out front you can take your pick from. I can drive. Well?"

"Doc wouldn't like it," Gunson argued feebly.

"So that's it. It's Doc that has the nerve. Maybe I should have held out for Doc. Maybe—"

Gunson growled, dug his fingers into her hair, pulled her face close to his. "I don't need anybody. Doc or anybody else. I didn't knock down a dime store on my last one because I was chicken." He slid the .45 into the waistband of his trousers. "You're sure you can drive?"

"Been driving since I was fifteen."

"Okay, baby. You're spoiling for action. Let's go get some!"

FIVE
Stick-up

An unshaded bulb that swayed gently in the night breeze spilled an uncertain yellow light down onto the service station. Liz swung off the road, braked to a stop in front of the pump, tooted the horn.

Through the grimy window, she could see the attendant scowl, fold the paper he was reading, head for the door. He took his time about coming out, started to leer when he saw the girl in the driver's seat. The leer froze when his eyes made out the size of the man with her.

"How many?"

"Fill it up," Liz told him.

When the station man went to the rear of the car, she passed the gun to Gunson. "I'll go in to the john," she whispered. "When he comes in, follow him. I'll make sure there's no one else around."

Gun nodded. His face was a white blur in the semi-gloom of the car. He watched the girl cross the concrete apron, push her way into the small office. She disappeared behind a paint-peeled door inside.

After a few minutes, the attendant walked up, drying his hands on a grimy rag. "That'll be three-twenty, mister."

Gunson nodded, dug into his pockets, brought out the small roll of bills. He separated four ones, pushed them through the window. "You got any cigarettes in there?"

The garage man nodded. "A machine."

Gunson opened the car door, followed the man to the office. As they closed the door behind them, the door to the washroom opened, Liz stepped out. "He's alone," she said.

The station man started, swung around. Gunson pulled his hand out of his jacket pocket far enough to show it held a .45.

"What is this?" the man blustered.

"Save your breath, mister. Get the dough out of the register and pass it over." He broke off, scowled at the close scrutiny the victim was giving him. "Stop staring. You got any ideas you'll know me the next time you see me, forget it."

"I don't have to remember very hard. I know who you are," the man snapped. "I seen you around."

A pinched look crept into Gunson's eyes, hard lumps formed at the sides of his jaw. "That's your tough luck, mister." He closed in on the station man, pushed him toward the washroom door. "Get in there."

The man staggered back against the door, looked for a moment as though he was going to struggle, didn't. His eyes were welded on Gunson's face as he backed into the small room.

"What do we do with him, Liz?" Gunson wanted to know in a low voice.

"You can't leave him to blow the whistle."

Gunson's eyes left the garage man, turned on Liz. He couldn't control a jerking muscle in his cheek. "Risk a murder rap for the lousy couple of bucks we're getting out of this?"

The man came to life. "Wait a minute. You wouldn't kill me. I—I wouldn't talk. Honest."

Liz reached across her companion, pulled the gun out of his hand. "All I know is that he made you. Ten minutes after we get out of here, every state cop's after us. That's why it's got to be this way."

Her finger whitened on the trigger, the big gun bucked and roared. The garage man laced his fingers over his stomach in a futile attempt to stem the flow of red that started to seep through his fingers. He went to his knees, fell forward on his face, didn't move.

Liz didn't pay him a second glance. She wheeled, walked to the cash register, punched a key. She scooped up the bills, ignored the change in the drawer. "Let's get going," she snapped.

Gunson nodded, pulled open the door, sprinted after her toward the car. She slid into the driver's seat, ground the car into gear. It roared away, skidded onto the highway, headed south.

The man beside her wiped the faint film of perspiration from his forehead and upper lip with the side of his hand. "Maybe knocking him off wasn't such a hot idea, Liz. There's going to be an awful lot of heat about it." He winced as she swung the car around a slow-moving truck, narrowly missed a car headed in the opposite direction.

"They'll have these plate numbers out on the air in an hour or so," she told him matter-of-factly. "The cops will probably tie it up with the stickup."

Gunson groaned. "I never thought of that. What do we do?"

"Ditch this heap as soon as we can get another."

Gunson nodded uncertainly. "But as soon as we get another, the owner'll report that one missing, too. Maybe we better try making it on foot."

The girl tossed a contemptuous glance at him. "Not the way we'll do it. The owner won't be notifying anyone." She returned her full attention to the road. "Ten miles or so up ahead we hit a long flat stretch. The first decent-looking car we see, we take." She picked the gun out of her lap, handed it over to the boy. "This one's on you. Like that, neither of us is likely to do any talking."

Gunson looked down at the gun, licked at his lips. "Maybe—"

"Take it," the girl snapped.

"Okay, if you say so."

"You got a better idea?"

He shook his head. "No ideas at all." He dropped the gun into his jacket pocket, fumbled around, came up with two cigarettes. He lit them, stuck one between the girl's lips. He slumped back, smoked with short, jerky puffs.

He was on his fourth cigarette when the girl grunted softly. She nodded ahead through the windshield to a small triangle of white light a mile or so ahead.

"Looks like our pigeon up there." She pushed down on the accelerator, started to eat up the space between her and the car above. As the red tail light of the front car started to grow in size, Gunson shifted uneasily, pulled the .45 from his pocket, fumbled with it.

"Suppose another car spots us, and—"

"No other car will," Liz growled. "That's why I picked this stretch. You can see a couple of miles in both directions." She looked over at him in the half-light of the car, giggled. "I thought you were so tough. You sound like you're going chicken on me."

"Don't worry about me," Gunson growled. "I'll hold up my end."

The driver of the car ahead gave no indication that he was aware of their approach. As Liz swung out to pass him, he flicked an incurious glance at them, returned his concentration to the road ahead.

Liz brought her car abreast of the other car, waited until her front fender was out ahead. Then, she swung the wheel, felt the jar as the fender crumpled against the other car. There was a squeal of brakes, the sound of scraping metal. Then the two cars came to a jarring stop.

The driver of the first car was out in the road coming at them. He was a medium-sized man, showing signs of a spreading waistline. His face was white, pinched in the dim light.

Before he could reach the car, Gunson was in the road, gun in hand.

The little fat man did a double-take at the sight of the gun in the boy's hand. "Wh-what is this?" He looked from Gunson to the slim girl who had joined him in the road. "If—if it's a stickup, I haven't got a thing. I—"

"We're not after your money, mister. We need a car. Bad," Liz told him. "We thought you might like to lend us yours."

The man's eyes hopscotched from the girl to the car she'd been driving and back. The question in his eye was unasked.

"It's hot," Liz told him. "We need a new one."

The little man licked at his lips, nodded jerkily. "Take the car. I won't give you any trouble."

"And leave you out here all alone?" Liz asked. "Not a chance, mister. You're coming with us."

"But, wait a minute, girlie. I won't—"

"Turn around," Liz snapped.

"Please," the perspiration glinted on the man's forehead and upper lip. "Don't make me. I won't give you any trouble. I—"

"You heard what she said. Turn around," Gunson growled. He caught the little man by the arm, swung him around.

The little man stiffened at the touch of the gun muzzle in his back. He offered no resistance as Gunson reached around him, relieved him of his wallet.

"What are you going to do with me?" he quavered.

Gunson handed the wallet over to the girl, she riffled through it, replaced the papers. She nodded to Gunson.

He lifted the barrel of the .45, brought it down alongside the little man's ear. It knocked his hat rolling into the road, his legs crumbled under him, he fell face forward, didn't move.

Gunson turned him over on his back with his toe, bent over him. A thin stream of red was already beginning to well from an ugly, jagged wound just inside the little man's hair line.

"He won't give us any trouble," the boy growled. "Like he said."

"Never mind admiring him. Get him into the car," Liz snapped. She waited until Gunson had loaded the little man onto his shoulders, led the way to the rear door of the car. "Ditching that hot car should give us a couple of days' head start with any luck." She slid in under the wheel, kicked the motor into life.

"How far's he going with us?" Gunson wanted to know.

"Not very." She backed the car onto the road, swung around the car they had been driving, continued south. "You ever been to New York, Gun?"

Gunson shook his head. His hand shook as he stuck a cigarette in the corner of his mouth. "Not yet."

"Me neither," Liz told him. "I always told myself I'd be going there. And now

I am." She flicked her eyes downward at the gas gauge. "How much did we get out of the service station guy?"

Gunson pulled a wadded roll of bills from his pocket, wet his thumb, counted them. "Sixty-eight bucks."

"That'll pay for the gas." She tossed her head toward the back seat. "That joker can pay for the food. There are of couple of tens and some ones in his wallet." The car hugged the inside lane of the highway, swung wide as it started to climb. A deep gully between two hills had been bridged by a white metal span that gleamed skeleton-like in the moonlight. Liz braked the car to a stop in the center of the bridge, looked in both directions.

"I think our pal is going to leave us here, Gun," she said.

Gunson looked out, nodded. He flicked his cigarette out into the darkness, watched it clear the low railing of the bridge, disappear like a falling star into the chasm below. From somewhere down there came the sound of running water, the gurgling of a fast stream.

Gunson got out into the road, pulled open the rear door. The little man lay in a heap the way he had been thrown. He was breathing noisily, almost as though he were snoring.

Gunson reached in, caught him by the arm, pulled him out. He lifted him to his feet, dragged him to the side of the bridge. The little man's head kept falling forward onto his chest, his feet dragged along the road.

Liz watched, waited until they had reached the railing. For a moment, she could make out the two figures. Suddenly the bigger of the two gave a heave, then there was only one. Gunson walked back to the car, reached in, brought out the little man's hat. He scaled it over the railing into the depths below.

SIX
Blood Lust

A big, hand-painted billboard announced the fact that Pine View Court was 150 feet ahead. The court turned out to be a mean little cluster of shacks huddled together under a small group of desiccated pines. A noisy neon light that stained the road a dull red chattered the fact that a vacancy was still to be had.

Liz guided the car off the highway toward the small shack marked: *Office*. She stopped the car, watched while an old man inside the shack walked to the window and peered out at them.

"You'd better handle this, Gun." Liz cuddled closer to the man in the front seat, turned her face to his.

The door of the office creaked open, the old man limped painfully over. He carried a dog-eared ledger with him.

"Evening, folks." He rested the ledger on the side of the door, peered into the front seat. "Got a nice one for you. Single bed." He held up the key in his hand to catch the faint light from the office. "Number 12. Can show it to you, if you like." The tone of his voice implied that he'd prefer not to.

"Don't go to any trouble, mister. We're not fussy," Gunson told him. "What'll it cost?"

"Five for the night, or any part of it," the old man told him. "In advance, son." He turned his head, spat.

Gunson brought out the thin roll of bills, separated a five from the rest, handed it over. "You needn't put in a call for us in the morning. We're going to sleep in. Got a lot of traveling to do tomorrow night."

The old man grinned lewdly, stuck the ledger in the window, waited while Gunson scrawled an indecipherable signature. "Just follow the road on back. Number twelve's the sixth one to the right." He folded the five, stuck it into his vest pocket. "You decide to leave before it's light, put the light on so's I'll know in case I get a chance to re-rent it." He turned, shuffled back to the office.

"What a dump," Gunson growled.

"Stop kicking," Liz told him. She eased the car into gear, bumped the hundred yards to where a stake in the ground bore the numeral 12. She swung the car between the two cottages, killed the lights. "A guy who runs a wide open place like this must get along okay with the local cops. We'll be safe here for awhile."

Gunson growled deep in his chest, led the way to the cottage, opened the door with the key, fumbled until he found the light switch. A pale ineffectual yellow light spilled from a single bracket in the ceiling, revealing a huge, badly made bed, a rickety wooden dresser and a speckled mirror hanging askew over it. At the back of the cabin, a door led to the lavatory.

Liz walked over to the mirror, set it straight, examined herself in it, seemed satisfied. "We'll hole up here until tomorrow night and then hit the road again. We can make better time traveling nights."

Gunson walked over to the bed, tested it. "I can use some sack time." He grinned up at her, patted the side of the bed. "Come on over and relax. It's been a big night."

Liz walked to the window, peered out, pulled down the shade. "Just like that old character to be a peeper. I've had some experience with old guys like that." She walked over to the door, felt for a latch, found none. "There's no way of locking this trap from the inside, Gun."

The boy shrugged. "So what?" He patted his pocket. "Nobody's going to bother us."

"I don't care about being bothered. I just get nervous with an audience." Her hand brushed the light, flooded the cabin with darkness. "Tonight was just the start, Gun. We're on our way to New York and nothing's going to stop us."

"Yeah." Gunson's voice didn't sound too sure. There was the scratch of a match. His forehead was ridged in the pale light as he applied it to a cigarette.

"Maybe we ought to take it a little easier, Liz. That's two killings tonight. How long do you think—?"

"Don't go chicken on me, Gun," there was a hard note in the girl's voice. "I'm tired of being kicked around. There's only one way to keep from getting kicked around and that's to be so strong that nobody would lift his leg to kick at you. You don't get that strong by being chicken."

"I wasn't thinking of running out. It's just that—"

"You're tired, that's all. Don't forget, Gun, you're in as deep as I am. They get me for that garage job, they get you for the guy on the road." She walked over, picked cigarette from between his lips, took a deep drag on it. "But what are we talking like this for? Nobody's running out, are they?"

The girl sank down onto the bed beside him. She slid her arm around his neck, pulled his mouth to hers. Her lips moved against his, she began to moan softly. Her nails dug into his back, she quivered deliciously. After a moment, she placed the flat of her hand against his chest, pushed him away.

"You wouldn't run out on me, would you, Gun?" Her breath came in short gasps. "We can go places together. Right to the top."

"I'm not leaving," Gun grunted.

The girl fumbled with her belt. There was the soft rustle of material as she pulled the dress over her head. She wore nothing under the dress. The whiteness of her body gleamed in the half-light of the cabin. He legs were long, sensuously shaped. Full, rounded thighs swelled into high-set hips, converging into a narrow waist. Her breasts were full and high, their pink tips straining upward.

As she stood there, she raised her hands slowly from her sides, and loosened the pile of hair on her head, letting it cascade down over her shoulders. She stood proudly in front of Gunson.

"You'll never leave me, Gun." She dropped into his lap, loosened the knot on his tie. "I know you won't."

A long splinter of yellow sunlight ran from under the shade to the foot of the bed. Liz stirred uneasily, rolled over onto her back. Half awake, she had the sensation of an alien presence. When she opened her eyes, the old man from the office was standing at the foot of the bed leering at her.

She made an ineffectual attempt to pull the covers over her. "What are you doing in here?" She nudged Gunson into consciousness. "We got company, Gun."

Gunson started, his hand snaked under his pillow, reappeared with the .45. "How long's he been here?"

"Long enough," Liz snapped. She looked back to the old man. "What about it? What do you want?"

The old man wiped the wet smear of his mouth with the back of his hand. "Just trying to do you a favor, that's all." The bristles on his chin glinted whitely. "You can put the gun away, young fellow. You're in enough trouble."

Liz sat up in bed, paid no attention to the cover as it dropped away. "What's that supposed to mean, mister?"

The old man couldn't tear his eyes away from the girl's nakedness. "Just had a visit from some friends of mine. State patrol. Real nice fellows."

"Get to the point."

The old man wiped his lips again. "Seems like they're looking for a 1950 Plymouth. A blue '50. With maybe a broken right headlight."

The girl's eyes narrowed. "So?"

The old man shrugged. "Okay. If it don't mean anything to you, forget it. Seemed to me one of your lights was out when you drove in last night. I just had me a look on the way in. It's a blue Plymouth. A '50."

Liz squirmed out of bed, pulled the dress over her head. "What are they chasing a blue Plymouth for?"

"Murder." The old man's eyes looked a little disappointed at the dress, contented themselves with concentrating on the deep neckline. "They found another car twenty, thirty miles back. They figure whoever was driving it pushed the Plymouth off the road, took it over." His eyes went from the girl to Gunson and back. "The other car was used in a stickup last night. Garage man killed." He turned, started for the door.

Liz caught him by the arm, swung him around. "Spit it out. What's on your mind?"

"I figure long's as you folks got nothing to lose, I'll tip off my friends on the patrol."

Liz motioned with her head, Gunson stuck his feet out of bed, circled around the old man, stood between him and the door.

"Maybe you just ought to figure on staying here for an hour or two until we put some distance between here and us."

"Now you're talking dumb," the old man told them. "The patrol's got road blocks all over the place. You wouldn't get twenty miles either direction."

"We could grab one of the other cars, Liz," Gunson snapped; "and—"

"What good's that if there's a road block. They'll be checking licenses." She looked back to the old man. "How come you tipped us off?"

The old man leered. "Hate to see anything happen to such a nice-looking young couple." His eyes followed the lines of Liz's figure, coming to stop at the breasts that bunched over the low-cut neckline. "Thought I'd be friendly."

"How do we know he's telling the truth, Liz? He might've seen the busted fender and done a lot of guessing. I vote we—"

Liz shook her head. "He might've guessed everything but the stickup back at the garage." She cocked her head at the motel keeper. "How'd the cops know it was a '50 Plymouth—a blue '50?"

"When you forced the other car off the road, you scraped fenders. There was a lot of flaked blue enamel worked right into the fender of the car you left behind. And the glass from the smashed headlight matches the headlight glass used by Plymouth in its 1950 models." He shrugged. "It didn't take a Sherlock Holmes."

"But you were willing to cover for us. Why?" Liz wanted to know.

"Hate to see a nice young couple like you get in trouble. Murder's a tough one to beat. Don't seem right a pretty young gal like you should get hung."

Liz looked at the man for a moment, then walked over to the dresser. Her lips worked smoothly under the fabric of the dress, her breasts traced a wavy pattern as they swayed. She picked up her belt, snugged it around her waist.

"And outside of the goodness of your heart, what's your angle?" She picked a cigarette from the pack on the bureau, stuck it between her lips, lit it. The smoke floated lazily from between her lips.

"Might be able to use a smart young couple like you," the old man admitted. "I have a friend up in Waynesburg always on the lookout for a smart girl, and," his eyes flicked to Gunson, "a smart young fellow."

"What's this friend of yours do?" Liz wanted to know.

The old man shrugged bony shoulders. "A little of this, a little of that." His eyes narrowed. "You particular?"

"Yeah. I don't work in houses," Liz snapped at him.

The old man licked his lips back into a smile. "You don't have to be smart to do that. I mean a real smart girl."

"I might be interested."

"You've got to be. But right now the idea is to lay low. Till those cops cool off."

SEVEN
Hostages

The coffee shop was a small shack set a few yards north of the motel office. Liz followed Gunson in, took a rickety table against the far wall. She waited until Gun slid onto the bench opposite her. "Cigarette me, will you, Gun?"

Gunson's good looks had disappeared. His face was swollen, his eyes puffy. The once carefully combed hair hung lankly over his forehead. The corners of his mouth drooped sullenly. He dug a battered pack of cigarettes from his blouse pocket, held it across the table.

Liz selected a cigarette. "You used to light them for me."

Gunson grunted, hung one in the corner of his mouth. "How long we going to hang around this dump, Liz? It's getting on my nerves."

The girl caught his wrist, pulled the lighted match over to her cigarette, took a deep drag. "What are you complaining about? We've been safe here, haven't we? You can read the papers. The heat's really on."

Gunson growled deep in his chest, touched the match to his cigarette, blew the smoke in twin streams from his nostrils. "I still think we should have kept going. We'd have been halfway to New York by now." He subsided as a waitress waddled up to the table, dropped two coffee-stained menus in front of them. He pushed it away. "Just bring me some coffee," he growled.

Liz nodded. "Me, too. Toast with it."

The waitress sniffed, shuffled back to the counter.

"I don't like the old guy that runs this place, either. You been spending a lot of time with him," he grumbled.

"You think I like it? He's keeping us under cover, ain't he? What do you want me to do? Spit in his eye? All he's got to do is tip those friends of his on the state patrol and we're in the soup."

Gunson raked his fingers through his hair. "But how long do we have to stay buried here? When does the heat go off?"

"How do I know? But as long as it's on, we stay under cover." She speared a crumb of tobacco from her tongue with the tip of a shellacked nail. "Now they found that guy you threw off the bridge, they've got to put on a show."

"I threw off the bridge. Now, look—"

Liz tossed her head impatiently. "You look. We're both in this together. You start getting the jumps, just think of that guy you tossed off the bridge. That'll calm your nerves."

Gunson chain-lit a fresh cigarette from the half burned butt in his hand. "Okay, okay."

The waitress was back with two cups of coffee. She spilled half the cup into his saucer as she slid it in front of him. The toast was black and brittle-looking. "Anything else?" she wanted to know.

Gunson shook his head.

She dropped a punched check on the table, waddled back to her perch behind the counter.

Gunson took a sip of the coffee, burned his tongue, cursed softly. "I can't take much more of this dump, Liz," he warned. "Things don't cool off by tomorrow, I'm getting out. You can either come with me or stay. Suit yourself."

Liz took her cigarette from between her lips, studied the carmined end with distaste. "You'd be asking for an awful mess of trouble, Gun. Hunt says—"

Gunson slammed his cigarette to the floor, ground it out with his heel. "I don't give a damn what Hunt says. How do we know he's not snowing us? Why shouldn't he try to keep us here? He's been having himself a picnic with you, and—"

"Is that any skin off your nose? Look, don't forget it's not only my hide I'm taking care of, it's yours too. And all you do is bitch." She ground her cigarette out in the saucer. "So I'm nice to the old guy. I'd be nice to any guy who saved my skin."

"So what am I supposed to do? Sit and watch?" Gunson's voice was low, tense. "What's that make me out? My girl with a guy old enough to—"

Liz leaned back, laughed mirthlessly. "Your girl? Grow up, Gun. I told you

I'd be nice to any guy who helped save my skin. I needed you to get away from Mickey's place. That's all. You got no complaints."

Gunson jumped up from his bench. "Just like that, eh?"

"Just like that."

Gunson glowered at her for a moment, then spun on his heel, stamped across the shack to the door. He shouldered his way past the old man from the office on his way in, headed for Cabin 12 and didn't look back.

The old man hobbled painfully across the floor, sank onto the bench across from Liz with a grunt. "What the hell's wrong with him?"

"Nerves," Liz grunted. She tested the coffee. "He wants to get out of here, Hunt."

The old man shook his head. The bristles on his chin glinted whitely in the morning light. "He wouldn't get twenty miles. State cops have the whole area sewed up." He signaled to the waitress to bring him coffee. "He don't know when he's got it good."

"Got a cigarette?" Liz wanted to know.

The old man dug a pack from his pocket, dropped it on the table in front of the girl. "Nerves like that can get us in trouble," he complained. "Might blow his stack and drag us all down with him." He peered at her. "Can you handle him?"

Liz shrugged. "I don't know." She lit the cigarette, let the smoke drift from between parted lips. "This friend of yours you've been talking about. Can't he get us out of here?"

"Wouldn't try," Hunt shook his head. "Not with all this heat on." He pursed his lips, stroked the bristles along his chin with the tips of his fingers. "I told him about you. He can use a kid with your brains and your looks."

"How about Gun?"

The old man shrugged. "Punks are a dime a dozen. And punks with bad nerves aren't even worth that." He waited while the waitress shoved the coffee in front of him. "He have to be part of the deal?"

Liz shrugged. "Not if he cracks up."

The old man shoveled sugar into his cup, stirred it. "My friends on the state police tell me the heat's going to stay on. Maybe get worse."

"How much worse?"

Hunt left the spoon in his cup, lifted it to his lips, sipped noisily. "A lot. They're going to put out a dragnet for the Plymouth."

"What's that mean, Hunt?"

"The works. They'll search every garage and every cabin court and any place the car might be hidden." He swirled the coffee around his cup, stared down at it. "They'll be reaching here tonight or tomorrow." He looked up. "They're going to find it."

"Isn't there any place we can ditch it?"

The old man shook his head. "Too late now. It'd be suicide to drive that heap on a state road with every cop in the county on the lookout for it." He put the cup up to his lips, watched the girl over the thick rim.

"What are we going to do, Hunt?"

The old man shrugged. "You ain't leaving me holding the bag. That's for sure." He set the cup down, wiped his lips with his sleeve. "I got an idea you might go for."

Liz's eyes narrowed. "Spill it."

"This punk. This Gunson—he's cracking up. Right?"

"Go on."

The old man shrugged. "Guy like that, he gets caught, he'll pull us all down with him." He picked up a cigarette, wet the end with his tongue, stuck it between his loose lips. "Maybe we can fix it so's he takes the whole rap."

"You just said he'd pull us all down with him."

The cigarette waggled when he talked. "Suppose he wasn't talking?"

Liz dropped her eyes to her cup, chewed on her lower lip. "You're not getting to me, Hunt. I don't see how that gets us off the hook."

The old man looked around, leaned across the table, dropped his voice. "Nobody knows how many people was in that car the night the two guys were killed. Right?'

Liz considered, nodded. "Right."

Hunt shrugged, raised his hands palms up. "So the cops get the car and a guy in it. Maybe with the gun that killed the garage guy. So they're satisfied. The heat's off, and you're in the clear. I can set you up with my friend, and Gunson's nerves don't have to jump."

"How does that satisfy the cops?" She rolled her eyes upward, studied the old man from under her lids. "Suppose Gun does talk?"

"Leave that to me." The old man reached over, laid a clammy hand on the girl's. "I told you I got friends, didn't I?"

Liz slid her hand free. "How?"

Hunt looked around again, satisfied himself no one was within earshot. "I tip my cop friends that the punk came in. Then we tip Gun off that he's got a chance to break clear." He grinned, leaned back. "He tools the heap out into the highway. When the cops move in, they'll move in shooting. All they want is a killer to shut up the newspapers. The gun and the stolen car will clinch it."

"That the only way, Hunt?"

The old man shrugged. "You know yourself the punk's not dependable. He might even try to cop a plea by dumping all the blame on you. Suit yourself. It's an out."

Liz thought for a moment, took a last drag on the cigarette, ground it out. "What do I do?"

"Go on back to the cabin and keep him busy." The rheumy eyes dropped to the bulging breasts, his tongue licked at his lips. "You shouldn't have any trouble doing that. Leave the rest up to me."

Liz nodded. "Okay. I'm leaving it up to you." She got up, walked to the door. The old man's eyes fastened on the smoothly working hips hungrily, followed her until she disappeared through the doorway.

The door to Cabin 12 didn't open when Liz turned the knob. She rapped at it with her knuckles.

"Who is it?" Gun's voice growled.

"Liz."

"You alone?"

Liz scowled at the door. "Of course I'm alone. Let me in, Gun."

There was the sound of heavy furniture being moved, the door swung open. Gunson stood back in the room, the .45 in his hand. "Get inside, Liz."

The girl stepped in, watched him with a frown as he shoved the washstand against the door. "What's this all about?" she wanted to know.

"I'm taking no chances," Gunson growled. "They got us cornered here like rats. Me, I'm not being taken." He walked back, dropped on the side of the bed, fondled the gun. "Where've you been so long?"

"Having coffee. Remember? You walked out on me, you know."

Gun's lips twisted in a sneer. "You weren't very lonely. I saw the old creep going in to you. What'd he have to say?"

Liz shrugged. "If you wanted to know, why didn't you stay?"

Gunson got up from the bed, caught the girl by the arm, swung her around. "I said what did he say?" His fingers dug cruelly into the flesh of her arm.

"He said he heard some of the heat was going off." She removed his hand from her arm, massaged it. "He heard the police figured the car got through the road-block some way."

"I figured it," he growled. "When'll he know for sure?"

Liz shrugged. "Why?"

"I told you why. I'm getting out of this dump." He stared around. "It's worse than being in stir. I'm getting out, and I'm getting out alone."

The girl stared at him. "What about me?"

"Let the old man take care of you. You seem to like it better that way. Okay, I'm giving him a clear field. Besides," he shoved his face close to hers, "I think you're bad medicine. I think you're a spoiler. Anything you touch, you spoil."

"You, for instance?" the girl sneered. "You never were anything but a cheap punk. All you were any good for was to help me get away from Mickey."

Gun's hand flashed in an upward arc, caught her on the side of the face, sent her reeling backward. Her lips peeled away from her lips, showing her teeth.

"You're nothing but a punk, a cheap punk," she told him.

He moved in on her, slapped her across the cheek again, back-handed her face into position. She went to her knees, stared up at him with bright eyes. "Hit me again, Gun," her voice was low, husky.

When he turned to walk away, she caught him around the knees. "Hit me again," she moaned.

He buried his hand in her hair, pulled her face upward. There was a strange excitement in her eyes, her lips were parted, moist. He cracked the palm of his hand across her cheek, felt the strange surge of excitement spreading through him. He couldn't stop. His hand slashed at her again and again. His eyes became glazed, his breath whistled through his lips.

Liz whimpered, she stared at him with strange hunger. She reached up, caught her dress at the neckline, tore it away. Her breasts spilled out. Then she threw herself at him, moaning softly.

EIGHT
Booby Trap

The noise reverberated through the cabin like thunder. Gunson opened his eyes blearily, decided someone was trying to knock the door off its hinges. He stared around the dimness of the room, estimated that they had been sleeping hours. The small rectangle under the shade where it didn't quite reach the window sill showed it to be dark out.

He reached over, touched the tip of the uptilted breasts of the girl beside him. "Liz," he shook her.

The girl moaned softly, stretched. "Yeah?"

The rapping came again, loud, demanding.

The girl came fully awake, sat up in bed, sheet up to her neck. "Who is it?" she wanted to know.

"I don't know. Find out," he snapped.

The girl wrapped the sheet around her, padded to the door. At the door, she stopped, turned around. Gunson stood behind her, the .45 ready. He nodded.

Liz pulled the washstand back, tugged the door open.

The old man from the front office stood in the doorway. He stepped in, kicked the door shut behind him.

"That's a fine way to greet a man bringing you good news," he whined. His eyes hopped from the gun to the girl. "What's the matter with you two?"

"What do you want?" Gun growled. "What's the good news?"

The old man pulled off his fedora, wiped his forehead with the back of his hand. "They're calling off the roadblock. The cops figure the killers slipped through."

"Don't use that word," Gun's finger tightened on the trigger.

The old man held his hand up. "Don't get nervous." He looked to the girl. "My friends told me they're looking for two people. No roadblock, just regular patrols. I figure you two can get into town, ditch the car."

"Thanks, old man. Only, it'll be me ditching the car. Not two of us. You just said they're looking for two people, didn't you?" He stuffed his legs into his trousers, shrugged into a shirt. "You got any kind of a car? Pickup truck?"

The old man nodded. "An old Chevvy. Why?"

"I'm taking it," Gun told him. He stared at the old man, the .45 pointed at his belly buckle. "Any objections?"

Hunt shook his head. "What about her?"

"She's your guest," Gunson growled. "She's bad medicine. I'm traveling light." He stuck the gun into his belt, lifted a jacket off the back of the chair, put it on. "Where's the heap?"

The old man stared at him, loose lips working.

"Where is it?" Gunson growled.

"Behind the office. Key's in it."

Gunson nodded, pushed past them to the door. "So long, baby," he twisted his lips at Liz. "I'm getting while the getting's good. You're poison to men. Anybody that touches you is a dead duck." He flipped a glance at the old man. "Why don't you try it? What've you got to lose?"

He stepped outside the cabin, looked around. There were no lights on in any of the other cabins. At the far end of the court, the neon sputtered fitfully. A yellow square of uncurtained window identified the office.

Gunson circled around to the back of the cabin. The weeds grew knee high, effectively covering the accumulation of beer cans and whisky bottles.

Slowly he picked his way behind the cabins toward the rear of the office. Once he thought he heard the sounds of motion, froze into the shadows of a building, gun clenched in fist. There was no sign of life anywhere else in the court.

The car was standing where the old man had said it would be. It was a prewar Chevvy, looked to be painted black in the darkness. He eased the door open, satisfied himself that the key was in the ignition as the old man had promised. He stuck the .45 into his waistband, slid behind the wheel.

The car responded to his foot on the starter, roared into life. He flicked on the lights, speared a beam toward the back of the office. Nobody seemed to have paid any attention to the motor starting. He swung the wheel, headed around the office to the road. At the highway, he swung to the right, pushed his foot on the accelerator.

He had barely cleared the entrance to the court when from somewhere close he heard the sound of a siren moaning softly. It reached for a high note, died away.

Gunson swore under his breath, jammed down on the gas. The small car seemed to leap forward like a thing alive. The sound of the siren was closer now, behind him.

He devoted all his attention to his driving, pushed the car for every ounce of speed. Suddenly, he saw the road block.

It was about a hundred yards in front of him, manned by two patrol cars. He kicked at the brake, the old car skidded to a stop.

A bright light knifed at him from a truck at the side of the road. Gunson debated the advisability of turning back, heard the approaching moan of the patrol car behind him.

He tugged the .45 from his belt, started shooting wildly at the spotlight on the truck. There was a sputter as a bullet found the bulb, then darkness descended like a shroud.

Gunson jammed on the gas, started toward the road block. Two men with riot guns materialized in the beam of his headlights. The guns in their hands started to belch orange flame. Little holes appeared in the windshield in front of him, then the windshield came apart.

He raised the .45, kept squeezing the trigger. The state police stood in front of the onrushing car, pumping round after round into the front seat. Suddenly the small car started to slew crazily from side to side. There was a screech of metal, the smashing of glass as it headed for the side of the road, came to a shattering stop against the trunk of a big tree.

When the troopers pulled Gunson from behind the wheel, they stretched him out on the grass alongside the wrecked car. His lips were pulled back from his teeth in a mirthless grin, his eyes looked up at a darkened sky he would never see. One of the slugs had torn a jagged hole through the side of his jaw, taking out a piece of cheekbone on the other side where it had passed through.

Jed Hunter sat behind the oversized, unpainted desk in the cabin court office, squinted owlishly at the two men in trooper's uniform that sat across the room. He turned his head, spat at a waste basket.

"We got the bastard, Hunt," one of the troopers grunted, "but Nelson stopped one. Pretty bad, the doc thinks."

Hunt shook his head, wiped the wet smear of his mouth with his sleeve. "You got the guy that did it, though. That's something."

The older of the two troopers nodded. "We got him, all right. And if that heap he left here when he lifted yours is the one we're looking for, we can start getting some sleep nights." He walked over to where an old water cooler was muttering to itself against the far wall. "You got anything to take the taste off this mud water?"

Hunt reached down, pulled a half-filled pint from the bottom drawer, set it on the top of the desk. "I guess I'm plumb lucky to be sitting here, if that guy was the killer you been looking for all this time."

The younger trooper grunted, yawned. "Just a punk kid." He got up walked over to the desk, took the top off the pint bottle, smelled it. "Make it yourself?"

The old man behind the desk grinned, winked. "That's against the law, Bob. Me, I buy my liquor."

The other trooper brought back three paper cups filled with a brackish water, set them down. He uncorked the pint, smelled it, grimaced, filled his glass to the brim. "How long you think them experts are going to be, Bob?" he growled to his partner.

Bob shrugged, tilted the bottle to his lips, swallowed twice. He washed it down with the water, crumpled the cup, tossed it at the waste basket. "They got to prove they're experts, don't they?" He walked to the window, peered out into the darkness toward Cabin 12 where the beams of flashlights threw the Plymouth into relief. "Looks like they're getting set to come in."

The older trooper downed his drink, dropped the cup into the basket. He straightened his tie, waited.

After a moment the door to the office opened, a tall man in a rumpled blue suit walked in. "That's the car all right, Hunter," he grunted. There was a faint shadow of a beard along the side of his jaw, he chewed continuously on a wad of gum. "Looks like the kid was the one we wanted."

Hunt nodded unconcernedly. "Glad to help, Sergeant." He indicated the bottle with a toss of his head. "Take the chill off?"

The sergeant turned to the two uniformed men. "You fellows better help Stack and Ryan get the car back to the barracks." When the two troopers had left, he picked up the pint, walked to the water cooler. "Tell me what happened again, Hunt." He filled a paper cup from the bottle, half-filled another with water.

Hunt spat at the waste basket, leaned back, laced his fingers behind his head. "It's like I told you, Sergeant. This young fellow drives in late last night. I don't spot the car until this afternoon. I start to ask him questions and he pulls a gun on me."

The sergeant took a deep swallow of the whisky, nodded for him to continue.

"He takes the keys to my old Chevvy and tells me to keep my mouth shut. Soon's it's dark, he's taking off, and if the cops come for him, he's taking me with him." He wiped his mouth again. "I sneaked away, phoned the barracks, warned them not to come into my place shooting. Too many innocent people."

"Like you, for instance."

Hunt grinned loosely. "Like me, for instance."

The sergeant finished the whisky, tossed off the glass of water. "So the desk promised you a stake-out. That it?"

Hunt nodded.

"And he was all alone. Nobody with him?"

"All alone."

The sergeant lifted the battered fedora from the back of his head, scratched the bald spot it covered. "I guess that wraps it up." He walked to the door, stopped with his hand on the knob. "That car of yours won't be a helluva lot of good any more. It's shot full of holes."

Hunt managed to look sad. "Only way I got of getting around, too."

"Maybe there'll be a reward," the sergeant grinned at him. "I'll let you know." He stepped out of the office, closed the door after him.

The old man stared at the closed door for a moment, then pulled himself painfully to his feet. He walked to the office door, watched the tail light of the police car grow smaller and smaller until it finally disappeared around the curve in the highway. He limped back to the water cooler, picked up the pint bottle, held it up to the light, measured what was left. Then, he held it to his lips, let the contents gurgle down his throat.

He walked back to the desk, picked up the phone, gave the operator a number. When the connection was made, he asked for Lew Barker, identified himself.

"Yeah?" the receiver wanted to know finally.

"Lew? Jed Hunter out at the motor court. That little matter's all taken care of."

"The punk?" the receiver wanted to know.

Hunt nodded. "State police knocked off the guy."

"How about the girl?"

"I told her about you. She's dying to meet you."

There was a pause, then. "What did you tell her?"

"Nothing. Just that you could use a smart gal." He turned his head, spat at the waste basket. "I'll have her out there tomorrow night."

"Have her here tonight."

"Aw, have a heart, Lew," he old man whined. "Give me a little break, too. I handled this for you and—"

"Tonight," the receiver snarled at him. "At the place. No later than eleven."

"Eleven? That don't even give me time to—"

The receiver laughed at him. "You're too old for that kind of stuff, Hunt. You've lived a long time. Just do what you're told and maybe you'll keep on living." There was a click as the connection was broken.

Hunt dropped the receiver back on its hook, sat glaring at it, cursing fervently.

NINE
The Blue Angel

Lew Barker operated the Blue Angel, an old frame building on the outskirts of town that had been converted into a roadhouse. Liz's first view of it was from the winding road that led from the state highway to the flapping canopy covering the short flight of stairs to its entrance. To the left of it was a parking lot filled with cars of all ages. A battery of cleverly hidden floodlights bathed the front of it, succeeding in hiding the fact that it was a tired old gray frame building anxious to relax without its makeup.

The cab dropped Jed Hunter and Liz in front of the entrance. He grudgingly shoved two bills through the front window at the driver, led the way up the stairs. A heavy-shouldered man in a faded purple overcoat decorated with gilt braid made a production of opening the door for them.

A small foyer led into what had once been the main parlor of the building, now converted into a bar room. Liz looked around, approved. The room was filled with small groups of chattering patrons dressed formally. Overhead a pall of smoke stirred restlessly in the draft from the opened door.

"Might's well have a drink while we're waiting," Hunt grunted. He led the way to a bar that ran the length of the room, found elbow space for himself and the girl, signaled for the bartender.

"Hi, Hunt," the man in the white jacket grinned at him. "All decked out tonight, ain't you?" He dried the bar in front of them with a damp rag that left oily circles. "What'll it be?"

Hunt rubbed his fingertips over the unfamiliarly smooth sides of his jaw, peered at the backbar. "Any good corn whisky?"

The bartender turned, studied the labels, nodded. "Right good." He selected a bottle from the back bar, lifted an eyebrow at the girl. "And your friend?"

"Scotch," Liz told him.

The man selected two glasses from under the bar, dumped a lump of ice into each. He slid the glasses over in front of Liz and the old man, tilted the bottles over them. He filled Hunt's glass too full, scowled, lifted it, swabbed the bar dry. "Looking for anyone special, Hunt?"

The old man nodded. "Lew Barker. He's expecting us."

The bartender raised his eyebrows, looked from Hunt to the girl, nodded. "I'll tell him you're here."

Liz picked up her glass, smelled it, tasted it. It tasted as good as it smelled. She turned her back to the bar, took inventory. The operators of the Blue Angel had retained as much of the original flavor of the parlor as had been feasible. At the far end an archway had been broken through the wall into what looked like a game room beyond.

"Quite a spot," she told Hunt. "Your friend owns it?"

Hunt shrugged. "He represents the people that do." He nodded toward the room beyond. "They got some real games running in there." He held his glass to his lips, swallowed deeply.

A muted buzzer sounded behind the bar. The bartender picked up the house phone, muttered into it, nodded, replaced it on its hook. Then, he walked down the bar to where Liz sat. "The boss says it's okay for you to go up now." He looked at Hunter. "He wants to see her alone."

The old man started to argue, thought better of it, licked at his lips. "Should I wait for her?"

The bartender shook his head. "The boss will get in touch with you, he said."

The old man drained his glass, set it back on the bar, turned and left without a word.

"Where do I go?"

The bartender pointed to a flight of stairs in the entrance foyer that led to the upper stories. "At the head of the stairs Mr. Barker's partners will take care of you." He seemed to lose interest in her, picked up a glass, started polishing it.

Liz finished her drink, set the glass back on the bar. She took a last look at her-self in a hand mirror, was satisfied with what she saw, started for the staircase.

At the head of the stairs, a 200-pound fashionplate in a midnight blue tuxedo stood waiting, a red carnation in his buttonhole, a lazy smile pasted on his lips.

"I'm looking for Mr. Barker," Liz told him.

The big man's eyes took inventory of her obvious assets. "I'm Vic Doss, Lew's partner." He sniffed at the carnation in his lapel. "I think you're going to do just fine." His hand was soft, moist where it caught her arm. "What did you say your name was?"

"I didn't. It's Liz Allen."

The lazy smile grew broader. "We ought to be able to do better than that." He led the way down the corridor toward a closed door. "I'll let Lew talk to you now. But I hope I'll be seeing you later." He knocked on the closed door, turned the knob and pushed it open. "Here's the girl, Lew."

The room beyond was half office, half den. It was a big room with knotty-pine paneling and Indian rugs. In an old fieldstone fireplace a comfortable fire hissed and puffed on the stone hearth.

Lew Barker was sprawled comfortably in an armchair. He waved to the girl to come into the room. "Hello, baby," he drawled. "Nice of you to come." His voice was silky, smooth with just a trace of deep-south drawl to betray his Al-abama origin. He was long, loose-jointed. His sandy hair had receded from his brow to the crown of his head, exposing a freckled pate. He had a ready smile that plowed white trenches in the mahogany of his cheeks. "Sit down."

Liz walked over to one of the easy chairs facing the man, dropped into it. "Thanks." She gave no sign of resenting the way he looked her over. "Hunt thought you might be able to help me get on my way to New York. He said you had a lot of friends up there."

"Business friends, mostly," Barker nodded. He seemed satisfied with the re-sult of his examination. "Where are you from, Liz?"

Liz pursed her lips, shrugged. "I've been a lot of places." She reached over, picked a cigarette from a humidor on a small table next to her chair. "I'm a lot more interested in where I'm going than in where I've been."

Barker nodded absently, his eyes going over her. "That the only dress you've got?"

Liz grinned, smoothed the skirt over her thighs. "Yeah, and it's not even mine. Hunt dug it up from one of his girl boarders."

"We'll have to get you some clothes," the man in the chair mused. "Mind standing up and turning around?"

Liz shrugged, hung the cigarette from the corner of her mouth. She stood up, turned around slowly. "Do I pass?"

Barker grunted, reached over to press a button at his elbow. "I think so. The most important thing is that you're not known here." He turned as the door to the den opened and the man with the red carnation came in. "You've met her,

Vic. What do you think?"

Vic Doss sniffed at the carnation, puffed out his lips. "Take a little dressing-up, maybe. But she ought to fill the bill."

"Mind telling me what I'm supposed to be doing?" Liz wanted to know. She looked from the big man to the man in the chair.

"You particular?" Barker drawled.

Liz thought it over. "Depends."

"We heard you had a narrow escape from the police," Barker told her. He fished a long cigarette holder out of his breast pocket, tilted it in the corner of his mouth. "You want to get as far away from here as possible. We want to help you." He chewed on the stem of the holder. "We understand each other?"

"You still didn't tell me what I'm supposed to do."

Barker looked over to his partner. "Tell her, Vic."

"We want you to keep a pretty close eye on a friend of ours. If he were to get out of line any way, we'd like to know about it." The lazy smile was still pasted on the man's lips. "The further out of line he got, the better we'd like it."

Liz tapped a thin collar of ash from the end of her cigarette with her index finger, watched it float to the rug. "And if he didn't get out of line, you wouldn't object to my making it look like he did?" She looked up through her lashes at the big man.

"I couldn't have put it better myself," he nodded. He walked over to a small bar in the corner, spilled some liquor into three glasses, brought it back, handed one to the girl. "You see why we had to find a girl who was unknown in these parts?"

Liz accepted a glass, set it down on the table. "Who is this man?"

Vic looked at the man in the chair, raised his eyebrows questioningly. Barker shook his head.

"It's not necessary that you know right now."

Liz shrugged. "Okay. Then count me out." She started toward the door. Barker waited until she had her hand on the knob.

"The police still aren't convinced there wasn't a girl in the car with the punk when he killed that garage man," Barker told her softly. "They'd love to have that girl."

She turned, studied him through narrowed eyes. "And you'd give her to them?"

Barker shrugged. "I wouldn't. But don't you think that Hunt, as a good citizen, should cooperate with the police if he can?" He sipped at his glass. "I just heard something else tonight that might be of interest to you. They think the girl that was with him was a waitress at a joint called Mickey's. That's where the first car was stolen from."

Liz walked back to the chair, dropped into it. "They wouldn't know her name?"

Barker shrugged. "What's in a name? It could be changed easily enough." He swirled the liquor around in his glass. "Besides, they're looking for a vag, a waitress. With some fresh clothes and the services of a hairdresser, nobody would ever know you."

Liz nodded. "You've sold me."

"Then you'll do it?"

"You mean I've got a choice?" Liz picked up her drink, drained the glass. "You finger me as being in the car with Gun when it pulled into Hunt's cabin court and I'm a cinch to take the rap for at least one killing. I don't figure to have too much to lose, do I?"

Barker looked to his partner, smiled. "The old man was right. She is smart." His eyes swiveled back to the girl. "But I hope for her sake that she's not too smart."

TEN
Experiment in Passion

A car picked Liz and Viv Doss up at the back door to the Blue Angel, headed for town. Liz watched the character of the neighborhood through which they were riding change from big estates to smaller suburban developments. They shot past the blank faces of closed stores, past unlighted homes and empty stretches of wooded country.

Liz leaned back against the cushions, let the cool wind wipe the fatigue from her eyes. In the other corner of the back seat, the big man sat, smoking silently.

"Do I get to know what I've let myself in for, Vic?" Liz asked finally. "Where are we going now?"

"We're going to find you a place to live. Then we're going to get you some decent clothes. And then we're going to set you up with a whole new identity." He rolled his eyes upward at the roof of the car. "Liz Allen, eh? We certainly should be able to do better than that."

Liz reached over, picked the cigarette from between his fingers, took a deep drag, exhaled it in a feathery stream. "Not that I'm crazy about the name myself. But why change it?"

Doss shrugged. "For one thing, somebody might recognize it. You heard what Barker said. Somebody put the finger on you back at that joint where you used to work."

"Mickey," the girl growled.

The big man grinned. "What's the matter? He throw a pass that didn't complete?"

"Mickey was a she. She tried to peddle me off into a stable." She took another drag from the cigarette. "That's not for me."

Doss nodded. "That's for the birds. No gal with your equipment and any brains at all would have to take that kind of a set-up.''

"No? What kind do you have in mind?''

"Suspicious, aren't you?'' The big man twisted his head, sniffed at the carnation in his button hole. "Only, we don't have to recruit girls this part of the country. We got more amateur talent volunteering than we could book.''

"But you sent for me?''

Doss nodded. "The job we want takes a gal with some nerve and some brains. The local talent hasn't got either. All their equipment is below their neck.''

"You still haven't told me the job.''

"There's a man in town been giving us some trouble. We want to fix it so he doesn't.''

Liz wrinkled her forehead, pursed her lips. "You want someone to put him on the spot?''

"Sort of. But not for a hit. It would bring too much heat if anything happened to him.'' The lazy smile was pasted back on his lips. "We want to be able to talk turkey to him. Right now he's pretty high and mighty dealing with us. We figure he ought to be brought down to size.''

"And I'm supposed to do it?'' Liz asked doubtfully.

"You can do it, baby,'' the big man assured her. "This guy has a weakness for the bottle. But he's plenty cagy who he's with when he hits the stuff. We haven't been able to get near him.''

"Who is this character?''

"The county attorney. His name's Ben Lewis. One of those big deal reform characters. Got himself elected by promising to run all the rackets out of the county.''

"That doesn't make it sound easy.''

Doss chuckled. "You don't know Ben Lewis. He's going to run all the games and all the girls out of the county, sure. But only those that belong to Lew Barker.'' He pursed his lips. "He's been giving us a bad time and we've got to get to him before the big boys up north figure we can't handle it by ourselves.''

"That would be bad, eh?''

"That would be fatal.'' Doss stared out the window. "The big boys don't take any excuses. Barker gets the franchise to run down here, they expect their cut. Every week. With Lewis beginning to put the heat on, we're beginning to fall off.'' He looked back at the girl. "Lewis has to be brought in line.''

Liz nodded. "Okay. But what do I get out of it if I pull it off?''

"You'll be taken care of,'' Doss promised. "You pull Barker off this hook and you can write your own ticket in this town. How's that sound?''

"You've got yourself a girl.'' She looked out the window as the car started to pull through more and more densely populated areas. "We coming into town now?''

The big man nodded. "We'll be where we're going in a few minutes. It's just a place for you to hole up until we can get you some decent clothes and find you a spot to stay." He grinned broadly. "You don't have to worry about this place. No one will bother you there."

"When will I hear from you again?"

"You probably won't, Liz. We'll get word to you through some of our people. There's a girl named Les that runs this place we're going to. When the time comes, she'll give you your instructions. Do what she says. She'll take care of getting you your clothes and setting you up in a hotel. We'll take it from there."

"Okay, if you say so. What'll I do for money to pay for the hotel and for eating?"

The big man reached into his pocket, pulled out a small roll of bills. He passed it over to the girl. "There's enough there to take care of what you need, and not enough to make it worthwhile blowing town. You play this one smart, baby, and you can have enough of that green stuff to paper a room. But—" he paused meaningly.

"But what?"

"Like Barker said—if you play it too smart, there'll be too much red spilled on that green to make it any good for using."

"Don't worry about me. You just see to it that I get next to your friend Lewis and I'll take care of him." She lapsed into a silence, settled back, stared out the window. After a few moments, the car pulled up to the curb in front of an old stone house. Over the doorway, a paint-peeled sign announced it as "Les Wells' Cellar." The door was three steps down from the street, opened into a small vestibule that had been converted into a check room. A heavily painted blonde presided over the coats hanging on the wall. It required a close second look to identify the check room "girl" as a man.

Vic Doss led the way through into a huge room that served as a combination bar room and dance floor. The lights were low, orange colored, spilling deep shadows all over the place. A bar, set against the far wall, was empty except for two Marines and a heavy-set man in drag.

Doss walked over to the bar, beckoned to the bartender. He was heavy, fleshy. His eyes were almost hidden behind discolored pouches, his lips were a thick, wet smear. But at least he affected trousers.

"Where's Les?" Doss wanted to know.

"Entertaining a friend." The eyes rotated to Liz, the bartender made no attempt to veil his dislike. "She's a spook, isn't she?"

"She's not here to get sociable. See that nobody bothers her."

The bartender bared discolored teeth in what passed for a smile. "Don't flatter her. Nobody'd give her a second look." There was a trace of a lisp in his simpering tone. "I'll tell Les you're here."

"What's a spook?" Liz wanted to know as soon as the bartender had swished off in the direction of the telephone.

"A girl who's not queer. They don't see many of them in here."

The bartender waddled back to where they stood. "Les says she's busy right now. She'll be down in a minute." He reached under the bar, brought up a bottle and two glasses. "Have a drink on the house. Is there anything else I can do for you?"

Doss grinned at him. "Not the best day of your life. Leave the bottle here. We'll call you if we need you."

The bartender's eyes receded behind their discolored pouches, a muscle flicked in the side of his throat. The fat wet lips puffed in and out in indignation, leaving a little bubble between them. For a moment Liz thought he was going to retort, but instead he turned and flounced back to the far end of the bar where the two Marines and the gowned man were getting gay and loud.

Liz was on her second drink and fourth cigarette, when a slim young man with thick, wavy black hair crossed the room, touched Vic Doss on the elbow. He was wearing a powdered blue suit and a flaming red tie, his eyes were large and liquid, his lips full and sensuous.

"Sorry to keep you waiting, Vic." When he talked, his voice was low, intimate—almost as though he were whispering. He turned the full power of the big eyes on Liz. "Is this your friend?" His eyes flicked from Liz's hair to her lips to the high breasts, down over the rounded thighs to the well-shaped calves. "It seeme a shame to waste something nice on a slob like Lewis."

"Don't mention names, Les," Vic growled. "Nothing must go wrong with this set-up. Too much is riding on it."

Les smiled, a slow, tantalizing smile. It came as a shock to Liz to realize that despite the mannish get-up, Les was a woman. Her hand was soft and moist as she took Liz's in it. "Nothing will go wrong."

A worried look creased the big man's eyes. "Don't get any ideas, Les. Barker will tear you apart if you lay a hand on her. Lewis or no other man would touch her if you did."

The low voice drawled insinuatingly. "They wouldn't have to. She wouldn't let them."

"Never mind trying to prove it," Doss snapped. "Tomorrow you set her up with all the clothes she'll need. Barker tell you how he wants that handled?"

Les nodded, didn't take her eyes off Liz. "I've got it all set up. All we'll need is the size." The eyes caressed the girl's shape again. "That shouldn't take too long."

Doss nodded impatiently. "Okay. Then see to it that she's registered into the Spotlight Club." He turned to Liz. "You're a out of work cigarette girl. Maybe you used to sing or something. You set it up the way you like it. Just so's you have a reason for living in the Spotlight. Got it?"

Liz nodded. "How do I make contact with this Lewis?"

"Leave that to us. You just check into the Spotlight, answer any ads for a cigarette girl. We'll take care of the rest. That clear?"

Liz nodded.

The big man turned back to Les. "Then I'll get out of here before somebody spots me with her." He picked up his glass, drained it, set it back on the bar. "Play your cards right, kid, and you can hit the jackpot in this town."

"She'll be all right." Les squeezed the girl's hand. "She looks real smart to me. Don't worry about a thing, Doss. Everything's going to go all right."

Doss started to say something, checked himself, nodded. He walked across to the door, passed through to the street.

"Another drink, honey?" Les wanted to know.

Liz shook her head. "I'm kind of tired."

The mannish girl shrugged. "I'll show you to a room." She slipped her hand under Liz's arm, led the way through the welter of tables. At the far end of the room a disguised stairway led to the upper story. At the top of the stairs, there was a long hallway with closed doors, an overpowering smell of perfume and cologne, the muffled sounds of revelry. Les led the girl to the end door, pushed it open. "You can have this room." She waited until Liz had stepped in, closed the door behind her.

"I won't stay long," Les told her in the low, intimate voice. "I just wanted to get your size."

"Twelve," Liz told her.

The other girl's eyes were amused, a grin played with the ends of her lips. "Afraid of me?" she challenged.

Liz was aware of a strange fascination, a combination of excitement and revulsion. She unzipped the dress, slid it back off her shoulders, stood in front of the other woman. She was aware of an unfamiliar shyness, a feeling she had never felt standing before a man.

Les walked over to her, slid her arm around her. Her hand was like soft, warm water over her breast. As the arm around her waist tightened, Liz turned her face away. The lesbian's lips missed her mouth, settled for the hollow of her neck. Liz got the flat of her palms against the other girl's chest, pushed her back.

Les's long, wavy hair had come loose from over her ear, had fallen down over the side of her cheek. She was breathing heavily, her eyes and lips shining. When she tried to move close again, Liz pushed her back.

"I'm a spook, remember?" Liz told her.

ELEVEN
Change of Address

The next two days were busy ones for Liz. A string of messengers arrived with packages of clothes, some new, some used. A hairdresser who had all the earmarks of a regular habitué of Les's place arrived, changed the long bob to an abbreviated gamin cut. Liz pored through a pile of back issues of *Variety* and *Bill-*

board, acquired an intimate knowledge of the backstage gossip of New Orleans and its environs.

On the evening of the second day, she was standing at the window, staring down into the alley that ran behind Les's place. There was a knock at the door, and Les walked in. It was the first time Liz had seen her since the night of her arrival.

"Everything ready?" Les wanted to know. There was a distant note in her voice.

"All set. When do I move, Les?" Liz wanted to know.

"Tonight. The plane from New Orleans gets in at 9:30. You're supposed to be on it. We'll get you out to the airport, you'll take a cab back. There's a room for you at the Spotlight Club. You know what you're supposed to do?"

"Answer any ads for a cigarette girl."

Les nodded. She stuck a cigarette in the corner of her mouth, snapped a wooden match on her thumb nail. "One other thing. That Liz Allen tag is out. You can use the same initials. Call yourself Lorna Andrews. Can you remember that?"

"Lorna Andrews." She walked over to the lesbian, took the cigarette from between her lips, took a deep drag. "Thanks for everything, Les. You're not sore?"

Les's eyes narrowed. "Not now." She turned on her heel, left the room, slammed the door after her.

"Lorna" checked her watch, frowned at the realization that she had less than two hours to get to the airport. She hastily packed the two bags that had been provided her, checked the room to make sure she had forgotten nothing.

She walked down to the bar, could see no sign of Les. The fat bartender cast her a surly glance, applied himself to polishing a glass. Lorna walked over, leaned against the bar. He twisted his lips petulantly, finished the glass he was polishing, set his cigarette on the upturned bottom of another glass. There was a faint flush of disapproval on his face as he waddled back to her.

"Let me have a drink, will you?" she asked him. "And have somebody bring my bags down from the back room. I'll be taking a cab."

The bartender sniffed, tossed his head, brought a bottle up from under the bar. His hips waggled as he came from behind the bar, crossed the room to the stairs.

Lorna finished her drink as the bartender puffed down the stairs carrying the two bags. He walked out to the front door, dumped them on the top step, returned to his post in back of the bar. He hung the half-smoked cigarette between his lips, went back to his glass polishing with no sign that he was aware of her presence.

She dropped a bill on the bar, walked to the front door. A group of men in uniform were sitting in the end booth drinking beer. As she passed, none of them looked up. A group of mannish-looking women in the next booth turned to watch her and she was aware of their eyes on her legs and hips as she walked through the door.

It bothered her as she waited for the cab. She remembered what Vic Doss had said about the touch of a lesbian warding off all male interest. She wondered if the encounter she had had with Les in her room that first night had tainted her. She was relieved when the cab skidded to a stop at the curb and the driver climbed the three short steps to get her bags.

The cabby was a short, fat little man with a greasy chauffeur's cap shoved on the back of his head. The frayed end of a toothpick protruded from between his lips. He looked Lorna over with knowing eyes. He waited until Lorna had gotten in, leaned back against the cushions.

"Where to?"

"The airport," Lorna told him. "I've got to be there no later than 9:30. Can we make it?"

"In a breeze, lady." He squirmed around on his seat, studied her curiously. "You a stranger in town?"

Lorna nodded.

"It figured. You don't look like their regular trade in there." He made a grimace, shrugged his shoulders. "Never could figure how those babes got their kicks. They make a pass at you?"

"Mind taking me to the airport?" Lorna cut him off.

The cabby swung around in his seat, jammed the car into gear. "Nothing personal. I just figured maybe you didn't know what kind of a dive it was you were walking into." He glanced up into the rear view mirror. "Now, if you were going home because you ran out of dough, I know a couple of places where a gal like you—"

"The airport," Lorna snapped.

The cabbie threw the toothpick through the window in disgust, turned back to his wheel. He didn't say another word until he'd wheeled the cab into the hack stand at the airport. "You're making a mistake. This is a live town if you got the right connections," he told her sadly.

Lorna shoved a bill through the window at him, joined the few strugglers heading for the airport administration building. Once inside, she walked to the window, satisfied herself that the cabby was on his way back to town. She walked over to the newsstand, selected a magazine, sat down to wait.

The 9:30 through flight from New Orleans was posted as ten minutes late. As the loud speaker announced the plane's arrival, Lorna squeezed toward the barrier, took up a position near the exit gate. The landing platform was wheeled to the big ship's side and soon a trickle of passengers started debarking. She waited until a group carrying baggage debarked and headed for the exit gate. As they came through, she picked up her baggage, followed them to the hack stand. She permitted the redcap to wave down a cab for her, climbed in and settled back.

"The Spotlight Club, driver," she told the cabby. "Know where it is?"

"Yes, ma'am. Right in the heart of town. Be there in no time."

The Spotlight Club was an old-fashioned residential hotel, an old brownstone house set in a row of similar brownstone houses. It had a faded awning that showed signs of having waged a losing battle with time and strong winds. Nobody had bothered to patch the gaping rips that flapped noisily in the evening breeze. The stone façade was dirty, neglected looking.

The prim little lobby had the requisite number of tired rubber plants, a few chairs obviously not intended to be sat upon, a general air of decay. The impression was borne out by the shabby registration desk and the old man who presided over it. He blew his nose noisily as Lorna crossed the lobby, deposited her bags in front of it. He favored her with a jaundiced look, raised an eyebrow.

"I'm Lorna Andrews. I think I have a reservation?"

The expression on the old man's face indicated that he didn't share her optimism, but he decided to check. He came up with a reservation card, managed to look annoyed.

"From where?"

"New Orleans," Lorna told him.

He shoved a dog-eared registration book in front of her, stowed his dingy handkerchief in his hip pocket. "How long you going be staying?" he wanted to know. The girl wrote "Lorna Andrews" in the ledger, scowled at the ink stain on her thumb. "Depends on how soon I can find some work."

"What do you do?"

Lorna shrugged. "A little of anything. Been hustling butts mostly."

The man behind the desk looked mildly disappointed. "Thought every girl in New Orleans was a strip teaser," he complained. He unhooked a key with a cardboard tag, banged on the desk with the flat of his hand. "Your room number's 335. No cooking in the rooms." He dug at a back molar with his thumbnail, seemed to forget her presence.

A pimply faced kid with blue shiny pants and an open bellhop jacket materialized at her side. He picked up the bags, tucked one under his arm. "What's her cell number?" he asked the man behind the desk.

The old man didn't deign to answer, shoved the key across the desk. The bellhop picked it up, glanced at the number, grunted. "This way, sister," he told her. He led the way to an old-fashioned, open grillwork elevator.

He started the ancient contraption wheezing upward, leaned back against the elevator wall, looked the girl over approvingly. "We're getting a better class people, looks like. In town long?"

Lorna shook her head. "Just came in on the 9:30 flight."

The elevator boy nodded. "Not stuck-up, either. From N'Orleans?"

"And points north, east and west."

The elevator boy wet his slack lips with his tongue. "That's what I'd like to do. Keep moving." His eyes flicked around the dingy elevator disgustedly. "Me, all I ever see is these four walls."

The elevator came to a shuddering stop at the third floor. The hop slid the grillwork door back with a shrill creak, propped it open. He picked up the bags, led the way down a long, bare corridor, stopped in front of her door. He fitted the key, pushed the door open, stepped aside.

Lorna walked in, looked around. "Looks pretty nice."

The elevator boy wrinkled his nose and looked around. "It's a dump and you know it." He deposited the bags on the bed.

"Well, I didn't come here to write the place up for *House Beautiful*, that's for sure." Lorna dug into her bag, came up with some silver.

"Thanks." The boy's watery eyes undressed her again. "My name's Willy. Case you want something—" He licked at his lips again. "I know a lot of guys who get kind of lonesome, and—"

Lorna caught him by the shoulder, pushed him to the door. "If I want anything, I'll call you." She closed the door after him, turned the key in the lock.

TWELVE
Cigarette Girl

The ad appeared in the "Help Wanted—Female" column in the local newspaper on the second day of her stay at the Spotlight Club. She was leafing through the back section of the paper when it seemed to jump out and hit her in the eye:

CIGARETTE GIRL WANTED
Must be experienced, young, pretty.
Good salary, Good tips, Uniform pro-
vided by management. Apply in person.
Café Laurence

Lorna cut it out with a long, pointed thumbnail, studied it with a frown. Obviously, this was the ad she was expecting. Yet, how could she be sure? She dismissed the idea of calling Les, decided to follow instructions and answer the ad.

She picked up the phone, asked for room service. "Willy on?" she asked the metallic voice at the other end.

"Willy? Yeah. He's around. Want something?"

"Some orange juice and coffee. Ask him to bring it right up." She could hear the sniff of disapproval at the other end, dropped the receiver on its hook.

A few minutes later there was a knock on the door. "Come in," she called.

The door opened, and the pimply faced bellboy sidled in, a cup and saucer and glass on a tray. He walked over to the bureau, set it down. "Anything else, Miss Andrews?"

Lorna walked over to him, held the clipping out.

"What kind of a spot is this Café Laurence?"

The bellboy took the clipping, read it with moving lips, then whistled. "Tops. That's the real cream." He handed it back, shook his head. "You get to work there and you're rubbing shoulders with the cream, what I mean."

"That good, eh?" Lorna caught her full upper lip between her teeth, worried it. "Who runs the place?"

"Big Larry. Larry Bauer, that is." He licked at his lips. "He used to be a big wheel in the rackets. Real big." He shook his head again. "Boy, you get in there and you got something."

Lorna picked up some change from the dresser, gave it to the boy. "Thanks, Willy."

"You going to try for it?"

Lorna nodded. "What can I lose?" She glanced at her wristwatch. "It didn't say what time to show up. Think 4 o'clock's too early?"

"Don't waste any time. Get right down there," the bellboy counseled. "So you wait awhile. That's better'n getting there too late." The slack lips puckered up into another soundless whistle. "The Café Laurence. Boy, that's something."

Lorna pushed him toward the door. "Keep your fingers crossed for me."

The boy's face relaxed into a loose-lipped grin. "Yeah, I'll do that. And maybe you better keep your legs crossed. There's going to be some heavy competition for that job."

The Café Laurence was a chromium-plated supper club with a multicolored canopy that extended to the curb. During hours, a giant in the full regalia of an admiral acted as doorman, and hidden lights bathed the front in a soft glow. At 4 o'clock in the afternoon, shorn of all its glamor, it was just a blank-faced store front, a tired old building relaxing with its glamor make-up off.

Lorna left the cab at the curb, crossed the sidewalk to the entrance. She pushed through the thick glass door into the foyer. A dozen or more girls, of all sizes, shapes and hair coloring, clustered at the rope thrown across the entrance to the dining room. A bored-looking man in a tuxedo stood guard at the rope with crossed arms. The smell of perfume in the enclosed space was almost over-whelming.

"When do we see the guy doing the hiring?" a plump blonde demanded pettishly. "I been here almost an hour."

"If you got someplace more important to be, don't let us keep you," the man in the tuxedo grunted. "Mr. Bauer will be out in a few minutes and he'll decide who he wants to talk to."

The blonde subsided with a lot of mumbling.

The tuxedoed guard's eyes fixed on Lorna. "You just get here?"

Lorna nodded.

"You fill out a card?" he demanded.

Lorna shook her head, walked up to the rope, accepted an application blank. She retired to the back of the foyer, braced the card against the wall, filled in the blanks. In the space marked "Experience?" she filled in, "Cigarette girl, Valentin Café, New Orleans, three years." When the card was filled out, she returned it to the man at the rope. He added it to the small batch he had in his hand.

Two more girls joined the group before Larry Bauer came out. He was a big white-haired man in a wheat-colored cashmere jacket, blue corduroy shirt and blue slacks. He paid no attention to the girls who surged forward as he appeared, held his hand out for the filled-in cards.

The man in the tuxedo handed them to him, lost interest.

Bauer leafed through the cards. "Who's Ann Ledge?"

The buxom blonde tossed a triumphant glance at the other girls, stood up. "That's me."

"Sorry, sweetheart," Bauer told her. "You haven't done enough hustling—of butts, that is." He tapped the card on his thumb. "We don't want to have to break anyone in."

The blonde turned on her heel, elbowed her way through the rest of the girls, flounced out the door.

"The ad meant what it said, girls. Any of you haven't put in a couple of years in a good spot, you're wasting our time."

There was a low murmur from the girls, then one by one they started for the door. Only three were left—a tall drugstore redhead who was waging a losing battle with the crow's feet and lines at the corners of her mouth, a young full-blown blonde and Lorna.

"What's your name, sweetheart?" Bauer asked the redhead.

"Ginger, Mr. Bauer, Ginger Carr."

The white-haired man flipped through the cards, selected hers, glanced at it. He looked up from the card, studied the woman. "Been around awhile, eh, sweetheart?" His voice was kindly. "Worked the old Chateau Chance out in the county. That ain't recent."

The redhead shook her head. "Ten years ago," she dropped her eyes to her hands, started to dry-wash them. "I got married while I was working there. I married Ben Duffy."

"I remember Ben. A good boy. I heard about what happened to him. Too bad."

"Things happen," the redhead shrugged. "Well, thanks anyway." She started to turn away.

"Wait a minute, Ginger," Bauer told her. He plucked at his lower lip with thumb and forefinger. "It doesn't have to be hustling butts, does it?"

The redhead stopped, shook her head. "I'd take anything, Mr. Bauer. It's not as easy to get a job as it used to be."

"How about working with the girls out back. Helping them with their costumes and stuff? Maybe you can teach them to keep that place looking decent. How about it?"

She was dry-washing the hands again. "I'd take anything."

"Okay, sweetheart," he winked at her. "You got yourself a job. Louie here can show you where to hang your hat."

The man in the tuxedo unhooked the rope, waited until the redhead had followed him through, hooked it again. He led the way toward the back of the big room.

The white-haired man looked at Lorna. "What's your name, sweetheart?"

"Andrews. Lorna Andrews," she told him.

He found her card, squinted at it. "You worked the Valentin in New Orleans, eh? Three years?" Lorna nodded. "Who was playing the place when you left?"

"The Lambertis. They've been there almost a year." Bauer nodded, flicked a glance at the other girl. "How about you, sweetheart. What's your name?"

"Lucille Flair, Mr. Bauer." She watched while he dug out her card, studied it. "I have a lot friends who'd like to see me get the job and they'd—"

"They're going to be disappointed, sweetheart," Bauer told her. He tapped the cards on his thumb. "I want a cigarette girl, not a hostess. Some other time," he dismissed her with a glance. He unhooked the rope. "Come on into the office, sweetheart," he told Lorna.

Lorna followed the white-haired man down a small corridor that ran parallel to the dining room to a door marked "Private." He pushed it open, held it for her.

The room was small, contained a large, highly polished desk, a small sofa and two leather chairs. Lorna sank into one of the chairs, waited.

The big man crossed to the desk, hoisted one hip on the corner, studied her. "Can you start tonight?" he wanted to know.

Lorna nodded. "Any time you say. I don't have any uniform."

"We'll provide that. Mind standing up?"

Lorna stood up.

"Lift your skirts."

The girl grinned at him, pulled her skirts to her knees.

"The costume's shorter than that."

She hiked the skirt another inch, then at a signal a little higher. "If the costume's any shorter than that, no use my wearing it," she told him.

"You'll do," Bauer grinned. He got off the end of the desk, walked around, pulled open the top drawer. He pulled out a picture. "You're a stranger in town, probably never saw any of our local celebrities." He tossed the picture across the desk. "That's our county attorney. Name's Ben Lewis. Nice fellow—real nice. Gets a little bit unreasonable at times, though."

Lorna picked up the picture, studied it. A man was sitting at a ringside table.

He wore his hair long, plastered back over his ears. His face was long and horse-like, shrewd in a thin-lipped, pinched-nose sort of way. She familiarized herself with his features, tossed the picture back on the desk. "Wouldn't exactly call him a country boy, would you?"

Bauer snickered, picked up the picture, dropped it back into the drawer. "Not twice, you wouldn't. He's a smart operator." He slammed the drawer shut, locked it with a key on his chain. "Hard man to reason with, too. Giving a lot of boys a real headache, Ben is."

"And you?"

The white-haired man raked his stubby fingers through the thick white mane. "Not me, sweetheart. Ben doesn't bother old Larry. Not yet, anyhow. Doing most of his picking's on the county boys—Lew Barker and Vic Doss. Fellows like that. But you wouldn't know them, you're a stranger in town."

"Yeah, that's right. I wouldn't know them." Lorna got up. "Anything else I ought to know, Mr. Bauer?"

"Call me Larry, sweetheart. Everybody does. All my friends, that is."

"Okay, Larry. What time am I due back?"

"Around ten will do. Nothing much happens at dinner. Most of our business starts around eleven or eleven-thirty. We run until about four."

"I'll be here at ten." She turned, started for the door, stopped halfway to it, turned around. "Nothing else I ought to know?"

Bauer shook his head. "Any time I think of something I'll pass it along. Right now, you handle things the way you like. If you look like you're getting off the track, I'll let you know."

THIRTEEN
First Bite

At night, the supper room of the Café Laurence was filled, the tables packed closely together around a large dance floor. Lorna stood in the entrance, squinted through the smoke at the floor where, as the band blared out an introductory chord, the lights went down.

A long, yellow spot stabbed through the dimness of the room to outline the figure of the girl emcee. She undulated out onto the stage, waited for the overhead mike to be lowered into range, broke into a brassy song of welcome. Her voice was husky, roughened by whisky and overuse.

After the song, a long line of girls scampered onto the floor in spangled brassieres and satin tights. They went through a tortured routine, twisted and squirmed under the colored spot, their bare legs flashing, their bare stomachs undulating. They ran off the stage to a smattering of applause, gave way to a piano singer that played and sang a series of double-entendre songs in a manner that left them open to only one interpretation.

The line of girls was back with different costumes, the same bare midriffs and insufficient brassieres. This time they made way for the brassy-voiced emcee. She leaned against the piano, threw her head back, gave herself over to wails of unrequited love. She permitted herself to be coaxed into an encore by a half-hearted round of applause, then bowed her way back to the stage door.

When the house lights went up, a thick pall of smoke swirled near the ceiling. Close by there was a hum as the air-conditioning fought a one-sided battle to fill the place with fresh air.

Lorna walked back to the check room, hooked a tray of cigars and cigarettes around her neck. Her long legs were unencumbered in a pair of breathtakingly brief shorts. Above, she stretched a white silk peasant blouse to the limits of credibility. She started making her way through the tables, stopping every so often at an upraised hand or on a signal from a waiter. On a previous tour of the floor, she had spotted County Attorney Ben Lewis sitting alone at a table near the dance floor. To date, he had given no sign of being aware of her presence.

From the corner of her eye, she saw Larry Bauer cross the floor, pull out a chair at the prosecutor's table. The night club man pulled a cigar from his breast pocket, offered it to Lewis, then fumbled at the pocket, came away empty-handed. He raised his hand, two waiters sprang to the table.

One of the waiters walked over to where Lorna was giving change on a sale of cigarettes.

"Better get over. The boss is fresh out of rope," the waiter told her.

Lorna nodded, started for the table. She threw a little motion into her walk that made her hips swing, her breasts trace patterns on the blouse. She stopped at the table, gave the white-haired man her best smile.

"Ran out of smokes, sweetheart," Bauer told her. He picked four Coronas off her tray, dropped a five. "Keep it for the piggy bank." He looked to the county attorney. "Maybe you ought to have some for the road, Ben?"

When Lorna leaned over so the prosecutor could select some cigars, the neck of the blouse sagged enough to prove that nature had needed no assist in the magnificence of her façade.

Lewis took his time about selecting his cigars, made no attempt to disguise the inventory he was taking of her assets. "A new girl, Larry?"

Bauer looked up at Lorna, nodded. "The redhead got too friendly with some of the customers. It got bad for business, Ben. I talked to her about it and she flew off the handle. I had to get rid of her."

The horse-face man nodded, didn't take his eyes off the girl. "I haven't seen you around before, have I?"

"Not unless you've been to New Orleans lately," Bauer told him. "She just got in the other night. Used to work the Valentin down in the Quarter."

Lewis nodded, grinned. His teeth were big, discolored. "I hear that's quite a town, that Orleans. Why'd you leave?"

Lorna looked from Lewis to the night club man and back. "I just got tired of it. I get tired of lots of things, mister. Like getting asked questions."

"Don't mind me, baby," Lewis grinned. "I can't help asking questions. I'm the county attorney. It's second nature to me."

"Is there anything else you want, Mr. Bauer?" Lorna turned to her employer.

The white-haired man shook his head. She swung on her heel, swivel-hipped her way back through the tables. The effect from the rear was just as satisfying as it had been from the front.

"Not bad, Larry, not bad," the county attorney commented. He bit an end off the cigar, spat it on the floor, kept his eyes on the girl's hips. "Where'd you get her?"

"An ad in the paper. Turned up about thirty girls. Most of them I wouldn't hire to work in the kitchen." He stuck his cigar between his teeth. "Hired another one, too. Remember old Ben Duffy?"

The county attorney nodded. "I remember old Ben. A pretty good boy. Always did suspect that county mob of Lew Barker's knocked him off. Wish I could prove it." He lit his cigar with a silver lighter, blew a stream of smoke across the table. "What about Ben?"

"His wife turned out in answer to the ad."

Lewis raised his eyebrows. "Ain't she a little old?"

"Broke, too. I put her on in the wardrobe. She can help the girls get dressed and keep their stuff in order. Old Ben was a pretty good lad."

"To get back to that new butt hustler. Know where she's staying?"

"Spotlight Club. Why?"

"I like a girl with a little spirit. I thought maybe I might get to know her a little better." He rolled his cigar between thumb and forefinger in the center of his mouth. "I suppose you checked her experience?"

"Yeah. I wired down to the Valentin. They said she was one of the best. Why?"

"It's like I said. Asking questions is like a second nature to me. I just like to know who I'm dealing with." He clamped his teeth into the cigar, leaned back, smoked contentedly.

At four o'clock, the big supper room was a ghost room. Chairs were piled on tables, huge lights had been wheeled in to help the scrub women in their cleaning. The orchestra stand was deserted, the music racks standing gauntly like skeletons.

Lorna pushed through the door to the street. The cool breeze flapping the awning out front felt good after the closeness of the club. She looked up at the sky and decided it was a good night for walking. She was halfway up the street when a man tapped her on the arm.

"This is a bad time to be out walking by yourself, miss," he told her. "Good thing for you I happened along."

"Who are you?"

"Sergeant Fry. I'm attached to the county attorney's office." He raised his hand in a signal and a big black sedan pulled away from the curb down the block, came toward them. It came to a noiseless stop abreast of them, the back door swung open. Ben Lewis, the county attorney was in the back seat. He grinned at her.

"Give you a lift?"

Lorna looked in at him, grinned back. "You talked me into it. I didn't really want to walk anyhow."

She stepped in, sank down on the soft cushions of the back seat. Lewis reached across her, pulled the door closed. "You'd better grab a cab, Sergeant. You've got to get up early in the morning."

The sergeant grinned, touched his fingers to the brim of his hat.

"Where do you go?" Lewis wanted to know.

"Home."

The car roared into motion, pulled away from the curb. "Where's that?"

Lorna cocked a humorous eyebrow at him. "The Spotlight Club." She dug into her bag, brought up a pack of cigarettes, slit the cellophane with her thumbnail.

"Swag?" Lewis wanted to know.

"What's the use of being a cigarette girl if you can't have a cigarette now and then?" She stuck one between her lips, accepted a light from his silver lighter, leaned back.

"Planning to stay in town very long?" Lewis wanted to know.

Lorna shrugged. "Until I get bored. Then I move on." She looked at the man's profile. "Any reason?"

Lewis shrugged. "Just curious. An occupational disease." He pulled one of the cigars he had bought from her from his pocket, bit off the end. "Like a night-cap?"

She looked at him, held her wrist up to the light. "It's after four-thirty. I thought all the clubs closed at four in this town."

"They do. But there are some private clubs—bottle clubs that might ac-commodate us." He lit the cigar, exhaled. "What do you say?"

"Not tonight, if you don't mind. I'm a little tired. I'll take a rain check on it."

Lewis shrugged. "Suit yourself." He leaned forward. "Drop her off at the Spotlight Club, Ed."

The driver grunted his assent.

"I'll see to it that Bauer lets you off a little earlier," the prosecutor told her. "It's not much fun when you're too tired."

"Don't go losing me my job. I need it."

Lewis chuckled. "Nobody fires you if you're a friend of mine—any more'd anybody'd hire you if you weren't."

The car pulled up in front of the Spotlight Club, he leaned over and opened the door. "Be seeing you, baby."

She stepped out, closed the door behind her, watched the car pull away.

"And they call you a smart guy?" she muttered under her breath. "Anybody could sell you the Brooklyn Bridge."

She walked into the club, headed for the elevator. Willie was sitting on a stool, dozing. She pushed his shoulder. "Let's go, Bright Eyes."

He slammed the grillwork door, started the car on its laboring way. "You in a jam?" he wanted to know.

"Not that I know of. Why?"

"Cops. Guy from the prosecutor's office. Big guy named Fry. He shook your place down. Took that paper you got the ad out of."

Lorna chewed on her lip. "Anything else?"

Willy shook his head. "Just asked a lot of questions. What time the plane from N'Orleans gets in. What time you got here. Whose hack. All that kind of stuff." He licked at his lips. "You in a jam?"

Lorna shook her head. "No. I guess they were just checking my application," she grinned. When he started to leave the elevator with her, she pushed him back in firmly, pulled the door closed. She walked down the hall to her room, unlocked the door, walked in. There was no sign of any search. She leaned her back against the door, shook her head. "I take it back, Horse Face," she murmured. "That guy that sold you the Brooklyn Bridge is probably still working out his time."

FOURTEEN
Black Magic

Ben Lewis was a regular ringsider at the Café Laurence for the next two weeks. Every night his car waited outside the club to drive Lorna home. Finally, about two weeks after she started working in the club, Larry Bauer called her into his office.

When she walked in, Ben Lewis was draped in one of the big leather chairs. Bauer nodded to her to close the door behind her.

"The prosecutor thinks you've been working too hard, Lorna," Bauer told her. "Thinks you ought to have a night off."

"I like to work hard," Lorna told him.

The white-haired man took a cigar from the humidor on his desk, tossed one to the man in the chair. "I think he's right, Lorna. You ought to take a night off." He bit the end off the cigar, spat it at the waste basket. "Go on out and see the town. Ben here makes a good guide."

Lorna unhooked the cigarette tray from around her neck, deposited it on Bauer's desk. "If you think I'm going to argue, you're nuts. Just as long as someone makes up my tips."

"Don't worry about your tips, baby. Sweetheart here will make sure you won't lose anything." His eyes pivoted to Bauer. "Won't you, sweetheart?"

The white-haired man grinned around the cigar clenched in his teeth. "We'll take care of that for you," he promised.

She smoothed the brief shorts down over her thighs. "What are we waiting for?"

"You," Lewis told her.

"I'll be ready in fifteen minutes. Where'll I meet you?"

"I'll have the car out front," the prosecutor told her.

"What's so special about tonight?" Lorna wanted to know.

"There's a little party I think you'd get a kick out of. Every so often they're real good. Tonight's one of the nights," the prosecutor told her. He turned to Bauer. "I understand Mama Laveau is having one of her séances tonight across the county line." He turned back to Lorna. "You ought to get a special bang out of it, baby. She's real N'Orleans. Real voodoo. You ever seen it?"

Lorna shook her head. "Heard enough of what went on down in Congo Square. Never got to see any."

"You will tonight. And the cork'll be out. This is a special closed party." He winked lewdly. "No ribbon clerks."

Lorna looked to Larry Bauer. "It's all right with you?"

"Sure. I just wish I was in on it," Bauer grinned. "I been hearing about that voodoo babe."

"I'll get dressed," Lorna nodded. She turned, left the room.

She was just shrugging into her dress when the door to the dressing room opened. Larry Bauer squeezed in, closed the door after him. "Look, sweetheart, this could be it." He pulled a small vial out of his jacket pocket. "Whatever you do, get him to go up to your place with you. Give him some of this stuff. We'll handle the rest."

"But suppose he won't go up to my room?"

Bauer showed his teeth in an amused grin. "You kidding? After he sits through that performance out at Laveau's place? Don't worry about it. Just refuse to go to his place and he'll go to yours."

Lorna held the vial up to the light. "What's in this stuff?"

A hard note crept into Bauer's voice. "That's our part of it. Your part is to see that he gets it." He opened the door a crack, applied his eye to it. "I'd better get back to the office." He slipped through the door, closed it after him.

For a moment after he left, Lorna stood staring at the vial. She unscrewed the cap, smelled it. There was a heavy, disturbing musky odor to it. She wrinkled her nose, put the cap back on, dropped it into her purse.

Ben Lewis was sprawled on the back seat of the black sedan outside the Café Laurence. When Lorna slipped onto the seat alongside him, he patted her on the knee. "Tonight you'll get something to write in your diary, baby." He leaned forward. "Take us to that voodoo doctor's place across the county line, Ed."

Lorna leaned back against the cushions, stared out the window. For once, her companion didn't seem to feel like talking. He sat in the other corner, chewing on an unlighted cigar.

About forty minutes from the café, the car swung off the macadam onto a narrow blacktop road that rambled back for a mile through a stand of old moss-bearing oak. After a while the headlights picked out the boarded window of an old gray house.

"Here we are," Lewis grunted.

Lorna stared at the ramshackle house. "This is it?"

The prosecutor chuckled. "What'd you expect, neon lights and a brass band?" The driver guided the car around the building, braked to a stop in a weed choked parking place. There were ten or twelve other cars parked there. The driver cut his motor, doused his lights. After a moment, he flicked his lights on and off.

A door in the rear of the building opened, spilled a triangle of yellow light across the yard toward the car. Lewis leaned across the girl, rubbed his arms across her breast. "Come on, baby. This is something to see." His voice was huskier than usual.

They crossed the yard to the open door. A tall Negro, bare to the waist, his black skin gleaming in the half light, held the door open. He waited until they were in, then closed the door after them.

"You-all a membuh?" he asked in a guttural voice.

Lewis scowled at him. "I'm better than that. I'm the county attorney. Get Mama Laveau out here."

The Negro looked faintly troubled, rapped his knuckles against the wall loudly.

After a moment, a woman materialized in the doorway beyond. Her hair was long, silky, black, hung down over her shoulders. She was dressed in a flowing, snow-white robe that complemented the café-au-lait color of her skin. "What is it, Leben?" she addressed the big Negro. Her voice was low, sultry, the kind that sent chills up and down the spine.

"Man say he got to see you, Mama. He police."

The woman's eyes seemed out of focus as she turned them on Lewis and the girl. "You are Mr. Lewis?" Her sensuous lips parted in a welcoming smile, her voice caressed him. "I have been told you would be with us tonight. Will you come with me?"

She turned and glided back in the direction from which she had come. She led the way across what had obviously once been a large kitchen, now unused and dust ridden, to a corridor that ran to the front of the house. As they crossed the old butler's pantry, Lorna became aware of a dull monotonous beat that made the old house vibrate. It grew louder as they approached the front of the house.

The woman in the white robe stopped at a long black curtain that hung from ceiling to floor, sealing off all light from the room beyond.

"We will start the ceremony in a few minutes," the octoroon told them. She held back the curtain, motioned for them to enter. As they walked in, the dull beat of what sounded like a tom-tom enveloped them like a physical thing.

The room was huge. The ceiling and floor of the room above had been torn out, making it one large, two-storied room. The walls were draped from ceiling to floor in a heavy dark blue material, and a thick pile rug completed the sound proofing of the room.

There was no direct lighting, the room seemed diffused with a blue light that turned the faces of its occupants into leering gargoyles. There was no furniture, men and women of all ages were draped over cushions scattered along the walls. In the center of the floor was a cleared space on which had been spread a white tablecloth.

Lewis caught the girl by the hand, led her to a couple of cushions at the side wall. Nobody paid them any attention, there was an air of supercharged excitement throughout the room. When they were seated, a Negro brought them two small glasses filled with colorless liquid. Lorna held the glass to her lips, sniffed, took a sip. It was sweet and heady. "What is it?" she whispered to Lewis.

The prosecutor grinned. "Probably a cross between Spanish fly and hashish. They use that to get the party really going. You don't have to drink it."

"I won't," Lorna told him emphatically. She set the glass down, settled back to wait.

It wasn't a long wait. A cleverly disguised door in the front of the room slid open. Two tall, statuesquely built colored girls emerged. They were bare to the waist, their well-formed breasts oiled and tipped with a bright carmine, their heads were wrapped in the traditional tignon of the Creole. They placed lighted candles at each corner of the cloth in the center of the room. Then, as a centerpiece, they placed a shallow, woven basket filled with herbs and tiny bones. Around the basket they scattered tiny white pellets, bits of corn, dried peas and more bones.

In the far corner, a dried-up old Negro started to scrape a long, rough bow across the strings of a primitive fiddle. The instrument had a long neck, its body was three inches in diameter, covered with a mottled snake's skin. It gave off a weird, insidiously disturbed sound.

Another man was astride a cylinder made of cypress staves hooped with brass and headed with sheepskin. With two sticks he beat away at it with a monotonous deep-throated beat. One of the tall Negresses took her place at his side, sat on a low stool and pounded out an accompaniment on the side of the cylinder with long shank bones. The primitive orchestra was rounded out by a man twirling a long calabash made of a native gourd a foot and a half long filled with pebbles. The combined effect added immeasurably to the room's charge of electricity.

The concealed door opened again, and the café-au-lait girl who had admitted them glided out, took her place at the head of the cloth in the center of the room.

The drumbeat started to increase in tempo, the café-au-lait girl started to chant in a throaty voice. As she sang, she seemed to grow in stature, her eyes began to roll in frenzy. The feverish beat of the drums and the screech of the fiddle reached a new pitch and the men and women around the floor picked up the beat, pounding their clenched fists against the floor.

As the high priestess stepped up the tempo, two white women, uttering screams, jumped to their feet, began to gyrate wildly. One of them, a young brunette, whirled onto the cloth, her hair flying, her body undulating and throbbing in time to the music. Her motions became more and more abandoned until suddenly, with a shrill scream, she collapsed into a heap on the floor, lay there. Nobody paid any attention to her.

Lorna could hear the heavy breathing of the man at her side. He had his hand on her thigh, squeezing the flesh between his stubby fingers. He was watching the action on the floor, eyes wide, perspiration glinting on his forehead.

Suddenly, the café-au-lait girl at the head of the cloth started to twist and squirm in frenzy. She raised her hands, lifted her long hair, let it cascade down over her shoulders. Without moving her feet, she started to undulate from head to foot; first slowly, then with suggestive abandon.

The music hit a wild, barbaric note and the pounding on the floor sounded like thunder in the soundproofed room. More and more of the occupants of the room joined the wildly gyrating group in the center of the floor.

Suddenly, the tall woman in front broke off her chant. She slid the white robe back over her shoulders, let it slide down past her legs, stepped out of it. In the dim light, her body glowed a golden brown. Her legs were long, sensuously shaped. Full rounded thighs swelled into high set hips, converged into a narrow waist. Her stomach was as flat as an athlete's, her breasts full and round.

She dug her long fingers into her hair, shook it down over her face. Her body twisted and squirmed suggestively. As though it were a signal, the tempo of the dancers stepped up to a new high in hysteria. The tall woman's body throbbed and swayed in time to the music.

The dancers tore at each other's clothes, ripped them from their bodies until soon the floor was filled with naked, gleaming bodies wriggling, twisting, undulating sensuously.

As they danced past the high priestess, she held out a large silver flask for them to drink out of. One of the tall Negresses picked up the lighted candle. Then she filled her mouth from the flask, spat it in a fine spray at the candle. The vapor exploded into a bright flame, brought a roar from the throats of the dancers.

The café-au-lait woman turned to the orchestra, urged it to greater fury with clenched hands. The lights in the room started to fade until the gesturing bodies were no more than shadows.

"Quite a show." Lorna was shaken to find her voice quavering. "Now what?"

The man at her side licked his lips. "Let's get out of here." He caught her by the hand, pulled her to her feet. They had to step over some of the bodies squirming on the floor on their way out.

They didn't talk until the cool night air slapped them in the face, drove some of the exotic fumes of the temple from their nostrils. Ben Lewis wiped the thin film of perspiration from his upper lips with the back of his hand.

"That N'Orleans must be some place."

Lorna nodded. "It sure is."

"You're from N'Orleans. Maybe we ought to go to my place and talk about it. You could tell me all about it." His fingers dug into her arm.

"Better make it my place," Lorna told him. "I make it a rule never to go to a strange man's apartment."

"Nothing strange about me. I'm the normalest guy you ever saw," Lewis told her. He slid his arm around her, bent her against him. His lips worked against hers.

She pushed him away. "Wherever we're going to go, let's go there now. This is no place. I get nervous with an audience."

FIFTEEN
Seduction

Willy's watery eyes widened when he recognized the man that stepped into the elevator with Lorna. He made a production of keeping his back turned, working the controls of the rattletrap elevator as it wheezed its way to the third floor.

Lorna led the way down the hallway to her room, opened the door with her key, stepped aside. Ben Lewis walked in, tossed his hat at a small table near the entrance. He nodded for Lorna to bolt the door after her.

Downstairs, Willy rushed over to the old man behind the registration desk. "Did you see who that was with Lorna?"

The old man brought his eyes back from a blank study of the racing form spread on the desk. "I didn't see anybody."

"That was Ben Lewis, the county attorney. I seen his pictures in all the papers, and he's the guy—"

The old man dug at a molar with a fingernail. "I didn't see a thing. And if you want to live to a ripe old age like me, that's the way you should be. You don't see a thing." He dropped his eyes back to the racing form, dismissed the bellboy.

Willy licked at his lips, then dried them with the back of his hand. "Okay. I see what you mean." He shuffled back to the elevator cage.

Upstairs, Ben Lewis had settled himself comfortably on the couch. He watched hungrily the smooth play of the girl's hips against the tight fabric of her skirt.

"How about a drink, baby?"

"Sounds good to me." She walked to the small curtained alcove that contained the silk, brought a bottle of bourbon out, held it up critically to the light. "How about bourbon?"

Lewis nodded. "With water. Got any ice?"

"I could get some easily enough."

"By calling downstairs? Never mind. The tap water ought to be cold enough." He watched while she splashed two fingers of bourbon into each of the glasses, then softened it with water from the tap. "Not too much water."

She brought the glasses, set them down on an ancient coffee table in front of the couch, sank down beside him. "That was sure some show out there. Some of those people are going to hate themselves in the morning."

He reached over, snagged a glass. "But they had fun tonight. That's the important thing. Fun tonight." He held his glass up to her in an unspoken toast, tasted his drink. "Good bourbon."

Lorna grinned. "It should be. It's some of the Café Laurence's." She reached over for her glass, settled back. She leaned her head back on the couch, her breasts jutted forward, straining the fragile material of her dress. "How'd you ever get in politics, Ben?"

The prosecutor shrugged. "It was the only way I could get what I wanted." He took a swallow from his drink, set it down. "It was the only way I could fight the mob that was trying to put me out."

"I don't follow you."

"I was doing all right in town here. Me, and a lot of other independents like Larry Bauer. Then the syndicate moved in."

"The syndicate? I thought that was strictly big-town stuff like New York and Chicago and New Orleans."

Lewis snorted. "They take over wherever there's any money to take. There's plenty in this town. Plenty of mills, plenty of big plants." He took a cigar from his pocket, jammed it between his teeth. "They came to us and gave us a chance to cut them in. When we didn't do it, they put the heat on us, started freezing us out." He grinned humorlessly. "I was born in this town, they were newcomers. I got myself elected and now I got the law behind me. After I run them out, I'll take over again."

"I heard they play rough."

"With a competitor, maybe. But I'm the law. Anything happens to me, and the heat would really go on. I'd bring the Governor into it. They couldn't stand that." He chewed on the end of the unlit cigar. "That joint tonight. The only reason it runs is because I let it. And I let it run because it's cutting in on Lew Barker. Cutting deep. And there's not a thing he can do about it."

Lorna took a deep swallow from her glass, twirled the liquid around the sides. "Suppose they framed you? It sure wouldn't have looked good in the papers if you'd been seen at that place tonight."

The humorless smile was back. "They couldn't make it stick. I'd yell frame and everybody would believe me." He pulled the cigar from between his teeth, studied the ragged end. He pasted back a loose thread of tobacco with the tip of his tongue. "I'm the local boy trying to make good. They're the outsider. It makes a big difference."

"Well, let's not get too serious." Lorna worked at a grin, made it. She wondered if Barker's plan had taken the county attorney's invulnerability into consideration. She held up her glass. "Bottoms up."

Lewis picked up his glass, clinked it against hers. They both drained the glass.

Lorna started to get up, Lewis caught her by the arm, pulled her back into his lap. His mouth found hers, his hand fumbled at her breast. She pushed him away, slid off the couch.

"Give a girl a chance to breathe." She pushed a loose tendril of her hair back into place. "Mind if I go in and comb my hair?"

Lewis shook his head, loosened his tie at the neck, unbuttoned his collar. "Take your time, baby. We've got all night." His eyes caressed her. "While you're in there, why don't you get into something comfortable?"

"Maybe I will." She crossed the room to the bedroom, softly clicked the lock after her. She lifted the receiver off hook, dialed the private line at the Café Laurence. There was a click as the receiver at the other end was lifted.

"Yeah?"

"This is Lorna. He's at my place."

She could hear the soft intake of breath at the other end. "He had the powder yet?"

"No. I'm beginning to think that—"

"Don't think," the voice at the other end snarled. "Give him that powder. I'll have a couple of boys over in an hour to give you a hand." The receiver clicked, the line went dead.

Lorna dropped her receiver on its cradle, then she opened her purse, took out the bottle. She slipped out of her dress, left on a bra and pants, shrugged into a housecoat. She dropped the bottle into her pocket.

When she came out of the bedroom, Ben Lewis was chewing on his cigar, staring morosely at the ceiling.

"Took you long enough," he complained.

"I have a lot of hair," Lorna grinned. She walked across the room, picked up the glasses. "I know something to sweeten your disposition." She walked back to the sink. When her body blocked his view of the glasses, she slipped the bottle from her pocket, dumped the powder into his glass. She quickly drenched it down with bourbon. "As much water this time?" she called over her shoulder.

"None."

She spilled in a little more bourbon, made her own.

Then she rejoined Lewis on the couch. "One bourbon straight," she held his glass out to him, wondered if he could see her hand shaking.

Lewis took the glass, set it down on the table. He pulled her toward him, his hand darting into the gaping front of the gown. He scowled as his fingers encountered the straps on her shoulder. "You can't be comfortable with those things." He hooked his fingers into the straps tore them away, spilling out her breasts.

She made no effort to resist, held up her glass. "To us."

Lewis picked up his glass, tilted it over his lips, drained it.

"What was in that drink?"

"Bourbon. You wanted it straight."

His fingers dug cruelly into her arm. "It tasted funny. You wouldn't try to pull anything on me, would you?"

"You're hurting my arm," Lorna whimpered. She leaned toward him. "You're hurting me."

He twisted harder. "You didn't answer me."

Her eyes were bright, her tongue kept darting at her lips. She moaned softly. "You're hurting." She threw herself at him, her mouth covering his, her teeth nipping at his lip.

He relaxed his grip on her arm, pulled her toward him. He could feel her body pressed against his. After a moment, he pushed her away, rubbed the back of his hand across his eyes.

"There was something in it." His voice was thick. "You bitch! I won't do you any good. I'll—" He sank his face into his hands, shook it, tried to clear it. He was muttering to himself now.

The girl squeezed back into the corner of the couch as he tried to struggle to his feet. He stood there swaying for a moment, then toppled forward, smashing the coffee table under him. He lay face down, didn't move.

Lorna walked out into the kitchen, poured herself a straight shot of bourbon, downed it. She grimaced, coughed, welcomed its warming glow in the pit of her stomach. She walked back to where the prosecutor lay, turned him over on his back.

Ben Lewis's face was white, his breathing deep. A film of clammy perspiration made his forehead damp, cold. She caught him under the arms, tugged him to the couch, dumped him on it.

She was on her third cigarette and a fresh shot of bourbon when the telephone rang. Her gait was a trifle unsteady as she walked into the bedroom, lifted the receiver.

"This is Larry Bauer, sweetheart. Everything okay?"

She giggled. "Of course. My friend went to sleep on me."

"Good. We'll be right up." The receiver clicked.

A few minutes later there was a discreet knock on the door. Lorna turned the latch, opened the door to admit Larry Bauer and Vic Doss from the Blue Angel.

Doss winked at the girl, pushed past her, walked over to the couch, grinned down at the unconscious prosecutor. "That's the most peaceful I've ever seen him look."

Larry Bauer seemed more nervous. He latched the door behind them, deposited a large leather carrying case on the floor. "How long'll that stuff keep him out, Vic?" he wanted to know.

"He's good for twelve hours," Doss grunted. "Get the camera ready."

"What are you going to do?" Lorna wanted to know.

Doss pasted the lazy smile back on his lips, sniffed at the ever present carnation. "We're just going to make sure our friend here doesn't give us any more trouble." He grinned down at the man on the couch. "He's been a real bad boy." He looked over to where the white haired man was fumbling with the leather case. "Let's get going with that camera, Larry. We got a lot of work ahead of us."

Bauer grunted, pulled a Polaroid camera from the case, fumbled with it. "You sure this will do the trick?"

Doss nodded. "All you do is take a picture, wait a few seconds and you pick it out of the back, all printed. Try it."

Bauer, adjusted the flash on the camera, aimed it at the couch, clicked the shutter. "Now what?"

"You just wait a second and you have the picture. Try the back."

The white haired man touched the catch on the back of the camera, brought out a clear cut shot of the man on the couch. "I'll be damned. Science is wonderful all right." He handed the picture to Lorna. "You take a good picture, sweetheart."

Ben Lewis was pictured sprawled unconsciously on the couch. In the background of the picture, clearly identifiable were Lorna and Vic Doss. On an impulse, she slipped the picture into the pocket of the robe. In the excitement, neither of the men noticed.

"Better get his clothes off," Doss ordered. "Help me, Larry." They set about stripping the clothes from the man on the couch.

"I still don't know what the pitch is," Lorna complained. "What are you going to do?"

Doss grinned up at her. "Take some pictures. Of you and him. Real cozy pictures."

"Now, wait a minute," Lorna protested. "Nobody told me—"

"Nobody told the cops that the babe who killed the garage guy and that guy on the road was sitting like a duck right here, did they?"

Lorna licked at her lips. "It won't work. He won't back down for just a set of pictures. He'll yell frame."

"Let us worry about that, baby. You just get that robe off and get ready to smile pretty." Doss looked up at her, waited. When she made no move to strip the robe, he got up menacingly. "Look, babe. I don't want any trouble with you. You're going through with this, one way or another. Get that?"

"Be smart, sweetheart," Larry Bauer told her. "We've gone too far to back away now. Do like the man says."

"I thought you were working with Lewis against the syndicate," she flared at Bauer. "You and the other independents."

Doss grinned again. "Larry found out if you can't lick them, join them. You ought to get smart, too, baby." He started toward her. "How do you pose for the pictures? Conscious or unconscious?"

She slid the robe back off her shoulders, stepped out of it. "Okay, Rembrandt. You talked me into it. What do I do?"

"Just like you're told," Doss grinned at her. "And you know what? You're not even going to have to wait to see how you photograph. We'll have a full set for your scrapbook tonight."

SIXTEEN
Frame

A while later, Lorna shrugged into the housecoat. She went out into the kitchen, poured herself two fingers of bourbon, drank it neat.

"You sure do take nice pictures, baby," Doss chuckled from the other room. "Want to see them?"

"I don't have to see any pictures. I was there. Remember?" She wiped her mouth with the back of her hand. "Okay if I put some clothes on?"

"Getting bashful?" Doss wanted to know.

"No. Just cold." She walked to the bedroom door, latched it behind her. She took the picture from the house coat pocket, slipped it into her handbag, then got into a dress.

When she returned to the living room, Doss and the white-haired man were dumping a limp Ben Lewis back into his clothes.

"It won't work," Lorna told them. "He expected to be framed some day. He'll fight you on it—and he'll win."

Doss grunted, looked up. "If he's in any condition to fight."

"Meaning?"

The big man shrugged, picked up the stack of pictures from the end table. "Maybe when he saw the spot he was in, he couldn't face it. Maybe he decided to take the easy way out."

"You're crazy. Lewis wouldn't kill himself."

"We were afraid he might get stubborn, too. So we're going to help him make up his mind." He helped tug the prosecutor into a sitting position. "Tomorrow, when they find him with the pictures spread out in front of him and a gun in his hand, our troubles are over."

A cold chill trickled from the base of Lorna's skull the length of her spine. "But me? What about me? I'm in those pictures."

Doss didn't bother to look up. "Yeah."

There was a tapping of heels across the floor, the opening and slamming of the door. When Doss looked up, the girl was gone.

"Vic!" Larry Bauer yelled. "The girl! She's gone."

Doss cursed bitterly, jumped to his feet, started after her. His foot caught a piece of the smashed coffee table, he crashed headlong to the floor. By the time he reached the door, the corridor beyond was empty. He ran to the elevator shaft, heard the whining of the cage as it labored upward. As it passed the third floor, he could see that it was empty except for the pimpled operator.

"You see the Andrews girl?" he asked the boy.

Willy shook his head. "I got a call to bring a paper up 405. I been in the lobby all night."

Doss nodded, stamped back to the room he had just left. "She went down the stairs, I guess. She won't get far. Meantime, I don't want to raise too much of a fuss. She won't do any talking—not with what we've got on her."

The night club man plucked at his lower lip with thumb and forefinger. "But what about the set-up? It's supposed to look like Lewis bumped her for shaking him, then knocked himself off."

"So it won't be so fancy. So he just knocked himself off when he saw the broad had him over a barrel. We'll take care of her some other way." He spread the pictures around the floor at the prosecutor's feet. Then he pulled a .38 from his pocket, carefully wiped it with a handkerchief. "Just take a look out, make sure the hall's empty."

Bauer crossed to the door, opened it a slit. He turned back, nodded.

Doss put the gun in the unconscious man's hand, smeared his fingerprints over it. Then he placed Lewis's finger on the trigger. He picked up a small cushion from the couch, put it against the side of the prosecutor's temple, put the gun up to it.

The shot was muffled by the pillow, the bullet knocked the unconscious man sideways on the couch. The heavy breathing stopped, a thin stream of red ran from the corner of his mouth to join the pool that was forming under his head.

When Lorna ran out of the room, she slammed the door behind her, hoping to slow up pursuit. Instead of heading for the staircase, she ran to the far end of the hall where the corridor turned to the north. She was standing flattened against the far wall when Vic Doss questioned Willy.

After the big man had returned to the room, she crept out, headed for the stairs. She passed the elevator well just as the cage was descending.

"Pick me up on the second floor," she whispered to Willy.

The pimply faced operator nodded, braked the car for the second floor. When she got into the car, he headed for the basement.

"What's going on up there?" he wanted to know.

Lorna shook her head. "I don't know. All I know is that if they catch me, they'll kill me." She waited until the car settled to a stop in the basement. "I've got to hide until I can get out of town, Willy. Where can I go?"

The elevator operator scratched at his head, shrugged. "Why not stay right here? Nobody ever comes down here but me. I can bring you down some food and stuff." He led the way out of the elevator into what seemed to be a small room, evidently a catch-all for the hotel above. Odds and ends were stored in confusion. Old furniture and crates were piled to the ceiling.

Willy picked his way through the crates to a small room fixed up as a bedroom. The bed was unmade, piles of lurid-cover pulp magazines were dumped around it.

"This is where I stay," he told her. "When I get off, I'll get you out of here."

There was a muted, metallic buzzer from the direction of the cage. Willy swore at it. "I got to go. If you want anything, buzz the elevator."

"Just a minute, Willy." Lorna pulled the photograph out of her pocket. "Can you get some copies made of this? Photostats or anything?"

Willy studied the photograph, whistled. "Hey, that's—"

"I know who it is," Lorna silenced him. "Can you get some copies made?"

Willy scratched his head. "I guess so. Soon's the places open up." He studied the picture again, oblivious to the impatient buzzing of the elevator. "He looks like he's dead."

"He wasn't then. I wouldn't guarantee anything now. You better go before they get curious about where you are." As the boy started to leave, she caught him by the arm. "Take care of that picture. That may be my out."

When Willy had left, Lorna threw herself down on the bed. In spite of what had happened, she fell asleep, slept soundly. When consciousness returned her first impression was that someone was shining a bright light into her eyes. She jumped up, looked around wildly. A bright shaft of sunlight was knifing its way from a partially covered window right across her bed. Her watch showed eleven-thirty, she had been sleeping almost seven hours.

The only sound in the basement was the hum and creak of the old elevator. She wondered where the elevator boy had gone, since he usually went off duty at seven. She got up, walked to the window, stood on a chair and looked out. The window gave out onto a large cemented area backing on the hotel. She pulled the curtains together, blocked off the light, sat down to wait.

It was almost noon when she heard footsteps approaching. She jumped from the chair, flattened herself against the wall, waited.

Willy's voice was low, hoarse. "Hey, Lorna. Where are you?"

Lorna let her breath out with a whistle. "In here." She waited until the pimply faced boy came in. "Did you get them?"

"Five copies." He held the copies out toward her. "And this."

The newspaper's headlines were an inch high: "County Attorney Kills Self In Girl's Apartment" and a subhead explained "Lewd Photos Given as Reason for Suicide."

Willy's mouth and chin were wet as he watched her read. "And hell sure broke loose around here last night." He licked at his lips. "I got a look at some of those pictures. You sure know your way around."

"Don't get any ideas, Junior," Lorna warned him. "Those pictures were taken with a gun at my head. You saw the condition Ben Lewis was in, didn't you? Those pictures were framed."

"Then why should he kill himself?"

"He didn't," the girl snorted. "They killed him. They just used the pictures as the reason. I think they intended to kill me, too. Make it look like Ben killed me when I tried to shake him down." She got up, paced the room. "I've got to get out of this town."

"But how?"

The girl stopped pacing, grinned at him. "Lew Barker and Vic Doss are going to help me."

The boy's jaw sagged open. "But you said—"

"I know." She held up the picture. "This changes things. It ties Doss in with Lewis and me. It shows he was there. This could upset the whole frame-up."

"How you going to handle it?"

Lorna grinned at him. "I'm going to write the whole story of what I did and who for. I'm going to put a copy of this picture in and address a copy to the newspapers, another copy to the police, another copy to the D.A. and the fourth copy to the Governor."

"What about the fifth copy?"

"I'm going to give that to Lew Barker with my compliments. If anything happens to me, the other four copies get mailed. Don't you see? It's better than life insurance. Then I'm blowing town."

"Take me with you, Lorna. I can drive, and I know my way around. I always wanted to get out of this burg."

Lorna pursed her lips, considered. "Maybe I will. But don't get any ideas about me, Junior. You're too nice a kid to have it happen to."

"Have what happen to?"

"What's happened to all the rest. I'm bad luck. Any guy that's ever laid a hand on me hasn't lived long enough to talk about it."

"There are worse ways of dying," Willy grinned.

"Maybe, but I don't want you to die just yet. I'm going to need you. Can you get me four envelopes and some paper?"

The elevator boy nodded.

"Okay, now listen closely. I'm going to write a statement and enclose one of these pictures in each one. As soon as they're written, I want you to take them and get out of here." She consulted her wrist watch. "You call the desk here at exactly three. If I'm okay, there'll be a message for you."

"And if there's no message?"

"Then mail those letters and we'll blow this town wide open—even if I'm in no condition to know it."

Willy licked his lips uncertainly. "What do I get out all this?"

"You said you wanted to get out of this town, didn't you?"

He brightened up. "You mean you're going to take me with you?"

Lorna shrugged. "Why not? It's like the giant said who married the midget— at least it's somebody to talk to."

SEVENTEEN
Blackmail

Lew Barker lived in an apartment over the Blue Angel. The cab dropped Lorna in front of the place, she walked up the steps to the entrance foyer, pounded on the door.

Vic Doss's jaw dropped when he recognized the caller. He pushed open the door, grabbed her by the arm, pulled her in. "Well, well. Welcome home. You were beginning to worry us. A gal like you on the loose could give us a bad time."

"Mind taking your hand off my arm, Doss? The material wrinkles."

Doss affected the lazy smile. "Nice of you to save us the trouble of looking for you." He pushed her to the stairs. "Go on up. Barker'll be glad to see you." Lorna walked up the stairs leisurely. "I wouldn't get rough if I were you, Doss. Something tells me you're about to lose your girlish laughter."

Doss chuckled. "Don't kid me, baby. You were the only loose link in the set-up. Everything's gone just the way it says in the book. Did you see the papers?"

"I saw the papers. You keep your eye on tomorrow's papers."

Doss grabbed her by the arm, swung her around. "You been to the papers?"

"Not yet."

His breath whistled through the big man's teeth. The grin was back. "I wouldn't count on getting there." He shoved her along the upper hall to a closed door, knocked. At a mumbled command, he pushed it open, shoved her in. "Look what the stork left on our doorstep, Lew."

Lew Barker sat propped up in an oversized bed, an open newspaper spread out on his knees. The sandy hair was mussed, a worried frown wrinkled his broad forehead. When he saw the girl, a relieved smile dug white trenches in the mahogany of his cheeks.

"Well, nice of you to come." The Alabama drawl was more pronounced. "We were thinking of going out to look for you." He folded the papers, dumped them into a heap at the side of the bed. "You gave us a bad night." He turned his eyes toward Doss. "Anyone with her?"

Doss shook his head. "All alone."

The sandy-haired man's eyes jumped back to Lorna. "You should have stayed. It'd be all over by now," he told her. He swung his pajamaed legs out of bed, fitted his feet into slippers. "We got to get her out of here, Doss. With those pictures around, her face is better known than Joe DiMaggio's. Any of the boys around?"

"I can raise a couple. They're—"

"Don't you think you ought to find out why I came here, of all places?" Lorna wanted to know. "Do you think I'd walk in if I weren't a lead pipe cinch to walk out?"

Barker looked amused. "You think you're going to tell us that you'll tell the cops it was a frame-up and—"

Lorna opened her bag, pulled out a picture, tossed it at him. "Take a look at that, wise guy."

Barker stared at her for a moment, his eyes gone bleak. He bent over, picked up the picture, studied it. His lips straightened out into a thin line, hard lumps formed on the sides of his jaw. He looked up at Doss. "You goddam idiot!" His voice was hard, cold. "If anybody ought to get chilled, it's you."

"What are you talking about?" The big man walked over, pulled the picture out of his partner's hand, looked at it. The color drained from his face, his hand shook.

"Where'd she get that?" Barker demanded.

Doss shook his head mutely. He stared at the picture, then, in a rage tore it to pieces. "I don't know where she got it, but—"

"Start acting your age, will you, Doss?" Lorna sneered at him. "That was just a stat. There are five more of them, all in envelopes waiting to be delivered to the newspapers, the D.A., the police and the Governor."

A muscle jumped in Lew Barker's left eye. He turned, walked back to the night table, picked up his cigarette holder, fitted a cigarette to it. "So what's that got to do with me? I'm not in that picture. Doss is."

The big man started to curse, subsided.

"Here's what it has to do with you, Mr. Big," Lorna told him. "Even a blind man could see that picture was taken just before the shots Ben Lewis was supposed to have posed for. It kicks over the suicide plant." She looked at Doss, glaring at his partner's back. "I can't see your pal here standing still for a murder rap without blowing the whistle."

Barker turned around, tilted the holder in the corner of his mouth. "Suppose Doss and you both had an accident?"

"The police and newspapers would get the story. Maybe you'd wiggle out of it," she conceded.

"So what's it go to do with me?"

"You didn't let me finish," Lorna told him. "You might wiggle out of it with the cops. But how about the syndicate? With all the heat it'd bring down, they'd get their tail burned. I don't think you'd be very popular—or very healthy. I understand from what I read that they're very narrow-minded about people who cost them money."

The sandy-haired man ground his teeth on the cigarette holder. "What do you want?"

"A car and some money. A couple of guns. Some introductions in New York." She ignored the glare of the big man. "I've just decided you men are lousing up the rackets. What they need is a woman's touch. I'm figuring on moving in."

"See that she gets what she wants and get her out here," Barker snapped at his partner. "See if you can do it without screwing up the details."

Lorna smiled at him sweetly. "One other thing. Don't go getting ideas. The day anything happens to me—even if it's just a case of ptomaine from eating in a hash joint, those letters get mailed."

"Get out of here, will you?" Barker's voice was low, taut. "Get out before I tear you apart myself."

"By the way, thanks for the car. I've always wanted one of my own. And it better not be a hot one—because like I said, the minute anything happens to me, you're going to get awfully unpopular."

Barker growled deep in his chest, grabbed a glass from the night table, threw it at her. It missed, hit the wall, shattered into a hundred pieces.

"You don't know what a favor I did you by ducking," she taunted him. She turned, walked out.

The bartender who had been behind the bar the night Hunt first brought her to the Blue Angel was polishing glasses. He was working in shirtsleeves, hadn't yet donned his white coat. Lorna walked into the bar room, perched on a tall stool. "Could you rustle me up a scotch?"

The bartender looked uncertain. "Bar isn't open yet, miss. We don't open until seven."

"I'm sure Mr. Barker would want you to buy me a drink," she told him. "Why don't you check him?"

The bartender set the glass down, started to pick up the house phone, decided against it. "I guess one won't hurt anybody." He picked up a dry glass, spilled some scotch into it, dumped the ice in and washed it down with soda. "Ain't I seen you someplace before, miss?"

Lorna sipped at the scotch. "I was in here a couple of weeks ago." She shrugged. "I didn't think I'd made such an impression."

The bartender screwed his face up in concentration. "Seems like it's lately." His face cleared. "Wait a minute." He walked over to where his coat lay folded over the back of the chair, pulled out an evening paper, smoothed it out. "Your picture was—" He broke off, looked up with stricken eyes.

"Let's see it," Lorna told him.

He passed the paper over. Her picture stared up at her from the front page under the caption, "Have you seen this woman?" It was just a head shot, obviously taken from one of the pictures made the night before.

She was still looking at the picture when Vic Doss came up behind her. She started as he tapped her arm. "Have you seen this?" she wanted to know.

Doss looked at the picture, shrugged. "I got troubles of my own."

"You'll have plenty more if somebody spots me from this picture," she told him. "And you'd better take care of your boy back there. He's already spotted me."

Doss flatfooted down to the other end of the bar, leaned across and spoke to the bartender in a low, urgent tone. The bartender was unconvinced, but he nodded vigorously.

Doss came back, picked up the girl's drink, took a deep swallow. "I've got a car out front."

"Hot?"

The big man shook his head. "I bought it myself. For a girl I used to know." He dipped his hand into his jacket pocket, pulled out a blank registration stub on which the license number had already been imprinted. "Fill this out. You won't have any trouble." He handed her his pen, watched while she made the registration form out in the name of Lorna Andrews, gave her address as an empty lot three doors up from Les's Place.

"Know anybody I can contact in New York?"

Doss's face looked pinched. "That's a tough contract, baby. Why don't you leave well enough alone? You start getting into the big leagues and things can happen to you."

"You better see to it that they don't."

"Look, baby. I've been a professional gambler all my life. Take my word for it, even though you've got aces back to back, don't push too hard on one pair."

"I've done a little gambling too," Lorna told him. "I have a few rules of my own, Doss. Such as never bluff when there's no limit on the table stakes. Anything happen to me, it'll be tough on you, a lot tougher than it'll be on me."

Doss tried to stare her down, dropped his eyes. "Okay, have it your way." He reached into his jacket, pulled out a .45, passed it over to her. From his hip pocket, he took a snub-nosed .38. "Anything else?" he growled.

"The money. Remember?" She held her hand out, he dropped a flat packet of bills into it. "Not very much, is it?"

"Enough."

"I guess so," she conceded. "After all, I can probably get more if I need it. I understand some of the syndicate brass have gone artistic, collect pictures. I'll bet I've got one they'd love to have in their collection."

He added another packet to the bills in her hand. "When you get to New York, let me know. I'll try to arrange some contacts for you."

The car was a black Chevvy sedan with a South Carolina license plate. Lorna walked out of the Blue Angel, slid behind the wheel, kicked the motor into life.

She headed toward town, watched in her rear view mirror for some indication that she was being followed. Twice, she pulled off into side roads, waited. There was no sign of a tail.

On the outskirts of town, she checked her watch, found it near three. She stopped at a gas station, motioned for the attendant to fill the car, headed for the phone booth. In a moment she was connected with the Spotlight Club.

"Do you have a bellboy named Willy?" she tried to sound nasal, old.

She recognized the raspy voice of the old man at the registration desk. "Yes. But he's not on duty now. Who's this?"

"Would you tell him his aunt called? He's supposed to meet me at the bus station at three-thirty. I wanted to be sure he wouldn't forget."

The desk clerk grunted. "If I see him, Ill remind him." He didn't wait for her answer, dropped the receiver on the hook.

Willy was waiting outside the bus station when she skidded the car to a stop at the curb. He pulled open the door, slid in alongside her. "Everything okay?"

She grinned at him. "Why not? We had cards and spades."

He swabbed at the wet smear of his mouth with the black of his hand. "Those were pretty tough boys you were muscling." There was a note of respect in his voice. "Ain't many men would go up against them, let alone a girl."

Lorna grinned, swung the car out into the stream of traffic heading south. "I'm just beginning to learn something I wish I knew a couple of years ago."

"What?"

"You can have everything you want. You just have to reach out and take it."

Willy shook his head doubtfully. "You can collect an awful lot of bruised knuckles that way."

"You can also get away with a lot of things you never thought possible." They were approaching the main coastal highway. Lorna pulled to a full stop, then started south.

"Hey, that goes to the south. I thought we were heading for New York."

"So did they. And they'll have a reception committee waiting. When I get around to going to New York, I don't mind a reception committee—but not the kind with sawed-off shotguns." She eased the little car around a big oil truck, pushed the gas pedal down. "I've been hearing so much about New Orleans lately, I think I'd like to look it over."

EIGHTEEN
New Orleans Woman

The Hotel Delcort was an old, weather-beaten stone building that nestled anonymously in a row of similarly weather-beaten stone buildings a few blocks uptown from the Old Absinthe House on Bourbon Street in New Orleans.

Wrought iron grills decorated the small balconies outside each room with delicate metal embroidery. A small plaque on the side of the entrance dispelled any doubts as to its character by labelling it a hotel.

A theadbare and faded carpet ran the length of the lobby. Overhead, a large four-bladed fan stirred up the humid air, made it hotter rather than cooler. The man behind the desk wore no jacket, his shirt collar was open at the neck. A pair of wide blue suspenders kept his trousers from sliding over his paunch. He was fanning himself with a dusty woven palm fan.

He watched Lorna and Willy walk the length of the lobby, step out into the blinding afternoon sunshine. "Damn waste. Gal like that with a skinny little runt," he said to nobody in particular.

"Let's get on over to the French Market," Lorna suggested as soon as the hot street air hit them in the face. "Might at least be a breeze." She started up Bourbon, Willy panting at her heels. "Besides, we can talk there without anybody getting close enough to listen in."

A heavy heat haze shimmered over the city as they worked their way across the Quarter to Jackson Square, then down to the market. They gratefully accepted a seat in the shade, sank into it and let the breeze from the river cool them.

Down Royal Street, they could see the spire of the Cathedral St. Louis almost obscured by the haze as it stood eternal guard over the old Place d'Armes. In the other direction, rows of squat houses, with their uniform balconies, sweltered in the sun. But in the market, it was cool.

Lorna looked at a coffee-stained menu, tossed it aside, waved down a waitress. They both ordered large coffees, black, with a double order of doughnuts. When the waitress was out of earshot, Willy leaned forward. "Where do we go from here, Lorna? Our dough's getting mighty low. I thought we'd have some action before now."

Lorna shrugged. "So did I. What would you suggest? Going out and robbing mail boxes? We'll get some action when we've got something lined up." She stared over at where longshoremen were loading crates on waiting trucks. "Something worthwhile."

She leaned back, waited while the waitress deposited two mugs of coffee, a plate piled high with hot doughnuts. She added two glasses of water and pattered off.

"I know, I know," Willy nodded. "But until we make the big strike, we've got to have eating money."

Lorna turned cold eyes on him. "What's the matter, Willy? Don't you like the way I do things?"

He dropped his eyes, licked at his lips. "It ain't that. But I was just thinking there must be a lot of small jobs—"

"Stop thinking. I'll take care of that end." She started to taste her coffee, stopped with the cup halfway to her lips. At the other end of the market, two men were leaning across a table, immersed in what appeared to be a confidential conversation. She ridged her forehead, tried to figure out why one of the men looked familiar.

Willy followed her eyes, scowled at the two men. "What's the matter, Lorna?"

She shook her head, pursed her lips. "I don't know. One of those guys—" She broke off, did a mental check of her memory files. "I'm sure I know the bigger one. You recognize him?"

Willy studied the man's features, shook his head. "Never saw him before."

One of the men at the table pulled a folded paper and a pencil from his pocket, started drawing a diagram on the picture. The bigger man dug into his pocket, pulled out a pair of horn-rimmed spectacles, stuck them on his nose, studied the drawing.

The frown on Lorna's forehead smoothed out. She snapped her fingers. "Doc! That's who it is!"

Willy managed to look more confused than usual. "Huh?"

"I just remembered where I know him from. He was a friend of an old friend of mine. I wonder if he'll remember me?" She got up, smoothed her skirt over her thighs. "I'll be right back, Willy."

Lorna skirted the tables, crossed to where the two men sat. As she approached, one of the men looked up, frowned, covered the paper on which he was writing with his arm. Doc looked up incuriously as she stopped at their table.

"Hello, Doc," she smiled at him.

The man with the horn-rimmed glasses stared at her for a moment, then recognition flooded his eyes. "Say, I remember you."

Lorna pulled out a chair unasked, slid into it. "Of course you do. Fancy meeting you here."

Doc looked around, dropped his voice. "Fancy meeting you anywhere. You were hotter than a fifty-cent pistol right after that caper with Gun." He nodded to his friend. "This is Kurt Davis." He wrinkled his forehead again. "I don't remember your name."

"Lorna. Lorna Andrews."

Doc turned to the other man. "You remember Gunson. The kid that did some time with us."

"The one who thought he was hot stuff," the other man growled. He looked

Lorna over. "His doll?"

"Nobody's doll," Lorna told him curtly. "I did a job with Gun. He went chicken, tried to run for it and ran right into a road block."

Doc slipped the glasses off his nose, chewed on them. "That's not the way I heard it."

"That's the way I tell it," Lorna told him.

Doc stared at her, shrugged. "He wasn't much of a loss anyway. What are you doing down here?"

"Looking for a connection."

Doc pursed his lips, looked over at the other man. "You know, Kurt, we might be able to use her, at that. A babe casing that place wouldn't stand out like a guy."

Kurt snorted. "Fluff? She'd probably fold the minute a cop looked hard at her. I'm not taking any chances with—"

Doc laughed. "Fold? Let me tell you what little I know about this fluff. First place I met her's a joint called Mickey's. She blows with Gun one night and I find out she's wanted for blasting a hick sheriff in another county. Then word's out the cops are looking for her for a garage stickup with a killing." He chuckled. "Anybody isn't going to fold on this job, my money's on her."

Kurt's eyes flicked past her to where Willy was sitting at the table alone, sulkily dunking doughnuts. "Who's the creep with her?"

Doc looked over, shrugged, turned to Lorna.

"A kid I can depend on. He's a good driver, he's not afraid of a gun. And I can trust him."

Kurt looked thoughtful. "We could use a good driver. He know his way around town?"

"It wouldn't take him long to learn." She lifted Kurt's arm off the diagram. "What's the job?"

Kurt looked to Doc, who nodded. "See what she thinks about it."

Kurt looked unconvinced but removed his arm from the diagram. Lorna leaned over, studied it. "Break it down for me, Doc."

Doc pointed to a long straight line that ran diagonally on the paper. "This is Canal Street." He jabbed to the right of the line. "This is the Quarter, right here. There's a horse room right about here in the 300 block on Dauphine." He looked up. "It's the biggest book in New Orleans. We're going to take it."

"Just the two of you?"

Doc shrugged. "There's plenty of guns who'll hire out if we need them." He cast a speculative eye at Willy's table. "Maybe if that guy's as good a driver as you say he is, we won't need any. Get him over."

Lorna waved to Willy, motioned for him to join them. He dropped some change on the table, shuffled over. He nodded in response to the girl's introductions. "Stop sulking, Willy," she snapped. "You've been spoiling for action. Doc and Kurt here might have some cooking."

Willy managed to look interested, hooked a chair from a nearby table with his toe, pulled it up to the table. "What kind?"

"A horse room," Lorna told him. "It's loaded."

"Lorna says you're a good wheelman on a getaway car."

Willy shrugged. "Nobody can push a heap faster. I been driving since I was a kid. Where's the car?"

"We'll get that when we're ready for it. We'll have one all picked out." He turned to Lorna. "How about iron?"

"We've got a .45 and a .38. Willy can have the .38."

An admiring grin split Kurt's face. "Say, she is an operator. You mean to say she uses a .45?"

Lorna ignored him. "You've got the place all lined up?"

Doc shook his head. "Just generally." He pointed to the map. "We've been trying to figure a getaway route." He bent over it, ran his thumbnail along the line that represented Canal Street. "I figure we blast out of Dauphine onto Canal, head for the Lake Shore Highway out near the Yacht Basin. It's pretty open country."

Lorna didn't like it. "Too open. You're giving them all the odds. Suppose they radio ahead and set up blocks. You're dead."

Doc grinned at her. "You don't think these guys are in any spot to yell copper, do you? They got to take it and like it."

The girl chewed on the inside of her cheek. "Maybe. Suppose there's some shooting and the cops declare themselves in?"

"There doesn't have to be any shooting if the job's cased right," Kurt growled. "Of course, if you don't like the way we're setting this job up, you don't have to come in."

Lorna shrugged. "Have it your own way. I'd do it differently."

Kurt started to sneer, Doc waved him to silence. "How would you do it, Lorna?"

She pointed to the paper. "I haven't been here long but I've noticed that Dauphine Street's pretty narrow. All those Carré streets are. You have to figure an outside chance that the cops will crash the party." She looked up, frowned at the look of impatience on Kurt's face. "Look, it's better to figure on it than to try to outrun a cop car."

"She's right, Kurt. Let her finish," Doc snapped. "So the cops decide to cut themselves in. We're dead. No?"

Lorna pursed her lips, shook her head. "Not necessarily. Suppose you do have to take off in a hurry with a cop car on your tail." She pointed to Dauphine Street. "You're heading for Canal. Let's say this is the horse room. It's in the 300 block?" She looked up.

Doc nodded.

"That means you've got two and a half blocks on Dauphine. Okay. Suppose an innocent little gal from South Carolina has her car parked right here in the

200 block?"

Kurt frowned his lack of comprehension. "So?"

"So right after you pass, the little girl pulls out and the cops either have to stop or ram her." She grinned at them. "Either way, the gal throws a wing-ding, gives you enough time to hit Canal, head for Rampart and ditch the car." She looked up, waited for the reaction.

Doc reviewed it to himself with moving lips, looked to Kurt. "Well?"

Kurt rubbed the heel of his hand along the side of his chin, tried to punch a hole in it. "It ain't bad," he admitted. He leaned over the map. "Break it down for me again."

Nobody interrupted while Lorna went through the plan. When she was finished, they all nodded.

"You got a car with a South Carolina plate or do we have to get you one?" Kurt wanted to know.

"If I didn't have one, it wouldn't be any good. They'd have me on a stolen car," she explained. "I've got a car and a registration that will stand up." She grinned at them. "You know, those cops are going to be pretty mad."

"Where are you staying?" Doc wanted to know.

"The Delcort."

He nodded to Willy. "With him?"

Lorna stared him down. "Not that it's any of your business, but we're both at the Delcort. And we might as well get this settled right now. If I go in with you on this or anything else, it's strictly a business deal."

Doc shrugged. "Have it your way. The only thing I'm thinking about is you ought to get out of that fleabag. Like you said, the cops are going be a little tee-ohed. They'll probably do a check on you. You ought to be in a decent hotel and it ought to look like you just arrived."

Lorna considered it, bought it. "When do you figure to do the job?"

"As soon as it's lined up. How fast can you case it?"

Lorna checked her watch. "I can start this afternoon. Give me three days to get the lay of the place. Maybe four. I'll let you know."

Doc nodded. "Okay. You'd better pack up today and check in the Roosevelt or the St. Charles. What name will you use?"

Lorna shook her head. "I've got to use the name on my registration, don't I?" She picked up the pencil from the table, scribbled the name "Lorna Andrews" on a corner of the paper, tore it off, handed it to Doc. "I'll be at the Roosevelt. How do I reach you two?"

Kurt looked to Doc, shook his head. "You won't. We'll keep in touch with you."

NINETEEN
Horse Room

The horse room was behind a small cigar store that looked out on Dauphine Street through two dusty plate-glass windows. A small counter ran the side of the cigar store, presided over by a gnome-like little man in shirtsleeves, with black arm garters; no collar. At the other side of the room, a large rack featured a collection of magazines—all well thumbed, all featuring a cover portrait of an unbelievably busty blonde.

The little man behind the counter looked up as Lorna walked in. He twisted his mouth in a caricature of a smile that bared-the brown stumps of his teeth. "Yes, miss?"

Lorna gave him the full benefit of a smile. "I understood I could get a little action on the horses. I'm a stranger in town, and—"

The old man sucked noisily at a tooth, considered. "Know anybody in town could speak for you?"

Lorna shook her head. She reached into her bag, brought out a bill, started folding it until the corner numeral was easily visible. "I don't think so. I just got into town, and—"

The man behind the counter reached over, took the bill from between her fingers. "I guess it'll be all right." He reached under the counter, pushed a button. There was a clicking noise. "You go in through the phone booth." He tucked the folded ten into a pocket, adjusted the garters on his arm.

Lorna walked into the phone booth, pushed on the back wall. It swung open, she stepped through into a large room. There was a hum of conversation, an undertone of excitement. A few slot-machines against the wall were getting a moderate play.

As the door closed behind her, it started the smoke eddying near the ceiling. No one gave her a second glance as she walked in. She stood for a moment, watching the man at the board post prices and positions. Suddenly, a loud speaker blared the results of the sixth race at Fair Grounds. There was a groan of disappointment from most of the players, several pushed their way gleefully to the wooden cashier's cage at the end of the room. Lorna wandered around, watched the pay-offs being made. She dropped several quarters into one of the machines, failed to hit a playback, waited until the entries were posted for the last race of the day.

She joined the small crowd that pushed its way to the cashier's booth, put down two fives, picked up a ticket on "Sombrero," number seven on the board.

Number seven ran out of the money, but by the time she left the room, Lorna had staked out in her mind the location of the cash box, the number of guards placed around the room. On her way back to the hotel, she marveled at the apparent lack of precaution on the part of the operators of the room.

The next day she returned in time for the first race, managed to pick three winners and came out a few dollars ahead. The men she had pegged as guards were in the same relative positions as the day before. There were no more security measures taken than had been in evidence on her first visit.

She returned two more days in a row until she was recognized as a regular customer, was now able to pick out without any question the house men, the guards and the location of the cash box. She was able to estimate a day's receipts in excess of twenty thousand from her observation of the four days' play.

The night of the fourth day she was sitting in the Blue Room of the Roosevelt sipping a Ramos when she heard herself being paged. She signaled for the boy, asked for a phone.

"This is Doc, Lorna. Getting anyplace?"

Lorna looked around, nodded. "Everything's ready, I'd say."

"You're sure?"

"As sure as I'll ever be. It looks pretty ripe."

She could hear him draw the breath in through his teeth. "Let's get together tonight and go over it." There was a whispered consultation on the other end of the phone. "Do you know how to get to West End Park near the yacht basin?"

Lorna bit at her lip, shook her head. "Better give me directions."

"The park's in the new section of town. Take Canal to the Pontchartrain road. You'll come to the Delgado Museum. You can't miss it. Check your speedometer, go three miles on the nose, you'll come to a dirt road marked dead end. Turn in there. How soon?"

"I can leave any time."

"Good," the receiver approved. "It'll take maybe a half hour, forty minutes. We'll be there."

Lorna nodded at the receiver, dropped it on its hook. She signaled the bellboy, gave him a folded bill. "Would you ask the garage to bring my car around front? I'm Miss Andrews."

The bellboy touched his fingers to his cap in a salute. "What kind of a car is it, Miss Andrews?"

"A '53 Chevvy. Black, with South Carolina plates."

A cold, penetrating drizzle had started by the time she picked the car up in front of the hotel. Most of the store fronts were dark along Canal as she headed out of town. She passed the Boston Club, where the Mardi Gras King greets his Queen on Mardi Gras day, headed uptown toward the lake.

As she rocketed past the famous light stanchions, each decorated with the four flags that have flown over the city in its turbulent history, the character of the neighborhood slowly changed. The business district, the Vieux Carré, fell behind. She drove into a district of big estates, their gardens running riot with roses and fragrantes. The houses themselves were huge white porticoed ghosts set far back from the road, half hidden by the giant moss-bearing oaks. Soon the estates too fell behind. She swung into the City Park with its famous duelling oaks and the ghosts of hundreds of gallants who had died there.

It took almost forty minutes to reach the Delgado Museum, a huge Greek temple that housed a priceless art collection. She cut her speed, checked her speedometer. Three miles farther she came to the dirt road meandering off to the left, a weather-beaten sign proclaiming it to be a dead end.

She swung the Chevvy off the macadam road, fitted its wheels into a rutted track that led back though a clump of trees. The car bumped along a road that was barely wide enough for one car's passage. After a mile or more of jouncing, she came out on a small promontory set high above the scenic highway, completely surrounded by trees and dense underbrush. Another car was standing there, without lights. She cut her lights, turned off the motor. The door of the other car opened. Doc walked over to her.

"Lorna?"

She rolled down the window. "Willy and Kurt with you?"

Doc nodded.

"Bring them over. I've got the layout pat. I'll spell it out for all at once, save a lot of re-telling."

Doc raised his aim in a signal, was joined by the other two men. They all scrambled into the back of the Chevvy.

"How's it look?" Doc wanted to know.

"Too easy," she told him. "Anybody got a cigarette?"

Doc gave her a cigarette, held a light. "What do you mean?"

She took a deep drag, let the smoke dribble from half-parted lips. "There are only two guards and the cashier. They act like they're pretty sure of themselves." She took another deep drag, blew the smoke at the ceiling. "As far as I can tell, there are no peep holes or guards upstairs or any place. Just the floor men."

Kurt nodded. "Just two." He looked to Doc. "That's what I told you. It's a pushover."

Doc explained. "Kurt got the layout from a guy he served time with. Guy used to be a floor man, got caught trying to nick the cash box. That's how come we picked the place." He plucked the cigarette from between the girl's fingers, took a puff, started to hand it back.

"Keep it. Give me a fresh one."

Doc colored. "What's the matter? I got something contagious?"

"I like to smoke my own cigarettes," Lorna told him. "Give me a fresh one."

Doc stared at her defiantly for a moment, muttered under his breath, brought out another cigarette. The girl lighted it from the one in his hand.

"You got the layout?" Kurt wanted to know.

Lorna nodded. "There's an old guy in the cigar store. The buzzer's under the counter. You've got to keep him away from it. I think there's a warning button there, too."

Doc nodded sulkily. "What then?"

"You let yourself in through the back wall of the phone booth." She snapped on the map light on the dashboard, pulled out a prepared map of the back room. "Right here where the X is stands the cashier's booth. He won't give you any trouble. He keeps the cash in a big valise right between his feet." She looked up, the men nodded. "Now there's a row of chairs right over here," she drew a line with a pencil. "The guy in the end chair is a guard. The other guard usually stands over here," she marked the paper again, "right next to the board. That way, anybody who goes near the cashier's box is covered from two directions."

Doc stared at the diagram for a moment. "Makes it pretty tough to cover both at once, doesn't it?" He puzzled over it for a moment, looked up at the girl. "Got any ideas?"

"One that may work. It could be risky, though."

"Let's hear it," Kurt invited.

"Okay. I said, there's an old guy out here who handles the buzzer. He looks to me like the kind of old guy intends to keep on living for a while."

Doc took a last drag on the cigarette, flipped it through the window. "So? How's he help us once we're inside?"

"If you could get him to call out the fellow that stands right here," she indicated the mark signifying the guard at the end of the board, "you'd only have to worry about the other guard and the cashier."

Doc considered it, shook his head. "The other guard would be keeping his eye on the door. He might get suspicious if his buddy didn't come back."

"But suppose he does go back? Kurt's about the same size as the guard near the board. You get the old guy to pull the guard out, Kurt walks back in, keeps his back to the other guy. When you come in, you walk right to the back of the room when you can cover this guard, Kurt takes care of the cashier from where he stands. How about it?"

Kurt stroked the point of his chin between thumb and forefinger. "Suppose the other guard makes me?"

"He might. Chances are he won't. I've watched them for four days. They hardly pay any attention to each other. They keep their eyes on the cashier." She folded up the map, handed it to Doc. "Long's he sees a guy who looks like his buddy come back in and take up his position, he won't give it a second thought."

"Might work. How about clothes?"

Lorna shrugged. "The guard near the board always wears a dark blue tropical and a big, brim-down panama. You can take his hat—one blue suit looks pretty much like another."

Doc turned to Kurt. "Well?"

"We got to get one of the guards out of the way some way. Sounds like it might work." He turned to Lorna. "How about Willy?"

"He sits at the wheel of the car out front, with the motor running. I'll be in the 200 block with the crash car in case anything goes wrong. If anything does go wrong, you ditch the car around the corner on Rampart, separate and lay low for a couple of days." She looked at Willy. "Otherwise, in a day or two you contact me like you did tonight and we set up to meet wherever you're holed in."

Willy nodded. "I'll take care of that, Lorna."

"You've got everything else figured out," Doc snorted. "Maybe you've got the time figured out."

"Yeah. Matter of fact, I have. But I don't like the way you said that, Doc. Maybe you think you could do it better without me?"

Doc started to retort, looked around, got no encouragement, backed down. "No. I guess I'm not used to taking orders from a woman. I'll go along with your set-up. What time?"

"The last race goes off at five forty-three. Lots of the players don't cash their wins until after the last race. There'll be twenty thousand or better in the box right around them."

Doc whistled noiselessly. "Twenty grand."

"I told you it was rich pickings, Doc," Kurt told him. "Real rich."

Doc wiped little beads of perspiration off his forehead and lower lip. "This is really it. Twenty grand!" He looked around. "I'm set. How about the rest of you?"

Lorna nodded. "I'll be at my spot at five-forty on the head. If anything goes wrong, when you hit Bienville, lay on that horn. Then as soon as you get past, I'll seal that street up like King Tut's tomb."

TWENTY
Getaway

The clock on the dashboard of the Buick said five-thirty. Willy fitted the car expertly in the middle of the narrow street, headed west on St. Louis toward Dauphine. In the back seat, Doc sat nervously cracking his knuckles, watching the colorful street slip past the window. Kurt, wearing a blue tropical suit, was absorbed in chewing his thumb.

At Dauphine, Willy swung west, pulled to a stop in the middle of the 400 block. He twisted around on the seat. "The cigar store's in the middle of the next block. Maybe I better park here for ten minutes or so, not to tip them off?"

Doc considered, nodded. He signaled for Kurt to follow him to the sidewalk. At the front door, he stuck his head into the window. "Just be in front of the store at five forty-three. Have that motor running and be ready to move."

Willy nodded, licked at his lips. He watched the two men walk slowly down the street toward the cigar store, wondered if Lorna was in position two blocks away to balk any pursuit.

At the entrance to the cigar store, Doc took an imperceptible glance in both directions, walked in. Kurt stood in the doorway. The old man behind the counter seemed to sense something amiss, started toward the middle of the counter, froze at the sight of the gun in Doc's hand. "Easy, pal." He slid around the counter, ran his hand along the edge until he found the twin buttons. "Come in, Kurt," he called softly.

When the man in the blue suit came in, the old man's eyes widened. There was a gray pallor in the hollows of his cheeks, his fingers crept nervously to the garters on his sleeves.

"Look, I just work here. I'm not making any trouble."

Doc nodded. "Good. We walk out, you walk out. Anything happens to us, you won't be around when the papers tell about it. Got it?"

The old man nodded his head jerkily. The pupils of his eyes were white-rimmed with fear, his forehead was glistening moistly. "What do you want me to do?"

"Back up into the phone booth," Kurt told him. "Don't try anything." He followed the old man into the phone booth, turned, nodded to Doc. There was the stutter of an electric latch, the inner door swung in, a thin yellow ribbon of light appeared.

Kurt dug the snout of his gun into the old man's back. "Get the guard out here. Anything goes wrong, you get it first."

The old man started to shake, Kurt bored the gun deeper into his back. "Get him," he snarled.

The old man stuck his face in the open door. "Murph," he called softly.

The guard near the board turned, scowled at the open door. "What?"

The old man licked his lips. "A call for you. The boss."

The guard pushed his panama on the back of his head, looked over to where the other guard sat, nodded. He walked to the door, pushed his way through, shoved the old man out of his way. When he saw Kurt behind the old man, he opened his mouth to yell.

Kurt's fingers dug into his Adam's apple. He gagged, gasped for breath, sank to his knees. Kurt caught the guard by the tie, dragged him out of the booth. The guard struggled feebly to get to his gun, succumbed to a vicious rabbit punch at the base of his brain. His face hit the floor, he didn't move.

Kurt picked up the panama from the floor, pulled it down over his eyes. He nodded to Doc, waited until the door to the horse room had been opened, slipped in. When he took up the guard's position, the other guard tossed him a cursory glance, went back to watching the cashier who was slipping rubber bands around stacks of bills.

Outside, Doc forced the old man to drag the unconscious guard out of sight behind the counter. He waited until the old man had deposited the guard at his feet, then as the old man was about to straighten up, he brought the barrel of his gun down on the old man's head. He knocked him to his knees with the first blow, beat him to the floor.

Nobody paid much attention when Doc entered the horse room. He took up a position against the wall, seemed lost in contemplation of the figures chalked on it. From the side of his eye, he saw Kurt walk past the board toward the cashier's desk.

The other guard stiffened, watched Kurt cross the room. While he was watching Kurt, Doc walked up behind the guard, stuck the snout of his gun against the back of the man's neck. The guard stiffened, didn't move. Doc reached over his shoulder, tugged a .45 from the hammock under his left arm.

"Don't make any fuss," Doc told him in a low voice. "Get up and walk out front. I'll be right behind you."

The guard seemed to hesitate for a moment, got to his feet reluctantly. He shuffled to the door of the store, slid through. Before he could get out of the booth, Doc slashed at the back of his neck with the butt of the gun. There was a dull crunching sound, the man crumpled to the ground a loose bundle of arms and legs. He lay there, his head at an awkward angle.

Inside, Kurt was showing the cashier his gun. His body blocked the view of the horse players behind him who sat watching the board with rapt, open-mouthed attention.

"We're leaving. You, me and the bag," Kurt told him.

The cashier stared down at the gun with morbid fascination. His eyes rolled up to Kurt's face. "Don't shoot. I just work here."

"Fill the bag."

The cashier's hand shook as he dumped pile after pile of bills into the bag. Finally, he looked up. "That's all."

"Head for the store and keep going. Do what you're told and you'll walk away from this. Get brave and you'll be a dead hero."

The cashier looked sick, nodded. He picked up the bag, sidled out of the cage, headed for the entrance to the store. His eyes appealed hopelessly to the horse players who never saw him leave. In the telephone booth he stumbled over the body of the second guard. His face glowed damply as Doc tugged the bag from under his arm, motioned with the snout of the gun toward the street.

Outside, Willy sat at the wheel of the car, smoking nervously. Almost at the same moment that he saw Kurt, Doc and the cashier heading for the car, he spotted the patrol car in the rear mirror. Surreptitiously, he signaled for his partners to hurry.

The patrol car rolled to a stop, the driver got out, walked up to where Willy sat. He leaned on the window, looked the driver over. "You got a registration for this car?" he wanted to know.

The door to the store slammed, Doc and Kurt crossed the sidewalk, herding the cashier in front of them. They saw the cop at the same instant he saw them.

The cop went for his gun. Kurt raised his and fired. The slug caught the cop in the face, threw him backward into the street. Doc and Kurt jumped into the car, sent the cashier sprawling on his face in front of the police car.

Willy jammed down on the accelerator, the car leaped way from the curb. Behind him, the other cop in the car was recovering from his momentary paralysis, was sliding into the driver's seat.

Willy rocketed the car down Dauphine, leaned on his horn as he approached the intersection. Ahead of him he could see the black Chevvy pulling away from the curb. As he drew near, the black Chevvy seemed to go out of control, climb the sidewalk as the girl behind the wheel fought for control. Willy raced past, kept the pedal to the floorboard.

Behind him, the second cop had the car in motion. He raced to close up the distance between him and the escaping car. He saw the Chevvy climb the sidewalk, then before he could get out of its way, it swerved off the sidewalk, right into his path.

There was a squealing of brakes, the tearing of metal and smashing of glass. The impact drove his car over the curb where it came to a shattering stop against a store front.

The bandit car two blocks away, skidded onto Canal, disappeared from sight.

A white-faced cop shoved open his door, stalked over to where the smashed Chevvy stood almost across the road, spilling water in a steaming stream from its shattered radiator. A girl sat behind the wheel, wide-eyed with shock, a thin red stream trickling down the side of her mouth.

"You all right, miss?" he wanted to know.

The girl stared at him uncomprehendingly.

"Get her some help, someone. I've got to call headquarters." He raced toward a store near the corner, put the details of his partner's murder on the wire.

Almost as he was calling in the alarm, a car pulled to a stop two blocks away, three men alighted, walked rapidly in different directions. One of them carried a small valise. In less than a moment, they were lost in the throng of tourists and sightseers that ebb and flow from one end of the Quarter to the other, day and night.

That evening, the newspapers announced that three armed bandits had robbed a cigar store on Dauphine, had killed a policeman in the course of the holdup. Their getaway car, stolen, had been recovered two blocks away after a pursuing prowl car had collided with a Chevrolet driven by a young tourist from South Carolina.

TWENTY-ONE
Top Guy

Lorna sat up against the pillow, in the white hospital room, managed to look wan. An interne hovered over her, fixed the two men on the chairs at her bedside with a baleful glare.

"Of course, Captain," his voice sounded very important, "our giving you permission to speak to the patient is done with the understanding that she has suffered great shock. You must be brief."

Captain LaFleur nodded impatiently. He was heavyset, with a thick shock of white hair. His face was red, thin purple veins stood out prominently on his nose. "We understand, Doctor. It's just routine. The district attorney's office has to have her testimony." He nodded to his companion, a thin man with a bobbing Adam's apple. "Mr. Deal will be as brief as possible."

Mr. Deal nodded, his Adam's apple jumped agonizingly. "Now, Miss Andrews, all we need from you is any description, if possible of what happened this afternoon."

Lorna bit at her nail, looked helplessly from the assistant district attorney to the interne. He nodded encouragingly. "It's all pretty hazy, Mr. Deal," she said finally. "I was driving down Dauphine Street. It's such a narrow street, you know." She found a wisp of a handkerchief under her pillow, held it to her nose. "I saw this car coming at me at a high speed. I tried to get out of its way and I lost control of my car. The first thing I knew I was on the sidewalk." She shook her head in confusion. "I must have frozen with my foot on the gas. I swung the wheel to get off the sidewalk and the police car smashed into me. I—I don't re member much after that."

The police captain nodded. "You see anything of the men in the first car, Miss Andrews?" he asked gruffly.

The girl shook her head. "It all happened too fast."

He tugged a memo book from his pocket, consulted it. "You're staying at the Roosevelt?" He looked up, got a nod, went back to his notes. "It there anybody you'd like us to notify at home?"

The girl shook her head again. "I'd rather not. I'm quite all right now." She turned the full power of her her smile on the interne. "Everybody's been so wonderful to me here. The doctor tells me I can leave soon."

"You've been a very lucky girl," the interne told her solemnly. "It could have been very serious."

"It was—for one of my boys," the police captain grunted. He pulled himself out of his chair. "Well, thanks for your cooperation, Miss Andrews. I'm sorry this had to happen to mar your trip."

"I hope you get the men responsible, Captain." She held out her hand.

"We will." The police captain waited until the thin man with the bobbing Adam's apple finished making some notations on a card. "Ready, Mr. Deal?"

The assistant D.A. got to his feet. "I'm afraid there's nothing much we can do to reimburse you for the damage to your car, Miss Andrews. I am familiar with similar cases where—"

"I'm fully insured for collision," she cut him off.

"Good, good." He turned, led the way to the door. The police captain followed.

When they left, Lorna turned to the interne. "Thanks for standing by."

He grinned his pleasure. "Glad to." He dropped into the chair just vacated by the district attorney's man. "Going to be in town long?"

Lorna shrugged. "I don't know. All this has taken the edge off my vacation. I'll have to think about it."

The following afternoon, Lorna signed herself out of the hospital, took a cab back to the hotel. There was no message for her at the desk from Willy or either of the other two. She recovered a package from the safe, took the elevator to her floor, headed for her room.

A man was sitting in the armchair against the wall, a smaller man was standing at the window looking out across Canal Street when she walked in. She started to withdraw, stopped at his command.

"Inside," he snapped at her. He was heavy-set, glowering. There was a large strip of adhesive tape over his right ear. In the dimness of the room she had no difficulty in recognizing him as the guard that had been stationed by the board.

The man at the window turned around, studied her carefully. "That's her, all right, Murph." He was the cashier.

"What's this all about?" Lorna wanted to know. "I'll call the police and—"

The man in the chair grinned crookedly. "Yeah. Why don't you do that? A cop was killed in that little caper. Cops can be awful narrow-minded when a cop gets killed." He waved at the phone. "Go on and call."

Lorna chewed on the inside of her lip for a moment. "What's this all about, anyway?"

The man in the chair looked to the cashier. "She wants to know what it's all about, Pete." He looked back at Lorna, growled deep in his chest. He touched the bandaged area over his ear. "Me, I almost got my brains beaten out. Pete there gets shoved around. What do you think it's all about, sister?"

"Look, mister, I've had a bad time, too. My car's smashed up and—"

"Mighty convenient you happened to block that street off right then. Those guys never would have made it. How come you just happened to be there?"

Lorna looked from the guard to the cashier and back. "I was on my way to the cigar store. I played there every day. Ask him."

"I don't have to ask him. I saw you there." He got up out of the chair. "Only, the time you were on your way there, the last race was on. What were you going to play? Parchesi?" He started toward her.

Lorna watched his approach without flinching. "Look. I don't know what kind of crazy idea you've got about me. Only let me tell you something. Things happen to guys who lay their hands on me. Bad things. You got something to say, say it. You got something to tell the cops, tell them. Only don't get any ideas you can push me around."

The guard reach out, grabbed a handful of her hair. "Tough, eh? Okay, baby—"

The cashier walked up behind him. "Lay off, Murph. The boss won't like it. He told you he wants to see her."

Murph pulled her face close to his. "Don't think you're getting away with it, baby. I owe you something for this crack on the head. I always pay my debts." He pushed her away from him. "We're going to pay a call on somebody. You're coming with us."

She met his glance, didn't flinch. "Suppose I don't."

He twisted the corners of his lips up in a sadistic grin. "I'm hoping you won't." He stuck his hand into his pocket, brought out a set of knucks. "The boss said you either come or else. Me, I'd rather the or else." He slipped the knucks over his fingers, polished them in his palm.

"You talked me into it, Murph," Lorna told him. "Maybe we can have our little dance some other time."

"Any time, baby. Any time." He turned to the little man. "Call Lombardi. Tell him we're bringing in the broad. Tell him she's the one."

The cashier nodded, headed for the phone.

"Lombardi?" Lorna managed to look unconcerned. "Who's he?"

"He's Steve Lombardi," the guard told her. "He's number one boy in this town. You sure picked yourself the wrong guy to play games with, baby. Steve don't like people who try to take money away from him." He chuckled. "Steve's going to be real glad to meet you, baby. Real glad."

Steve Lombardi lived in the swank Carter Arms, an expensive pile of stone and plate-glass that towered over Lafayette Square. The lobby was furnished in aggressively modernistic style. Brightly colored couches and chrome tables tastefully complemented the soft, restful, ankle-deep pastel carpeting. Murph led the way across the lobby to an ornate registration desk where an impeccably dressed man was absorbed in adjusting the edge of a cuff that peeked from the end of his morning jacket.

"Ring the penthouse and tell Mr. Lombardi that I'm on my way up with his guest, will you?"

The clerk raised his eyes, nodded. "Of course, Mr. Murphy."

Murph caught the girl by the arm, led the way past a bank of elevators to one marked "Penthouse." He pushed a red button on the panel, leaned back against the wall. The elevator glided to a noiseless stop at the penthouse, the doors slid noiselessly open. A man sat at a small desk paring his nails with a gold penknife. He glanced at the girl incuriously, went back to his nails.

"The boss is expecting you, Murph." He tossed his head in the direction of a closed door. "The study."

Steve Lombardi sat behind a desk that looked as if it had cost important money. He looked up as they walked in.

"This is the broad, Steve," Murph told him. "Name's Lorna Andrews."

Lombardi looked her over. "Nice of you to come over and see me."

"You mean I had a choice?"

Lombardi chuckled. "That Murph. Real persuasive, isn't he?" Lombardi's face had probably once been lean and wolfish, now it was blurred by a soft overlay of fat. Flat, lustreless eyes peered from beneath heavily veined, thickened eyelids, but the soft discolored pouches beneath them took away the menace. "What's your real name?"

"The one you've got will do," Lorna told him.

Murph caught her by the arm, swung her around. "Mr. Lombardi don't like smart broads. He asks a question, he expects an answer."

"Leave her alone, Murph. I like a girl with spirit." He studied her from under the heavily lidded eyes. "Who were the boys that knocked over my joint, Lorna?"

She shrugged. "Why, don't you ask this guy? He was there, I wasn't."

"We're not going to play games, are we?" Lombardi sighed. "There are ways to make you talk, you know that." He tossed his head at Murph. "I could ask Murph to have a little session with you. He'd like that."

"You don't believe I don't know the guys?" Lorna asked.

The man behind the desk shook his head. "I don't believe."

"But why? Just because I happened to hit the cop car, and—"

"Cut it out, baby. You had it and you know you had it. Both Pete the cashier and Murph here made your picture when it broke in the papers this morning. You've been casing that room for almost a week. You just didn't happen to bump that cop car. You were planted there for that." He looked her over, pursed her lips. "It took nerves and brains to do what you did. Enough brains to know you're not going to get away with it."

"Can I have a cigarette?" Lorna wanted to know. The man behind the desk pointed to a humidor. "Be my guest."

She walked over, picked out a cigarette, hung it from the corner of her mouth, looked to Murph for a light.

Lombardi grinned. "Give the lady a light, Murph."

The guard growled, pulled out a pack of paper matches, scratched one, held it for her. She took a deep drag, blew the smoke into his face. She turned to Lombardi. "Suppose, just for the sake of argument I did happen to know who pulled that job? What happens to me?"

Lombardi leaned back in his chair, laced his fingers at the back of his head, pursed his lips. "The same thing that happens if we have to beat it out of you. Only quicker." He smiled, shrugged. "It would be bad for business if word got around that somebody could pull a deal like this on Steve Lombardi and walk away from it."

"It would be worse if word got around that you couldn't even make a girl spill." She opened her huge dangling handbag, took out a handkerchief, touched it to her nose.

Lombardi started to laugh, the laugh froze when she returned the handkerchief, her hand reappearing with a big .45.

The heavy-lidded eyes widened. He turned on Murphy venomously. "You didn't frisk her for a gun?"

The guard's mouth hung open. He licked at his lips, started to shuffle toward her. "Who figured her to be heeled? She was in a hospital, and—"

Lorna's finger tightened on the trigger. "He comes one step closer, Lombardi, and there's going to be a new boss in this town."

"Keep away from her, you fool," Lombardi snarled at the guard.

Murph stopped shuffling, glared at the girl. "They shook her stuff down at the hospital. They always do. I didn't figure—"

"If this guy's a sample of your mob, Lombardi, it doesn't look like much of a future for you," she sneered. "He didn't think I could case a gun in my room? He doesn't know Lorna!"

"You're a pretty smart broad, at that," Lombardi nodded. "Maybe I could use you in my set-up." He flashed a venomous glance at Murphy. "Like you said, with knuckleheads like him on the payroll there's not much I can grab. How'd you like a place in my organization?"

"What's it cost?"

Lombardi shrugged. "I want my dough back. And somebody takes the fall. It don't have to be you."

Lorna considered it. "I'll get you your money back and throw you the guys that pulled the heist. The driver and I walk away."

Murph drew a whistling breath. "You're not going to let this little twist get away with that after—" He broke off as the girl turned to him, her finger white on the trigger. He licked at his lips, subsided.

"Okay, baby. You've got a deal. You turn over the guys who pulled the heist, turn back the dough and we'll work out a spot for you." He kept his hands laced behind his head, his eyes on the unwavering muzzle of the .45. "It was your idea? The crash car?" She nodded. "I can use a gal who thinks up gimmicks like that."

TWENTY-TWO
Double Cross

The knock on the door was light, almost imperceptible. Lorna turned the latch, opened it a crack. Willy was standing in the hotel corridor, shuffling his feet nervously. She opened it wide enough for him to slip in, closed it after him.

He wiped his mouth with the back of his hand, looked around. "You okay, Lorna?"

She nodded. "How about you boys?"

Willy walked over to the armchair, sank into it. "Not so good. Doc and that other guy been drinking pretty heavy." He found a cigarette, lit it with a shaking hand. "That little guy, that Kurt, had no call to shoot that cop. That's where all the heat's coming from."

"That's what you think." Lorna walked over to the bureau, took a fifth of bourbon from the top drawer. "You know who owned that horse room we knocked over?"

Willy shook his head. "Who?"

"A guy named Steve Lombardi. Runs this town." She spilled some liquor into a glass on the bureau, disappeared into the bathroom to bring out another glass. "They grabbed me the minute I got out of the hospital."

The color drained from the boy's face, leaving it murky. "How'd you break loose?" He looked around wildly. "They'll be looking for you here, and—"

She handed him a glass. "I made a deal with Lombardi, Willy." She sat on the edge of the bed, swirled the liquor around in her glass. "I'm giving them the money and the two boys. We walk away from it."

Willy's hand shook. "What'll they do to them?"

Lorna took a deep swallow from her glass. "The same thing they were going to do to me. The same thing they'd do to you." She frowned down at the glass, swirled it. "Lombardi's top dog in this town. He wouldn't be, if he let a couple of punks push his organization around."

Willy chewed on his cuticle. "Kurt should have told us who we were going up against. He should've told us."

"Well, what about the deal with Lombardi?"

Willy shrugged. "You're the boss." He took a deep swallow from his drink. "How do we know Lombardi'll live up to it? Maybe he'll wait until he gets back his dough, then he lets us all have it."

"It's been done," the girl admitted. "I think he'll be satisfied to get his money back and clean the slate with Doc and Kurt. Nobody has to know anybody else was in it."

The boy shook his head. "Suppose you decided not to go through with it. What then?"

"I don't think we'd make it, Willy. Lombardi's getting a little soft from the looks of him, but not in the head. I think we've grown a tail from here on in." She finished her drink, set it down. "Good or bad, we've made a deal and it looks like we're stuck with it. Unless you want to make a run for it. If you do, you're strictly on your own."

"I'm with you."

Lorna nodded. "I thought you'd be." She walked to the window, looked down into the street. "They'll be expecting some word from me. They must have seen you coming in."

Willy licked his lips, stared hungrily at her hips, the long clean line of her thighs silhouetted against the window. "When do they take them?"

"Tonight." She turned back to face him. "Where are they holed out?"

"An old shack out on the Bayou St. James road. Some place Kurt knew about."

"Where on the Bayou road?"

Willy licked his lips, drained his glass, set it down. "About two miles past the highway crossroads. It's set back from the road, got a picket fence around it. There are no other houses near it."

Lorna nodded, walked over to the telephone. She lifted the receiver, gave the operator a number. When Steve Lombardi's heavy voice came through, she relayed the information.

The shack stood about a hundred yards back off the road. It was surrounded by a decayed fence from which most of the pickets had fallen to rot in the weed-choked front yard.

"That must be the place, Murph," Pete, the cashier, told the man sitting beside him on the front seat. He drove the car behind an old moss-bearing oak where it would not be visible from the house, turned off the motor. There was no sign of life in the house itself.

Murphy tugged a .45 from his holster under his left arm, signaled for the thin man to follow him. They headed across an overgrown field, approached the house from an angle that gave them the most cover.

At the house they melted into the shadows along the wall, waited. Murph slid along the wall to the small porch, tested the wooden steps before he put his weight on them. He tried the doorknob, turned it quietly, found it locked. He brought out a thin steel rule, slid it into the doorjam. After a moment, it clicked, the door opened. The room beyond was in pitch darkness.

Murph stepped in, the thin man followed. He felt along the wall, located the switch. He waited for a second, then snapped the switch, spilling a yellow brilliance into the room from an unshaded overhead light.

The two men lay sprawled across an unmade bed, fully dressed. Doc started, rolled over. When he saw the two men standing at the door, guns in hand, his own hand streaked for the gun on the table near the bed.

Murph's .45 jumped. The heavy slug caught Doc in the side and slammed him back against the bed. He tried to get up again; another slug caught him in the belly, folded him over. He slid back, laced his hands over his middle, tried fruitlessly to stem the flow of red already seeping through his fingers.

The shots had blasted Kurt awake. He lay there, hands in full view, staring into the muzzle of the .38 in the cashier's fist. He watched Doc's body slowly fold over his hands, pitch forward on its face, then turned to Murph, waited expectantly.

"Weren't expecting to see me again, were you, sucker?" Murph asked in a deceptively mild voice,

"So I'm seeing you again," Kurt shrugged. "That's the chance you got to take."

"Pretty tough cookie, ain't he, Pete?" Murph asked the cashier. "I'll bet he's a real hard guy. Me, I like hard guys." He looked back at the man on the bed. "Where's the dough, sucker?"

Kurt motioned toward a closet at the other side of the room. "In there. All of it."

"Get it, Pete," Murph snapped. He waited until the smaller man had crossed to the closet, pulled out a valise. Pete opened it, fingered through the stacks of bills.

"Looks like it's all here, Murph."

Murphy nodded. "Lombardi'll be glad to hear that. Me, I got something more important on my mind than the dough." He reached up, fingered the bandage on the side of his head. "You and me have a little settling up to do, sucker."

There was a strained look in Kurt's eyes. "Look, there wasn't anything personal in it. I was doing a job, that's all."

Murph nodded. "That's what I'm going to be doing, just a job. Nothing personal, just a job." The gun came out of Murph's pocket only a few inches from Kurt's face. The blast filled the room and there wasn't any more face.

TWENTY-THREE
Setup for Sin

Steve Lombardi was sitting behind the desk when Murph walked in. He motioned for him to set the valise down on the desk.

"Have any trouble, Murph?"

Murph grinned, shook his head. "No trouble. It was a pleasure." He looked over to where Lorna sat polishing her carefully lacquered fingernails against the side of her palm. "I still think we ought to finish the job."

Lombardi pulled the valise to him, opened it, stirred the packets of bills with a pudgy finger. "We made a deal, Murph. A deal's a deal. Besides, we got our dough back and you got even.''

"Yeah, but I still think—''

"Stop thinking,'' Lombardi cut him off. "I take care of that end.'' He nodded his head toward the door. "I'll see you tomorrow.''

Murph nodded, left without a backward glance.

The man behind the desk pulled out the packs of money, piled them on the desk. "Would have been a nice piece of swag, at that.''

Lorna looked up from her fingernails, shrugged. "Another day, another dollar. You can't make a pass every roll.'' She got up from the couch, walked over to the desk. Her body was lush, ripe. Swelling breasts showed over the top of her low-cut dress; a small waist hinted at the full hips, the long shapely legs concealed by the fullness of her skirt. The sway of her hips had the calculated effect on Lombardi. "What about Doc and Kurt?''

Lombardi shrugged. "What's the difference? They knew what they were walking into when they tangled with Lombardi.'' His eyes undressed her. "You made a bad mistake. You know that.''

The girl nodded. "I sure did. Next time I'll be more careful about those license plates.''

"What license plates?'' Lombardi scowled.

"On the getaway car.'' She picked up a pile of bills, riffled through them. "Doc had Willy steal that car the day before we pulled the job. The owner must have reported the plate numbers. That's what fouled us up. The cop was questioning Willy about the car when Doc and Kurt came tearing out. If it hadn't been for those plates, it would have been as clean as a whistle. I never would have had to show in it.'' She looked almost wistful as she tossed the money back on the desk.

"That's a risk you got to take. So a cop spotted the plates. It wouldn't happen in a million years.''

Lorna shook her head. "Next time I'll know better.'' Lorna walked to a small table, picked up a silver cigarette box, weighed it in the palm of her hand. "I just figured it out.'' She set the box down, continued wandering around the room aimlessly, picking up small objects, examining them, setting them down. "What about us, Steve?''

"Us?''

Lorna looked at him, nodded. "Willy and me.''

"Yeah. What about that? What's with you and that pimply faced kid? You two shacking up?'' His voice made it pretty plain he didn't think so.

"Not that it's any of your business,'' she told him calmly, "but the kid's like a good-luck piece to me. He was nice me once when I needed help, and he didn't expect to paid for it. Any way. That doesn't happen often.''

"Okay, okay. No need to get sore.'' He stared at the top of her dress where her breasts swelled out. "I'll find a spot for both of you.'' His eyes narrowed. "You're figuring on staying, right?''

Lorna shrugged. "Why not? With you I can make important money. On my own, I might end up pitching for pennies."

Lombardi nodded. "You're being smart." He tapped on the edge of the desk with pudgy fingers that had dimples for knuckles. "You know why I made a deal with you, Lorna?"

"You can use some brains in this outfit, I guess."

He considered it, puffed out his lips, nodded. "I need somebody smart I can trust." He hit himself in the chest with the side of his hand. "I set up this organization. Some of my boys think it's time I moved over. I need somebody I can trust."

"Maybe I'll get ambitious, too. Maybe you'll have to get someone to watch me."

He submerged his neck into his shoulders, held his hands palms up. "Why? You ride with me, you got everything you want. Besides, the mob would never stand still for a woman running it. You got nothing to gain." The flat lustreless eyes studied her face. "Well?"

"You're the boss, Lombardi."

"Steve. It sounds cozier. You and me are going to work close together. Real close."

"That part of the deal?" Lorna wanted to know.

"That's the deal," Lombardi told her. The heavily veined lids all but closed his eyes from view. "All or nothing."

"And if I want out?"

Lombardi shrugged. "You get out." The lids unveiled the cold eyes. "But you got to realize one thing. Murph out there can't let you go walking around knowing he knocked off those two friends of yours. I can hold him off you if we got a deal. No deal, I couldn't keep him away from you."

Lorna shrugged. "I'm a hard luck gal, Steve. Something usually happens to guys that get cozy with me. Something bad."

Lombardi grinned. "Like Typhoid Mary? Me, I been vaccinated. I'll take my chances. Is it a deal?"

The girl sighed. "It's a deal."

He reached over, pushed a button on the corner of his desk.

The door opened, Murph walked in. "Where's that pet poddle of hers?"

Murph frowned. "Her which?"

"The kid. Pimples. Where is he?"

"Oh, him." Murph's face cleared. "The boys got him stashed down on the fifth floor waiting until you make up your mind."

"I made it up. You and him go over to Lorna's room at the Roosevelt. Check her out."

Murph grinned. "Then what?"

"Then nothing. Bring the stuff here. She's moving in with me."

The grin drained from the guard's face, leaving nothing but a venomous look.

"Okay, if you say so."

"He just said so, Murph," Lorna snapped at him. She walked over to where the guard stood, stopped in front of him, hands on hips, feet planted akimbo. "Seems to me you do a lot of griping around here. A smart guy might figure it'd pay Steve better to take on a couple of independents that could make his hired guns look sick than to keep on a guard that's dumb enough to be taken by amateurs."

Murph was about to retort, saw the look on Lombardi's face, subsided. "We weren't looking for anybody to be crazy enough to try to hit one of Steve Lombardi's rooms," he growled defensively. "You got to be crazy to pull something like that."

Lorna grinned at him. "Crazy like a fox." She looked the guard over from head to toe. "You know what'd be crazier?"

Murph didn't answer, stood glaring at her.

"It'd be crazier to think Lombardi's ready to move over, alive or dead. That'd be crazier."

"What's she talking about, Steve?" Murph appealed to the man in the chair. "She must be nuts."

"Maybe not so nuts, Murph," Lombardi told him. "You like the way the organization's set up, Murph?"

Murph's shrug was elaborate. "Why not? I been getting along. I got the biggest horse room under my belt, I carry my own weight."

Lorna spoke. "Some day you might even be number-two man in the set-up, eh, Murph?"

"Is that bad?"

The man in the chair puffed out his lips. "Sometimes guys get ideas. A little something like the stickup the other day, they think things are getting out of hand. They think they could do better, Murph." The eyes had receded behind their pouches, glittered under their lids. "That's bad when that happens, Murph."

Murphy wet his lips. "What are you telling me all this for?"

"Like Lorna said. Maybe some day you'll be number-two boy in this town."

The guard shrugged. "So I said is that bad? I'd be plenty satisfied. Hell, you know I'd—"

Lombardi shook his head. "No guy likes to stay second man all his life. He gets to looking at the top man, he gets to figuring he could do a better job." Murphy started to argue, Lombardi waved him to silence. "You don't have to tell me, Murph. I was number two once. My boss met with a bad accident." He played with the diamond ring on his finger. "He was getting soft, Murph. You're not figuring I'm getting soft, are you, Murph?"

"What's this all about?" Murph looked from the man in the chair to the girl and back. "You want to bring her into the organization, that's okay with me, boss. I just thought—"

"I told you to let me do the thinking," Lombardi said coldly.

The guard's forehead glistened damply as he nodded. "Sure, sure. Anything you say, boss." He looked at Lorna, licked his lips. "No offense. It's okay with me."

"Mighty generous of you." Lorna turned her back on him, walked to the couch, dropped onto it, crossed her knees. "Now suppose you pick up Willy and get my things over here."

Murph nodded, turned on his heel, hurried through the door. Lombardi sat for a minute, staring at the closed door. "You don't think he'd have the nerve?"

Lorna shrugged. "He's dumb enough." She rubbed the palm of her hand along the side of her arm. "Suppose somebody did decide to try for you, Steve. Got anything set up?"

Lombardi considered for a moment, shook his head. "I usually take Murph or one of the other guns along when I go anyplace. Here," he looked around the room, "who could get at me here?"

"Any one of them," Lorna told him. "He had a gun on him right now. Any time he comes up here, he's heeled. Right?"

The man in the chair looked thoughtful, nodded. "I can't tell him to go around without a rod. What good would he be to me?"

"He doesn't need one here. Nobody else uses that penthouse elevator?"

Lombardi shook his head.

"Okay. I've got a spot for Willy. When I found him he was jockeying an elevator. He'll run the penthouse car."

"What good will that do?"

Lorna grinned at him. "No one gets up here unless they check their artillery with Willy on the way up."

TWENTY-FOUR
Catherine the Great

Lorna stretched out on the divan on the penthouse's sundeck, lazily watched Willy making the drinks. He handed one to her, sat on the edge of the divan, looked out over the low roofs of the old city.

"Where's Lombardi today, Lorna?" He wanted to know.

Lorna shrugged. "Out checking some of the horse rooms with Murph." She put her arm up under her head, her breasts strained upward against her nylon blouse. "The take's been falling off. Steve's getting worried."

Willy had difficulty tearing his eyes away from the soft lines of her bosom. In the two months he had been working for Lombardi he had started to fill out. His pimply face gave promise of clearing up. His mouth was still slack-lipped, damp. "Figure the boys have been sticking their fingers into the till?" He sipped noisily at his drink, wiped his mouth with the back of his hand.

Lorna shook her head. "No, the numbers and policy boys are beginning to go big. The marks have only so much money. Every dime they drop on the numbers is a dime they can't play on the horses."

"Lombardi could be through, Lorna." Willy leaned toward her, put his hand on her knee. "Maybe we better get out from under."

When she felt his breath against her face, Lorna's eyes rolled down from a contemplation of the soft summer sky, to where his hand lay on her thigh, a few inches below the hem of her linen shorts.

His eyes followed hers, he removed his hand reluctantly. "When do I gets a break?" he pouted sullenly. "You think I don't go crazy knowing that fat slob has you in here all to himself?" Suddenly, impulsively, he tried to grab her. She sat up, broke his hold with an upward and outward thrust of her arms, pushed him off the divan.

"You flipped?" she growled at him. "Since when did you get so big you think you can put your hands on me?" She swung her legs off the divan, stood over him. "I've been pretty nice to you, but don't let that give you any ideas."

Willy got to his feet sulkily, brushed himself off. "You're not that hard to get along with when Lombardi whistles. Me, you're like an ice cube with—him you play house with."

Lorna started to get mad, shrugged. "Look, Willy, I like you. Or I wouldn't have bailed you out when Murph wanted to give you the same medicine he gave Doc and Kurt, would I?"

Willy shook his head, licked at his lips. His eyes were fixed hungrily on the deep cleft exposed by the V-neck of her blouse. "Then why don't you give me a break? I go crazy seeing you every day and being allowed to look but not touch."

Lorna walked over to the portable bar, spilled some bourbon over ice cubes, softened it with a touch of water. "I've never let a man lay a hand on me unless there was a reason for it, Willy." She drank deeply, studied him over the rim. "All my life men have pushed me around. I made up my mind I'd push back to get what I wanted." She looked around the luxuriously appointed sundeck. "Lombardi gives me this and the contacts I need. Lewis gave me a hold over Lew Barker and Doss. Before that there was an old man who ran a drive-in, and a kid named Gunson. They all served their purpose."

Willy shuffled closer to her. His voice was tense. "I've got to have you, Lorna." He grabbed out for her, caught the fragile fabric of the blouse, ripped it away.

The sight of her firm, pink-tipped breast drove him into a near frenzy. A stream of saliva coursed down his chin as he struggled to pull the girl into his arms. His hands fumbled over her breasts frantically, he tried to press his wet mouth against hers.

As he strained her to him, he was pleasantly surprised to feel the resistance oozing out of her. He slobbered against the side of her neck, tried to reach her mouth.

Lorna seemed to go completely limp. Suddenly she brought her balled fist up in a vicious uppercut. His arms slipped from around her, he folded them over his stomach. She straightened up, chopped at the side of his neck with the edge of her hand. He grunted, went to his knees, stayed there, gasping for breath.

"Don't ever try it again, Willy." She turned to the bar, poured two fingers of straight bourbon into a glass, held it out to him. "You don't play in that league."

Willy drained the glass, coughed. After a moment, he was able to get up, sit on the side of the divan. His eyes were watery, sick. "Okay, I'm sorry."

Lorna nodded, walked over to the grilled railing, looked down into the heat haze below. "Let's forget it, Willy. I don't want to be mad at you. You're the only friend I ever had." She turned, grinned at him. "Okay?" For the first time she seemed to be aware of the torn blouse and of what it exposed. "I'd better find something to put on. I'll be right out."

When she returned a few minutes later with a tightfitting sweater, he had dried his eyes. He watched her as she walked over to pick up her drink. The shorts were tight, clung to her hips.

"I read about another girl like you once," he told her.

She looked surprised. "Like me? How?"

He shrugged. "She liked to make men suffer, too. Her name was Catherine the Great. She was a Russian. Not a Commie. There wasn't any commies in her day."

"How was she like me, Willy?"

"I guess she was a pretty hot package. Anyway, she could have any man she wanted. And as many at a time. Maybe it was because she was the queen," he conceded. "She used to have a personal bodyguard, all six-footers. Every night, she'd pick the biggest and shack up with him. The next day he'd turn up dead."

"And that's like me?"

"Ain't it?"

"I'm a hard luck girl."

"A hard luck gal's a gal things happen to. You make things happen. Why?"

Lorna crossed her arms over her breasts, rubbed the backs of her arms. "You're wrong, Willy. I don't make things happen. They just do."

He raked his hair back into place with his fingers, stood up. "I better get back to the cage."

She stuck her hand out. "No hard feelings, Willy? We understand each other?"

Willy nodded, shook her hand. "No hard feelings." He walked to the door leading into the den, turned around. "I'll buy what you said about using all these guys. But you'd better never go for one of them where I get pushed outside."

"Don't worry about it, Willy. If I ever pick a man to fall for, I'll fall for you.

Okay?"

He turned, stalked through the den toward the front of the penthouse. She stared at his departing back with a puzzled frown for a moment, then shrugged.

She was stretched out on her back on the divan when Lombardi came in an hour later. He walked out onto the sundeck, swabbed at his forehead with a balled handkerchief.

"It's plenty hot down there," he growled. "Got anything cool to drink?" He shrugged out of his jacket, tossed it at a gaily colored aluminum chair. Half moons of sweat darkened his shirt at the armpits; it clung clammily to his back.

"Got just what the doctor ordered, Steve." Lorna crossed to the bar, dropped chunks of ice into the shaker, poured liquids from several bottles.

Lombardi dropped into a chair, watched her back and hips as they bounced in time to the cocktail shaking. When she was finished, she poured a frothy white drink into a glass, held it out to him.

"How about the rooms? Find out what's going wrong?"

He sipped at his glass, left a mustache of white foam on his upper lip. "We're losing money by the bucket in most of them. The customers are staying away in droves."

"Why?"

Lombardi shrugged. "They get bigger action for their money on the numbers and in policy." He wiped the foam off his upper lip, scowled. "I had a chance to move into numbers when it first started to get a play. I muffed it."

"Who runs it?"

"A gunsel named Rivero. He's got his finger in policy, too. Those Riquenos out in the parishes go heavy for it." He took another swallow from the glass. "If I had that, I could bail myself out for the drop in the rooms."

"What's stopping you?"

Lombardi mopped at his face again. "Rivero's a pretty tough number. He wouldn't stand still for it if I moved in on him." He finished the drink, handed the glass back. "It would mean a war with packages left on every corner in town."

"And one of them might be you. That it?" The corner of the girl's lip curled slightly. "What do you think the boys are going to do if they get the idea you're ducking a fight, Steve?"

"I'm not ducking any fight," he snapped at her. His eyes couldn't meet hers. "Give me another drink."

Wordlessly she refilled the glass, handed it back to him. "What happens when the Syndicate starts to ask questions about receipts dropping off?" she persisted.

Lombardi swabbed at his face again. There was a faint greenish tinge about his jowls. "They gotta understand. It's not like the old days. They can't expect me to go around blasting everybody that tries to muscle in—"

"Maybe not, but from what you've told me, the big boys don't expect excuses, either. They expect results." She chewed on the tip of a lacquered nail. "You've got to do something, Steve. You've got to stop him some way."

"What can I do?" He set his glass down, paced the sundeck. "I've put all the heat on my boys they can take. It's the same answer every place. They don't come in, they can't drop money." He stopped in front of her. "You're a smart girl. Maybe you got some ideas?"

"How about this Rivero?"

Lombardi shook his head. "Tough. Real tough." He wiped his damp palms. "He brought most of his own mob with him from Puerto Rico. Anything happen to him, those spics would go crazy. He's their padrone." He shook his head. "Hitting him's not the answer. That would only make it worse."

"Maybe you can hit him without having him hit."

Lombardi scowled at her. "Break that down into English."

"You just said Rivero's their padrone. Anything happens to him they'd go crazy. That's because they think he's all-powerful. Right?"

Lombardi nodded impatiently. "I just told you that."

"Okay, maybe if we prove to them he's not so important, maybe they'll stop thinking he's God Almighty and we can start moving in." She shrugged. "After all, we know he's human. He must have some weak spots in his set-up. It's up to us to find them and break a hole through."

Lombardi considered it, sighed, shook his head. "You don't know him. He's hard, cold and careful. He has no outsiders in a key spot in his set-up. Just Riquenos. And you can't get to them."

"The way you talk we might as well throw in the sponge," Lorna snapped at him. "Whose side are you on?"

Lombardi clapped the palm of his hand against his forehead. "Whose side am I on, she asks?" He scowled at her. "Don't you think I've been laying awake nights trying to figure an out? Don't you think I know that the boys in New York will be sending one their trouble shooters to take over if I don't find an out?"

"So what are you doing about it?"

"Worrying."

"That's what I thought. Worrying won't do you any good. When you open your eyes he'll still be there. I still say you've got to move in on him. It'll slow him up, anyway."

"If I move in on him, it'll mean war. And we haven't got the manpower to stand up against him in an all-out war."

"You can have the Syndicate send in some outside troops, can't you?"

Lombardi shook his head. "No. That'd be admitting I was in trouble. They wouldn't wait. They'd send in one of their enforcers to take over."

"But this way we might all go down."

Lombardi grinned at her crookedly. "This way we might go down. If they send in an enforcer, I'm sure to go down." He walked over, stuck his face close to hers. "Don't forget, baby, that when the showdown comes, we all have to think of Number One." He jabbed at his chest with a pudgy finger. "That's who Lombardi's thinking of. Number one."

TWENTY-FIVE
Assignation

Lorna melted back into the shadows of the doorway. Up the street, a taxi pulled to the curb, disgorged a lone passenger. He stood at the curb, irresolutely looked both directions. When the cab had swung into a U-turn and disappeared in the direction from which it had come, the man turned, walked toward the doorway where she stood.

He stopped almost abreast of the doorway, stuck a cigarette into his mouth, scratched a match, touched it to it. In the weak light, she could recognize Murphy's profile.

"Make sure I'm not being tailed, then follow me. I've got Room 318 in the hotel around the corner. I'll be in the room." He flicked the match toward the curb, continued walking.

The girl stayed in the doorway for five minutes, saw no evidence of a tail on the guard. She stepped out, walked unhurriedly in the direction he had gone.

On the corner, a hotel neon was clicking on and off tirelessly, alternately dyeing the street in light or drenching it with darkness. It was a small, well-kept hotel.

The girl pushed through the door, walked to the elevator. The man behind the desk didn't take his eyes out of the magazine he was reading. It was a self-service cage—she pushed a button, rode to the fourth floor. Then she walked to the red bulb that marked the staircase, descended to the floor below.

Room 318 was in the front, looked down on the street. She knocked softly, the door was opened immediately. Murphy pulled her in, stepped into the hall, looked in both directions. His right hand was sunken in his jacket pocket where it bulged suggestively. He closed the door, snapped on the lock.

"Okay. What's the fever? Pimple face made a big deal you got to see me. What's it all about?" he asked cautiously.

"Give me a chance to get my breath, will you?" Lorna complained.

Murphy caught her by the arm, swung her around to face him. "Look, baby, never mind the strip tease. You got a pitch to make, make it or your audience is going to walk out."

She shook her arm loose from the man's hand. "Don't handle me, Murph, I don't like it." She walked over to the only chair in the room, dropped into it, crossed her knee. "You want it fast and hard, okay. I think Lombardi's opening at the seams."

The man sneered at her. "You get me all the way across town to tell me that.

He's been going soft for months. Right now he's shaking like jelly because a two-bit chiseler has moved in on him."

"Rivero?"

Murphy's eyes narrowed. "What do you know about it?"

"Lombardi's scared of him. Unless somebody stops Rivero, he's going to move in and take Lombardi over."

The man cursed volubly. "Try talking to your fat boy about slapping Rivero back in line, he shakes himself to pieces."

"What are you going to do about it?"

His jaw sank. "What am I going to do about it? Why should I do anything about it?" He watched her through narrowed eyes. "He's the boss. You know that."

"He may be the boss, but you're next man from the top."

Murphy dropped onto the side of the bed, stared at her. "So?"

She shrugged, looked him right in the eye. "Something happens to the fat boy, and you're in the saddle. You make the moves and we can stop Rivero dead."

"We?"

The girl shrugged. "You and me. Or maybe you'd rather not have me as a partner?" She stood up, smoothed her skirt against her thighs. Standing against the light, it was apparent she wore nothing under the dress.

"Just a partner?" He took no pains to conceal the obvious inventory he was taking of her assets.

She walked over, stood close to him. "You'll be the boss. You call the turns." She reached down, lifted the cigarette from between his lips, covered his mouth with hers. He reached up, caught her, swung her down into his lap.

"You levelling with me?" he demanded.

She nodded. "I wouldn't cross you, Murph." She reached up, loosened his tie, opened his collar. "I've got too much to lose. We start this thing, there's no turning back."

He stared down into her upturned face for a moment, then his forehead clouded. "It won't work," he growled. "Too many of the boys will ride with the fat boy, right or wrong. Anything happen to him, and they'd burn us down on the spot."

"Suppose it happened in the suite, and—"

He grinned at her glumly. "You fixed that, sweetheart. You and that idea of checking all guns before seeing him. Nobody could get a gun up there, not even you."

"You don't have to get a gun in. I've been looking the situation over. There's a spot on one of the floors of a building across the square where you can see right into the penthouse den."

"That's a pretty long shot, all the way across the square. Suppose it missed?"

"It mustn't miss. What kind of a shot are you?"

He let her sit up, got up, paced the floor. "Pretty good. But—"

"It'd be a cinch with a reacher."

He stopped pacing, stared at the girl. "A reacher?"

"A silenced rifle with a telescopic sight. It'd be like knocking bottles off a stone."

Murph raked his fingers through his hair, resumed his pacing. Once, he stopped, started to say something, went back to it. Finally, "No, it's no good. Even if I do manage to pot him, how long will it be before they find him? Then all hell breaks loose."

The girl shook her head, her eyes followed the man. "It can be forever before they find him, if we work it right."

He stopped pacing, walked over, sat down beside her. "How?"

"Leave that to me." She took his face in her hands, looked into his eyes. "You do trust me, don't you?"

Murph considered, shrugged. "You got too much to lose if it goes wrong. I've got to trust you."

"I'll take it on that basis." She pressed her lips against his. "As far as the rest of the boys know, Lombardi has taken off on a trip, maybe even to report to the Syndicate."

His eyes were clouded with doubts, but he nodded. "Go on."

"While he's away, you take over. You move fast and hard, show the big boys what you can deliver. When Fat Boy doesn't come back, you're it on a permanent basis. How's it sound?"

Murphy pursed his lips, tried to punch a hole in it, couldn't. "Just one thing. Even if you can count on Willy to load him into the elevator, the only place that cage goes is to the lobby. You going to walk a stiff through that lobby?"

She sealed off any further questions with her lips. As they started to move against his, the man caught the zipper in the back of the dress. Her skin was smooth and cool to his touch. He started to pull it from her shoulders, she pushed him away.

"Easy, Murph," she grinned. "I've got to walk out of here in the morning." She slipped out of his arms, stood up, looked around. "Do we need all this light?" She walked to the switch, flipped it off.

TWENTY-SIX
Penthouse Blues

Steve Lombardi was scared.

It showed in the little twitch under his left eye, it showed in the nervous, staccato way he talked.

Lorna sat, feet folded under her on the couch, watched him pace the room. "You know you haven't been out of this place in over three weeks, Steve? The boys are beginning to wonder."

He stopped, scowled at her. "They think I'm scared?" He hit his chest with the side of his hand. "Me? Steve Lombardi? I'm not scared of anybody or anything. They know that."

"You could fool me," Lorna told him mildly. "From what I hear, Rivero has been really taking over. Murph tells me—"

"Murph talks too much," Lombardi snapped. "Maybe he thinks he could stop Rivero, huh?"

"Maybe. It's a lead pipe cinch you can't stop him hiding away up here." She unfolded her legs, stood up. "That elevator out there looks like you're expecting an invasion. The minute anybody gets into it, two or three guys squeeze in behind them, fan them. It doesn't look good."

"I like it that way."

Lorna walked over to the piano, helped herself to a cigarette. "Willy used to handle the job all by himself. It didn't cause so much talk." She lit the cigarette, exhaled blue fog, squinted at him through it. "Don't you trust Willy? Next thing you know you won't be trusting me."

"Maybe I don't," Lombardi spat at her. He pulled a cigar from his breast pocket, bit off the end. "I don't trust anybody." He resumed his pacing, chewed on the unlit cigar. "I'm staying put right here until I get this thing licked. And I'll lick it, baby, don't think I won't."

"Maybe. If you don't shake yourself loose at the seams first."

He stared at her for a moment, then walked over to her. His right hand flashed upward, slammed her across cheek, knocked her head to one side, backhanded it into position. "When I want funny sayings I turn on the television." He turned his back, stamped out of the room.

She watched him disappear into the den, glared after him murderously. She swore at him under her breath, rubbed the tips of her fingers along the angry red stain on her cheek.

She walked out onto the sundeck, squinted into the heat haze that seemed to have settled permanently over the city. The blueness of the sky gave no promise of any relief. She walked to the rail, studied the buildings across the square. Only one of them, a tall office building, towered over the spot where she stood. She wondered what progress Murph had made in the two weeks since the plan had been hatched. On an impulse she walked back into the living room, picked up her bag.

"I'm going out to see a movie, Steve. Okay?" She called in to him.

"Go to hell for all I care," he growled back.

The elevator cage was sitting at the penthouse floor. Willy looked up from a picture magazine as she walked out. He stared at the red mark on her cheek. "That fat bastard been teeing off on you again?"

Lorna shrugged. "Let him have his fun."

The car dropped silently toward the lobby. "What's with him, anyhow?

He's got a whole troop down in the lobby frisking everybody that goes up. Nobody ever sees him come down. What's with him?"

"He's scared. Rivero has been taking over district after district. The fat boy figures if he stays up there and prays maybe a miracle will happen and Rivero will pick up his marbles and go home."

Willy snorted. "This mob's going to fall apart if the boys don't get some action pretty soon."

Lorna grinned at him. "They'll get action. Real soon."

The car slid to a smooth stop, the door swung open. She walked out into the lobby, passed the two hard-eyed men who sat on a couch ostensibly reading newspapers.

As she stepped out into the street, the heat hit her in the face like a hot towel. She waved down a cab, gave an address in the Vieux Carré, settled back, let the superheated air fan her face. On the sidewalks women were shuffling along listlessly in thin cotton dresses, men were in their shirtsleeves, collars open.

The cab swung off Canal into one of the narrow streets of the Quarter, ambled to the 300 block, pulled up in front of a reproduction of an old-time saloon, authentic down to the swinging doors.

Lorna pushed a bill through the window to the driver, crossed the sidewalk, pushed through the swinging doors. Inside it was cool, dim. There was sawdust on the floor, small tables were scattered around in organized confusion, overhead a large-bladed fan lazily stirred the air.

She crossed the floor to a telephone booth set against the rear wall, entered, dialed a number. When Murphy answered, she told him where she was, asked him to meet her. Then, she slid into the rear booth, ordered a Tom Collins.

She was on her fourth cigarette when Murphy pushed through the swinging doors, stood in the entrance squinting into the dimly lit room. She waved him down, he crossed the room, slid into the booth opposite her.

"What's happened?" he wanted to know.

"Nothing. That's what's killing me. I can't put up with much more of that fat slob. He's shaking himself to pieces."

Murphy grinned. "The great Lombardi." A waiter sauntered over, he ordered a fresh Collins for the girl, a bourbon and water for himself. "I got a real good cure for the shakes. Permanent, too."

Lorna nodded. "I know all about it. But when? We wait much longer and that Rivero will have such a grip on this town, no one will shake him loose. You included."

Murph scowled at her. "I'll shake him loose, baby. Don't worry about that." He leaned back as a waiter slid the drinks in front of them, waited until he'd gone back to his station. "I don't want to muff this job by being too anxious. It's got to go right."

Lorna grunted. "Wait much longer and he'll die of old age. When are you going to be ready?"

"Saturday night."

The annoyance seeped out of the girl's face. "This Saturday?"

Murph nodded. "We got things pretty well sewed up. It wasn't easy. We ran into a lot of headaches."

"Okay, so you'll get a merit badge. Fill me in."

"I cased all the buildings facing the penthouse. Only one that's any good to us is the big office building."

"I figured that."

"Me and Pete went from floor to floor until we got the right level. It's the 20th floor." He took the cigarette from between his lips, blew a stream of smoke toward the ceiling. "There are four offices facing Lombardi's sundeck. One of them's a textile outfit, closed Saturdays."

Lorna listened, nodded. "Can you get in it?"

Murph nodded. "A cinch. We were in there the other day. Made like we were looking for some textile quotes. It's perfect. I could see you walking around in the den clear as day."

"Wonderful." She picked a fleck of tobacco off the tip of her tongue, rolled it thoughtfully between thumb and forefinger. "Saturday, eh? That gives me just three days to take care of my end."

"There better not be any slip-up there, baby," Murph warned her. "The Syndicate gets the idea Lombardi was knocked off, they'll start smelling around. It mightn't be too good for either of us. That idea of yours better work."

"It will."

Murph took a swallow from his glass, watched the girl chewing on her fingernail. "I hear he's got some outside troops watchdogging him. That going to kick it over?"

Lorna shook her head. "No. All they do is check anybody going in. They don't check anybody going out. Besides, after midnight they're off."

"How come?"

"Lombardi has the penthouse cage brought up to the penthouse at midnight. You can't get up there any other way."

"I hope you're right."

"I hope you get your hope," she told him. She crushed out her butt in the ashtray, picked up her bag. "I've got to get moving. Does Pete know what he's supposed to do?"

Murph nodded. "He'll be standing by." He looked up at the girl. "Don't forget that I'll be over there waiting. It's up to you to get him up. Don't get between him and the window. Got it?"

Lorna nodded. "Got it." She bent over, covered the man's mouth with hers. "I'll be seeing you Sunday."

TWENTY-SEVEN
Dead Pigeon

Murphy checked his watch against the clock in the lobby of the office building, headed for the bank of elevators.

The starter raised his eyebrows. "Who were you going to see, sir?" He smiled apologetically. "Some of the firms are closed on Saturday."

"I have an appointment with a buyer in Sun Chemicals." He checked his watch. "For eleven forty-five."

The starter consulted his sheet, nodded. "Yes, sir. Sun's on the eleventh floor." He motioned to the end cage. "They have the whole floor, sir."

Murph left the elevator at the eleventh floor, waited until the cage had dropped out of sight, started for the stairway. He trudged slowly up the nine flights, stood on the landing of the twentieth floor, leaned against the wall to catch his breath.

He opened the fire door a few inches, satisfied himself the floor was empty. Quickly, he walked down to the office he had selected, went to work on the lock with a small pick. It surrendered easily, he stepped into the one-room office, closed the door after him. The air was heavy, stale, hot. He opened the window, pulled up a chair, sat down to wait.

At two o'clock, he opened his valise, started to assemble the rifle. He attached the silencer, adjusted the telescopic sight. Then he walked over to the sink, washed the oil off his hands.

He returned to the seat by the window, resumed his vigil, the rifle leaning against the window sill.

The afternoon seemed to drag on interminably. After what seemed years, the shadows began to grow longer, the sun started to go down, a red merciless molten ball in a clear blue sky. He watched it reflect off the windows across the way, wondered idly if Lombardi could see the blank space on this building front represented by the open window. He wondered what the fat boy would think if he knew death would soon come blasting out of that window to mow him down.

By six o'clock, dusk had fallen sufficiently so that in some windows across the Square electric lights started to shine. In the penthouse, someone switched on the light on the piano near the window, also the lamp behind the divan.

Suddenly, Murphy stiffened. The blinds were being drawn in the penthouse windows, blocking out any view of the interior. He raked his fingers through his hair, started to swear. He wondered if the girl had suddenly gone crazy.

Lorna sat on the couch, watched Lombardi pull the blinds. She could feel the little beads of perspiration forming at her hair line, the moistness in her palms.

She made no comment.

The weeks of self-imprisonment had left their mark on the fat man. There were discolored circles under his eyes, the skin hung in folds along the sides of his jowls. The constant twitching under his eye had become more marked. He ignored the girl, stamped over to pick up the folded newspaper on the table in the foyer. He flipped through the pages as though looking for something, growled, bunched the paper up and threw it at the waste basket.

Lorna got up from the couch, walked over to the big window, opened the blinds, looked down into the twinkling of lights twenty stories below. Lombardi started to yell at her, checked himself. He walked over behind her, hands going around her to her breasts, lips to the back of her neck. "I guess it hasn't been easy being cooped up with me here, baby. I'll make it up to you. You just trust old Steve."

She removed his hands from the front of her gown, nodded. "I do, or I wouldn't be here." She turned around. "That whole city should belong to you if you'd take it." She moved aside, left him standing at the window looking down at the network of lights, the glare in the sky that marked the Quarter.

There was a tinkle of glass, the faint hum of an angry bee. Lombardi's body shuddered. There was another hum, and his head jerked back. His knees folded under him, he hit the floor face first.

Lorna pulled the blinds shut, used all her strength to turn the big man over on his back. There was a rapidly spreading dark spot on the front of his jacket, a blue-black hole over his right eye. He was beyond help.

She opened and closed the blinds twice, the pre-arranged signal to tell Murph that the second phase of the operation was due to get under way. She checked her watch. It was almost seven o'clock.

She walked into the bedroom, brought in a blanket, dropped it over the dead man, sat down to wait.

It was nine o'clock before the telephone finally rang. She dried the palms of her hands along the side of her thighs, walked to the phone, lifted it from its receiver. She tried to make her voice sound casual. "Yes?"

"This is the desk, miss," a metallic voice informed her. "We've just been notified by the garage that there are two men from the Superior Rug Cleaning Co. down there. They say they're expected."

"Who?"

"The Superior Rug Cleaners, miss."

"Just a minute." She held the mouthpiece a little away from her mouth, called out. "Steve. Do you expect anyone from a rug cleaners?" She waited a moment, then: "Oh, I didn't know. Which rug? The Persian?" She put her mouth back to the instrument. "Yes, Mr. Lombardi expects them. Will you send them up?"

The man at the other end coughed indecisively. "There's a little difficulty about this, miss."

Lorna could feel the cold finger of fear running down her spine. "I don't understand," her voice was cold. "Perhaps you'd like Mr. Lombardi to—"

"Oh, no," the voice assured her hastily. "It's not that serious. You see, our freight elevator doesn't go to the penthouse."

Lorna took a deep breath, wiped the perspiration from her upper lip. "So?"

"Would it be all right if they used Mr. Lombardi's private elevator to bring the rug to the floor below, then load it on the freight elevator?" He paused for breath, raced on. "In that way, it could go right to the garage, wouldn't have to go through the lobby."

Lorna pretended to consider for a moment, nodded. "I think that'll be all right. Please send them right up." She dropped the receiver back on its hook, walked to the nearest chair, collapsed into it.

Two men in gray whipcord windbreakers and peaked hats walked up from the garage entrance, crossed to the penthouse elevator. The clerk behind the registration desk favored them with only a passing glance, went back to a dreamy contemplation of the entrance to the lobby.

The two men entered the elevator. Willy's eyes widened as he recognized Pete and Murphy. His slack mouth stayed open, the question still unspoken at a hard glance from Murph.

"This elevator take us to the penthouse?" Murph wanted to know.

Willy nodded, waiting until a tired-looking man who had been reading a paper on the couch, joined them in the elevator. "Going to see anybody in particular, bud?" the newcomer asked Murph.

Murph frowned, dug a carbon of an invoice from his jacket pocket. "Lombardi." He looked up, made no effort to resist when the tired-looking man picked the flimsy from between his fingers, read it. He stepped out of the elevator, looked down to the desk. When he couldn't catch the clerk's eye, he snapped his fingers.

The clerk turned an annoyed glance his way, nodded when the guard pointed to the elevator. "They're expected," he snapped.

The tired-looking man stepped back into the elevator, nodded for Willy to take it up. "Don't suppose you're packing any artillery?" he drawled.

Murph looked to Pete, then back to the guard. "What is this?" He held his arms out from his sides. "You think I'm heeled, take a look."

"I was figuring to," the guard nodded. He fanned Murph expertly, turned to Pete, did a similarly thorough job on him. "The boss is nervous about guns. Especially when anyone else has them. I run the checkroom for them."

Murph pulled off his cap, wiped his forehead and face on his sleeve. "I'll be glad when tonight's over." He led the way to the penthouse door, knocked.

Lorna opened the door a splinter, looked out. She unhooked the chain, pulled it open, closed it after them and latched it. "Am I glad to see you? You must have taken the fifty-cent tour through the Quarter on your way over."

"Look, baby, don't give me a hard time. It's been a bad day." He walked across to the window, lifted the blanket off Lombardi, grinned down at him. "Well, what do you know? He bleeds just like common people." He dropped the blanket. "Not bad shooting, eh?"

"Let's take the bows tomorrow. Tonight, let's just get him out of here. He's been giving me the willies."

"Why? He can't bother you." He nodded for Pete to help him, caught the dead man by the shoulders, Pete caught the feet, carried him to the center of the big Persian rug. Without a word, they moved all the furniture back.

"What are you going to do with him?" Lorna wanted to know.

Murph shrugged. "There's lots of the old burial vaults out in the old section. We'll jimmy one open and stick him in. They'll never find him." He looked around, spotted a bottle of bourbon on the desk, walked over, titled it over his mouth. "Use one, Pete?"

The smaller man nodded, took a slug. "Maybe we better get moving, Murph. That meatball down in the lobby might start getting curious if we stay up here too long."

Murph nodded, they started rolling up the rug, the dead man in the center. When they were finished, Murph straightened up, wiped the sweat off his forehead. "We take him off the private elevator at the next floor. Right?"

Lorna nodded. "Willy will show you where the freight elevator is. It runs right down to the garage."

"Good. Get him up here." While the girl was ringing for the elevator, Murph helped himself to another slug from the bottle.

Willy had the cage up to the penthouse floor in record time. He stepped out, looked around. "What the hell's going on around here?"

"Help us get a rug out and keep your mouth shut," Murph growled at him. He led the way into the apartment, nodded for Willy to get one end while he and Pete got the other. They lifted it with a grunt, the rug sagged in the middle.

"That's sure a heavy rug. It weighs almost as much as—" Willy broke off, his eyes shot from Lorna to Murph and back. "Almost as much as Lombardi."

"A coincidence, no doubt," Murph growled. "You here to help or to talk?"

Willy licked at his slack lips, caught his end of the rug, tugged it toward the elevator. "What happens now?"

Lorna patted him on the arm. "You wanted some action, didn't you? Well, under the new management, you'll get plenty."

"New management?" His eyes swept to Murph.

"Yeah. Any objections?" Murph growled.

Willy shook his head. "No objections." They dumped the rug into the elevator, Willy started to close the door, Murph caught his arm.

"The guards go off at twelve?" he asked.

Lorna nodded.

"I'll be back. You can use this car to pick me up at the tenth floor at one o'-clock. We'll get rid of the guards permanently in the morning."

Willy's watery eyes flashed. "You don't waste any time taking over, do you, Murph?"

Murphy caught him by the front of his jacket, pulled him up on his toes. "You heard what I said. The mob is under new management. Me. I'll do all the thinking and deciding and even the criticizing around here." He pushed Willy back against the wall of the cage. "Now get this thing going before I decide Lombardi needs company."

TWENTY-EIGHT
Disappearing Act

Steve Lombardi's disappearance failed to create a ripple. On Sunday morning, Murph called down to the guards in the lobby, releasing them from their vigil. Since they had never seen Lombardi, they accepted the telephone order at its face value.

As the days passed, Lorna and Murph sat tight waiting for the inevitable query from the Syndicate. It came one day in the form of a visit from an attorney.

The telephone rang, Lorna answered it. The desk informed her that a Mr. Sylvan Brode of New York was calling to see Mr. Lombardi. Some of the color drained from Lorna's face, she held her hand over the mouthpiece, relayed the information to Murphy. His lips thinned out, hard knobs formed on the sides of his jaw.

"Send him up."

Lorna relayed the instructions to the desk clerk, hung up the receiver. "What if he tumbles?" she wanted to know.

Murph shrugged. "How could he? If they were suspicious they would have been here before now."

She nodded, led the way to the sundeck. He picked a chair halfway across the porch from the divan, filled a glass with bourbon and soda. She nervously poked at her hair, waited.

When the knock came at the foyer door, she started, caught her lower lip between her teeth. Murph picked up his glass, crossed his fingers. She took a deep breath, crossed to the door, pulled it open.

Sylvan Brode was a tall man with a thick shock of white wavy hair. He stood in the doorway smiling, his lips pulled back from a perfect set of white teeth. The smile failed to defrost the icy blue of his eyes. He held a brief case under his arm, wore a jacket and managed to look cool.

"I'm Slyvan Brode. Is Mr. Lombardi in?"

Lorna shook her head. "Not right now, Mr. Brode. I'm Lorna Andrews. Steve's secretary, you might say."

The white-haired man stepped in, waited until she had closed the door behind him. "Will he be back soon?"

"I don't know," she told him frankly. "I expected him before this." She looked into the icy blue eyes. "He's been gone several weeks."

The shadow of a frown marred the man's forehead, the smile faded until it was no more than a tilting of the corner of his lips. "Where is he?" He looked around. "Haven't you had any word?"

She shook her head. "Murphy, his right-hand man, just dropped by to ask about him, too. He's worried about the way things are going."

"Frankly, so are we. That's why we're here." He looked past her toward the sundeck. "Is that Murphy? I'd like to meet him."

Lorna took the brief case, dropped it onto a table, led the way to the sundeck. Murph looked up incuriously as the white-haired man came out. He didn't show any signs of resenting the careful looking-over the other man gave him.

"Murph, this is Mr. Brode. He's a friend—" she raised her eyebrows inquiringly.

"A business associate of Steve's," Brode corrected her. He walked over to a chair, sat down, crossed his knees, laced his fingers in front of his chest. "I'm from New York, Murph."

Murph's eyes widened, his manner became a shade more respectful. "I didn't know." He looked the white-haired man over curiously. "Syndicate?"

Brode nodded. "We've been curious to know what's been going on down here. Receipts have fallen off alarmingly. Now I find that Steve's among the missing. Why weren't we notified?"

Murph shrugged. "Steve's the boss. I wouldn't go over his head, Mr. Brode. He wants to take a trip, who am I to ask him where or how long?"

The white-haired man considered that, liked the sound of it. "You're right, of course." He looked at the small bar. "I wonder if I could trouble you?" he asked Lorna. "A little gin and tonic if you have it." He returned to his scrutiny of Murphy. "Any idea of why the receipts are so bad?"

Murph took a deep swallow from his glass, set it down. "I'd rather you asked Steve, Mr. Brode."

"I'm asking you." There was no change in his expression, but his voice was hard. "Why are the receipts off?"

Murph rubbed the heel of his hand along the point of his chin. "We been having competition. A guy named Rivero moved in and has practically taken over all our territories."

The white-haired man frowned. "Why wasn't he stopped?"

Murph shrugged, looked to Lorna. The white-haired man followed his glance. "Why wasn't he stopped?" he snapped.

Lorna placed a glass in his hand, sat down on the edge of the divan. "Something's been happening to Steve, Mr. Brode. He's gone soft, scared of his own shadow." She shrugged. "Before he went away, he wouldn't go out of this place for weeks. He imported guards to search everybody that came up here."

Brode smelled the drink, tasted it. It tasted as good as it looked. "I'm familiar with that. What was he scared of?"

"Rivero. He couldn't think of anything else," Murph volunteered. "Every time anybody would suggest doing something about him, Steve'd have a fit."

"What did you have in mind to do?"

Murph grinned, shrugged. "I only know one thing, Mr. Brode. A guy gets in my way, I stamp him flat."

The white-haired man tapped on the side of his glass with the tips of his well-manicured fingers. "I don't know if now is the time for open warfare. Public sentiment is always aroused when there's a lot of unnecessary killing. Who knows that Lombardi's missing?"

"Nobody. Except Murph and me, he hasn't been seeing anybody for months. I didn't know what to do," Lorna shrugged. "For all he told me, he might have been on his way to New York to report to you."

Brode shook his head with annoyance. "What's the morale of the organization down here?"

Murphy scratched his neck, twisted his lips in a thoughtful scowl. "It'd be a lot better if the boys would get some action. We lost a couple of our runners to Rivero last week. He's offering more money."

The white-haired man set down his glass, walked over to the rail, stood with his hands clasped behind his back, stared down at the city. Finally, as if arriving at a decision, he turned, faced Murph. "I want you to take over for Lombardi, Murph. I want you to put the organization back on its feet."

Murph almost lost the battle to keep a triumphant grin off his face. "What do I tell Steve? He'll think I muscled in. There are a lot of boys who'll do anything he says."

"You'll leave Lombardi to us, Murph. If he shows his face back in New Orleans, which I doubt, you're to refer him to New York. That clear?"

Murph nodded.

"You don't think he's coming back?" Lorna wanted to know.

Brode pursed his lips, shook his head. "I think we'll find that Steve has been converting a lot of his holdings into cash and ran out when the going got tough. He probably figures he's safe in Sicily or South America or somewhere. We'll find him." The smile was back, the eyes cold, menacing. He turned to Murphy. "All right, now what will you do about this Rivero? No open warfare, you understand."

Murph looked out over the railing, scowled. He chewed on the inside of his lip, struggled desperately to come up with a solution.

"Can I make a suggestion?" Lorna wanted to know.

Both men looked at her, Brode's eyes questioning, Murphy's relieved. "Go ahead," the white-haired man invited.

"The way I've always heard it, an organization is only as good as the protection it gives its members. Right?"

Both men nodded.

"Okay. So we start giving Rivero's boys a bad time. We knock over his policy banks, we beat up his collectors, we keep hitting him where it hurts. Pretty soon, his boys are going to look to him for protection and then it's up to him to move. We keep him off balance long enough and make him look bad enough and we'll move back into the saddle."

Brode thought it over, nodded his head slowly. "Very smart. Very smart, indeed. Too bad Lombardi didn't listen to you."

Murph broke in. "He did, in the beginning. She did all his thinking for him." He grinned at her. "As long as I'm taking over, the job of secretary is open, Lorna."

"I'll think about it," she promised.

Brode shook his head. "None of that thinking about it. We can use a girl like you that can think on her feet. You're staying."

"I was hoping to, anyway," she grinned.

Brode picked up his glass, held it up in a toast. "Here's to a new combination." He drank to the toast. "I'll be in touch with New York and tell them we've a new management down here. I wish you luck. We can all use some."

TWENTY-NINE
Moving In

Avenue Caribe is the Fifth Avenue of Little San Juan in New Orleans. A long row of soot-stained, uniformly dingy three-story buildings stretch from one end of the street to the other. At all hours of the day and night a slow-moving tide of whites, yellows and blacks ebbs and flows the length of the street.

Lorna drove the length of Avenue Caribe, carefully avoiding the kids of all sizes and colors that darted across the road without warning. At her side, Murph stared out the windows, studied the expressionless faces that shuffled past on the sidewalk.

"That's the house over there," he nudged Lorna. "Number 56."

"You're sure?"

Murph flipped a half-smoked butt from the window, nodded. "Willy tailed the old guy here last night. Practically put him to bed." He turned on the seat, continued to look back at the house.

"What are you going to do?"

"Start giving Rivero a bad time like we agreed." He faced front again, reached over to the glove compartment, pulled out a blackjack and a snub-nosed .38. "This old guy's Rivero's right-hand man. Some kind of a relative, or something. We start with him."

Lorna looked worried. "Take it easy, though. You know what Brode said about killing." She turned, studied Murph's profile. "You're a little too fond of killing, Murph."

"Leave that up to me," the man growled. "Sure, he's chicken about starting an all-out war. Maybe because he figures Lombardi's coming back. We don't have to worry about that." He signaled for her to pull over to the curb. "When he sees results, he won't worry either."

"Want me to pick you up?"

He shook his head. "Turn that corner up there and wait for me. It shouldn't take too long." He got out of the car, slammed the door, stuck his head in the window. "Just don't worry about a thing."

Murph melted into the stream of humanity that flowed along the avenue. A yellow-faced girl in a bright red dress fell into step alongside him. She whispered to him suggestively, tugged at his sleeve. He grinned at her, haggled playfully.

The girl detailed her many specialties eagerly. "You come with me, Chu-chi. *Que lindo tu eres*." She rolled her eyes lasciviously. "Me, Rosa, much fun."

As they were coming abreast of number 56, Murph was about to send her on her way, when he suddenly stiffened. A man he hadn't noticed before stood leaning against the building across the street from 56. He was working on his nails with a small pocketknife, glanced up every so often at the entrance to 56.

The girl tugged harder on Murphy's arm. "You come with me, no?"

Everything about the man with the knife spelled gunman to Murph. He debated the advisability of continuing past the house to return another time, realized this was part of a regular detail.

He was about to shake the girl's hand off impatiently. "Where do you live, *chiquita?*"

She caught him by the arm, pointed to a house two doors up from number 56. "You come, no?"

Murphy saw the man across the street flick him a sudden, interested glance. He nodded to the girl, put his arm around her waist, walked past 56 with her. The man across the street curled his lip at them, went back to his nails.

Number 48, Avenue Caribe, was identical with its neighbors on either side from its front façade to the mixture of odors that hit them in the face when they walked into the vestibule. It was an odor compounded of equal parts of Spanish cooking, inadequate toilet facilities and human effluvia. The girl stuck a warm damp hand into his, led him into the dark hallway, up two flights of stairs to the top floor. Her room was in the front of the building. She pushed open the unlocked door, led him into a darkened room. She flicked a light switch, spilled a dismal yellow light in to flood everything but the far corners. She looked around proudly. "Pretty room. *Verdad?*"

Murph looked around, nodded. "Real pretty."

The girl took him by the hand, led him to the side of a mussed bed. She unbuttoned his shirt, stuck her hand inside, tickled his ribs. "Rosa like you." She watched with a frown while he walked to the hall door, opened it, looked out.

"That go to the roof?" he pointed to a low flight of steps.

She walked over, looked over his shoulder, shrugged. "Rosa don't care about this." She put her head against his arm. "Rosa like you, but—" she managed to look sad, "Rosa very poor. She need money. You like Rosa, you give her money, she be very nice to you."

Murph growled deep in his chest, dug out a roll of bills, separated two fives, handed them to her. The girl's eyes lighted up, she ran into the small lavatory off the bedroom.

Murph opened the door softly, crept down the hall to where the steps led to the roof.

A short wall separated the roofs of the houses along Avenue Caribe. Murph crossed two roofs to number 56. He tried the roof door, it opened with a creak, he made his way down to the third-floor landing. Rivero's collector had a flat on the second-floor rear.

Murph descended the stairs carefully, listened at the door. He could hear sounds of someone moving around inside. He tried the door; it was locked. He rapped his knuckles against the wood, pulled the .38 from his waistband.

"Juan?" a voice on the other side demanded.

He grunted assent, heard the key turning in the lock. As the door started to open, Murph put his shoulder against it, pushed. The man on the other side was thrown off balance, staggered backward. Murph walked in, covered him with the gun.

The other man was tall, incredibly thin. The teeth he bared in a snarl were ivory white in contrast to the darkness of his skin. His eyes were little, mean and bloodshot. He didn't say a word, stared at the gun in Murph's hand.

Murph reached with his hand behind him, turned the key in the lock. "You're not very hospitable. Don't you ask company in?"

"Who are you?" The old man's voice was heavy, guttural. "What you want?"

Murph looked around elaborately. "I hear this is where Rivero's policy bank drop is. I could use some money. Where do you keep it?"

The old man's lip curled in a sneer. "You crazy. You don't get out of here alive. Who are you?"

"A guy that Rivero owes something to. A guy who's come to collect."

The old man's bloodshot eyes continued to study Murph's face. "I know you next time I see you."

"Turn around," Murph growled.

The old man shrugged, turned his back. Murph pulled the sap from his back pocket, brought it down with all his strength on the old man's head. His knees started to cave, Murph hit him again, beat him to the floor. "All you spics got hard heads," he grunted. He raised the jack and brought it down again. It made a soft, hollow sound. The old man didn't move.

Murph walked around the apartment, went through the papers in the drawer of the table, found a list of locations of the major drops. He folded the papers, stuck them into his pocket. He was going through the contents of a tied batch of envelopes when he looked over to where the old man lay. He hadn't moved since he had hit the floor.

Murph walked over, turned him on his back. The old man's red eyes stared up at him malevolently. There was a bright red stream from the corner of his mouth, down over his chin. Murph swore, tried to find the beat of the carotid artery, swore some more. The old man was dead.

He went back to the package of envelopes, satisfied himself they all contained money, was about to pack them into a small canvas bag when a knock came at the door. Murph stiffened, tugged the .38 from his belt. The knock came again. He walked over to the door, did his best to imitate the old man's voice. "Juan?"

A voice on the other side answered with a flood of Spanish. Murph unlocked the door, pulled it open. The man outside was the guard that had been posted across the street. Surprise dulled his reflexes. Before he could move, Murph was on him, slashing at his face with the barrel of the gun. The guard covered his face, reeled backward. Murph kept on top of him relentlessly. The other man hit the rotted old banister, it gave way. He fell to the first floor landing with a thud. Murph looked down the stair well, the man lay there a tangle of arms and legs. Murph ran into the room, grabbed the canvas bag, raced for the third floor and the stairway to the roof.

Once on the roof, he ran across the adjoining roofs in the direction of the corner where Lorna waited. At the end house he tried the door leading to the third floor. It resisted his efforts. He pulled out the .38, smashed the small glass pane, reached inside, slipped the bolt.

He walked slowly down the stairs to the vestibule. On the stoop, he looked up the street toward 56. Already there was a crowd forming out front, a policeman came running from the far corner escorted by a little brown man who was gesticulating wildly.

Murphy walked down to the sidewalk, headed for the corner. The car was parked halfway up the block. He walked up, slid in alongside Lorna. "Let's get out of here."

She nodded, kicked the car into life, put it in gear. "Any trouble?"

Murph shrugged. "A little."

She stole a worried look at his profile. "No killing?"

"I'm not sure. But it couldn't be helped." He pulled the sheafs of paper out of his breast pocket. "It was worth it. Here's a list of all Rivero's policy collectors. It's worth—"

"Who'd you kill? Not the old man?"

Murph grunted. "I didn't mean to. I guess I hit him too hard." He shoved the papers back into his pocket. "With this list, we can move in on Rivero, give him a run for his money."

THIRTY
Death in the Family

Rivero was small, dark. He stood impassively in the hallway of 60 Avenue Caribe, watched with no display of emotion while the men from the medical examiner's office lifted the old man's body to a stretcher.

A homicide detective walked over to him, offered him a cigarette. "He was your uncle, that it, Rivero?"

Rivero waved aside the cigarette, brought a small brown cigarro from his pocket. "Sí. My uncle."

The detective motioned in the direction of the broken banister. "The other guy. Know him?"

The little dark man shrugged. "A friend of my uncle." He scratched a wooden match, held it to the cigarro, exhaled a dark blue smoke. "I have seen them together often."

"But you didn't know him?" the detective insisted.

Rivero rolled his eyes to the ceiling, showed the whites. "I think I hear him called Juan. Is a very common name, Juan." He shook his head. "I do not know any more about him."

"Any idea why anyone would want to kill your uncle?"

The small man shrugged, lifted his hands palms up. "Why would any one kill an old man? Maybe they thought he had money?"

The homicide man failed to look convinced. "Okay, Rivero. If there's anything else we need, we'll contact you." He walked to the door, stopped with his hand on the knob. "There's not going to be any trouble, is there? The Commissioner won't stand for any wars. You know that."

Rivero smoked placidly. "There will be no war." He shrugged elaborately. "My uncle, he is dead. We bury our dead."

The detective nodded. "Fair enough. We'll do everything we can to find the man or men responsible. Leave that up to us and we'll all get along. Try taking over and there'll be trouble."

The little man nodded, there was no change in his expression as the door closed behind the detective. He walked over to a chair that lay on its side, righted it. He sat down to wait.

He drummed with spatulate fingers on the edge of the table, stared at the far wall without expression. Around him he could hear the creaks and the muffled conversation of an old, overpopulated house, smell the many odors that went with age. He watched the erratic progress of a cockroach descending the wall, showed no signs of impatience.

Finally, the door opened. He looked up as one of his men pushed a young girl in a red dress into the room. He questioned the man with his eyes.

"She is Rosa, a *puta*. She was seen with the one who killed the old man."

Rivero's eyes swung to the girl. She tried to hide her fear under an impertinent grin, wasn't quite able to wash the terror from her eyes.

"Who was this man?" Rivero's voice was deceptively low.

The girl shrugged her shoulders. *"Mi pichonsita."* She pulled her arm loose from the man's grip, faced Rivero. "He was my sweetheart."

Rivero's eyes roved from the kinky hair down over the clinging dress to the exaggerated heels of her strap slippers. "You're a liar. Who was he?"

The girl started to protest, the man at her side buried his fingers in her hair, pulled her head back. "Rivero ask you who was the man?"

Her face turned a murky yellow under the tan. "I do not know him. My hair, you are hurting."

"Where did you meet him?" Rivero wanted to know. He signaled for the other man to release her hair.

"I meet him on street. He smile at Rosa, and—"

"What did he look like?"

Rosa wet her lips, shrugged. "I did not see him long, Señor Rivero."

Rivero stood up. He dropped the butt of his cigarro to the floor. "You will know this man again?"

The girl nodded. "I will know him."

"Bring her with you," he instructed the man that had brought her. "We will see how good is her memory."

Sylvan Brode sat on the sundeck of the Carter Arms, enjoyed the fresh breeze that was a welcome newcomer to New Orleans. He held a tall, cool glass in his hands, clinked the ice against its sides.

"That list you picked up proves very interesting, Murph," he conceded. "Almost worth your disobeying my orders." The icy blue eyes were fixed on a spot inches above Murphy's head. "Any explanation?"

Murphy cracked his knuckles, shrugged. "I didn't intend to kill him. I guess he was just old." He looked over to where Lorna sat studying a Tom Collins in her lap.

Brode considered it, seemed satisfied. "There have been no retaliations from Rivero?"

Murph shook his head, grinned. "He's yellow. I knew it all along. He won't hit back."

The white-haired man shook his head judiciously. "He's not yellow. It took a lot of guts to calmly walk into a town and buck the Syndicate. It took more than guts—it took brains to get away with it."

"So far."

"So far," Brode conceded. "But don't underestimate him. He knows as well as we do that dumping packages all over town won't do anybody any good, will just goose the authorities into action."

Lorna rolled her eyes upward. "In the meantime, Rivero's taking a bad loss of face with his organization. The old man was his uncle and everybody's waiting to see what he's going to do about it."

"What are we going to do about it?" Brode countered. "True, his prestige has been nicked. How are we going to follow up on it?"

Murph grinned broadly. He tugged the list from his slacks pocket, smoothed it out on his knee. "Rivero's drops. We're going to knock them off one at a time. We'll drive him crazy, and word will go out that he can't protect his own men. How about that?"

The white-haired man took a deep swallow from his glass, licked at his lips. "For a long term proposition, it'll do." He looked disappointed. "I was hoping you'd be able to follow up the raid on Rivero's uncle with something equally spectacular."

Murph chewed on his thumb, looked over at the girl, who shrugged. He looked back to the white-haired man. "Got any ideas?"

Brode held out his hand, Murph passed the list to him. He underscored one address with his thumbnail. "That's Rivero's own place," he said. "If we can knock that one over, that would really hit him where he lives." He handed back the list. "One score like that is worth a hundred little drops knocked over."

"He'd never be expecting us to hit him in his own joint," Murph nodded. He looked to Lorna. "We could throw him off balance by feinting a couple of scores on some of his places across town, then take this one when they're expecting us to hit someplace else."

Brode nodded his approval. "Sounds good. I'll leave the details to you." He finished his drink, set it down. "I'll be leaving for New York the first of the week. I'll be glad to tell the big boys how well you're filling Steve's shoes."

Murph grinned his thanks. "No word from Steve, yet, eh?"

"Maybe he don't like to send postcards." The white-haired man got up, nodded to them both. "Don't bother to show me out, I know the way."

They waited until he had disappeared into the foyer. Lorna got up, picked up the list, ran her eye down to the name Brode had underscored. "Diego's," she read, looked up at Murph. "You know the place?"

He shook his head. "It's a new one, I guess." He chewed on his thumb. "Brode hasn't just been sitting on his hands. He's been looking around." He ran the tips of his fingers along the point of his jaw. "It's not going to be easy, knocking over Rivero's own spot. That's probably his main bank. He'll have that sewed up tighter than Fort Knox."

Lorna nodded absently, walked over to the railing, stared down into the streets below. "But Brode's right. We pull that one off and Rivero's done for in this town. If he can't even cover his own place, nobody else is going to trust him to cover for them."

"Got any ideas?"

She turned around, walked back to the divan, folded her knees under her. She reached over, snagged a cigarette from the low table next to it, lit it. "Well, we could always load up a couple of cars and blast our way into the place." She smoked for a moment, watched the smoke curl upward. Murph sat quietly, didn't interrupt. Finally, she looked up. "Suppose we do what you said. Suppose we feint a couple of jobs downtown. Maybe even make a few fast scores just to let them know we mean business."

Murph nodded. "Go on."

She stared dreamily at the sky. "I just read about how the British tricked the Germans into thinking they were going to hit one place, pulled them off balance and hit another where they weren't expecting it."

"How?"

"They dressed a dead man in a major's uniform and planted a fake set of plans on him, dumped him into the water where the Nazis were sure to find him. German Intelligence thought they had the blueprint for the invasion, got up a welcoming committee—at the wrong place."

"You mean knock off one of our boys just so they'll think—"

"Not necessarily. How about a wallet falling out of some guy's pocket during a score? It's got all the places we've already hit with dates and stuff they'd know was authentic. Then there'd be the plans for a big score on one of the downtown places—" She picked up the list, ran her eyes over it—"on Hymie Lengel's place on Country Club Road."

"So what's that do?"

"It pulls them off balance. They'll send all the troops they can spare out to Hymie's place, they'll leave the uptown places with a skeleton guard. Then we hit Diego's—but hard."

Murph went over it in his mind, scowled. "Suppose they figure it for a plant and are laying for us at Diego's?"

"Then we'll move in and take Hymie's. We wait until they set the trap for us downtown and we lower the boom uptown."

"And how are we going to know whether they've fallen for the gag?"

Lorna grinned at him. "That's where a good casing comes in. I'll start casing Diego's before we plant the wallet so I get a pretty good picture of the security. Then, I can tell if they're pulling the men off to cover Hymie's when they find the wallet."

"Think we can pull it off?"

"Think we've got a choice?"

THIRTY-ONE
Once to Every Girl

Willy dropped the girl at the corner of Le Tourneau and Grand, watched her legs flash as she crossed the street. He lit a cigarette, waited until she had disappeared around the corner of Le Tourneau, headed the car for a parking lot.

Lorna melted into the thin stream of pedestrians along the avenue, stopped at several windows, appeared to be aimlessly window shopping. At the jeweler's window, she glanced up at the big clock, checked it against her watch. Four o'clock. She continued down the street, stopped in front of a large club that gleamed with chromium and newness. A huge electric sign that ran the full length of the front spelled out "Diego's."

She looked over her shoulder, failed to see Willy, decided to go ahead. Inside, Diego's was dim and cool. A large, gaily decorated cocktail lounge opened into what appeared to be a large club behind. The bar was a long slab of mahogany, upholstered in blue leather and brass nailheads. She walked into the bar room, sat on one of the heavily upholstered stools, looked around.

A man pushed his way through a swinging door behind the bar, smiled at her. The smile hit her with a strange impact, she suddenly felt unaccountably nervous. She made an attempt at returning the smile.

The man came over. "I'm terribly sorry, miss," there was the faintest trace of a liquid accent in his voice. "Ladies cannot be served at the bar."

Lorna colored slightly, started to flounce from the stool. She tried desperately to think of an answer, found herself almost tongue-tied.

"I hope you understand, miss." He was tall, his shoulders seemed to balance precariously on the slimness of his waist. "Would you permit me to buy you .a cocktail," he waved to one of the tables in the lounge, "over there."

She tried to glare at him, was disconcerted by his large black eyes, the pencil-line mustache that separated his aquiline nose from the full, sensuous lips. She amazed herself by smiling and accepting.

She walked back to one of the tables near the wall, sat down. In a moment, he was walking over to her, a drink on a tray. "I know it must be annoying to be told ladies are not permitted to sit at the bar, but you understand I do not make the rules."

Lorna's returning smile was almost shy. "Of course." She looked at the single glass on the tray. "Can't you join me?"

His teeth, when he smiled, were white, strong. He shook his head. "More rules. Equally silly, but rules," he shrugged. He set the glass in front of her, hovered over her. "Are you a stranger in New Orleans, miss?" he wanted to know.

Lorna nodded. Subconsciously, she wondered why she had taken the trouble to lie, couldn't find a reasonable explanation. "Just visiting."

"How about letting me show you the town? There's a lot to it they can't put in guide books."

Lorna tasted the drink, studied his face over the rim. She decided it was the way his eyes crinkled that made him look so young. "I don't know," she managed to look confused. "I'm not in the habit of—"

"Look, no one should visit New Orleans without a native to show them around. You'll never forgive yourself after you get back to—?"

"South Carolina."

"You'll never forgive yourself after you get back to South Carolina if you don't see the place while you've got a chance."

She caught her lower lip between her teeth, worried it. "I suppose it would be all right," she conceded. Mentally, she was assuring herself that it would be the best way to do a thorough job of casing the place.

"How about tonight?" he wanted to know.

She wrinkled her brow, considered, then nodded. "Okay. Where should I meet you?"

"I could pick you up, if you like?"

She thought fast, shook her head. "I'm with some other girls. I don't think they'd understand." She worked hard on the smile. "We're all small-town girls!"

The door opened, four men came in. They nodded briefly to the bartender, headed for a flight of stairs at the back of the cocktail lounge.

"You know, I don't even know your name," she told him.

"Jim Kanin. What's yours?"

"Lorna. Lorna Andrews." She accepted the hand he stuck out seriously, then broke into a grin. "Maybe it's not the way Emily Post would do it, but I'm glad to know you, Jim."

He started to say something, checked himself as four different men came down the stairs. One of them waved to him, he excused himself, went over and talked to each of the four. He pushed his way through the swinging door behind the bar, was back in a moment with a bulging canvas bag. The shortest of the four men accepted the bag, they all walked out together.

Jim walked back to the girl's table. "That's the day crew checking out," he explained vaguely. "We carry quite a bit of money here sometimes and they drop it off in the night vault on the way out."

Lorna pretended complete lack of interest. "You a native, Jim?"

He shook his head. "Native of Ponce. That's a town near San Juan in Puerto Rico. I'm not all Riqueno, though," he added. "My father was an engineer down in Puerto Rico. From Kansas. I grew up down there. Been here maybe two years now."

She looked properly impressed. "Do you work here?"

He laughed at her, shook his head. "I'm sort of a partner. Wife of one of the day men took today to have herself a set of twins. The other one's out sick, so

I've been spelling them. I'm glad they picked today to stay out."

She grinned at him. "So am I."

"Where and when tonight?" he pressed.

She pursed her lips, looked at the ceiling. "I don't know the town too well. Why don't you set the place and I'll meet you. I'll find it."

"How about starting with cocktails and dinner at the Roosevelt?" he suggested. "Tomorrow, we can see Jackson Square, maybe the Cathedral. How's that sound?"

She pursed her lips, considered. "It's a date. With one provision. I'm like Cinderella. I go home alone."

"At midnight?" he grinned. "Maybe that's when Cinderella's day ends, but here in New Orleans that's just when it's starting. I'd like you to see this place in operation."

"All right," she conceded. "I'd like to. But I don't want my friends to know that—"

He winked. "I'm the soul of discretion."

He walked with her to the door, watched her walk out into the blinding brilliance of Le Tourneau. She ambled down the street, stopping along the way to window shop. At the jeweler's window, she stood next to a thin man with a damp slack mouth.

"I got held up in traffic. Everything okay?" he asked without moving his mouth.

"I think it's going to be fine," she told him. "Get back to the penthouse, get enough of my clothes to register me into the De Soto. I've got a date with Diego's house manager for tonight."

Willy growled deep in his chest. "What for?" He started to turn, stopped at her hissed warning. "What's this date business?"

"I want to know him well enough to be shown around the place. There are four guards on eight-hour shifts, but I don't know where they're stationed. We'd get cut to pieces if we tried to take the place without knowing."

Willy was mollified. "Think they keep the collections there?" he wanted to know.

"I know they do. The eight-to-four shift takes the day collections with them. Four guns. I guess the four-to-twelve handles the evening collections and the early shift the gambling stuff."

Willy whistled, moved to the other window as an elderly man and woman joined them at the window. When they walked on, he got close to the girl again. "Why can't you come back with me?"

"I can't be seen anywhere near you or any of Murph's boys until this is over." She pulled a handkerchief from her pocketbook, held it to her nose. "Just make sure I'm registered into the De Soto under my own name. I'll keep in touch with Murph and you. I figure three days should be long enough to romance this guy into showing me the set-up. Then we plant the wallet downtown and start the ball rolling."

He was still standing in front of the jeweler's window when she circled around him, continued her window shopping down the avenue. For the first time in her life she was aware of a peculiar conflict within her.

She walked slowly, trying to reconcile the deep-seated hatred she felt for men with the peculiar reaction Jim Kanin had stirred in her. She rationalized the emotion by trying to convince herself that it was necessary to play a game of romance with the man in order to find the means of destroying him.

Yet, even as she rationalized, she was aware of a hope that it would prove impossible to knock over Diego's as the plan called for. She wondered what would be the reaction of Murphy and Brode if she failed to blueprint a method. Yet, she knew that she was less anxious over their reaction to her failure than to the possible reaction of the man in the bar in the event of her success.

She knew it was impossible, yet vaguely she wondered if she were falling in love with Jim Kanin.

THIRTY-TWO
Proposal

The next three days passed in a purple haze for Lorna Andrews. After the first night with Jim, she was no longer in doubt that she had fallen in love with the big man. She spent half her time plotting means of upsetting the plan to knock over the numbers bank for which he was responsible.

The first time he danced with her, she knew by the alien sensation that for the first time in her life she would be unable to sacrifice a man for her own profit. She fought against the sensation, succeeded only in becoming more deeply enmeshed.

On the third night after she had met Kanin, the telephone rang in her room in the hotel. It was Murphy.

"What's going on?" he growled. "Brode's needling hell out of me to get this caper on. What's holding it up?"

"I haven't been able to case the room where the guards are stationed," she evaded. "It takes time, Murph."

"Time we haven't got, baby. Our time is running out. Brode goes back north with a thumbs down and we're out. A new guy takes over from up there and we may find some of the boys selling us out."

She bit her lip. "I can keep Willy in line. Can't you handle Pete?"

"Sure. While we're in the saddle. Nobody can talk for nobody. Sometimes not even for themselves," the receiver told her.

"What's that supposed to mean?"

"It's supposed to mean I don't like all the delay. We're all set with the decoy plans on the downtown spot. We're waiting for you to give us the word."

The girl massaged her forehead with the tips of her fingers. "Maybe we'd better call it off, Murph. That place of Diego's is a fort."

"Call nothing off," Murphy growled. "You set this caper up in the first place. I'm on the hook for it with the Syndicate and we're going through with it."

"You never lost a thing listening to me, Murph," the girl pleaded. "I think it's a mistake to try for Diego's."

The voice on the other end was hard, cold. "I didn't ask you. I'm through asking you. I'm telling you—we're setting the decoy tonight with a raid on one of the downtown drops. The phony plans call for a raid on Hymie Lengel's tomorrow night. That gives you twenty-four hours to get cleared away."

The receiver banged in her ear, the girl stared at the phone for a moment, dropped it on the hook. She walked to the window, looked down into Perdido Street, marveled at how well its name described her position.

By the time she left the window, she had made up her mind. She was certain now of what she had to do, and how she had to do it. Calmly, she walked back to the telephone, picked the receiver off its hook, dialed a number. Now that the decision had been made, she felt strangely at peace with herself.

That night, three of Rivero's downtown drops were raided and smashed.

Rivero leaned across the bar, studied a map of the city unfolded in front of him. He chewed on the end of a small brown cigarro, his shoe-button eyes giving no indication of what he was thinking.

His index finger pointed to an address and a date. "That is Manuel's place. It was raided three weeks ago." His finger moved to the penciled date. "That is the date." He repeated the process with five other notations, looked up. "They are all accurate. This was a record kept by somebody who knew all of their moves."

"And tonight they're taking my place, Diego. You got to cover me," Hymie Lengel was big, gross. His jowls hung down over his collar, he looked as though he had been jammed into the huge armchair in which he sat. Damp, dark ringlets tried futilely to cover the baldspot that gleamed pinkly through them. His lips were thick, pouty. "I tied up with your outfit because you promised protection. I need it now."

Rivero ignored the complaint. "You saw these plans they made of your place, Hymie. They accurate?" He stabbed a finger at a hand-drawn floor plan. "A man could get in through that door?"

Lengel nodded, disturbing the rolls of fat under his chin. "They do like it says there, I'm ruined." He made the supreme effort, leaned forward. "Unless you give me enough guards to protect me."

Rivero pulled the cigarro from between his teeth, tapped its coarse ash to the floor. "They're using ten men." He pursed his lips. "We could take them with ten, maybe fifteen." He leaned over the map again, hit the bar with the heel of his hand. "We let them get in, then we seal them in and cut them down." He nodded. "I'll get you the men, Hymie."

"Where? I only got two guards of my own. Where you getting ten, twelve more?"

"I got eight in my place alone. I'll get the others. We smash that mob now, and we don't have to worry no more." He reached over the bar, snagged the phone, dialed a number. "This is Rivero. Jim there?" He made an annoyed face. "No, I don't know where I'll be. Give him this message. I want the eight guards— that's right, both shifts, sent out to Hymie Lengel's place at four." The voice on the other end sputtered frantically. "Don't worry about it. I know where they're hitting tonight. We'll be waiting for them." He slammed the receiver down.

Hymie nodded his satisfaction.

Lorna and Jim were chuckling over some private joke when they walked into Diego's that afternoon. Jim permitted himself to be flagged down by the bartender, seated Lorna at a table, headed for the door behind the bar. When he came out, there were strained lines at the sides of his mouth, a v-crease between his eyes.

"Sorry, baby, but I've got to make a call. I'll be right with you." He walked to the phone booth in the foyer of the lounge, tried three numbers unsuccessfully. He sat in front of the phone for a few minutes, then shrugged, joined her at the table.

"Something wrong?" she wanted to know.

His forehead was ridged, he shrugged. "I don't know, for sure. I just got a message from Rivero that doesn't sound kosher. Now I can't raise him." He looked worried. "I guess he knows what he's doing."

Lorna lit a cigarette. "Anything I can help on?"

He kissed the tips of her fingers, grinned. "I'm afraid this is outside the realm of your experience, baby." He signaled the man behind the bar to bring two drinks, waited until they were in front of them. "Ever think of leaving South Carolina, Lorna?"

She sipped her drink, hoped he couldn't see her hand shaking. "Constantly. Why?"

Kanin took a deep drag on his cigarette, blew it in twin streams from his nostrils. "I was talking to my folks in Ponce last night. I might go back down there." He tapped a thin collar of ash into a tray. "It's really beautiful country, Lorna. Blue skies, green hills, purple tassels in the cane brakes. You've never seen it, have you?"

She shook her head, couldn't say a word.

He looked around the cocktail lounge, pursed his lips. "I thought this was what I wanted. To be a big operator, live an exciting life of sleeping all day, gambling all night. When Rivero asked me to join him, I jumped at it." He shrugged. "Now I'm not so sure."

"Why?"

He considered for a moment. "I don't think a man living the kind of life I live has a right to ask a girl to share it with him."

She dropped her eyes, caught her breath. "Were you thinking of doing that?"

"I am doing it, Lorna." He reached over, covered her hand with his. "I'm pretty sick of this town, I'm pretty sick of this kind of an operation. I thought we could buy a little plantation and—"

She pulled her hand free. "You don't know anything about me."

He shrugged. "I don't have to. In fact, I don't want to. I'd rather keep on knowing you the way I do in my own mind."

She caught her lower lip between her teeth, was about to answer. The door opened, the four oncoming guards walked in.

"Pardon me," Jim got up, walked over to them. They talked in a low tone, then one went to the stairs. When he returned, the four day guards were with him. There was a low-voiced conversation, one of the guards shrugged. All eight left together.

Jim walked back to the table, leaned over it, dropped his voice. "Will you excuse me, Lorna? The guards are off, and I've got quite a lot of cash out back. I'd like to make sure it's put away. Okay?"

The girl nodded. "Go right ahead. I've got some telephoning I have to do, anyway."

He leaned down, brushed his lips against her cheek. "I won't be too long."

The girl watched him cross the floor, shoulder the door open, disappear through. She fumbled in her bag, brought up two nickels, headed for the phone booth. She dialed a number, waited.

The voice at the other end was tense. "Yeah?"

"No good, Murph."

"What do you mean, no good?" Murph screamed. "We're all set to take them."

Lorna shrugged. "Suit yourself. They must have tumbled. They've doubled the guards here. Eight of them up behind the peepholes and all carrying tommy guns. Something went wrong, I tell you."

She dropped the receiver back on its hook, dabbed at the thin film of perspiration along her hair line with a wisp of linen.

THIRTY-THREE
Reception Committee

Hymie Lengel's roadhouse was on the Country Club Road about two miles east of New Orleans in Victoire Parish. It was a rambling old Colonial that made little pretense of being anything but what it was, operated on an understanding with the local sheriff, who had neither the facilities nor the inclination to interfere with its operations.

Tonight the play was light. Less than a dozen people clustered around the roulette table in the game room, the slot-machines along the wall were getting little or no play. At the long bar in the lounge, the two bartenders were barely outnumbered by the customers. There was an air of expectancy hanging over the place.

Outside, the big doorman lounged against the entrance, his chair tilted back, his uniform cap on the back of his head. He dropped the chair to all fours as a small coupé pulled up to the entrance, walked down to greet the newcomers.

As he reached the driver's side of the car, a muzzle of a .45 stared him in the face.

"Stay where you are, pal," a voice from the inside of the car told him. "When my friend gets out, you'll get in and take this to the parking lot. Got it?"

The doorman nodded, waited obediently while a man got out of the car on the other side. Then he slid in alongside the man with the gun. As the coupé pulled away toward the parking lot, a large sedan pulled up, disgorged four men.

"Everything set?" the man from the coupé wanted to know.

The newcomer nodded. "Four more are hitting the back entrance through the kitchen."

The men assigned to cover downstairs ambled into the bar, waited for a signal from their leader. They whipped out .45s, covered the two bartenders and their customers. Simultaneously, five men appeared in the game room, herding the kitchen help in front of them. Between the eight men, the entire floor was completely covered. No one offered any resistance.

Upstairs, the two men assigned to Hymie Lengel's office were having similar luck. The one guard staked out in front of the office was reading a paper as they crept up the stairs. When he saw them, his hand started for his holster, froze inches from it. They ordered him to his feet.

"Turn around and face the wall and you don't have to get hurt," one of the gunmen snapped.

His partner crept up behind the guard, reached over his shoulder, tugged a .38 from the shoulder holster. He walked to the office door, listened for a moment. Then he grabbed the knob, turned it, pushed it open and fanned the room with his .45. It was empty. He pushed up the brim of his hat with the muzzle of his gun, scratched his head.

"No one there," he turned to his companion, froze, his eyes goggling. The .45 fell from his fingers to the rug.

"What the hell's the matter with you?" the other gunman growled.

"Don't turn around, Ed," the man at the door told him. "There are four of them. All with tommy guns. Right behind you."

Ed stiffened, started to turn slowly.

"Drop the gun," one of the men behind him ordered tersely.

Suddenly from below there came the bark of a few scattered shots, the authoritative chatter of a tommy gun, then ominous quiet.

The guard grinned at the two gunmen. "Guess one of your boys had to be convinced."

He waved them toward the office with the .45. "Inside. I've got a friend who wants to ask you jokers some questions. In fact Rivero has been waiting a long time to meet some of you boys."

Lorna dropped the cab in front of the hotel, started across the sidewalk. A figure materialized out of the shadows next to the doorway, met her before she reached the entrance.

"Hello, Lorna." It was Pete.

Lorna started, worked at a smile, didn't quite make it. "You shouldn't be seen talking to me, Pete. It might kick over the whole set-up."

Pete nodded amiably. "Whatever you say, Lorna. Only this one wouldn't wait. Murphy wants to see you. Now."

Lorna scowled impatiently. "I'll be over as soon as I can. Right now, I've got to—"

"He wants to see you now." Pete showed her the blade of the switch knife hidden by his sleeve. "I got orders to bring you now, one way or the other."

She stared at the small man's face, watched for some small sign of indecision. There was none. "All right, Pete. But I'm not forgetting this."

"You're not likely to, Lorna." Without taking his eyes off the girl, he signaled to a car parked against the curb halfway down the street. It pulled up, the rear door swung open. Willy was at the wheel.

The girl got in without a word, settled back against the cushions. "What is this, Willy?"

Willy wiped his lips with the back of his hand. "Murph wants to see you, Pete said." He looked at Pete. "Ain't that right?"

Pete nodded. "Yeah, that's right."

Murph was sitting on the couch in the den, glass in hand, when they walked in. "Well, well. If it isn't Lorna. And here I was worried that you'd walked out on us." He finished his drink, set it down.

Lorna ignored him, walked over to the portable bar, spilled some bourbon in a glass, drank it neat. "Now, why would I do that, Murph?" Her eyes were wary, the smile on her lips patently forced.

Murph shrugged. "Maybe because you thought the mob was finished. Maybe because you're going to be a nice respectable housewife."

Willy started to chuckle, broke it off in the middle as his eyes shuttled between the two.

"Maybe because you double-crossed all of us." Murph got up, walked across to where the girl stood. "You know what happened out at Hymie's place?"

Lorna didn't answer, stared at him.

"The boys walked into a stakeout. All ten of them! You set it up." His hand sailed through the air, caught her on the side of the face, knocked her back into the portable bar. He moved in to hit her again.

"Keep your hands off her, Murph." Willy stood, gun in hand, feet planted apart. "Hit her again and I'll blast you."

Murphy turned around, sneered at the little man. "Why? So she can marry that bartender down at Rivero's joint?"

Willy licked at his lips. "You're a liar. She wouldn't marry anyone." He looked to where Lorna stood. "Back around him, Lorna. Don't get between us. We're getting out."

Murphy snorted. "Tell the sucker, Pete."

"He's levelling, Willy. She's been playing house with that glass jockey. She called the job off at his place tonight, said it was lousy with guards. She's a liar. They were all out at Hymie's."

Willy's chin shone wetly. "Why would she do that?" His eyes fought to disbelieve, lost the decision. "Why?"

"She was afraid her man'd get hurt if we hit his place," Pete told him. "She rather have our boys walk into a tommy gun stakeout than take a chance on him getting hurt."

Murph hit where it hurt. "You're not good enough for her, Willy, you couldn't get near her. But a crummy bartender moves in and plays house. What's that make you, Willy?"

The slack lips moved, no words came out. A thin stream of saliva ran from the corner of his mouth to his chin. "You shouldn't have done that to me, Lorna," he said finally. "I always told you I'd go along if you was playing with these guys to get something. You shouldn't have fallen for any of them." The arm with the gun dropped. He wiped his chin with his sleeve. "I'll be seeing you." He turned and walked toward the foyer.

"You better go with him, Pete. He may need some help."

"Willy, wait a minute." Lorna tried to slip past Murphy, run after them. He caught her by the arm, swung her around. "You're not going any place, sweetheart."

He raised his hand, hit her across the face with the flat of his palm, knocked her sprawling. She lay there quietly, a thin trickle of blood running down her cheek.

"You and I have some settling up to do. You want to run out?" He drew his lips back from his teeth in a grin. "You can run that way," he waved toward the sundeck, "and keep right on going."

THIRTY-FOUR
The Last Laugh

The girl pulled herself painfully to her feet, dabbed at the side of her mouth with the side of her hand, stared at the red smear. "I told you once never to lay a hand on me, Murph," she told him.

He sneered at her. "You're finished telling me things, baby. When I'm done with you, you won't even know what time it is." He loosened his belt, pulled it off. "I'm going to fix you so your boy friend wouldn't even have you in the dark." He twirled the belt over his head, it whistled out, bit into the girl's skin.

She clenched her teeth, wouldn't give him the satisfaction of flinching. He raised his hand, lashed at her again. When she didn't break, he walked over to her, caught the front of her dress, ripped it down. She tried to struggle out of his grip, he brought back his clenched fist, hit her in the face, knocked her back over a coffee table. It shattered under her weight, went to the floor with her. She lay in the wreckage, glared up at him.

"You'll never break me, Murph," she panted. There were rapidly rising red welts across her breasts and ribs. She licked at her lips, tasted blood, spat it at him. "I'll still be around when Rivero gets around to you. I'll be around to hear you scream."

Murph dropped his strap, reached down to grab her by the throat. As his fingers dug into her flesh, her hand closed over a brandy decanter that had been knocked to the floor when the coffee table shattered. She raised the decanter, swung it wildly. It caught him on the side of the neck. He released his hold on her throat, went to his knees, gagging. She swung the decanter again, opened a gash on the side of his head as the bottle broke.

Frantically, she squirmed back out of his reach. When he started toward her on hands and knees, the blood running down the side of his face, she picked up the remains of the coffee table, smashed it over his hunched shoulders. It knocked him to the floor, gave her a moment's respite. She got to her feet, desperately tried to remember where there'd be a weapon. She ran to the desk, pulled out the drawers in the hope there might be a gun, drew a blank. As he struggled to his feet, stood swaying, she backed away to the bar.

It was there, the knife they used to cut lemons. A long-bladed, razor-sharp kitchen knife, its blade discolored by long use.

As Murphy stumbled toward her, she grabbed the knife, brought it around between them. She held it point up, waist high, in the manner of a knife fighter.

Her hand was steady.

"Come on and get it, Murph," she whispered. "You're a real brave guy. Come on and get it."

Murph stopped in his tracks. "Put up that knife." He tried to make his voice hard, couldn't keep out the panic. "Put it up."

She shook her head, showed her teeth through her bloody lips. "Not a chance, Murph. You wanted it so bad I'm going to see you get it."

He started to back away, she followed him.

"You won't be the first, Murph. There was an old sheriff. He pushed me around, too. I gave it to him in the belly. The way you're going to get it, Murph."

Murphy licked at his lips, stopped back-pedaling. He made a sudden, desperate dive for her, his hand going for her wrist. He felt the wrist under his hand, then it slipped away.

Lorna was waiting for the lunge with planted feet. As his hand went for the knife hand, she brought it up with all her strength. It went into the pit of his stomach.

He stood there swaying for a moment, a look of disbelief in his eyes. The knife handle protruded from below his ribs like some obscene horn. He looked down at it, caught the handle with both hands, tried to pull it loose. His knees folded under him, he crashed to the floor face first.

Lorna tottered to the bar, spilled some bourbon into a glass, drank it straight. The liquor burned her lips, made her cough. She stumbled to the phone, lifted the receiver, dialed the number of Diego's. She could hear it ringing, but there was no answer. There would be no answer, she realized, if Jim were alone in the bar and busy. She prayed that there were enough people in the bar to keep him safe until she could warn him.

She headed for her old closet and some clothes.

At this hour of the evening, the cocktail lounge at Diego's was almost deserted. Two men sat on stools at the bar, watching the good-looking man behind the bar mixing drinks.

Somewhere close a telephone kept shrilling. The bartender looked over toward the booth, scowled his annoyance, went back to his concoction. Finally, he poured it into two glasses, put them on a tray. A waiter picked them up, headed for the game room. The couple at one of the tables finished their drinks, headed back to the game room.

"Gets pretty quiet out here, at night," Pete told the bartender casually.

Jim shrugged. "Most of the action is in the game room after nine. Some nights we don't have anybody out here." He picked up a glass, polished it, set it on the backbar. "We get our biggest play here around four in the afternoon."

The phone in the lobby started to shrill again.

The bartender grunted. "I guess I might as well answer it. Some drunk, probably. He'll keep it up until he gets an answer." He dried his hands, walked around the bar, headed for the phone booth.

Willy glared at his back, tugged his gun from his waistband, started to follow him. Pete caught his arm, shook his head.

Willy growled deep in his chest, shook the other man's hand off. "I'm getting him right now."

Pete nodded. "Sure, but not with that." He reached across the bar, picked up an icepick. "This won't make as much noise."

The bartender slid onto the stool in the phone booth, lifted the receiver. "Diego's," he chanted.

"Jim, this is Lorna. You've got to get out of there right now and—"

Jim grinned. "Hi, baby. I been thinking of you—" He broke off as a shadow blocked the doorway to the booth. "Look, mister, I'm busy. I—" His eyes fell on the icepick, he tried to struggle to his feet.

Willy pushed him down, raised the icepick, jabbed down with it. Jim's body lurched forward, then slumped back onto the stool.

The receiver of the phone dangled. "Jim! Jim!" a metallic voice pleaded.

Willy dried his mouth with his sleeve. "You're not so pretty now, sucker." He shoved the body into the corner of the booth, closed the door.

Willy was sitting on the side of his unmade bed when she walked into his room. He had an almost empty fifth of bourbon in his hand, his eyes were bleary, his mouth slack and wet. He stared at her as she stood in the doorway. "You shouldn't have done it to me, Lorna. How much could I stand? You shoulda come with me." He tilted the bottle over his mouth.

"Murph's dead, Willy," she told him. "I killed him. Jim's dead, too, isn't he?"

Willy finished the bottle, threw it on the bed. "Yeah. Now there's just the two of us!" He stood up, swayed. "This time, nobody takes you away from me. You belong to me."

She stepped in, locked the door behind her. "That's the way you want it, isn't it, Willy? You've always wanted me."

He nodded drunkenly. "And now I'm going to have you." He reached down, fumbled under his pillow, brought up a gun. "This time I'm going to take you— for keeps."

"Of course you are, Willy," she told him. She reached up, caught the neck of her dress, tore it way.

His eyes devoured her nakedness. He started toward her, she scuttled around him. "Let me do it my way, Willy," she told him. She sank her nails into her side, dragged them up across her breast, leaving four red trenches. She moaned softly. "You never knew, Willy. I like to be hurt, Willy." She moved toward him. "Hurt me, Willy."

Willy licked at his lips, stared at her. She caught him by the arm. "You want me, don't you?" Her voice was low, urgent. "Hit me."

He brought back his fist, slammed it against her face, she went down on her back. She got to her knees, crawled to him. Her eyes were bright, feverish. She caught him around the knees. "Hit me again," she moaned.

He sank his fingers into her hair, pulled her to her feet. His chin was wet again, his eyes beginning to glaze. He lashed out at her face, kept lashing at it until it was a red blur.

The girl fell against him. "Hold me close, Willy." He stood there, arms dangling at his sides, staring at her. The gun hung forgotten in his hand. "Kiss me, Willy." As he raised his hand to encircle her, she caught the gun hand, her finger closed over his on the trigger. There was a roar. The girl staggered back.

The sound of the shot stunned Willy. He stared down at the raw hole in the girl's abdomen, a hole beginning to well with blood. She closed her hands over it for a second, the red seeped through her fingers.

Somewhere close, there was the sound of a siren, reaching for a high note, dying away. Willy turned, stricken, stared at the window.

The girl went to her knees, fell over on her side. "It's no use, Willy, I called them from the lobby."

He ran to the door, pulled it open. He could see down the stairs to where two uniformed cops were entering the lobby from the street. He slammed the door, ran to the window. The whole street was rapidly being closed off.

"Why? Why did you do it, Lorna?"

"I told you I'd kill you if you ever laid a hand on me," she panted. "Jim was part of me, the best part—" She watched with glazing eyes as the man darted from window to door. "They'll burn you, Willy."

"They can't prove I did it. They can't prove it."

She tried to laugh, it sounded like a hollow cough. "Your gun. These marks on me. They'll burn you for rape and murder. Mine!" She tried to sit up, sank back. "They would have burned all of us. And I wouldn't be found dead in the chair you sat in!" Her head sank back, her eyes glazed.

She was already beginning to turn cold when the cops broke the door in, found Willy cowering in a corner.

THE END

Syndicate Girl

by Frank Kane

Chapter 1

The big sedan swung off the macadam road onto a graveled driveway that twisted through a row of trees to the big house. It purred to a smooth stop in front of a double garage. Judge Carter pushed open his door, stepped out of the car, headed for the garage door.

A man stepped out of the shadows. The judge stopped, a look of surprise twisting his face. Surprise was still frozen on his face as four slugs slammed him back against the car door. He laced his fingers across his stomach in a vain attempt to stem the red stream that was already beginning to seep through his fingers. He slid to a sitting position, slowly toppled over on his face.

The gunman walked over to the body, turned it over on its back with the toe of his foot. Sightless eyes stared up at him, a red stain ran from the corner of the fallen man's mouth.

Some place a door opened. A puddle of light spilled into the driveway, spread over the two men. The man with the gun swore, a scowl marred his pleasant face as he whirled around. For a moment he stood trapped in the light.

A woman was framed in the open doorway. She opened her mouth to scream. The bark of the gun drowned out the scream; the heavy slug hit her in the midsection, knocked her backward out of the doorway.

The killer hesitated for a moment, as though debating the advisability of making sure of the second kill. Instead he sprinted across the lawn to a row of hemlocks that had been planted to insure privacy. He melted into the shadows, satisfied there was no immediate pursuit.

His car was parked on a back road that paralleled the house. He stamped on the starter, eased the car into gear.

By the time the startled servants in the Carter household had reached the police, the pleasant-faced killer was miles away.

Captain Marcy Lewis of the Jackson City Police Department watched with no change of expression while two men from the medical examiner's office transferred the body of the man in the driveway onto a stretcher. They strapped it into place, then one of the men walked over to the captain, held out a printed form.

"This is sure going to raise some hell, skipper. The papers have been hinting that the judge was getting ready to bust the department wide open on that ice investigation."

Lewis initialed the form, pushed it back at the man. "The only ice he knows anything about now is the ice he's getting put on." He pushed his fedora on the back of his head, scratched at his thinning hair with the nail of his index finger. "Snoopers have a habit of not living long. A guy like this takes himself seriously when they put him in charge of an investigation, stands to reason he's asking for trouble."

"How about his wife?"

Lewis shrugged. "Fielded a big one. The doc doesn't give her much of a chance."

"Think she saw anything?"

The police captain squinted at him. "Maybe. For all the good it'll do us. Unless someone knows how to work a ouija board."

The M.E.'s man bared the discolored stumps of his teeth in a broad grin. "That reform mob's been yelling for blood. Looks like they got it. Their own."

Lewis nodded. He took a last look at the body on the stretcher, crossed over to a small group clotted on the lawn preparing a footprint for casting. He watched while one of the tech men set a camera in a vertical position over the print, then laid a scale graduated in inches alongside of it. After the picture had been taken, his partner sprayed a thin coat of shellac on the surface of the print, waited for the shellac to dry, carefully sprinkled talcum powder over it. A third member of the team added some plaster of Paris, dropped in a few twigs of reinforcement, then covered them with more plaster of Paris.

"Any good?" Lewis wanted to know.

"Should be, skipper." The man in charge of the cast nodded. "It's good and clean. It'll match up with the guy when we get him."

"Anything else? Prints? Anything?"

The tech man shook his head.

Lewis grunted, swung away, recrossed the lawn to the side entrance to the house. He climbed the low set of stairs, pushed open the door and walked into what was apparently a study. His eyes hopscotched around the room, came to rest on a large, dark stain on the rug. A middle-aged woman stood near the desk, dry-washing her heavily veined hands, answering the questions snapped at her by a young plainclothesman. He broke off as the captain walked in.

"She see anything, Blake?"

The plainclothesman shook his head. "No, sir. Just heard the shots, came down and found Mrs. Carter on the floor." His pencil sought out the stain.

"Get everything she can give you. I won't need you any more tonight. I'll take the car with me. You get a ride back in with the other boys."

The plainclothesman watched his superior stride out with a puzzled frown. He shrugged, wet the tip of his pencil between his lips, snapped open his leather notebook and resumed his interrogation.

Captain Marcy Lewis handled the big department sedan as though it were a toy. He weaved his way in and out of the late evening traffic, headed for downtown Jackson City. About twenty minutes from the scene of the homicide, he swung off the street onto the sloping ramp of an underground garage. He turned the car over to a broadly grinning attendant who materialized from a small, brightly lighted office.

"Boss still around, boy?"

The Negro attendant flashed his startlingly white teeth. "Been here all night, Captain." He pointed to a long, sleek Cadillac against the far wall. "Ain't been out at all."

Lewis crossed the dankness of the garage to a small elevator set in the wall. He pushed a button marked 3. The car rattled to a stop, and the gate automatically swung open. He followed a balcony that looked down on a dining room and dance floor below. There was a smell of good food, expensive cigars and imported perfume. The dance floor was deserted, a few couples still huddled around tables, impervious to the rhumba beat being pounded out by the five-piece orchestra.

He stopped outside a door marked *Private*, knocked.

A muffled voice told him to come in.

The room beyond was half office, half den. It was a big room with knotty pine paneling and Indian rugs. In a huge fieldstone fireplace a comfortable fire hissed and puffed on the stone hearth.

There were three men in the room. One, young and pleasant-looking, sat on a couch, leafing through the pages of the current *Esquire*. The man who sat behind the desk was fat and soft-looking. Dark, damp ringlets futilely tried to cover the bald spot that glowed pinkly in the indirect lighting of the room. His eyes, two shiny black marbles, were almost lost behind the puffy balls of his cheeks. He seemed half asleep as he sat there, hands clasped across his middle, eyes half veiled by heavily veined lids. The third man was thin to a point of wispiness. His hair, beginning to show signs of receding at the temples was light and wavy. His lips pouting, unnaturally red. All three pairs of eyes turned to Marcy Lewis as he walked in.

"Well, Captain," the fat man behind the desk said in a throaty voice, "nice of you to drop by."

"Judge Carter is dead. Gunned," Lewis told him. His eyes jumped from face to face. "All hell is going to break loose." His eyes returned to the fat man behind the chair. "Why wasn't I consulted, Zito?"

Zito pursed his lips. "Maybe it came up too suddenly." He waved a pudgy hand at a chair. It had dimples instead of knuckles. "You know what Carter was about to do?"

The police captain stared at him bleakly, waited for him to finish.

"He was about to give the Grand Jury a complete list of all the ice being paid in Jackson City. Your name was on that list."

"You got the list?"

The fat man looked up. "It's in a safe place."

"That's what you thought before. But they got hold of it just the same."

"They won't this time."

The homicide detective scowled at the man behind the desk. "The woman is still living. I hope you know that."

The fat man looked at the pleasant young man on the couch. "Joey got stampeded. She opened the door and got a look at him. He didn't take the time to finish the job."

Joey managed a shy grin. "She did frighten me for a minute. How is she?"

"Pretty bad, but still alive." Lewis walked over, dropped heavily into the chair Zito had indicated. "If she got a good look at you, what happens if she comes out of it long enough to make you?"

"She doesn't," Zito told him amiably. "She doesn't make him, that is."

"How can you be so sure?"

The fat man's lips spread in a damp grin. "I have a lot of faith in you, Captain. A lot of faith. You make sure."

Marcy Lewis's forehead gleamed damply in the indirect lighting. "What do you expect me to do? I've got to show her pictures. If I leave your boys out—"

"Don't make a Federal case out of it, Captain," Zito raised his fat hands, palms up. "So you show her my boys. Yeah Joey too." He looked over at Joey. "He's a good boy. A little careless, maybe. But a good boy. You show her his picture."

The police captain frowned. "And if she makes him?"

"She will." Zito shrugged. "So you have her sign the back of the picture. Like this." He placed two sheets of paper together, put an X on the front sheet, turned them over, holding the two sheets together. "It's an old gimmick. Art dealers use it all the time. You take a good painting, paste a cheap copy on the back. You let the mark take it to an expert for appraisal. Then he writes his name on the back. Only he's writing his name on the back of the copy." He flipped the papers at the wastebasket. "You get it?"

Marcy Lewis licked at his lips. "But whose picture is pasted on the back of his?"

The fat man leaned back, smiled. "You got a boy in your department, a real ambitious boy. He could cause real trouble."

"Benson?" The police captain nodded morosely. "A real fink."

"He's been working with Carter. You know that?"

Lewis said he did.

"So, okay. Benson's picture is on the bottom. The woman makes him as the killer."

"You couldn't make it stick."

"No?" He gestured toward the phone. "Some time in the next hour, that phone is going to ring. When it does, the boys take a ride. Tomorrow they're going to find Benson. A suicide. Two and two always adds up, am I right?"

The police captain licked at his lips. He fought a losing battle to keep his eyes off the phone. It was exactly twenty-three minutes later that it rang.

Chapter 2

Captain Marcy Lewis stood at the side of the bed, looked down at the blood-less face of the woman in it. Her skin seemed transparent, had the shine of wax. Her breathing was barely perceptible beneath the sheet.

The white-jacketed intern walked over, checked the transfusion set-up that was funneling blood into her arm. He stood alongside Lewis, stared down at the woman, shook his head.

"Afraid she's not going to make it, Captain."

Lewis frowned. "Think she'll come out of it long enough to give us some idea who did it?"

The intern reached down, felt for the woman's pulse. "Could be. But she won't stay around long enough to give you any kind of a statement. She's had several lucid periods during the night, but they're getting shorter and shorter. That's why we notified your office."

The police captain ran the tips of his fingers along the stubble on his chin. "There's no way you could—"

The intern shook his head. He walked across the room to where a nurse was arranging her medical chart, whispered to her. The nurse looked over to where Lewis stood, nodded.

"Wait a minute, Doc," Lewis called. "I think she's opening her eyes."

The intern crossed the room noiselessly on rubber-soled shoes, picked up the limp wrist. He adjusted his stethoscope, placed it against the woman's breast, squinted up at Lewis. "I think she's coming around. Not too many questions, Captain. She's pretty weak."

"Okay if I just show her pictures? She doesn't even have to talk."

"That would be fine. Anything to save her exertion." He leaned over the woman in the bed. "Can you hear me, Mrs. Carter?"

The head on the pillow moved almost imperceptibly.

"Captain Lewis is here from the police department. He has some pictures. If you see the man who shot your husband, just nod. You're not to try to talk. Do you understand?"

Mrs. Carter moved her head again, her eyes opened.

Captain Lewis replaced the intern at her side, took a batch of pictures from his case, held them in front of her.

"I'll go very slowly, Mrs. Carter. If you see the man, just nod your head." One by one he held the pictures in front of her. On the fifth picture, her head nod-ded weakly. "This one?"

The head moved again.

"Doctor, would you come here, please?"

The intern joined him at the bedside.

"We have an identification here. I'm going to ask you to help Mrs. Carter sign the back of this picture. Then I'll want your signature as further identification."

The intern looked doubtful, but agreed. "I guess it can be done." He turned, motioned for the nurse. Between them they propped the woman up, placed a pen in her hand. Painfully she scribbled her name.

"Would you sign your name and the date under it, Doctor?"

The intern took the pen, wrote his name, returned his attention to his patient.

"I think you'd better leave, Captain," he said over his shoulder. He snapped an order at the nurse, seemed to forget the captain's presence. He was still bent over his patient when Lewis closed the door.

Blake was waiting in the department sedan in the hospital parking lot. His eyes searched Lewis's face curiously as the captain slid into the seat beside him.

"Get anything, skipper?"

"Plenty," Lewis said. "You'd better get me back to the office fast. I've got to talk to the D.A. This is loaded with dynamite."

Captain Lewis had a cubbyhole office on the third floor of the county court building overlooking Memorial Park. He walked into the office, shut the door in the face of the frankly curious Blake. He took the precaution of locking it before he opened his case and took out the picture Mrs. Carter had signed.

He stared into the pleasant face of Joey for a moment; then with his nail, he separated the two pictures, peeled the top one off. The bottom picture was that of a man in his early thirties, with a prominent nose and a pugnacious chin. He turned it over, laid it on his desk. On the back was the signature of Mrs. Carter, witnessed by her doctor. Carefully he tore the picture of Joey into little pieces, wiped the face of the bottom picture with a soft cloth until no trace of rubber cement remained.

Then he lifted the receiver from its hook and dialed a number.

"This is Captain Lewis," he told the answering voice. "Is the district attorney in?"

"One moment please, Captain," a pert female voice chirped. After a second, the district attorney answered. "Hello, Captain. I hope you've got something. The papers are really on my back."

Lewis answered grimly, "I've got something. A time bomb. I've got an identification of the killer from Mrs. Carter."

"Mrs. Carter is dead. I just hung up on the doctor."

Lewis wiped a thin film of perspiration from his upper lip. "We don't need her. She signed the picture and her doctor witnessed it."

"Good. Have you—"

"Mal, it's a member of the department."

There was a long painful pause. "A member of your department?"

"Benson."

He could hear the intake of breath from the other end of the phone. "That's crazy. Benson was very close to the judge. He was working with him on—"

"All I know is that Mrs. Carter identified him as the man she says she saw shoot her husband."

"Have you reached Benson? I'm sure he can clear this up."

"I thought I'd better talk to you first." He tugged a handkerchief from his hip pocket, swabbed at his forehead. "This one is loaded with dynamite, Mal."

"You think I don't know? The reporters have been camping on my front door."

"It could get worse. The judge was supposed to be uncovering graft in the department. Now his wife says he was killed by a cop."

There was a thoughtful pause at the other end. "I see what you mean. I think we'd better have Benson brought in here. Can you meet me at my office with that picture?"

"Sure."

"Good. Put out a line for Benson. Have him meet you here."

Lewis dropped the receiver back on its hook, got up and walked over to where a water cooler stood against the far wall, muttering to himself. He filled a paper cup with cold water, drained it, then crushed the cup in his hand. After a moment, he tossed it at the wastebasket, walked to the door and unlocked it.

"Blake!" he barked.

The young plainclothesman scuttled into the office. "Yeah, skipper?"

"I want you to find Sergeant Benson. He's to meet me in the D.A.'s office in an hour—"

"Benson's dead, skipper. We just got the flash on the hot shot. They think he did the dutch."

Lewis stared at his driver. "Suicide?" He could feel the small beads of perspiration on his forehead. "Where?"

"Looks like he had a little hideaway apartment over on the east side." Blake shrugged. "Proves you can't tell about a guy—"

"Who's handling?"

"It's still just routine. It hasn't gone out on the air yet."

"Get downstairs, see to it that it doesn't. We don't want a lot of reporters tracking this up." He waited until the plainclothesman had scuttled from the room, then wiped his forehead on the back of his sleeve. He picked up the phone, dialed the D.A.'s office, was connected immediately. "Mal, all hell's broken loose. They found Benson. Dead."

"What?"

"Sounds like a suicide. I'm taking it on personally to keep the lid on. I've kept it off the air."

"Where?"

Lewis shook his head. "I don't know. It's some hideaway apartment he was keeping on the east side. My driver's getting everything now. I'll pick you up at your office on the way."

Sergeant Benson lay on his back in the mussed bed, one arm hanging down the side of the bed, the other folded across his belly. He stared unblinkingly at the ceiling with unseeing eyes. A dark hole in his face was diagonally opposite the ragged exit on the other side of his jaw where the slug had torn away a piece on its way out.

District Attorney Malcolm Waters stared down at the dead man, swore under his breath. He watched while Captain Lewis bent down, inserted a pencil in the barrel of the gun that lay close to the fingers of the dangling hand and lifted the gun from the floor.

"The clincher will be if the bullets from this match the slugs the M.E. dug out of the judge." He laid the gun on the table. "I have a hunch they will."

Mal Waters bobbed his head unenthusiastically. "So do I."

"How do we handle this, Mal?"

The D.A. rubbed the heel of his hand along the side of his jaw. "How is there to handle it? If the bullets match—" He shrugged his shoulders helplessly.

Lewis walked over to the dead man's coat where it hung draped over the back of a chair. He went through the pockets, finally came up with a billfold from the breast pocket. He opened it, whistled softly. "Take a look at this. Must be a couple of grand there." He held the billfold out for the D.A. to see. "You don't get that kind of loot working for this man's police force." He tossed it on the table next to the gun. "How do you read it now?"

Mal Waters shook his head. "None of it makes any sense to me. Judge Carter trusted Benson. He must have known—"

"Maybe he didn't. Until last night. Maybe last night he got the proof that Benson was on the take. And he shoved the proof under his nose." He watched with narrowed eyes while the D.A. picked up the billfold, riffled through the wad of bills.

"I don't see how we can sit on this one, Lewis. It's too big."

The captain shrugged. "It's going to make a splash."

"It's unavoidable. We'll just have to live with it." He took a long last look at the body on the bed. "Nobody could ever have convinced me that Benson was a crooked cop. Nobody but him."

"I know someone who must have been even more surprised," Lewis said. "Judge Carter."

Mary Lister was comfortably upholstered, sloe-eyed, languorous. She affected a cigarette holder tilted from the corner of her full, pouty lips. Her luxurious hair was ash blonde.

She sat in Al Zito's office, tapping her foot impatiently. The small jeweled watch on her wrist showed 8:15. She was studying the polish on her carefully shellacked nails when the door opened and Zito waddled in.

"Been waiting long?" he asked as he crossed the room to his desk chair.

"Long enough," she told him coolly.

He settled into the chair with a sigh. "That was a nice job, Mary. A real nice job."

"They always are. That's why Murph sends me."

The fat man shrugged. "This wasn't an easy one. Benson was a smart cop."

"Not so smart. He's dead." She tapped the cigarette holder against perfect teeth. "Only thing, Murph doesn't like jobs that take this long."

"What difference does it make how long it takes as long as everything goes off this good?"

The girl sucked on the cigarette holder, blew a stream of smoke ceilingward. "It means hanging around a town too long. Too much chance of something going wrong."

"So it took a little longer than usual. Tell Murph I'm real satisfied." He leaned back, touched his fingers across his middle. "You're going back tonight?"

"On the nine o'clock flight." She checked her watch. "I'll want one of your boys to drive me."

"Joey'll take care of it."

Mary Lister dropped her eyes, studied the man in the chair from under carefully tinted lids. "Anything you want me to tell Murph?"

"Tell him not to worry about Jackson City. With Carter and his fly-cop Benson out of the way, everything is under control."

The girl pursed her lips. "He'll be glad to hear that. Some of the big boys in New York thought things were getting out of hand. They'll be glad to hear you've got everything under control again."

The fat man scowled. "They've never gotten out of control."

"You could fool us. We thought the reason the judge and Benson had to be cooled off was because they were getting too hot." She got up, walked to the door. "I'd better get going. I don't have too much time."

The fat man watched her sulkily. She stopped at the door, smiled sweetly. "I'll tell Murph how things are going." Then she walked out, closed the door behind her.

Zito swore under his breath, punched at the button on his desk. The door opened, Joey walked in.

"See that that bitch gets on the nine o'clock plane," he growled. "Make sure she gets out of town."

Joey nodded, studied the angry color of the fat man. "She's sure a wise broad. Some day she's going to talk out of turn and—"

The fat man leaned back, his eyes receded under the heavy lids. He shook his head. "Nobody'll do anything. Nothing will ever happen to that broad with what she knows. The Syndicate can't even afford for her to catch cold." The eyes seemed to close completely. "The time to take care of her was before she had so much on so many people. Now it can never happen."

Joey shrugged. "I better be careful driving."

"Yeah. You better be careful." The fat man pursed his lips. He didn't appear to notice when Joey walked quietly out of the room.

Al Zito could have done without Mary Lister from practically the first minute he'd met her. But it wasn't very likely that he would take any steps to achieve that end.

Zito had been a product of the closing days of the late unlamented Prohibition Era. With the fading of bootleg profits and the substitution of new rackets to keep the mobs' coffers lined, he had drifted west, ended up as number two man in Eddie Ryan's politico-gangland empire. Besides being number two man to Ryan, Zito soon had his own book going for him and a number of minor sources of income that sprang from his close association with Ryan.

But the juicy take was soon threatened by an invasion from a united organization with roots in the East known simply as the Syndicate. As it moved in Zito sat back and watched the efficiency with which those who resisted its take-over were dispatched. And was impressed. In the beginning, the Syndicate boys didn't bother Zito—only because they had a healthy respect for Eddie Ryan's power.

But it was obvious to everybody concerned that a showdown was inevitable. Eddie Ryan stood between the Syndicate and a complete take-over. So Eddie Ryan had to go. But since it was as obvious to him as it was to the members of the Syndicate, Eddie Ryan took no chances. He lived in a penthouse apartment in midtown, a penthouse that could be reached only by a private elevator manned by one of his men. And nobody rode that elevator who was not first searched in the lobby. Nobody, including Al Zito. But the fact that Zito made nightly calls at the penthouse to report activities of the day came to the attention of the Syndicate. And that was how he came to meet Mary Lister for the first time.

Sitting here in his office in Jackson City, he could remember that day as well as if it had been yesterday. He scowled at the memory.

She had been sitting in his office in Eddie Ryan's Democratic headquarters when he walked in, much as she was sitting here tonight. The cigarette holder was tilted from the corner of her mouth, her knees were crossed, exposing a generous expanse of nylon-sheathed leg. He flashed a questioning glance at the girl in the outer office.

"She said it was personal and important," the girl told him defensively. "Said it would be all right with you for her to wait in here."

Zito nodded, motioned for the girl to get out. He turned back to the girl in the chair. "Who are you and what do you want?"

The blonde shifted comfortably in the chair, turned the full power of the sloe eyes on him. "My name's Mary Lister. I'm here to do you a favor." She dropped her eyes, studied him through thick lashes.

"What's the favor?"

The girl looked around the room. "This is no place to talk about it."

"It's not bugged if that's what's worrying you."

"Neither is my room. The Morrison. 621."

Zito shook his head.

Mary Lister removed the stub of her cigarette from her holder, grinned languidly. "Not afraid of a girl, are you, Zito?" She blew through the holder, stowed it in her bag. "Make it neutral ground. You know where I am. Call me any time." She got up, smoothed the dress over her thighs. "It'll be worth your while." She flashed him the slow smile again. "I'll wait to hear from you. But don't take too long."

She turned, walked to the door, and left without a backward glance.

At eleven o'clock that night, Al Zito crossed the lobby of the Hotel Morrison to the bank of house phones at the far end of the registration desk. He selected one which gave him an uninterrupted view of the hotel switchboard, watched the operator as she plugged him in.

"Miss Lister. Room 621."

The operator's fingers skipped over the switchboard, plugged the third key from the left in the fourth row. In a moment, the sultry tones of Mary Lister came through the receiver.

"This is Zito. I'm in the lobby. I thought we could take a ride and talk."

There was no hesitation in the voice. "I'll be right down."

Zito dropped the receiver back on its hook, watched the operator at the switchboard. There was no call from 621 by the time the girl stepped off the elevator. She walked up to him, nodded coolly.

"You're smart. You didn't take very long to make a decision."

Zito grunted, turned, headed for the street. She tagged along beside him, didn't add a word as the doorman had his car brought up. She slid into the front seat, dug her holder out of her bag and fitted a cigarette to it. Zito stamped on the starter, eased the car into a stream of traffic heading south. At the first corner he made a right turn, turned left at the next. The girl offered no comment, smoked silently.

"You're not being followed. If we had wanted you, that would have been easy. You're just lucky that we need you to get Ryan. Find a place where we can talk. Any place."

"You're wasting your time. Nobody can get close enough to Ryan to get him."

"You can," the girl told him.

Zito shook his head. "I wouldn't last very long even if I could. Ryan has a lot of friends. But even I couldn't get a gun up to the penthouse." He looked sideways at her. "Do you know the set-up?"

She smiled. "It's not bad. The house elevator goes to the floor below the penthouse. Everybody going to the penthouse has to ride the private elevator for the last floor."

"Yeah. There's no other way to get up. And the guy on the elevator makes sure that nobody gets up without an okay. He's even got to clear me." He shook his head. "I couldn't get a gun up there if—"

"Nobody's asking you to make the hit. We have our own troops." She took a deep drag on the cigarette, let the smoke escape through half-parted lips. "You just have to set him up. We'll have one of our boys in a window across the street with a reacher."

"Eddie's not that dumb. Every gun that comes into town is spotted by his boys. The minute you brought in a guy who's good enough to do the job, he'd know about it."

"Not that the details are any of your business. But nobody will know these boys. They're being brought in especially for him." She smiled around the holder. "Mr. Ryan's an important man. He deserves special treatment."

"Brought in?"

"From Italy," she said. "They were deported years ago. They're in Tia Juana right now waiting for the word. They come in for the job and are back in Mexico before anyone knows Ryan's been hit."

"That leaves me holding the bag. If I'm up there with him when he gets hit, they'll have to know that—"

"Nobody will know that you had any part of it. Not the men who do the job or the men the Syndicate sends in to run things."

"You'll know."

The blonde smiled at him. "That's right. And that's something you should remember." She took the holder from between her lips. "The boys use me to run messages and to set up hits because they trust me. They have to." She unscrewed the butt from her cigarette holder, dropped it out the window. "You will too. You see, I've been in on a lot of these jobs. And each time I draw up a complete dossier on who was hit, who set it up and how. These statements will never turn up—unless something happens to me."

"You mean—"

"I mean that if I were to have an accident, friends will mail these statements to the F.B.I. and to the various police chiefs. A lot of important people in the Syndicate would have an awful lot to lose by that accident. Do we understand each other, Zito?"

Zito swung the car off the road, stopped under a tree, turned off his lights. "We understand each other."

"Good. And don't get any ideas that my insurance won't stand up. Bigger men than you have tried to find some way of getting out from under. It won't work. The minute Mary Lister disappears or turns up dead, every hit I've ever set up will be blueprinted for the police. So since we understand each other, we can drop it. Just as long as you never forget it."

Zito wiped the beaded perspiration from his upper lip with the side of his hand. "What do I get out of this?"

"You get the next territory opened up by the Syndicate."

"Not here?"

"No. This territory has already been given out. Besides we don't like the questions some of the boys ask when a number-two man takes over in a territory."

"What do I do?"

Mary Lister paused. "Today is Thursday. A week from tonight you'll find some reason to visit Ryan's penthouse at exactly nine o'clock. You'll arrange for him to be standing by the window facing south some time during the next half hour. We'll take care of the rest."

"But—"

Mary Lister ignored the interruption. "You will then call the desk and tell the assistant manager that Ryan is sending his rug out to be cleaned and that messengers from the Castle Rug Cleaners are to be permitted to pick up the rug the first thing Friday morning. He'll leave in the rug which will go down the service elevator to the basement."

"But what about the operator on the private elevator?"

"You said he's very faithful to Ryan. So what's more logical than when Ryan takes a run-out to escape the heat that he takes his stooge with him?"

Zito swabbed at his face again, nodded.

"Shall we go back?" The blonde settled back comfortably in her seat. "I'll be leaving in the morning. From here on, it's up to you. I think you understand that nothing must go wrong—for your sake."

Eddie Ryan's disappearance created a two-day wonder. Then the Syndicate moved in its well-oiled operation, and speculation as to Ryan's whereabouts died down. The Syndicate kept its word—Al Zito was given full control of the Syndicate's operation in Jackson City. Mary Lister kept her word, too. Soon after Eddie Ryan's death he received by registered mail a copy of the file she had made on the Ryan murder. Duplicates of it were planted in various places throughout the country ready for mailing in the event anything happened to her. A glance at it made it very obvious that from then on Al Zito had a big stake in the continued health and safety of Mary Lister.

Chapter 3

Jackson City took the news that one of its trusted police officers had been taking graft in its stride. It even accepted the theory that Sergeant Tim Benson had killed Judge Carter to prevent him from exposing the graft taking.

Jackson City had learned to take a lot in its stride since Al Zito took over as resident manager for the Syndicate. There had been exterminations, beatings and bombings of local free enterprisers until one by one they either fell in line, left town or took up permanent residence in the cemetery just outside town.

After Zito had eliminated competition, his first move was to supplant the questionably friendly administration with a "reform ticket," a ticket that could be expected to co-operate. A smoothly running Syndicate operation needs a lot of things, but publicity isn't one of them.

Ed London had been the ideal choice to head the reform ticket. He had always been articulately anti-administration, he had his heart set on running Jackson City. But his most important qualification in Al Zito's eyes was the fact that Ed London was ready to bargain. The reform ticket was swept in to office and calm descended on Jackson City—the citizens were able to indulge in their own forms of vice and the Syndicate was able to operate. Both with a minimum of official interference.

It was to Jackson City in this point of its development that Mal Waters returned. It wasn't that he wanted to return; it was the fact that it was fairly obvious that his father's days were numbered and that the old man's greatest ambition was that his son would some day take over his law practice.

Mal had left Jackson City a high-school football hero, had gone on to greater glory at Harvard. He interrupted his studies at law school there to serve his time as a squadron leader over Korea. When that "local unpleasantness" came to its inconclusive conclusion he returned to Harvard to complete his studies. A brief connection with the State Department had been interrupted by the news of his father's ill health, so he had returned to Jackson City.

When he had left, Rita London was a gangling kid whose only outstanding features were the braces on her teeth. When he returned, she was a tall, self-possessed young woman who wore her red hair piled on top of her head and who knew all too well the deadly effectiveness of her slanted green eyes.

They had found each other almost immediately following his return. An occasional meeting turned into a standing date and then it became unofficially accepted that Mal Waters had been tagged to become Mayor London's son-in-law.

When the time came for Ed London to pick his slate for his third term in office, Larry Conklin, the sexagenarian who had been district attorney for as long as anyone could remember, announced his intention to retire. It was a foregone conclusion that Mal Waters would be selected to succeed him on the slate. A foregone conclusion, that is, to everyone who knew that Rita London had plans for her husband to succeed her father in the mayor's office as a logical step in the direction of the governor's mansion in reasonable time.

Rita broke the news to Mal a week before primary at the country club dance. They had walked through the French doors that led to the terrace overlooking the swimming pool. She held a cigarette to her lips, waited for him to light it.

"I have such wonderful news, Mal." She leaned closer to him. "I shouldn't be the one to tell you, but I can't keep it any longer."

"That you love me?" He grinned.

"That's no news. You've known that for a long time," she told him softly. She took a deep drag on the cigarette, blew the smoke out in a feathery tendril. "Larry Conklin is going to retire as district attorney."

Mal frowned slightly. "I hadn't heard. I thought they'd have to wheel him out of office. What happened?"

"They found a perfect man for the job. And Conklin's getting too old. That's what Daddy said."

"Who's the man?"

"You."

Mal stood for a moment speechless, then shook his head. "That's crazy. I don't want to be district attorney."

"But I want you to be."

"But, honey, I'm happy doing just what I'm doing. I have a good law practice, I'm going to marry the girl I love, and—"

Rita covered his hand with hers. "That's just it, darling. I want to marry you and I want to be proud of you. I want to know we'll be going places. Together."

"You can't be proud of me as a lawyer?"

She pressed his hand, leaned over and kissed his cheek. "Of course I'm proud of you, Mal. You know that. But I know you can go places. Any place you set your mind to go. And I want to go with you."

Mal raked his fingers through his hair. "I don't know if I can explain this to you, Rita." He broke off for a moment, marshaled his thoughts. His mind went back to an air strip north of Seoul where as squadron commander he had sent flight after flight of jets north to the Yalu only to watch tattered remnants of them stagger back at night. He had sworn then that never again would he take a position where he could control other men's fate. And now—

He felt her hand on his arm. "Understand what? That you don't want a chance to be mayor? Governor maybe? No, Mal, I don't understand."

He led her to two chairs near the railing, waited until she was seated. "I never told you this, honey. But in Korea I had to send a dozen of my friends out on missions they couldn't hope to come back from. It was my job, but I hated every minute of it. Now you're asking me to take the responsibility of sending other men either to prison or to the chair. I don't want that kind of responsibility again, Rita. I don't want it."

Her voice was soft, caressing. "I didn't know, Mal. You never told me." She stood up, moved close to him. "But this won't be that kind of a job, Mal. The district attorney doesn't have to be anything else but a supervisor of his office. You'll have lots of assistants to handle the actual detail." She smoothed down his ruffled hair. "And it won't be for long. Daddy will be thinking of retirement soon. And who's a more logical man to succeed him than the district attorney?"

In the long run she prevailed and when Ed London's administration took over for its third term, Mal Waters was the newly elected district attorney.

He found the district attorney's office a pleasant backwash. His days were filled with unarduous tasks, his evenings with social functions through which he was expertly steered by Rita. The actual duties of his office were assumed by a corps of skilled assistants; he was buttressed from any unpleasantness by an experienced and hardened secretary who added nothing to the decor of the office but who had an instinctive feel for what was good for the political future of her boss.

Judge Carter's murder came as a bombshell. Up to then, Mal had dismissed Carter's activities as one of the sporadic clean-up drives that afflict all cities where one administration is too long in office. When Captain Lewis brought him the further news that Sergeant Benson had undoubtedly been the killer, Mal began to wonder uneasily about the rumors of graft and corruption the anti-administration forces had been circulating.

He wasn't naïve enough not to know that below the Line in the lower section of town, things were running relatively wide open. But he did buy the philosophy that "you can't legislate morals" and that it's better to have a section where you can keep eyes on things rather than to run vice underground and spread it into all sections of the city. Besides, it wasn't the function of his office to investigate vice—it was his function to prosecute it when it had been brought to his attention.

During the first few weeks after Judge Carter's murder, Mal made an effort to find out how far the judge's investigation had gone. But the judge had either kept no records or they had been destroyed. The investigation lengthened from days into weeks, then spilled over into months. Finally, even the newspapers lost interest.

All except the *Star*.

The *Star* had once been the most important newspaper in Jackson City. It had been the first to recognize and warn against the invasion of outside influence like Al Zito. Consequently it had been his first target. Advertisers in the *Star* were first threatened, then petty acts of vandalism were used to persuade them that their support of the *Star* was likely to cost more than the line rate. One by one they got the message and dropped out. Apologetically at first, then as the message from Zito interests got more pointed, without notice.

As revenue dwindled, the good staffers one by one were lured away by opposition sheets which had suddenly showed signs of affluence.

Max Everett had published the *Jackson City World* for years on what appeared to be a shoestring. It was a tabloid: lurid, scandal-mongering. The kind that might go in a city like New York or Chicago, but wasn't gaited for the more conservative tastes of Jackson City. A blind item column that hinted at backstreet activities of some of the town's less discreet businessmen was the only effective "advertising" the *World* used.

Then, one by one, the advertisers fell into line. The editorial columns softened their approach, the paper thickened as the *Star* thinned out. After a five-year assault on the *Star's* advertisers and its staffers, the *World* had finally emerged as the voice of the administration. It had successfully howled down, time after time, the *Star's* charges of corruption and vice in city affairs.

Mal Waters had had difficulty in reconciling the new importance of the *World* and the rejection of the *Star* when he first returned to his home town. When he had left, the *World* had been known as a scandal sheet and was forbidden in his home. Now the *Star* was a dying institution, its headlines growing larger as a means of filing the space that once had been filled by ads. The large staff was almost gone; a few old-timers stuck, some out of loyalty, but most because they were no longer useful to a more aggressive paper.

Because it had been such an important force in his boyhood, the *Star's* constant needling about the unsatisfactory solution to the murder of Judge Carter added to Mal Water's feeling of unrest. It hinted often and loudly that the murderer of Judge Carter had never been named, that Tim Benson had been framed.

Although it was the wrong political season to risk the reopening of an explosive case like the Judge Carter killing, Mal Waters, in one of those black moods, telephoned the *Star* to complain about the distortion of the facts of the case.

Chapter 4

Lou Stewart, editor and publisher of the *Star,* dropped the discolored phone back on its hook, stared at it for a moment. He dug a battered briar out of his top drawer, found a leather pouch of tobacco, scowled thoughtfully as he dug the bowl into it and tamped tobacco in with his forefinger. He leaned forward, depressed the lever on the intercom on his desk.

"Come in a minute, Harley."

When the city editor walked in, Stewart was leaning back in his chair, holding a wooden match to the pipe bowl.

"Just had an interesting call," he told the short, fat man who headed what was left of the copy desk. "From the D.A."

Tom Harley grunted. "What's he going to do, deliver the *coup de grâce* by tossing an action at us?"

Stewart rattled the juice in the stem of the pipe, sucked in a mouthful of smoke, blew it at the ceiling. "I'm not sure. But he actually sounded like he wanted to be shown we knew what we were talking about."

"And if we show him?"

"He'll do something about it."

The city editor stared at the man behind the desk for a moment, shook his head. "Nuts. He's in it up to his ears. Just like the rest of them. He's got to be."

"Figures to be," the editor conceded. "But there's always an outside chance he could be on the level."

"If he were, what's he doing with that gang?"

Stewart smoked for a moment, considered it. "He's set to marry the mayor's daughter, for one thing. They might just be taking care of him. After all, the frame on Benson did look pretty good. It's just possible they keep Waters too busy being the prospective son-in-law to bother looking beyond the obvious."

"I don't buy it," Harley said.

"Maybe I don't either. But it doesn't cost anything to window-shop." He chewed on the stem of the briar. I want you to hold for a possible replate on the front page."

"For what? To announce that the D.A. doesn't like the things we're saying about him?"

Stewart shook his head. "This is the first time any member of the administration has taken official recognition of what we've been screaming. I want an answer to just one question. Does he plan to do anything about the vice and graft in Jackson City? If he says he doesn't, it makes news. If he says he does, it makes even better news."

Harley massaged the tip of his jaw with his fingers. "You think you can get such a statement?"

"The question brings either a yes or no."

"Like the oldie 'Have you stopped beating your wife?'" The city editor grunted. "Well, did you ask him?"

"Not yet. I'm meeting him for lunch. I'll ask him then—where he can't hang up without answering."

A slow grin twisted the corners of the city editor's mouth upward. "You're meeting him for lunch? I wonder if the mayor knows that?"

"I'm sure he doesn't. And neither does Max Everett of the *World*. So whatever we get, one way or another, we reopen the Benson murder tonight. And we ride it as an exclusive."

The political crowd patronized a little bar in the shadow of City Hall known to its habitués as the Pit. Mal Waters walked into the cool dimness of the bar, ran his eyes along the line that stood elbow to elbow clinking glasses, talking in low muted tones. He walked in, elbowed himself a place at the bar, nodded to Harry the bartender for his usual martini.

He looked around, saw nobody he was interested in talking to, picked his martini from the bar, sipped it slowly. He had had the feeling before that although he was of the political crowd, he had never actually been accepted as a part of it. The old-timers, while friendly and cordial, had a habit of changing the subject when he joined the group. It had bothered him in the beginning, then he shrugged it off indifferently. The average political hack bored him anyway.

He was on his third cigarette and second martini when a heavy-set man in a rumpled blue suit, gray fedora perched on the back of his head, stopped alongside him.

"Mr. Waters?"

Mal turned, noticed the faint white glint of stubble on the older man's chin, the heavy lidded eyes, the tired droop of the lips. He nodded.

"I'm Stewart," the newspaperman told him.

"Oh yeah." Waters didn't offer to shake hands. "Want a drink before we eat?"

Stewart shook his head, waited until Waters had drained his glass, dropped two bills on the bar.

"I have a room in the back reserved where we can talk," the D.A. told him. He led the way to the rear of the Pit where private dining rooms were available for the more private dealings of its patrons. Waters was aware of the speculative glances that followed them the length of the bar, ignored them.

A waiter in a black jacket with a butcher apron tied around his waist smiled at Waters, led the way to their room.

"Drink, gentlemen?" he inquired as they settled down.

Waters raised his eyebrows questioningly at the newspaperman, drew a nod.

"Dewars on the rocks."

"I'll have the same, Pete," Waters told him. "You'd better bring a refill. We want to do a little talking before we order."

The waiter nodded, withdrew, closing the door behind him.

For a moment, neither man spoke. "You have plenty of courage. Being seen in public with me," Stewart told him.

"Possibly."

The newspaperman pulled his pipe from his pocket, fumbled for his pouch. "I think you said over the phone you wanted to talk to me about the Carter murder."

Waters watched the older man fill the pipe bowl from the pouch, waited until he had clenched the stem between his teeth. "What I wanted to know is whether these insinuations about his death spring from anything more tangible than a personal dislike of me?"

Stewart scratched a wooden match, applied it to the pipe bowl. "I have no personal dislike of you, Mr. Waters. I don't know you well enough to either like or dislike you. I don't think many people in Jackson City do." He sucked in a mouth full of smoke, exhaled in a blue-gray cloud. "We're not attacking you. It's what you represent we're attacking."

The district attorney dug a battered pack of cigarettes from his pocket, shook one loose. "And exactly what do I represent?"

"A do-nothing policy. A public official who is content to let a brutal murder go unpunished because he's afraid of a scandal that would hurt his political bedfellows."

Waters stuck the cigarette in the corner of his mouth where it waggled when he talked. "That's your opinion."

"Not my opinion. The facts." Stewart started to elaborate, broke off at a knock on the door.

"Come in," the D.A. instructed. His eyes never left the newspaperman's face.

The waiter walked in, placed a drink in front of each of the men, placed two more on the small serving table. "Just ring when you're ready, Mr. Waters."

Mal waited until the door had closed behind him. "You say the murder of Judge Carter has gone unpunished. I say you're ignoring the facts. Benson was found with the gun that killed Carter—"

"A plant," the editor growled. "And a goddam clumsy one at that." He pulled the pipe from between his teeth, jabbed the stem at Waters. "But even if he did kill Carter, calling off the investigation because of the judge's death was just putting the cork back in the bottle."

"The investigation wasn't called off," the D.A. told him heatedly. "There wasn't a thing we could find that would justify continuing it."

Stewart stared at him coldly for a minute. "I should have known I'm wasting my time." He jammed the pipe between his teeth, chewed on the stem. "The only reason I came was because I knew your father. I figured maybe there was some of him in his son." He started to get up.

"Sit down," Waters snapped. "You've made some big statements. Before you leave here, you're either going to back them up or back down."

"That'll be the day. Your gangster friends haven't been able to shut me up. It's a cinch you won't."

The D.A.'s eyes met his and held. "I'm not trying to shut you up," he finally growled. "I want the truth as much as you do."

The older man dropped back into his chair. "Do you?"

"Yes."

"Even though it's going to hurt some of your in-laws? Some of your social friends? Some of the people who put you where you are?"

Waters scowled at him. "Leave my friends and my fiancée and her family out of it. I'm the one you're gunning for. Remember?"

The newspaperman shook his head. "You're only a small cog. The ones we're gunning for are the mobsters who operate the dives and the dens below the Line. And the fancy self-satisfied hypocrites who own that property and are getting even fatter off what goes on down there." He leaned forward. "Why do you think there's an alliance between people like your prospective father-in-law and a racketeer like Zito? They have a common stake."

"You're a liar."

Stewart grinned at him. "Then why has nothing been done to clean out that area? Why has it been allowed to run wide open with no police interference?"

"Because as long as there has to be vice, it's better to have it in a regulated area where we can—"

"You're insulting my intelligence. Controlled area! That place is wide open. It's a sewer." He leaned back, glowering. "You know the reason. Rents down there are sky high and your friends own the land. The take from the games and the rackets is fantastic. And that goes to your boy Zito."

"Don't call him my boy, goddam it." Waters glared. "I've never laid eyes on the man." He crushed his cigarette out angrily. "If there were such a conspiracy, why should you think I'd be part of it?"

"Want me to be honest or polite?"

Waters snorted. "I want to know what you know, not what you've dreamed up."

"All right. The reason you're part of the conspiracy is because your fiancée has her heart set on the governor's mansion. You go up against Zito and his Syndicate or the hypocrites that control this administration, and you couldn't get yourself elected dog-catcher."

"That's what you think?"

"That's what I know!"

Waters took a swallow from his glass, swirled the contents around the sides. "All right. If I weren't part of this conspiracy, what would I do?"

"Reopen the Carter case."

"You know that's impossible. We had a deathbed identification of Benson by Mrs. Carter, he committed suicide with the same gun that killed the judge. On what basis could I reopen the case?"

"On the basis that Benson never killed the judge. In the first place it was never proven the gun was his. In the second place none of the tenants in that building had ever seen him before. But the rent on that apartment had been paid weeks before."

"And the deathbed identification?"

The newspaperman's face clouded, he rattled the juice in the stem of his pipe. "A dying woman. Benson's face might have been familiar to her from his working with the judge. She might have been confused," he added lamely.

Waters shook his head. "A deathbed identification is almost irrefutable. That plus the other factors convinced us we had the right man."

"And did it also convince you that there's no graft and corruption in the police department and the administration? That everything became lily-white the day Benson blew out his brains or had them blown out for him?"

"I have no proof that there's any graft or corruption in the police department."

"And if there were, would you be prepared to help stamp it out?"

Waters drained his glass, set it down before him. "I believe that's the sworn duty of my office."

"You haven't answered me, Mr. Waters. Would you be prepared to help stamp it out?"

"Of course," Mal snapped angrily.

"May I quote you on that?"

"Certainly you can quote me on it."

Stewart studied the younger man's face. "And if the *Star* would present evidence that warrants the reopening of the Carter murder, would you be willing to act on that, too?"

"It would have to be highly conclusive. In view of the facts—"

"It would be conclusive."

"Before I committed myself, I would have to know the nature of the evidence."

A half grin twisted the newspaperman's lips. "Of course. And probably you just thought of some hedge on the corruption angle, too?"

"No hedge. You bring me evidence of graft and corruption that will stand up and I'll take action."

"The list of ice payments that Judge Carter was getting ready to make public? Naming the cops and how much they got?"

"You know of such a list?"

Stewart shrugged. "We don't have it—yet. But if we can get it?"

"If it'll stand up, I'll impanel a Grand Jury and wipe out corruption no matter where it exists."

"And I can quote you?"

"You can quote me."

The newspaperman grabbed his glass, emptied it in one swallow. He knocked the dottle out of his pipe, stood up. "I don't think I'll stay for lunch, Mr. Waters. I've got a paper to get out."

Waters nodded.

Stewart started for the door, stopped, turned around. "Maybe we can get to understand each other better. We certainly can if you intend to stand behind what you just said."

"I stand behind everything I say."

The newspaperman shoved a gnarled hand at him. "We'll see what we see when the action starts." He turned, pushed open the door, shouldered his way through the men at the bar.

Waters got up, walked to the door, stared after him thoughtfully. He became aware of a tall redheaded man who smelled dankly of whisky standing in the doorway beside him. He recognized him as a ward leader close to Ed London.

"That was that creep from the *Star*, wasn't it, Mr. Waters?"

Waters turned, studied the watery eyes, the wet red smear of a mouth, the numerous blue veins that bulged the man's nose. "That's right."

"What's he want around here?"

"He wanted to know if I were against sin."

The watery-eyed man shook his head knowingly. "You got to be careful about guys like that, Mr. Waters. They twist everything a man says." He pursed his lips thoughtfully. "What does he mean are you against sin?"

Waters signaled the waiter to come in for his order. He turned back to the man at his side. "I didn't think you'd know." He walked into the private dining room and closed the door behind him.

Chapter 5

Malcolm Waters, District Attorney of Jackson City, dominated the front page of the *Star* the following morning. A 48-point headline shouted: D. A. PROM-ISES ACTION IN REOPENING GRAFT PROBE and a three-column streamer added, *Waters to Investigate Corruption and Tie-In to Murder of Judge Carter.*

His secretary, a thin woman with painfully prominent teeth, stood at the filing cabinet as he walked into his office. She pushed a grayish wisp of hair from her face, tucked it untidily behind her ear.

"Have you seen the papers, Mr. Waters?" she asked breathlessly.

Waters nodded. "I've seen them, Goldy. I guess everybody in town has."

Miss Gold crossed to her desk, picked up a memo. "The mayor has. That's for sure. His secretary called first thing this morning. He wants to see you as soon as you come in." She dropped the memo in her basket. "You didn't say those things, did you?"

Waters shrugged out of his topcoat, handed it to her. "What? That I'm against sin?"

She carefully arranged the coat on a hanger, stuck it in the small closet. "Being against sin is all right. As long as you don't specify what kind of sin. Then everybody can think you mean somebody else's, not theirs."

"But suppose there is such a list, Goldy? Suppose Carter was killed because he had a list of every crooked cop in town? Suppose they bring me such a list?"

"If you lay your hands on it—burn it." She glanced toward the door. "What about His Honor?"

"Call his office. Tell his girl I'm on my way up."

Goldy nodded. "Good luck." She picked up the receiver on her desk, dialed 224. "This is Mr. Waters' office. Tell the mayor Mr. Waters is on his way up." She dropped the receiver back on its hook, watched sympathetically as her boss walked out of the office.

Mayor Ed London had his office on the top floor of the three-story City Hall building. A thick, wheat-colored broadloom stretched from the executive elevator to the double, ground-glass doors that bore in gold the information *Mayor's Office.*

Mal Waters pushed open the doors into the outer offices of the suite. A cool-looking blonde in a tightfitting black dress looked up from her typewriter as he walked in.

"Good morning, Mr. Waters." There was no change of expression on her face. "I'll tell His Honor you're here."

She manipulated the key on the intercom carefully as though to avoid damage to her highly shellacked nails. "The district attorney is here to see you, sir."

A muted voice came back to her. "Yes, sir."

She smiled at Waters, a smile that exposed a perfect set of teeth, but worked no change of expression in her eyes. "He'll see you now." When she stood up, she was taller than she had appeared. The black wool did nothing to her curves for which it could be reproached. She led the way to the inner door, pushed it open.

As Mal entered the room beyond, the secretary closed the door behind him. It was a large room, had a beamed ceiling, a peculiar absence of sound—almost as though it were a vacuum. The floor was covered with thick gray-green carpeting, the furniture polished to a soft gleam. One side of the room was covered with a huge bookcase, and in the center, facing the door, an oversized desk dominated the room.

Mayor Ed London was short, stout. He had the perennially smiling expression of a Guy Kibbee. His skull was almost completely naked of hair save for a gray tuft that started behind each ear and met at the back of his skull.

As the door closed behind Mal, the perpetual smile had a strained quality about it. There were two others in the room—the tall, breathtakingly proportioned redhead Mal had every intention of making his wife, and an angry-looking, hawk-faced man who was chewing savagely on an unlit cigar.

"Come in, Mal, come in," the mayor boomed. He walked around the desk, poked a pudgy hand at the D.A. The mayor's hand was soft and wet.

Mal walked over to where Rita stood leaning against her father's desk. The slanted eyes were serious, the full lips slightly set as she offered him her cheek. "Hello, honey. You know Mr. Everett, the publisher of the *World?*" She indicated the man with the cigar.

"Certainly. Hello, Mr. Everett."

The hawk-faced man fixed him with a cold stare, bobbed his head. He continued to macerate the end of the cigar stonily.

"Have you seen that scandal sheet today, Mal?" the Mayor asked with deceptive geniality.

"*The Star?* Yes, I've seen it."

"Naturally the story is a pack of lies? You never made such ridiculous statements. We'll force a retraction that—"

The D.A. raked his fingers through his hair. "Just a minute." He looked from face to face. "What's ridiculous about saying I intend to live up to my oath of office?"

The mayor worked harder on his smile. "Nothing, of course. But you certainly wouldn't play into his hands by reviving a scandal designed only to embarrass the administration?"

"I merely said I'd be interested in seeing anything he has that could convince me that this administration is corrupt—"

Everett pulled the cigar from between his teeth, tearing off a piece of tobacco in the process, and interrupted, "What kind of pool are you playing, Waters?

A paper makes it a policy to take the hide off you and your party every chance it gets. So what do you do? Give them an exclusive interview! If the only way we can get co-operation from your office is to go to work on you, we can do that too."

"I'll bet you can," Waters snapped at him. "But when you do—"

The mayor held up his hand. "Wait a minute, Ev. No need to get so hot. I'm sure it was just a mistake that—"

The newspaperman pointed his cigar at the man behind the desk. "It sure as hell was a mistake. And your boy made it." He took a look at the torn end of the cigar, bounced it off the bottom of the wastebasket. "I've gone along with you fellows for years—"

"Wait a minute," Mal broke in heatedly. "Since when do I have to ask your permission to make a statement? Or anyone else's?"

"Stay out of this, Mal." The mayor's normally ruddy face was beginning to turn a cherry color. He swung back on Everett. "Sure, you swung along with us, and you've done all right—"

"I'm not staying out of this. Stewart claims he can prove this town is lousy with corruption. If it is, I took an oath to clean it up, and—"

"A goddam boy scout yet," Everett groaned. He squinted at Mal. "You took an oath to do what you're told. And I'm telling you to keep your mouth shut until you're spoken to. That article in that rag is going to cost the party enough support to run it out of office." He looked from Mal to London belligerently.

"Whose support?" the D.A. wanted to know. "Zito's?"

The fat man swabbed at his bald pate with a balled handkerchief. "Let's not start throwing names around."

"Why not? Your boy started it. Yeah, it's going to cost you Zito's support. And without it, you haven't got a dream. None of you."

"I don't want Zito's support if it means fronting for a gang of lousy racketeers. If we're letting them run wide open below the Line so a bunch of super-respectable hypocrites can—"

The redhead walked over, caught him by the arm. "Don't get so excited, Mal. Dad and Everett are thinking of your future as well as their own. They know this politics business better than you do."

"I'm glad they do. I have to look myself in the eye every morning when I shave. And I've got a weak stomach."

"This is politics, Mal. You play by the rules. You don't make them," the mayor said. "Sometimes you have to make concessions—"

"And don't forget the strange bedfellows bit. That's always good for a laugh," Mal broke in.

Max Everett got to his feet in disgust. "Looks like you're not as careful as you used to be in picking a man to sponsor, London. If this is your idea of the kind of man to succeed you as mayor, don't count on my paper to support him." He grabbed his hat from the corner of the desk, stamped to the door and slammed it behind him.

"You see what you've done, Mal?" A thin note of exasperation crept into the redhead's voice. "Everett's paper is real powerful. With him behind you you can have anything in this town. Or even in the state. But if you alienate him—" She studied the grim expression on Waters' face, squeezed his arm. "You're just excited. Tomorrow you'll call Ev and apologize, won't you?"

"For what? For wanting to know if the party I represent is covering up a murder? For saying I'd live up to my oath of office and stamp out graft in the administration? I should apologize for that?"

The mayor brought the flat of his hand down on the top of the desk with a loud crack. "Stop talking like a goddam idiot. What difference does it make what the people in the street think as long as the people who can do you some good know where you stand?" He stamped around his desk, dropped into the leather chair.

Mal walked over to the desk, leaned the flat of his hands on the polished surface, stared down at the fat man. He studied him for a minute. "I hope that didn't mean what it sounded like."

"What did it sound like?"

"It sounded like you were saying you'd go along with a rat like Zito." He tried to read the expression in the fat man's eyes. "I know that's not what you meant."

"Of course it's not what I meant," Ed London snapped. "That's as crazy as you standing there telling me that you're violating your oath of office by not spreading the filth from below the Line all over town." He picked up a pencil, pointed it at Mal. "There was a big reformer once did that. He woke up one day to find a house operating right across from him. You want that?"

"No I don't. But I don't want murder to go unpunished either." He jabbed his finger at London. "Judge Carter was a friend of yours. You appointed him to the job. He was murdered."

"By a crooked cop."

Waters raked his fingers through his hair. He wondered what he was arguing about. He had no proof that Benson hadn't killed Carter. He had a small nagging doubt that he might have been needled by a professional malcontent. But there was still the possibility

"If that's true, okay. But suppose Zito had Carter killed? What then?"

London bobbed his head in exasperation. "There's no proof of that. Not an iota. But there's all the proof in the world that Benson killed him. While you're seeing bogeymen, why don't you suppose that Al Capone got up out of his grave and killed him? It makes as much sense."

The redhead walked over to Mal, caught him by the arm. "Dad's right, Mal. This fellow from the *Star* is just using you to sell papers. He wants you to stick your neck out for him. Was he able to give you anything but his opinion that anybody but Benson killed Carter?"

"No, but—"

"Then why don't you wait until he does?" Rita suggested. "Don't you realize how much satisfaction he'd get if he could see you and Daddy at each other's throats like this? And for what?"

London dug a handkerchief from his pocket, polished his bald pate. "Rita's making sense, Mal. You're upset and I guess I don't blame you. You had an expert needler working on you and you haven't been in politics long enough to recognize it." He returned the handkerchief to his pocket. "Lou Stewart is just hoping you'll give him something that will sell enough papers to pull that rag of his out of bankruptcy. And you fell for it." There was a conciliatory note in the mayor's voice. "You know me well enough, better than you know Stewart. Whose word will you take?"

"I guess I sound like a chump. He did rile me up." The district attorney grinned ruefully at Rita. "I told you I wasn't cut out to be a district attorney, honey."

She squeezed his arm. "You're doing just fine, Mal. We're proud of you. Aren't we, Daddy?"

The fat man behind the desk pasted the customary smile on his face, nodded paternally. "Real proud."

"I don't know why you should be."

Rita looked at Mal. "You wouldn't be much of a man if you didn't get riled up over the stuff a man like Stewart prints. It's just because you're new in politics. You'll get used to taking things like this in your stride."

London nodded. "Stewart isn't interested in Benson or Carter or anyone else. He's just interested in Stewart. And the way he can do Stewart the most good is to do the administration the most harm. If he didn't use this, he'd use something else. But it won't do him any good."

"Incidentally," Rita added, "it wouldn't do Mal Waters any harm if he started thinking more about Mal Waters and where he's going. Because if you don't, nobody else will. Except me."

"Rita's right, Mal. Don't throw away your future," London said. "Make it up with Ev. He throws a lot of weight. Put yourself in his shoes. He's been supporting the administration against all the scurrilous attacks of the *Star*. Besides, when a county official has an important statement to make, who does he make it to? The paper who supports him—"

Waters raked his fingers through his hair. "Okay, okay. I get the point. No more statements to the *Star*."

"That's all we wanted you to say, honey," Rita cooed to him. "It's as important to you as anybody else that the administration gets all the support it can from men like Everett. You understand that."

"I know all that. It's just that I don't like for a guy like Everett to think he owns me."

"You're hypersensitive, honey," Rita scolded lightly. "Nobody is trying to own you. Unless it's me."

Mal grinned reluctantly. "That I'll buy."

She turned to her father. "You see? He's not really as hard to manage as he pretends."

"You should know," and the mayor beamed.

Chapter 6

The telephone on the night table started to shrill discordantly. Mal Waters groaned, cursed sleepily and dug his head farther into the pillow. The noise refused to go away.

He opened one eye experimentally; he could see by the half-drawn shade that it was still night. He glowered at the phone but it refused to be impressed and continued to shrill at him.

He tried to wipe the sleep from his eyes but it wouldn't wipe. The phone gave no indication of giving up, so he fumbled for it, located it and held it to his ear.

"Yes?"

"Mr. Waters? I'm sorry to call you this late but I have something I think will interest you."

"Who is this?"

"Stewart at the *Star*. You said if I could give you any proof that Benson didn't kill Judge Carter—"

Waters peered at the clock on the night table, groaned. "Do you have any idea what time it is? It's after three."

"I know. That's why I had to call you now. During the day, this evidence isn't available. Or aren't you interested?"

Waters raked his fingers through his hair, debated the advisability of hanging up. "Look, I've had a bad day. That paper of yours didn't help. And now—" He paused.

"And now I'm getting ready to bother you more by giving you facts to upset your preconceived conclusion. I should have known it was all talk," the editor said.

"What kind of proof could you possibly have at this late date?"

"Proof that Tim Benson never fired the shots that killed Carter. And if he didn't kill Carter, he didn't kill himself. But then, you wouldn't want to know about that, would you, Mr. District Attorney?"

"Stop making me out a heavy. Where is this proof?"

"Right in the files of your own police department. The safest place in the world to bury it."

The district attorney sighed. "Where are you now?"

"You know the all-night beanery across from headquarters? Place called

Benny's?"

"Yeah. I'll be there as soon as I can."

Waters dropped the receiver back on its hook, swore softly. He swung his feet from under the covers to the cold floor, then completed the waking-up process in the bathroom by dousing his face with cold water. He already regretted agreeing to meet the editor, remembered his promise to the mayor. He considered picking up the receiver, asking Information for the number at Benny's so he could call it off. He decided to play the hand out, expose the so-called evidence and get the newspaperman off his back once and for all.

He shrugged into his jacket and headed for the door.

Benny's was a small hole in the wall across from Police Headquarters. A few heavy-set characters, whose shoes practically wore a badge, sat huddled over coffee at the end of the counter near the door. At the far end, Lou Stewart sat swirling the thick liquid around the inside of his cup.

Waters walked the length of the counter, slid onto a stool at his side. Stewart looked up, nodded.

"You're beginning to puzzle me, Mr. District Attorney," he told him. "I sat down at this end because I've been expecting that phone to ring to tell me you couldn't make it."

"I thought about it. But I decided it would clear it up a lot quicker for both of us if I took a look at this evidence." He looked up as the counterman shuffled down to them, ordered a coffee.

"Fair enough. If you decide the evidence is phony or wouldn't stand up, bow out. At least you've given me a fair hearing. On the other hand—" He left it hanging there.

The counterman returned, sloshed a cup of coffee in front of Waters, dried his hands on his apron. "Anything else?"

Waters shook his head, the counterman shuffled back up the bar to where his half-smoked cigarette was balanced on an up-turned cup. He seemed to have lost all interest in them.

"Where is this evidence?" Waters wanted to know.

"In the files. You'll be able to see it. Right now."

Waters sipped at his coffee, burned his tongue, swore softly. "What's the nature of the evidence?"

"A footprint. The killer's footprint. And it's not Benson's."

The district attorney pursed his lips thoughtfully. "How can you be so sure it was the killer's?"

"The lab boys picked it up at the scene. It was fresh, just made. And it was on the lawn heading for the hemlock hedge the killer broke through to make his getaway."

"Where's it been until now?"

"Where it is now. They buried it in the files. We haven't tried to call attention to it because they'd find some way of destroying it."

"Who's we?"

"Me, Captain Cleary and a lot of other people who want to see Tim Benson's name cleared." The editor squinted at Waters thoughtfully. "I'm taking a big chance that my guess is right. That you're a stand-up guy, not just an administration stooge. I'm really tipping our hand because we need somebody like you to bust this open."

Waters nodded. "How about our seeing this evidence?"

The editor drained his cup, set it back on the counter. "Let's go." He waited until Mal had taken a deep swallow from his cup, set it back and dropped some change next to it. He led the way to the door.

They crossed the small Memorial Park wordlessly, headed for the side entrance to the County Court Building where two blue globes announced Police Headquarters.

Stewart pushed through the double glass doors, held them for the younger man. He waved to the sergeant who sat at the telephone switchboard handling the calls as they came through. Some he relayed to the captain on duty for special assignment, some to the lieutenant to be put on the air for the cars, some he sent directly to the detectives' bullpen where three men are always on duty to handle squeals.

"Hi, Lou," the sergeant grinned briefly at the newspaperman, studied Mal with interest. "Evening, Mr. Waters."

"Buzz Captain Cleary, will you, Dave? Tell him I've got the D.A. with me. Like to drop up and say hello if he isn't too busy."

The sergeant plugged in the captain's wire, murmured into it. He nodded, yanked the line free. "He says go on up."

"Thanks."

The sergeant stared at their backs until they disappeared up the stairs, then he plugged in an outside wire and started dialing.

Captain Matt Cleary was a grizzled veteran of twenty-five years of police work. His still thick white hair was parted almost geometrically in the center of his skull, flattened down. He sported heavy, bristling eyebrows and a mustache of matching color. His face was weatherbeaten to a texture of old leather, crisscrossed with lines and a jagged scar that ran along the side of his jaw, a memento of an encounter with a knife-wielding wino.

He looked up as the door opened, his eyes startlingly blue under the thick white of his brows. They jumped from the editor to Waters and back. There was an unspoken question in them.

"I told you he'd come, skipper," Stewart told him.

"That you did." He eyed Waters speculatively. "I had my doubts about one of Mayor London's official family being seen in public with the editor of the *Star*."

"You make it sound like a dirty word the way you say it, Captain," Waters told him. "You apparently don't think very much of the administration?"

The captain shrugged, leaned back in his chair. "I don't think the administration is very much worried what I think. Do you, Mr. District Attorney?" He looked around the office without bitterness. "They've arranged it so what I think or what I do won't make any difference. Twenty-five years and this is what I rate. Permanent twelve to eight, sort of a glorified clerk."

Mal studied the weatherbeaten face thoughtfully. "It couldn't be that this is a personal gripe?"

The blue eyes narrowed. "Real personal. When an honest cop is framed and buried as a disgraced man, that makes it personal, mister. Real personal." He stared at Waters for a second, got up and stamped to a small closet at the far side of the room. "You knew Tim Benson, Mr. District Attorney. Would you say he was a grafter and a killer?"

"I hadn't been close to him in years. People change."

The captain selected a key on his ring, opened the door. "That they do. I remember you, for instance. I knew your father. You were a good kid, a hard fighter and a clean fighter."

Waters grinned humorlessly. "And I've changed?"

The old man turned and faced him. "That's what we're going to find out." He held a cloth-wrapped object and a shoe. He brought them to the desk and set them down. He unwrapped the object, set a plaster cast of a footprint on the desk. "There's the print of the killer we lifted off the lawn the night the judge was killed. This," he held up the shoe, "was Tim Benson's shoe."

He fitted the shoe to the print, showed it to be several sizes too large, looked up.

"Tim Benson never could have gotten his foot into the shoe that left that print."

The two older men watched while Mal bent over, examined the shoe and footprint. Finally he straightened up.

"Why hasn't this been brought to my attention before?"

"Would it have done any good?" Cleary walked around the desk, dropped into his chair. "Or would it have disappeared?"

"Look, Cleary. I'm getting pretty sick of all the snide remarks about me and the administration. Give me a straight answer for once. Do you think I'm trying to cover a killer?"

The captain pursed his lips thoughtfully, scowled. "Maybe not you. Maybe the people behind you. It adds up to the same thing."

"Or is it because you've been put out to pasture here?"

The man in the chair jabbed a sausage-shaped finger across the desk. "Get this straight, mister. Anything they can hand out, I can take. They put me here because they can't handle me. Because I won't jump when they snap their fingers. Okay, that's their privilege. But killing one of my boys and smearing his memory, that I don't take."

"Who's they? Me, the mayor? Who?"

Cleary sniffed. "You kidding? London, you? You're just window dressing, mister. The Syndicate runs this town. If they say go, you go. If they say jump, you damn well better jump. If they say you die, don't start reading any continued stories."

"By the Syndicate you mean Al Zito."

"He's their local boy, sure. They have a local boy in every town like this. All he has to do is keep the town in line. Judge Carter started to stir things up, so he had to go. Benson knew too much, so they kill two birds with one stone. Carter goes and Benson takes the rap."

"You're still here."

Cleary shrugged. "I'm not very important. And my hands are tied. Even with the proof that Tim didn't do that killing, so far I haven't been able to do a thing about it." His eyes rolled to the editor's face. "That's why I let Lou talk me into taking a chance on you. I guess you're our last chance."

Waters stared at the cast, scratched his head. "You're forgetting one important thing. Mrs. Carter saw the killing. She identified the killer. She picked out Benson's picture. How about that?"

"I know, I know. The doctor witnessed her signature. Only he was more interested in his patient than in what he was doing. He didn't realize it but he was getting a fast shuffle."

Waters shook his head. "Not that fast a shuffle. He verified his signature at the inquest. There was nothing phony about—"

Cleary grunted. He reached into his top drawer, brought out a pack of gum. "The signature on the back for identification is one of the oldest con games in the world. And suckers keep falling for it." He stripped the wrapper from a piece of gum, stuck it between his teeth. "Art fakers use it all the time."

"You'll have to spell it out for me," Mal said, frowning.

"An art faker asks a ridiculously low price for a painting, offers to let the mark have it appraised. The appraiser values it at ten times what the faker is asking. When he brings the thing back to the original dealer, he's allowed to sign his name on the back to make sure he gets the painting he had appraised. Only pasted on the back of it is a cheap copy. His signature doesn't go on the back of the real painting but on the copy. You follow?"

Waters stared at him, mouth slightly open. "You mean—the picture she signed was pasted on the back of the real killer's picture?"

The captain nodded.

"But that would mean—" The district attorney looked from the police captain to the editor and back. "That would mean that Captain Lewis knows who the real killer is."

"I wonder if you're really as shocked as you look?"

Waters leaned on the edge of the desk, shoved his face into that of the police captain. "Why should Lewis be party to a frame-up of one of his own men?"

"Because Marcy Lewis is owned body and soul by Al Zito. He always has been. That's why they took me out of command and gave him my job. He follows instructions better."

Chapter 7

Mal Waters stood at the window in Captain Cleary's office, stared down into the darkness of the park across the street. A few puddles of yellow light spilled onto the path that wound through the park, light that reached tentatively into the darkness that surrounded it, dwindling away into shadowy areas under the trees. Finally he turned, faced the two men who watched him.

"Marcy Lewis is one of the top police officials in this county. You're asking me to take your unsupported word that he is on the payroll of Al Zito." He shook his head. "I can't buy it, Captain."

The old man's jaws chomped away on a wad of gum. "You can't buy it? Or you won't? Which do you mean?"

The D.A. walked back to the desk, rested his knuckles on it. "I mean what I say. I can't buy it. Unless you give me proof."

Lou Stewart dug the ever-present pipe from his pocket, put it to his lips, blew through the stem. "How much do you know about Marcy Lewis, Mal?"

Waters shrugged. "I haven't had too much contact with him. I had the impression he was a cop who knew his job."

"That he does," Cleary conceded. "He could have been a real good cop." He touched the tips of his fingers across his chest, leaned back, "Do you know who Marcy plays house with, Mr. District Attorney?"

"No. And I'm not sure it's any of my business."

The police captain considered it, nodded. "Maybe it isn't. But it's interesting. Marcy Lewis has a girl named Cora Harper. Ever hear of her?"

Waters squinted, nodded. "She's a dancer."

"Dancer, stripper. Just a matter of opinion. But the interesting thing is that Cora works for Barney Maurer. And Barney Maurer is just a front for Zito." He watched the district attorney's face. "And Cora doesn't come cheap. She'd never be available on a cop's salary."

"You ever been in Maurer's place, Mal?" Stewart wanted to know.

The district attorney shook his head.

"It's one of the widest open places in the county. Girls, gambling, after-hours sales. You name it, Maurer provides it."

"And his protection never fails," Cleary added.

Mal studied the old man's face. "You know, Captain, there's an old saying about a bird who fouls its own nest. You're supposed to be a cop. Yet all I've heard from you—"

The old man in the chair interrupted him with an explosive bang of the flat of his hand on the desk top. A red flush started at his collar, flooded upward into his face.

"I am a cop. I've been a cop for twenty-five years, and proud of it. But I'm sick to my stomach when I see what's going on here. And I'm not alone. There are a lot of men on this force that feel the same way. Tim Benson was one of them. He tried to do something about it and ended up on a slab. And before I'm through—"

"You haven't given me any proof," Waters told him.

"You've got eyes. If you want to see," Cleary growled. "Go out to Maurer's place yourself. Count the violations. Then explain to yourself how it is that Marcy Lewis walks in there night after night to pick up his woman and the place still runs wide open."

Waters looked from Stewart to Cleary. "Maybe I'll do that."

"I'd like to hear your answer."

The district attorney stared at him. "My answer will be a raiding party."

Cleary pounded on the wad of gum rhythmically. "With plenty of warning?"

Waters grinned at him, a grin that twisted the corners of his mouth, didn't reach his eyes. "Your confidence in me is overwhelming. Maybe you'd like to organize the party. You claim there are a lot of men like you who can be trusted. All right, if there's a leak—it won't be from me."

The captain missed a beat on his gum. "You mean that?"

"Yeah. I mean it."

Cleary resumed the tattoo on his gum. He looked to the editor, who nodded, then back to Waters. "You know, Mr. District Attorney, it's just possible that I've had you wrong. In that case you have my apologies. But if I was right in the first place, we're going to be sticking our necks way out." He raked his fingers through the thick white hair. "The minute the mayor finds out you were in Maurer's—"

"And how would he find out?"

Cleary shook his head in wonderment. "You wouldn't be in the place five minutes before Zito got word. And two minutes later the mayor would be getting his orders."

Waters started to retort, checked himself. "We'll see, Captain. We'll see."

Barney Maurer's was a sprawling white frame building perched above Lake Harding roughly ten miles outside Jackson City. A long, winding gravel driveway led from the state road to the entrance. Although it was now hours after legal closing, the parking lot was still filled with cars. As he approached the entrance, Mal Waters could hear the muted beat of an orchestra.

He turned the car over to the doorman, a giant in a maroon uniform, who waved a hamlike hand. A parking attendant materialized out of the gloom, climbed into the car and swung it expertly from the front of the building to the parking area beyond.

"Last show's already on, mister," the giant told him in a surprisingly gentle voice. "You want to see Cora, you better hurry."

Waters climbed the low flight of steps to the lobby. He elbowed his way through a chattering group of departing guests in the lobby, headed for the supper room beyond.

It had once been the living room of the old house, had been enlarged by breaking through the wall to the library. It was relatively small, intimate and airless. Tables were clustered around a postage-stamp-sized dance floor, foursomes and couples practically sitting in each other's laps.

On the floor, a tall full-breasted brunette who had apparently been poured into a dark red, strapless gown was strutting across the floor, her hips waggling with exaggerated rhythm. When she reached the far end of the dance floor, the drummer rolled off four sharp beats. She kept time with bumps. As she started back across the floor, she pulled open the snaps that ran the length of her gown. White flesh gleamed through. At the rhinestone curtain, she turned, grinned saucily at the crowd and pulled open the gown. She stood there for a moment in jeweled G-string and filmy bra as the house lights went down.

The place rocked with wolf calls and applause. When the lights went up, she stood in the middle of the floor. As the band stepped up its tempo, her strut became a wild swaying; her body undulated from shoulders to hips to ankles. The beat of the drum, the wail of the trumpet swelled in volume. Her motions became more and more abandoned. She danced wildly, her hair flying, her body twisting and squirming sensuously.

Then she stiffened, emitted a little scream, reached back and unhooked the bra. It fell from her, leaving her breasts as living things throbbing in time with the music.

There was a roar of frustration from the closely packed tables as the lights went down and the music stopped. This time the girl refused their coaxing for an encore. As the spotlight knifed through the darkness, it focused on the curtain; a hand came through holding a rhinestone G-string. Then a shapely leg protruded and was withdrawn. The applause continued for minutes.

When the lights went up, Mal was aware of a thin film of perspiration on his forehead and his upper lip. He wiped them with the side of his hand, looked around. Almost every table had liquor on it and, as the orchestra started to file from its podium, the waiters were back serving.

Waters wandered into the bar that adjoined the supper room, found himself space. The bartender did a slight double take as he swabbed the bar in front of Mal, a worried frown ridged his forehead.

"What'll it be?"

"Crow on the rocks." Mal dug a cigarette from his pocket, turned to survey the place. Many of the supper-room patrons were beginning to head for a door at the far end of the building.

The bartender made a production out of spilling some bourbon over the ice in his glass. He softened it with water, then headed for the end of the bar. Waters gave no indication that he was aware the bartender had pushed a button on the base of the phone. He sipped at his glass, approved.

A tall blonde with tired eyes slid into the space next to him. Her carefully made up lips twisted into a smile that didn't erase the fatigue in her eyes.

"Hello, honey. All alone?"

Waters let his eyes drop to the deeply cut décolletage that did a halfhearted job of concealing the magnificence of her façade, nodded.

"So am I." The blonde continued to work at the smile. "Like to buy me a drink?"

Before the D.A. could answer, the bartender was in front of them. He flashed a warning to the blonde with his eyes.

"Sorry, miss." He pasted a smile on his lips. "No unescorted ladies at the bar. House rules."

The blonde looked from the bartender to Mal and back. The smile was even more strained. "I'm sorry." She turned and melted into the crowd.

"Hope she didn't bother you, Mr. Waters?"

Mal eyed the bartender, shook his head. "Of course not."

The bartender appeared to lose interest in him, walked back to his post at the end of the bar. Waters was just finishing his drink, speculating on his chances of getting into the gaming room when he became aware of a heavy-set man in a midnight blue tuxedo who was approaching from the stairs. He wore the red carnation that was his trademark in his buttonhole. Waters recognized the 200-pound fashion plate as Barney Maurer.

Maurer stopped alongside him, greeted him with a broad smile. "We don't get to see much of you in these parts, Mr. Waters."

Mal signaled for a refill. "I've been hearing things about your Cora Harper. I decided to have a look for myself."

There was a note of relief in the fat man's voice. A knowing leer tinged his smile. "That's a lot of woman, Cora. A lot of woman." He eyed the D.A. speculatively. "I'd like to have you meet her, but frankly she's already spoken for. And her boy friend is pretty jealous." His eyes continued to study Mal's face. "But there are a lot of other girls—" He broke off.

The bartender slid the refill across the bar; Mal wrapped his fingers around it. He appeared to be considering. "I might take a rain check on that. If Cora's friend is here tonight, maybe—"

"It's an every night thing, Mr. Waters," Maurer told him apologetically. "You can't blame a guy for keeping something like that private, can you?"

"I guess not," Mal conceded. "As you say, that's a lot of woman." He dug into his pocket, brought up some bills, separated a five from them and dropped it on the bar. Maurer picked it up, shook his head.

"Your money's no good here. I'm glad I finally got a chance to meet you." He licked at his thick lips. "I'm sorry about Cora, but like I say there are a couple of other girls you might—" He broke off to signal to the cigarette girl. "Here's one I'd like you to meet. Bonnie Peters."

She was tall, loosely put together in a way that flowed tantalizingly when she walked. A pair of briefs did nothing to hide her long legs and she stretched the white silk peasant blouse to the limits of credibility. It was obvious she wore nothing under it. She swayed where they stood, smiled warmly.

"You want something, Mr. Maurer?" Her eyes strayed from the big man to Waters, and she seemed to like what she saw.

"This is a friend of mine, Bonnie. Mr. Waters. He's a real important man. He's the district attorney." The girl pursed her full lips, seemed impressed. "It's a pleasure, I'm sure." She patted the thick, glistening golden coils that were caught in a bun at the nape of her neck. "I've never met a district attorney before. Socially, I mean."

"Any time Mr. Waters comes in, Bonnie, be nice to him. He's a good friend of ours. Anything he wants—it's on the house."

The blonde smiled at Mal. "It will be a pleasure." She turned away as the bartender leaned across the bar, whispered to her. "Pardon me. A gentleman wants some cigarettes."

As she headed down the bar, the effect from the rear was as satisfying as from the front.

"Nice?" Maurer wanted to know.

"Real nice."

Maurer shrugged. "If you could hang around and relax awhile I could arrange to let Bonnie have the rest of the night off. Things are pretty slow, anyway."

"I don't think so. Not tonight. But I'll be back."

The knowing smile was back on the fat man's lips. "I thought you would be. Come in any time. Always honored to have you. Let me know and I'll have somebody stand in for Bonnie that night."

Waters drained his glass, set it down. "I just drove out here on impulse. It was worth the trip." He stared past the fat man. A heavy-shouldered man was heading down the hallway toward the rear door. It was Captain Marcy Lewis of the Jackson City Police Department. "Well worth the trip."

"Glad you came." Maurer pushed a pudgy hand out, shook hands with a surprisingly film grip.

Waters headed for the exit, stood at the entrance for a moment, filling his lungs with the cool air. Inside, Maurer stared at the door with a frown, signaled for a phone, started to dial.

Chapter 8

Mal Waters wheeled his convertible off the street under the carport of the big house, noticed with grim satisfaction that the light was burning in the mayor's study. He walked around to the front of the house, reached for the brass knocker only to have the door pulled open before his hand touched it. Framed in the doorway was the kimonoed form of his fiancée.

"We've been trying to locate you, Mal," she told him coldly. "Do you know it's almost six o'clock?"

"Yeah. I didn't know you were such an early riser, Rita." He walked past her into the hallway. She watched him with a puzzled frown. "Your father in the study?"

She eyed him curiously. "Have you been drinking?"

"Some." He waited for her to precede him down the hall to the study. After a moment, she shrugged, walked past him to the end of the hall, threw open the door, stood waiting.

Mayor London greeted him with a scowl.

"Looks like none of us got much sleep tonight, Mr. Mayor."

"Where've you been, Mal?" There was an edge to the mayor's voice.

"Don't you know?"

London's scowl grew more pronounced. "What's that supposed to mean?"

"I figured by now you'd been told to keep your protégé out of places where he doesn't belong. Or hasn't Mr. Zito phoned yet?"

"What were you doing in Maurer's?"

"You know what kind of a place it is," Rita chimed in.

"What kind of a place is it?" Mal wanted to know.

A frown marred the smoothness of the redhead's forehead. "What's gotten into you? You know it's a dive. A dive of the lowest sort. How do you think it looks for you, the district attorney, to walk in—"

"And you, Mr. Mayor. You know the place runs wide open, sells after hours, has prostitutes—"

"Mal!"

"I beg your pardon, Rita. I didn't realize the word would shock you. The condition apparently doesn't."

"Why should it? It's below the Line. It doesn't affect me."

"It does me. I'm going to close the place."

"You can't," London roared. "Are you crazy? Barney Maurer is very important to us."

"He's running wide open. Cops hang out there, the head of the department is living with the star of the show and everybody knows it. I'm closing Maurer down."

"I won't let you." The fat man locked glances with Waters, dropped his eyes first. "You're drunk, Mal. I want you to go home and sleep on it. In the morning, when you have a clear head, we'll discuss it."

"We'll discuss it right now. I'm going to close Maurer's and every other dive with violations—either with your help or without it."

"What's gotten into you, Mal? Are you trying to ruin everything?" Rita gasped. "You start making enemies like Barney Maurer and you've thrown away everything that we're working for."

Waters turned to the girl. "Suppose I tell you I'm now convinced that Tim Benson didn't kill Judge Carter. That he was framed for it and murdered."

"It's impossible. He was identified and—"

"I can knock that identification out, too."

The redhead stared at him. "You mustn't. Tim is dead. What good would it do him? It will ruin a lot of people who aren't dead. Why can't you leave it alone?"

"Because if Benson didn't kill Carter, someone else did. And that someone is walking around. I want him."

Rita looked from Mal to her father and back. She wet her lips with the tip of her tongue. "Mal, don't stir up a lot of dirt. It can't do any good. And it can do a lot of harm." She walked over, put her hand on his arm. "You've told me you love me, that you want to marry me. Do you think I could marry a man who would put my father in that kind of a spot?"

"Your father doesn't have to be in any kind of a spot. Not unless he was mixed up in the murder. And if he was, he's already in a spot."

"You know I had nothing to do with it," London growled. "I still believe Benson killed Carter. But regardless of who killed him, Rita's right. You can't do any good by stirring up a lot of dirt. Benson's dead and forgotten. Let him stay that way."

Waters shook his head. "There's a cancer eating at this town. You can cover it up, but that doesn't stop it from eating. The only way to fight it is to tear it out by the roots. That's what I intend to do."

The redhead turned her back on him, walked to the desk. She fumbled with her finger, dropped a ring on the desk. "If you go ahead with what you plan, we're through."

"You don't mean that, Rita."

"Every word of it. If you persist in smearing my father and holding this town up to disgrace, I'll never talk to you again." She turned around, faced him. Hollows showed under her eyes, her lips were unnaturally thin and compressed. "Everything has been running smoothly, just the way we wanted it. Now you, of all people, have set yourself out to destroy it."

"I thought you'd understand."

"Understand what? That you're going to set yourself up as a one-man vigilante committee? That you owe such an allegiance to the dead you'd sacrifice the living? Understand that?"

"It's not a one-man vigilante committee, Rita. There are a lot of decent people in this town who—"

The fat man snorted contemptuously. "Decent people? Is that why Maurer's and every other spot below the Line is jammed with them every night? If they're so unhappy with the way things are going, why do they re-elect us time after time?"

"Because Zito is organized and they're not. I intend to get them organized and run Zito and anybody like him out of town."

"You won't even last as long as Judge Carter did," London told him. "You talk like a kid out of law school. This is no debating society. While you're running him out of town, what do you think Zito will be doing?"

"I know. They play for keeps. I've heard all about."

"Then remember it." The mayor opened the humidor on his desk, pulled out a cigar and bit off the end, spat it at the wastebasket. "You go through with this harebrained idea and you can count me out."

"You can count me out, too," Rita told him flatly.

The D.A. looked from the girl's face to her father and back. They returned the scrutiny coldly. "You really mean that!"

"I mean it more than anything I've ever said."

"Like telling me you love me?"

"More than anything." Her eyes roamed his face, looking for a softening of the grimness. "It's not too late to change your mind, Mal. We had so many plans, so many—"

"I wouldn't ask you to live with a man who turned his back on a thing like this. I couldn't even live with myself."

Rita caught her lower lip between her teeth, turned and ran from the room. Mal stared bleakly as she slammed the door behind her. He turned back to the little fat man.

"I'm sorry this is the way it has to be."

London nodded airily, chewed on the end of the cigar. "I've got an idea you're going to be a lot sorrier before this is finished."

"Don't bother to let me out. I know the way."

As he closed the door behind him, Mal had a last glimpse of Rita London standing in the gloom of the staircase, her red hair gleaming softly in the half light. He waited on the step for a moment on the chance she'd come to the door. When she didn't he sank his balled fists into his pockets and headed for the carport.

In the study, Ed London swabbed his bald pate with a handkerchief. He walked over to the portable bar, mixed himself a stiff scotch, drank it neat. Reluctantly he headed for the telephone, dialed a number.

A mild voice on the other end identified itself as belonging to Joey, Zito's right hand.

"Let me talk to Zito," London told him. "I just had Waters here."

"Just a minute."

There was a slight pause, then the fat, choked tones of Zito came through. "You got everything cleared away, Mr. Mayor?"

London swabbed at his forehead. "No. He was stubborn. Somebody's gotten to him."

"That old creep down at headquarters. Cleary. Waters was in his office earlier with that newspaper guy. So what they got to him? You're getting to him now. I don't want any trouble with this guy."

"He won't listen."

"Maybe that's because he's only got two holes for ears. Maybe if we put another ear in his head—"

"You can't. That would blow the town wide open." The mayor licked at his lips. "There must be another way, Zito. There mustn't be any more killings. We were lucky with Carter, but—"

"Maybe we ought to have a meet. There are a lot of things going on I don't like."

"Do you think it's wise? I mean—"

"I'm glad you asked what I think," the fat man told him quietly. "I was beginning to get the feeling you were starting to do the thinking. That's my department. We have the meet."

"When?"

"Tomorrow night. I'll send someone for you." There was a click as the receiver was hung up at the other end. London took the instrument from his ear, looked at it. Then he dropped it on its cradle, walked over to the bar and poured another stiff shot.

Chapter 9

Al Zito sprawled on the couch in his third-floor office, hands clasped across his middle. He regarded Mayor Ed London coldly.

"He's popping off," he said. "Even if he did have the nerve to try to knock Barney's place off, Barney'd know about it hours before he could do any damage. So all that happens is the D.A.'s raiders have a ride in the country. Maybe the air will do them good."

The mayor polished his shining pate with a wadded handkerchief. "It might be a good idea to close them down for a while, Al."

The fat man on the couch blew bubbles between his lips. "And have the boys think we've lost control? What do you think they pay protection for? They run, just like always. And they won't be bothered."

London shrugged, worked at a grin with halfhearted success. "I just thought—"

"Let me do the thinking. This Waters character, he won't get out of line. I'll see to that." He dropped his eyes, studied the dimples in his hands where the knuckles should have been. "He won't get out of line."

The mayor licked at his lips. "Look, Al, there can't be any more killing. It was a lucky thing for us Benson was around to take the blame for Judge Carter, but—"

The expressionless disks of the fat man's eyes rolled upward, fixed on the other man. "We don't leave things to luck. And I didn't say he was going to get hit. There are other ways to keep a guy in line."

London's head bobbed in agreement. "Sure, sure. Whatever you say."

Zito's eyes seemed to lose interest in the other man. "You got somebody in Waters' office you can trust?"

"His secretary."

"Make sure she contacts you if she hears anything about any raids." He sighed at the inevitability of motion, leaned forward, lifted a cigar from the humidor on the table near his elbow. He bit the end off, spat it at the wastebasket. "I'll handle it from headquarter's end. After a few dry runs they'll get tired." He clenched the cigar between his teeth, leaned back. "You got anything else you want to talk to me about?"

"Nothing pressing. But about election—"

"What about election?"

"Waters. Will he be on the slate?"

The fat man touched a match to the end of the cigar, inhaled a mouth full of smoke. "By election, Waters can't even get himself arrested. Leave that to me." He blew a feathery stream of smoke at the ceiling. "That kid of yours— she still fixing to marry this guy?"

"No. She kissed him off last night."

Zito nodded his satisfaction. "Good." He squinted at London through the smoke. "You know something? A newspaper publisher's got as good a chance to become governor as a D.A. Ever think of that?"

"Meaning?"

The fat man shrugged. "I'm tired of taking chances with amateurs. Max Everett tells me the other day he's got some ideas about going into politics."

"Ev?"

"Why not? He's got a built-in press support, am I right? With that sheet of his backing him up and us behind him, he could go places."

The mayor ran the tips of his fingers along the side of his chin thoughtfully. "I guess he could."

"He can," Zito assured him. "So that kid of yours shouldn't feel too bad about brushing off the boy scout. He's strictly nowhere—and she looks like a kid who wants somewhere."

London started to protest, shrugged. "She is ambitious," he conceded. "But

Everett's a lot older than Rita, and—"

"Look, I'm not making like a cupid. Just a tip to the wise. Max is on his way. Somebody wants to hitchhike, now's the time to get aboard. Just a tip to the wise."

"Thanks."

Zito rolled the cigar between pudgy fingers, nodded. "So we got nothing to worry about." He frowned as the phone on the desk started to peal. "Joey!" he called.

The door opened, and the baby-faced gunman crossed quickly to the phone. He lifted it to his ear, murmured a few monosyllabic acknowledgments, dropped the phone back on its hook. He looked from Zito to the mayor and back.

Zito nodded impatiently. "You can talk."

"That was headquarters. They're fixing to knock over Maurer's place tonight. After hours."

The fat man pulled his cigar from between his teeth, studied the soggy end. He pasted back a loose piece of tobacco with the tip of his tongue, replaced the cigar between his teeth.

"Your boy scout don't waste time," he grunted at the mayor. Without moving his head, he rolled his eyes to Joey. "Get Maurer on the phone. Tell him to get the girls out, clean out the gambling lay-out and close on the dot."

"For how long?"

A shrug disturbed the rolls of fat around Zito's jowls. "Tonight. Tomorrow night if they're going to play cops and robbers again we'll give him plenty of notice. If he don't hear, he can run."

He turned back to the mayor while Joey dialed. "Like I said, he can't even blow his nose without we know. Just the same, if he keeps giving us trouble, we have to take him."

London was suddenly aware of the beaded perspiration on his forehead and upper lips. He wiped it with the side of his hand. "But you said—"

"He don't get hit. But just the same he gets discouraged. Permanently." He took a puff on the cigar; the heavy lids veiled the eyes as he listened to Joey passing along the instructions to Barney Maurer.

The following morning Mal Waters stood in his office, stared dejectedly into the street below. Finally, he turned, shook his head.

"There had to be a leak, Stewart. Maurer was expecting us. That place never would have been that clean if he hadn't." He walked back to his desk, dropped into his chair. "Where do you figure it was? Cleary?"

The newspaper editor chewed on his pipe, shook his head. "Matt's more anxious to nail them than you are."

"No one else knew. Except him and his men, you and me." He reached for a cigarette, stuck it in the corner of his mouth.

"I don't figure it. Matt claims he can vouch for every one of his men." Stewart rattled the juice in the pipestem. "You sure you didn't tip your hand in any way?"

"I might have. I blew my stack with Ed London, told him I was going to clean up places like Barney Maurer's." He lit the cigarette, took a deep drag. "Maybe if we hit a couple of other spots—"

"Pass Maurer's up?"

"Just for the time being. We keep them off balance. We keep hitting one spot after another. When word gets out that Zito's protection is no good, maybe we can move in for the kill."

The editor smoked silently for a moment, shook his head. "Sounds too simple. What will Zito be doing all this time?"

"What can he do? I'm district attorney, and until the next election I continue to be district attorney. Maybe they can vote me out then with their machine, but in the meantime we may just be able to throw a couple of monkey wrenches into it."

"It's worth trying," Stewart said dubiously. "But let's make sure there's no chance of a leak. We'll arrange with Cleary not to tell anybody which joint we're going to hit until we're on our way."

Waters considered it, nodded. "Let's get a county map in here and you can mark off the areas where there's a spot running wide open." He jabbed at the button on the base of the phone, held it to his ear. "Get me a county map in here, Goldy. Then call Matt Cleary at"—he consulted a penciled notation on his pad—"Crestwood 7-2209 and ask him if he can come over here as soon as possible."

The receiver assented metallically. Mal dropped it back on its hook.

"Let's pick a couple of the smaller spots, places they won't think we're likely to bother." Waters took a last drag on his cigarette, crushed it out in the ash tray. "They'll have it figured out we'll hit the big places for headlines. The little guys can scream just as loud as the big guys and they hurt easier."

"Sounds logical," Stewart agreed.

The door opened, Goldy brought in a map of the county. "Where do you want it?"

"On the desk here." Mal cleared the desk, waited while the woman spread the map in front of him. She watched curiously while he flattened it out, studied it. Finally he looked up. "When Cleary gets here, send him on in, Goldy."

She accepted the dismissal, stalked from the room, slammed the door after her.

The newspaperman joined Mal at the desk, started pointing out areas with a stubby forefinger. By the time Matt Cleary walked into the office, a slow moving fog of blue smoke swirled near the ceiling, the map was heavily marked with penciled X's and Mal Waters had listed half a dozen locations on a yellow pad.

Briefly they explained their strategy to the police captain. He listened without comment, pounded away on the customary wad of gum, scowled in concentration. Finally he nodded. "Sounds all right," he grunted. "If there's no tip-off."

Mal looked up at him. "Meaning?"

"We looked pretty silly last night, busting into Barney Maurer's without a violation in sight. Maurer's already complained about me and I could face a departmental trial."

Stewart groaned. "Matt, I'm sorry. If I'm the cause of you losing your job and your pension—"

"You're not the cause of it, Lou." Cleary didn't take his eyes off Mal. "I knew the chances I was taking. But if I'm being set up—"

Waters slammed his pencil down on the desk top so hard it bounced. "You back singing that tired old song, Cleary? Don't you think I looked as foolish as you did? Do you think it does me any good to read stories like that one on the front page of the *World* this morning?"

"I don't know. It didn't seem to do you any harm."

"That's what you think."

"Be fair, Matt," Stewart counseled. "Mal has as much to lose as we have. Why should he tip them off?"

"Up to now there haven't been any leaks. All of a sudden an outsider decides to play ball with us—"

"And I'm the outsider," Mal grumbled.

The white-haired police captain nodded. "You're the outsider," he told him grimly. "You're also the one who suggested the raids that may make it possible for them to do what they've always wanted to do and never could: get enough on me to force me out of the job."

Mal raked his fingers through his hair in exasperation. "If they succeed in turning us against each other, we don't have a chance."

"I'm not so sure we do right now," Cleary told him.

"String along with me on this, Cleary," Mal urged him. "We'll hit a few spots, keep them off balance and then move in on Maurer's. If we can get the evidence on them, I promise you I'll use my office to smash the whole set-up."

Cleary stared at him for a moment, then looked at Stewart.

"I'm with Mal," the editor told him.

"All right, count me in." The captain moved closer to the desk, studied the notations, copied the information into his leather notebook.

For the next hour Captain Cleary called a group of picked men to take part in the raids. Arrangements were made for the raiders to meet at headquarters shortly after midnight. Destination of the various cars was to be contained in sealed orders to be opened en route. No man in any party was to leave the car or to make any contacts until the raids were accomplished.

Cleary dropped the receiver on the hook after his last call, leaned back in Mal's chair. "We're all set, Mr. D.A. I hope nothing goes wrong this time."

"Nothing can," Mal assured him. "We'll hit three spots tonight, serve notice that we mean business. From now on all raids will be made under sealed orders."

Stewart said, "That means only we three will know what spots are to be hit." The other men nodded.

At seven o'clock, Mal and the other two men walked through the outer office on their way to dinner.

"You'd better lock up, Goldy. I probably won't be in until late tomorrow. Cancel any of my appointments."

The bucktoothed secretary nodded, watched them go. She walked into Mal's office, tidied up his desk. She studied the county map curiously for a moment, switched off the desk light. On her way home, she made a telephone call.

That night, three places were raided, no evidence was uncovered in any of them. Barney Maurer's, which was not affected by the raids, ran wide open.

Chapter 10

The morning following the raids, Mal Waters sat dispiritedly behind his desk, jabbed disconsolately at his fingernails with the tip of his letter opener. He tried to keep his mind off the thinly veiled accusations Matt Cleary had hurled at him the night before after the fiasco. For the first time, Lou Stewart had seemed to share the police captain's suspicions of him.

It had all the earmarks of a tip-off. In all three of the places they had been expected. And yet only the three of them knew the places to be hit—Cleary, Stewart and himself. It was unthinkable that the police captain should sacrifice his future and his pension. Stewart had even less to gain by leaking the information. But each of the three places had been tipped off!

The telephone rang.

He debated the advisability of not answering it, realized wearily that he would have to face Ed London's wrath sooner or later. He snagged the receiver, held it to his ear.

The clipped tones of the mayor's secretary came through the receiver. "Mr. Waters, His Honor would appreciate it if you would find time to drop by his office."

"I'll be right up." Mal dropped the receiver back on its hook, swore at the supercilious bleached blonde bastard and her sarcastic, "If you would find time." From here on, if the administration had its way he'd have nothing but time.

He stuck a cigarette in the corner of his mouth, ambled through the outer office toward the executive elevator.

The blonde in the mayor's outer office eyed him with no show of enthusiasm. Peeking from her wastebasket was a copy of the morning edition of the *World* with a headline that read: *Urge Probe of District Attorney's Office Following Se-*

ries of Raids.

"You're to go right in."

She made no effort to get up from her chair to open the door as she had in the past.

Mal pushed through the door into the curiously quiet room. The mayor was seated at his desk, a scowl of annoyance on his face. He nodded curtly, busied himself with some papers until the D.A. had dropped into a chair. Finally he looked up.

"You've been making a bit of a fool out of yourself. And us."

The district attorney met the bald-headed man's glare, held it. "By doing the job the people elected me to do?"

"Nobody elected you to break in on lawful, legally licensed premises to harass the owners." Ed London filled himself a glass of water from a carafe on the corner of the desk. "I understand the *World* has evidence that these raids were part of a scheme to shake down operators." He didn't look up, replaced the top of the carafe. "It may even ask the appointment of a special prosecutor to investigate your office."

"Busy little man, your friend Everett."

London regarded him with thoughtful eyes. "Not nearly as busy as you." He held the glass to his lips, took a deep swallow. "I suppose you know your friend Cleary may be relieved of his command? He's under investigation." He set the glass down on the desk, leaned back and pursed his lips. "If your resignation were submitted, I'd be inclined to accept it."

"Why should I resign?"

London shrugged. "You might save all of us some embarrassment if you did."

"I'll bet I would." Waters got up, leaned on the desk. "Try firing me, Mr. Mayor, and you'll find out what embarrassment really is. And get your special prosecutor in here. Maybe I can help him."

The man behind the desk pasted a painful little smile on his lips. "Don't be so hasty. If you resign, you can still practice law and make yourself a living. Some place else. But if we have to put you out of the job, we may have to go all the way."

"It'll be interesting to see you try it. Remember, you once told me there were two kinds of people—that you prefer the kind who get behind you even though they have an angle. You wanted no part of the other kind, the do-gooders who are too lazy to vote people like you out of office. Don't underestimate them, Mr. Mayor. It takes a long time to get them roiled up, but when they are—look out!"

The mayor's lip curled contemptuously. "They're sheep. Sure, they can get roiled up. But they listen to the last one who gets their ear. Don't you ever forget that. I wouldn't count on them to do anything but turn on whoever's trying to help them."

"We'll see." Waters got out of his chair. "Is that all you wanted to see me about? To ask for my resignation?"

"Mostly. I'd also like to make it clear that Rita doesn't want to hear from you or see you."

"Rita hasn't told me that."

"She asked me to." He opened his top drawer, took out a ring, slid it across the desk. "She also asked me to tell you that you forgot this the other night."

Waters picked up the ring, rolled it between thumb and forefinger. "Like that, huh?"

"Like that." The mayor leaned back. "You had a chance few young fellows your age ever get. You blew it because of stubbornness. You might still be able to right things—"

"How? By blaming the whole thing on Cleary and Stewart? By crawling out from under and promising your Al Zito to be good?"

"Don't bring Zito's name into this!" London snapped.

"Why? Am I supposed to genuflect when I say his name?" Waters sneered at the man behind the desk. "Tell Zito this for me. I'm not asking anybody to take the rap for what I've done. And tell him another thing—anything I start, I finish."

He turned, headed for the door.

"Waters!"

Mal stopped with his hand on the knob. "You've had your warning. Keep stepping on people's toes and there's nobody can help you."

Waters pulled the door open, slammed it after him. The cool blonde in the outer office eyed him unsympathetically as he headed for the double doors that led to the corridor beyond.

Goldy wasn't at her desk as he re-entered his own office. He started for the inner room, decided to check her pad for possible calls that had came in during his absence. There were no notations on the pad bearing today's date. He was about to turn away when two penciled numbers caught his eye. One, Crestwood 7-2209, was the number he'd given her to reach Cleary. Below it, the other number, Island 6-2230, was equally familiar.

It should have been. It was his fiancée's number. It was also the home phone of the mayor. And there was no reason for Goldy to have it, since it was unlisted.

He decided against questioning her about it, walked through into his room. He was seated behind his desk, chain-lighting a fresh butt when Goldy stuck her head into his office.

"I had to run out for a few minutes. I didn't think you'd be back so quickly."

Waters nodded. "It's okay."

She brushed her hair from her forehead, tucked it behind her ear. "Pretty bad?"

Mal grinned weakly. "Bad enough." He crushed out the spent butt in the ash tray. "Try to reach Lou Stewart at the *Star* and Matt Cleary. I think you have his number?"

Goldy nodded.

"Tell them I'd like to have a meeting here at about four this afternoon."

"Don't you think—" The woman broke off, frowned.

"What?"

"With all the heat that's on, don't you think you ought to kind of lay low? All Cleary and Stewart can bring you is grief."

Mal considered it. "That's probably what Zito and his boys will think too. So tonight we're going to hit them again. Only this time they won't be expecting it." He took a deep drag on the cigarette, blew twin streams through his nostrils. "See to it that Cleary and Stewart are here."

Goldy looked unhappy as she closed the door behind her.

Mal Waters pushed through the doors leading to the city room of the *Star*, which appeared to be in the state of semi-animation that afflicts a city room between editions.

Desks were scattered around the room in organized confusion, on them scraps of copy paper, crumpled newspapers, typewriters of varying vintages, telephones that had lost their luster.

A few men in shirtsleeves, their coats over the backs of chairs, were pecking away at typewriters, calling out periodically for the copy boys who were scooting between the desks picking up copy and distributing proofs.

At other desks men were sitting back, drinking coffee out of soggy cardboard containers or just staring ahead, organizing their thoughts for the follows they were to write on stories they'd already done for the early editions. Four copy men were working on the rim and two in the slot slashing copy down to size.

Mal Waters picked his way through the desks, headed for the frosted glass door in the rear stenciled *Editor*. He knocked, but when there was no response he decided the knock couldn't be heard above the general confusion, so he turned the knob and pushed the door open.

Lou Stewart sat behind his unpainted desk, studied a still wet proof of a headline. He looked up, recognized Mal Waters with no show of enthusiasm.

"What do you want?" he growled. He held up the headline so Mal could read it. It said in 48-point type:

CLEARY, VETERAN COP, FACES SUSPENSION FOLLOWING RAIDS ON SUSPECTED PREMISES

He scowled at Mal. "That what you came for? To get a few laughs?"

Waters closed the door behind him. "You know I feel as badly about Cleary as you do." He walked toward the desk, hooked a straight wooden chair with his toe, pulled it close to the desk. "It might make you feel better to know I've been asked to resign, too."

"But of course you won't," the editor sneered. "Look, I'm busy. Why don't you find some place else to gloat. You've done what your boss wanted done, now beat it." He crumpled the proof angrily, tossed it at the oversized wastebasket at his elbow. "If I were ten years younger—"

"If you were ten years younger, maybe you wouldn't be giving up so easily," Mal spat at him. "So they take the first few tricks. Now it's our turn."

"Look, don't press it. You've put Cleary out of the job and—"

"I didn't leak that information. My secretary did," Waters told him. "I just found out she called the mayor. He must have tipped Zito."

"What's the difference, whether you did it or your secretary did it? We look like fools and we have no defense."

"That's our strong card. We look like such damn fools." Mal leaned forward. "Now that we know where the leak is, we can capitalize on it." Before the editor could interrupt, he hurried on. "Remember the stunt the British pulled, feeding the Nazis information that they were going to hit one place and pulling them off balance so they could hit another?"

Some of the anger drained from Stewart's face. "You mean the 'Man Who Never Was'?"

"Right. They took a body, dressed it in uniform and put a lot of plans on it so the Nazis would find it. German Intelligence thought they had the blueprint for the invasion, got up a welcoming committee. At the wrong place."

The man behind the desk studied him thoughtfully. "It just might work," he conceded.

"It will!" Waters insisted. "We're supposed to have a meeting at my office at four. Have you gotten word?"

"I didn't take the call."

"Call back. Say you'll be there. Have Cleary with you. We'll lay out a plan to raid three places on the east end of the county. Maurer won't be expecting trouble and we'll crack down like a ton of bricks."

Stewart ran the tips of his fingers along the stubble on his beard. "Maurer's, eh? That would be worth cracking!" He stared at Waters for a moment, nodded. "I'm game to take one more chance."

"Good. Then I'll expect the two of you at my office at four. We'll discuss plans for the east end of the county but the sealed instructions will call for Maurer's. Ask Cleary to trust me just this once."

Stewart nodded. He got up, stuck his hand across the desk. "For all our sakes, I hope this time it works."

Chapter 11

The king-sized doorman lounged on the steps leading to Barney Maurer's. Beyond, the parking lot was filled almost to capacity. He ambled to the door of the coupé as it pulled up to the entrance.

As he reached the driver's side of the car, the muzzle of a .45 stared him in the face.

"I wouldn't try to get near any warning signal," Captain Cleary told him in a gentle voice. "When my friend gets out of the car, you'll get in and drive this to the parking lot like any ordinary car."

"What is this?" the doorman wanted to know. "A heist?"

"Even more surprising. A raid," Cleary told him.

The doorman waited obediently while a man got out on the far side of the car, then slid in alongside the white-haired police captain. As the coupé moved away toward the parking lot, a large sedan pulled up, disgorged four men. Mal Waters stood on the steps waiting for them.

"Everything set?" he wanted to know.

One of the men from the sedan nodded. "Four more are hitting the back entrance through the kitchen."

The five men walked slowly up the steps into the lobby of Barney Maurer's. They waited for a signal from Waters. As four men came from the kitchen, herding the kitchen help before them, Waters gave the signal.

"This is a raid, ladies and gentlemen. Nobody is to move."

The men with him pulled their guns. Between them and the men from the kitchen, the entire floor was covered. No one offered any resistance. Within an hour police vans had arrived to cart away the employees; guests had been questioned, required to provide identification, allowed to go. Captain Matt Cleary personally supervised the smashing of the equipment in the game room.

It made up for the frustration of the previous series of dry runs.

Al Zito got his first word of the raid an hour after it had been carried out, in the form of an aggrieved telephone call from Barney Maurer who had been booked in an outlying precinct. A friendly desk sergeant had made the call possible.

"What do you mean you got knocked over?" Zito growled. "Those boy scouts were supposed to be on the other side of the county."

"All I know is they busted up my place, scared hell out of my customers and tossed me into a cell," Maurer told him heatedly. "You told me it was okay to run."

"We'll make it up to you," Zito promised. "Sit tight. I'll have you out of there in a half hour. I'm sending Joey for you. I want to get this straightened out tonight." He dropped the receiver on its hook, turned to a waiting Joey. "Get London on the phone. Tell him they've got Maurer in the Glenwood precinct. I want him out right away. I don't care who signs the papers, I want them signed. Then tell London I want him here within an hour."

The fat man settled himself in his chair, spent the next twenty minutes on the phone.

When Ed London walked into the office, his first impression was that Zito had been jammed into the huge chair behind the desk. The fat man made no sign of greeting when the mayor walked in, followed by Joey, and sat down.

"How did it happen?" he wanted to know.

London's face gleamed wetly. "I don't know any more about it than you do, Al. Mal's secretary called to tell me they were getting set to hit the three spots in the eastern end of the county. How'd I know—?"

"They smashed Barney Maurer's place up. You know that?"

The mayor swabbed at his damp face. "They must have gotten wise to Goldy. Planted the phony information—"

"You should have guessed that before now. Maurer's on his way over here. We're stopping this D.A. right now." He looked inquisitively at Joey when a knock sounded at the door. Joey opened it a few inches, turned.

"Mr. Everett."

Zito nodded, waited until the publisher was in the room.

"You heard?"

"Got word from one of my district men. He followed the patrol wagon out. Says they busted hell out of the joint." He eyed Ed London. "Maurer carries a lot of weight in the county, Ed."

The mayor sighed, nodded.

"I told you that guy was no good," the publisher growled. "We should have dumped him last election and—"

"We're dumping him now," Zito told him. "And we're not waiting for any election to do it."

Everett looked from the fat man to London and back. "It could be dangerous, Zito. If anything happens to Waters this soon after he pulls a successful raid, there could be a lot of heat."

Zito's eyes were tiny black marbles, almost lost behind the puffy balls of fat. "There'll be a lot more heat unless we hit back fast." His voice was blubbery, as though choked by the heaviness of his jowls and chin. "Maurer was operating with the okay of the Syndicate. That means he had a right to keep operating." He swung his chair around, slid open a panel that disguised a built-in bar and refrigerator. "Use a drink?"

London nodded. "Sure could." He watched the fat man snag a bottle, some glasses and ice, deposit them on the desk top.

"It's definite, this business of him and your daughter breaking off, London?" He dumped some ice into each of the glasses, spilled whisky over them.

London nodded.

Zito looked up from the glasses to the publisher. "How about giving that a play in your paper, Ev? It's news, ain't it? Mayor's daughter kisses off the D.A. Gives him his ring back. Maybe on account of other women, eh?"

"Now, wait a minute—" London started to protest.

"You don't like the way I'm doing it? You've got an idea?" Zito asked him coldly. He stared down the mayor, turned his attention back to Everett. "Maybe that's the reason he knocked over Barney Maurer's, eh? He was sore because one of Barney's girls had given him the go-by. That a good story?"

Everett walked over to the desk, picked up a glass, swirled the whisky around the side. "Pretty tricky. Might have a tough time proving it."

"That's my job."

Everett shrugged. "I can handle the rest of it. When do you want it to run?"

"Tomorrow's paper."

The publisher whistled softly, checked his watch. "We can't make the early edition. Might catch the late one." He took a deep swallow from his glass. "I'll handle it personally. Anything else you need me for?"

The fat man puffed out his overripe lips, shook his head. "Not right now. But I think there'll be a big story for you. Pretty soon. I'll let you know. In plenty of time."

Everett drained his glass, set it down. "I'll be waiting for it." He looked over to where Ed London sat. "As long as the engagement's off, any objection to my calling on Rita?"

London shook his head. "She's a big girl now. She makes up her own mind."

"I'll do the best I can with that story on Waters, Al. It might take the wind out of the *Star's* sails on the Maurer arrest." He nodded to London, jammed his hat on his head, left.

"Have your drink. You look like you need it," Zito told the mayor.

They were still in that position, Zito squeezed into the oversized chair behind the desk, London sprawled on the couch, damp-faced, white, when an indignant Barney Maurer walked in. He looked from the mayor to Zito and back.

"What the hell goes, Al? I'm not paying the kind of ice I pay to have my joint knocked over and me locked up."

"You're out, aren't you?" Zito growled. He picked up the bottle, spilled a potent shot into one of the glasses. "Have a drink."

The nightclub operator glared at him for a minute, tossed the drink off neat. He picked up the bottle, refilled his glass. "Who makes good for the damage?"

"Don't worry about it."

"I am worrying about it, goddam it! They smashed the hell out of all my equipment—"

"I said don't worry about it." Zito hadn't raised his voice but there was a new hard note in it.

Maurer took a swallow from his glass. "You can't blame me for being mad, Al. In the old days—"

"These aren't the old days," Zito told him. "We got to keep the killing down until the heat's off."

"You mean this monkey walks away from this?" He swung on London. "How about him? He takes our money, promises we can run, then he okays a do-gooder like this Waters to raise all kinds of hell."

London licked at his lips. "How could I know? I thought he could be handled."

"He can." Zito leaned back, laced his pudgy fingers across his middle. "You told me you offered Waters a looker the night he looked your place over. Which one?"

"Bonnie. You know, the kid who hustles butts."

"Nice piece of material. He didn't buy?"

"I could have told you he wouldn't," London broke in. "He's not a chaser. You'll never pin him that way. I ought to know."

"Where's she live?" Zito asked.

Maurer shrugged. "I don't know offhand. I can find out."

"Find out and get the information over to Joey. I'll have him drop by and have a talk with some of her neighbors or whoever runs the place." He rolled his eyes over to London. "Make it fit in with the story Everett's running. This plaster saint of a D.A. of ours has been playing house with the cigarette girl at the joint he knocked over."

London swabbed at his face. "I still don't buy it."

"You will." He turned back to Maurer. "Let me know when she's got him coming up there. I have some arrangements to make."

Chapter 12

Mal reread the story in the *World*, crumpled the paper angrily and threw it at the wastebasket. For the fourth time he dialed Rita London's number in an attempt to get from her a denial that she had given the paper so distorted an account of their break-up. The redhead still refused to accept the call. He gave up in disgust, slammed the receiver down on its hook. Angrily he picked the paper out of the basket, smoothed it out on his desk top. He read the item again:

> ...although the mayor's daughter refused to comment, it has been a matter of common knowledge in City Hall circles that she and her fiancée have had numerous differences of opinion because of his back street activities with an employee of Barney Maurer's roadhouse. The return of his ring and the apparently retaliatory raid on Maurer's is rumored to have followed an ultimatum by the roadhouse operator to leave the girl alone....

Once more he crumpled the paper into a ball and flung it into the basket. He reached for the phone, dialed 216, the police department's R and I section.

"Lieutenant Davidson, R and I," the receiver chirped back at him.

"This is Waters, Dave. I want some information." He picked up a cigarette, tapped it on the edge of the desk. "Confidential."

There was a slight pause. "Sure, Mr. Waters. If I've got it."

"All nightclub employees are fingerprinted and on file. Is that right?"

"Yes, sir."

Waters stuck the cigarette in the corner of his mouth. "I want the present address of a girl working in Barney Maurer's place. Her name is Bonnie Peters. She's a cigarette girl there."

"It might take a little while."

"Rush it." Waters dropped the receiver on its hook, picked up a paper pack of matches, lit one. He blew out the spent match, flipped it at the basket.

The door to the outer office opened, Goldy stuck her head in. "Stewart from the *Star* is on the extension. You want to take it?"

Waters picked up the phone, punched at a button on its base.

"Mal? Lou Stewart."

"Yeah, Lou?"

"See the story in the opposition this morning?"

Waters grunted. "I've seen it."

"Looks like they're out to nail you. I can't quite figure the angle, but it looks like a set-up."

"To me, too. I can't reach Rita so I'm going to do the next best thing. I'm trying to get in touch with Maurer's cigarette girl."

"She the one they're referring to?"

"Must be. Maurer introduced her to me the night I was out there. Practically offered me a due bill on her."

"Be careful, Mal. Those boys play rough. Anything I can do?"

"Not yet. But if I can persuade her to talk, maybe you can put some space aside for me."

The dry chuckle came across the wire. "You got it. When do you expect to see her?"

"As soon as R and I comes up with an address. I'll be in touch."

"Right."

Waters dropped the receiver on its hook, took a last drag on his cigarette, crushed it out. He got up from his chair, wandered over to the window, stared down into the street below.

It was over a half hour before he heard from R and I.

He crossed the room in four steps at the first peal of the phone. "Yeah?"

"This is Davidson, Mr. Waters. I have that information."

Mal picked up a pencil. "Let's have it."

"Bonnie Peters, Sherbrooke Apartments on Cherokee. Apartment 408."

Waters jotted the information on the top sheet of his pad, tore it off, folded it up. "Thanks, Dave." He stuck the folded sheet in his pocket. "And, Dave—"

"Yes, sir?"

"Nobody has to know I wanted this."

"I understand."

The D.A. dropped the receiver back on its hook. He jabbed at a button on the base. After a moment the door opened, Goldy stuck her head in.

"If anybody calls, I'll be back about four."

The woman frowned. "Any place I can reach you?"

He shook his head. "No place."

The Sherbrooke Apartments turned out to be an old stone building on a side street off the Square. Its façade was dirty and neglected looking. Inside the lobby was dingy, lightless and dusty. A couple of discouraged-looking rubber plants had been placed around it in an attempt at decoration, half a dozen unsafe looking chairs were scattered around in an abortive attempt to make it cozy.

Mal Waters crossed the napless rug toward a self-service elevator in the rear of the lobby. Behind the desk at the right, an old man in a dark jacket dabbed at rheumy eyes with a wadded handkerchief. He watched Waters' progress across the lobby with no show of curiosity.

Mal entered the elevator, pushed the button marked 4. The ancient cage wheezed and jerked its way to the fourth floor. Room 408 was at the end of the corridor. The D.A. knocked on the door, waited.

After a moment, the door opened, the face of the cigarette girl appeared. Her eyes widened when she recognized the D.A. She tried to close the door, but she had delayed too long. Mal pushed his way in, closed the door after him.

"You'd better get out of here, mister, before you get me in a lot of trouble."

Mal grinned at her. "Why should I get you in trouble? Maurer said you were supposed to be nice to me."

The girl backed away from him. "That was before. Now you're poison. I can't afford to be seen with you." She looked down at the clinging dressing gown she was wearing which concealed little more than the brief costume she wore at the club. "Anyway you ought to give a girl some warning."

"It's not a social call, Bonnie."

She stared at him fearfully. "Look, Mr. Waters, if you've got something against Barney, don't drag me into it.

"You're already in it."

She shook her head. "I can't help you. I can't even help myself. Don't get me in any deeper."

"All I want you to do is tell me what you know about Marcy Lewis's connection with Maurer and any other cops Maurer has on his payroll."

She shook her head. "I don't know anything."

Waters ignored the interruption. "Maurer has a whole string of county cops and officials on his payroll. It's worth a lot to me to get a line on who they are."

Bonnie continued to shake her head.

Mal reached out for her arm, she shrank away from him. "Listen to me, Bonnie. Maurer and Zito are finished in this town. So are the Marcy Lewises and the other grafters. I'm giving you a chance to get on the winning side before—"

"You don't understand. I can't help you. Even if I wanted to, I can't."

"What have they got on you?"

Some of the color drained from the girl's face. "N-Nothing."

"They must have. Otherwise you'd jump at the chance I'm giving you to walk away from this whole mess clean."

The blonde turned, walked back to a coffee table set in front of the shabby couch. She reached down, snagged a cigarette. "You're a little late for that." She scratched a match, touched it to the cigarette. "So don't ask me anything. No matter what you do to me, I can't help you."

Mal scowled, tossed his hat at the couch. He watched the girl smoke with short, nervous puffs. "You've got me wrong. I don't intend to hurt you. I want to help you."

The blonde swung around, faced him. "Why should you?"

"Because you can help me."

"You want me to tell you everything I know about Marcy Lewis and Zito? You think they'd let me get away with it?"

"What could they do? Kill you?"

She took a deep drag on the cigarette, let the smoke escape through half-parted lips. "Worse than that."

The D.A. squinted at her. "Worse than that? What?"

Bonnie walked to the windows, pulled back the curtain, looked down through the dust-streaked window. "I come from a small town. A real small town. My mother and father are still alive. My sisters still live there. Everybody in town knows them and respects them."

"So?"

She dropped the curtain, turned to face him. "A couple of years ago, when I first came here, I got into trouble. Real messy trouble. Marcy Lewis has a whole file on it in his office."

"And they're holding that over your head? Why didn't you leave town?"

Bonnie smiled mirthlessly. "You know what he'd do? He'd swear out a warrant for me on charges of prostitution and send it to my home town. It would kill my people. Now do you understand?"

Mal reached down, helped himself to a cigarette. He tapped it on the back of his hand. "I didn't know."

"Well, now you do. And now you know why I can't help you."

Mal stuck the cigarette in the corner of his mouth. "Suppose that file no longer existed?"

Bonnie shrugged. "Why wish for the moon? It does. And as long as it does, I do what Maurer and Lewis want me to do."

Waters touched a match to the cigarette, took a deep drag, squinted at her through the smoke. "You didn't answer my question. Suppose the file no longer existed?"

"Ask me then."

"I'm asking you now." Mal studied the girl. "You want that file, I want that information. I'll make you a deal. You get what I want, I'll get what you want."

"I—I don't know. I—"

Mal grinned at her. "You'll never get a better offer."

"But if it doesn't work? If you can't get the file?"

"I'm the district attorney. I'll get it."

Bonnie crossed her arms across her breasts, massaged the backs of her arms with her palms. The cigarette dangled forgotten in the corner of her mouth. "If I could only believe it."

"You can."

The girl walked back to the couch, took the cigarette from her mouth, crushed it out. She rubbed the flat of her hand across her eyes, debated the advisability of the plan. Finally she looked up at Waters.

"It's a big risk. If it goes wrong, I'm in terrible trouble." She chewed on her lower lip uncertainly.

"It can't go wrong."

"All right. I'll take a chance. What do you want me to do?"

"I want to know the name of every cop and county official who hangs out in Maurer's and—"

"I can do better than that."

"What?"

She licked at her lips. "Barney keeps records. I know because I've been in his office when he added names to the list. I might be able to get that for you."

"That's even better. Tell me where he keeps it, and—"

The blonde shook her head. "It would be better if I got it for you. You'd never get past the guards on the grounds. They're used to seeing me come and go."

Mal studied her face. "It's a big risk."

"It's for big stakes."

"When?"

"The sooner the better. Tonight?"

"You think you can do it tonight?"

She nodded. "Can you get what I want by then?"

"Yes."

"All right. Where do we meet?"

Mal considered. "You wouldn't want to come to my office?"

"They know more about what goes on there than you do."

"Probably. You have any ideas?"

"Do you know the old Saw Mill Road on the north side of town?"

Mal grinned. "We used to call it Lovers' Lane. That the one?"

"I can be there by midnight."

"It's a date." The D.A. reached for his hat. "If for any reason you can't make it, call me. Don't leave any name. Just say the date is canceled."

The girl nodded. She watched him with clouded eyes as he crossed to the door, walked out. For the first time in years, she saw a way to break Marcy Lewis's hold on her.

At a quarter to twelve, Mal Waters guided his car along the rutted road that led to the parking field. There was only one other car parked there tonight. Mal drove to the edge of the field, cut his motor, turned off his lights. He watched the other car. After a moment, the lights flicked on and off. He picked up a package from the seat alongside him, pushed open his door. He took a last drag on his cigarette, flipped it out into the darkness. It cut an orange-colored arc through the black, ascending slowly, then gathered speed as it descended, shattering into a myriad of pinpoint sparks as it hit the ground.

He started across the short space that separated the two cars, could make out the form of the girl in the other car. She was alone. He was only dimly aware of the sweet scent of the grass, the rustling of the leaves. Suddenly he stopped, all senses alert. He started to swing around. He heard rather than felt the blow that hit him. There was a hissing rush of sound from behind. He tried to fall away from the blow. It hummed like a bumblebee, exploded on the side of his head with the blinding brilliance of a flare. He was dizzily aware of a sinking sensation, then the ground came up and hit him in the face.

The door to the other car opened, a white-faced Bonnie Peters ran over. She reached down, picked up the envelope Mal had dropped, looked through it, then up at Maurer and Joey. "It's all here. This is mine now. You promised."

Maurer grinned at her. "It's all yours." He reached into his pocket for his lighter, flipped it into flame, held it out. "Want to make sure nobody ever finds it again?"

She held the corner of the envelope into the flame, watched it consumed with all its contents. When it was nothing but ash, she dropped it to the ground, crushed it into dust with her foot. "Thanks, Barney."

The big man shook his head, lifted the carnation in his buttonhole to his nose. "A deal is a deal, baby. When you tipped us off what this creep was up to, I promised to take care of you, didn't I? I never break a promise."

Chapter 13

It seemed as if endless time had passed before consciousness came knocking at Mal Waters' skull. There was an acrid odor of gasoline and another odor, one he subconsciously knew he should recognize. He tried to remember where it had been that he smelled it, but the blinding flashes of pain drove all consecutive thought before it.

From somewhere close came the sound of voices. Waters fought to get his eyes open, finally succeeded. The familiar odor was stronger now. He wrestled vaguely with the memory, evoked a picture of the girl whose apartment was his last memory. It was a scent associated with that apartment and that girl. He tried to move, but some heavy weight pinned him down. He called out to the owners of the voices he heard, was surprised by the weakness of his voice.

One of the voices came closer, a note of surprise in it. "Hey, Jim. The guy's alive. I just heard him. We better get him out."

The D.A. was aware of a lot of activity outside where he was, then suddenly what had pinned him down was off him. He realized for the first time that he had been pinned behind the wheel of a car. Rough hands caught him under the arms and dragged him into the open.

He understood why the odor of the girl's perfume had been so strong. The object that had pinned him against the wheel was the smashed body of Bonnie Peters, a woman who in life had been beautiful, but in death was a grotesquely shattered doll.

He tottered dizzily, steadied himself against the car and looked around. The car had half climbed a tree, its windshield and grill shattered by what must have been a terrific impact. He wiped his mouth with the back of his hand, struggled to keep his eyes from the dead girl. The men who had dragged him out of the car stood watching him incuriously. They were dressed in the uniform of county sheriff's deputies.

"Got a cigarette?" Waters croaked.

The shorter of the two deputies, a squat, red-faced man dug into his blouse pocket, came up with a pack. He held it out to the D.A. "You sure sobered up in a hurry, friend."

Waters waited until he had the cigarette going, drew a lungful of smoke, let it out slowly. "I've been sober right along."

The second deputy grinned crookedly. "Sure. That tree just up and ran into your jalopy. Ain't that it, mister?"

"I wasn't drunk."

"Not drunk?" the short deputy snorted. "Then you must bleed a hundred proof. Get a smell of yourself."

Waters sniffed. The front of his shirt and jacket were saturated with liquor. "Somebody went to a lot of trouble to set up this picture. With a frame to match, And I'm sitting front-row-center."

The tall deputy grunted. "Sure. It's a Communist plot, no doubt." He walked over to where the girl's body lay sprawled on the grass, pulled down her skirt. "She might've been a real dish once, but that tree sure made hash out of her." He reached into the wrecked car, found a short bolero jacket, covered her face with it.

Waters turned his back, tottered over to the police car, leaned against the fender. His head was still spinning but his brain was beginning to come back to life. He had walked into a trap, and the girl had been the lure. The accident had accomplished two things—it had set him up as a drunken driver, guilty of at least vehicular homicide, and it had removed the only witness to the fact that it was a frame-up. He wondered if he had been intended to walk away from it.

A searing flash of pain shot through his head and he identified it as the screech of a siren. After a moment a car with red headlights skidded to a stop behind the patrol car. Another car roared up behind it, pulled to a stop in the rear.

The short beefy cop walked over to the car with the red lights, gave a report in a low voice. The door to the car opened and Captain Marcy Lewis stepped out. He walked over to the body, pulled the bolero from the dead face, stared at it bleakly. A man carrying a camera hopped out of the rear car, started snapping pictures of the wreck and the dead girl's body. Lewis held the bolero for a few moments, then re-covered the face and walked over to Waters. He did a double take when he recognized the district attorney. The cameraman trotted at his heels.

"You Waters?" Lewis grunted.

A light bulb popped in back of him, the cameraman busily reloaded.

"It's a frame, Lewis. I was sapped and—"

"Smell him, Cap," the cameraman hooted. He leveled the camera, another bright flash seared Waters' brain. "The guy who sapped him was the bartender who didn't eighty-six him."

"Better get in my car. I'll drive you to your office," the homicide man grunted. He made no effort to restrain the cameraman from taking a shot from another angle that included Waters, the wrecked car and the dead girl. The last shot the cameraman got was of Lewis helping the D.A. into the police car.

Mal Waters slumped in his desk chair, stared around his office bleakly. Captain Marcy Lewis stood at the window smoking, staring down into the street below. Neither spoke.

Lewis turned at the sound of the door opening, nodded to Mayor Ed London as he bustled in. The ever-present smile was missing from the mayor's face, a dull red suffused his face. Behind him, Max Everett chewed on the inevitable unlighted cigar. He carried a large manila envelope with him, walked over, dropped it on the desk.

"You take a good picture, Mr. D.A.," he grunted.

Ed London dropped into the chair across the desk from Waters, dug a handkerchief from his pocket, swabbed at his bald spot. "This is quite a mess, Mal. Quite a mess." He looked over to where Marcy Lewis stood. "I don't think we have to keep you, Marcy. I'll be responsible for Mal."

Lewis nodded, crossed the room and left. As soon as the door had closed behind him, London turned back to Waters. "If you didn't have friends, boy, this could spell the end of your career. You know that, don't you?"

Mal squinted at him. "What friends?"

"Me. Ev here." The mayor indicated the newspaperman. "Take a look at what he's willing to kill. Any paper in the state would give their right arm for shots like that." The D.A. reached over, dumped the contents of the envelope on the desk. There were five glossies, still damp. The camera had caught the scene at the wreck with disconcerting clarity. The smashed body of the girl, the bedraggled condition of Waters, the last damning touch of him being escorted into the police car.

"So Mr. Everett is willing to kill the story. How about Lewis—and the deputies? They were there."

London looked from the D.A. to the newspaperman and back. "They'll do what they're told."

"Like I should have done, huh?"

"Like you're going to do from now on," Everett told him from around the cigar clenched between his teeth.

Waters leaned back in his chair, raked his fingers through his hair. "And that's the price for walking away from this mess. How about the girl? Doesn't she matter? Or hasn't it occurred to you that a girl is on a slab in the morgue?"

"Take a look at the pictures and see who put her there," the newspaperman told him. "Don't go preaching a sermon to me. I'm not covering up because I've got any special love for you, Waters. But I'm playing ball because I'm part of a team. That's something you ought to learn."

"Part of a team? The whole rotten mess is one team. The police close their eyes to wide-open gambling and prostitution. The tax collector gives the joints below the Line special deals on taxes because they're owned by friends of the team. Other friends get the city contracts and go through the motions of paving roads and putting up buildings that a decent contractor wouldn't have his name on. But it's all done for the team—"

London put his hand up. "Just a minute, Mal. You're in no position to complain. The team's willing to go to bat for you. It's not a question of right or wrong. It's the way things are done. And, Mal—teamwork is a two-way street."

"So I have to play ball. Is that it?"

The mayor swabbed at his pate again, shrugged. "That's it."

Waters looked from the mayor to the newspaperman and back. "And if I say I want to fight this thing—prove that I was framed?"

"You wouldn't get it off the ground," Everett sneered at him. "Do you know what the so-called decent people that you're being such a hero for would do? They'd do what they're told to do. They'd do everything but lynch you."

"Mal, grow up," London pleaded. "I tell you, this is the way things are done. We all make compromises. I have to. So do you."

The D.A. shook his head. "I don't believe it."

"Nobody gives a damn what you believe," Everett pulled the cigar from between his teeth, pointed it at the man behind the desk. "You'll do what you're told or I'll personally crucify you. And if you don't think I can—"

"I think maybe you can," Waters told him calmly. "I think maybe you can. But I'm beginning to realize something I kept my eyes closed to. I think the first time I realized it was in Korea. Know what that is?"

"It's too late to wear your medals."

"I realized that I'm not very important. Except maybe to me. If I've got to go, my job is to take as many with me as I can. Maybe you will get me. But by the time I'm through things will be changed. The people you sneer at so much, the decent people, take a long time to get wise. But when they do, buddy, watch out."

"Mal, you're talking crazy. That stuff is all right in books. But this is no book. This is real. Goddam real." There was a note of desperation in Ed London's voice. His face gleamed with perspiration. "They'll get you. Don't ever think they won't. But they don't want to. They want to make a deal. You lay off and they'll lay off. Mal, you've got to think it over." He eyed the man behind the desk anxiously. "Even if you got them, there'd be others. Somebody always leads, others follow. And the leaders take the gravy. That's the story of the world, Mal. You can't fight it. You're crazy if you try."

Mal studied the fat man's face for a moment. "Your history's a little ragged, Mr. Mayor. Sure—there's always someone to lead. Caesar, Nero, Hitler, Mussolini. And the rest followed. But then something happens. The little guys, the followers, get tired of these leaders running things their way. And when the big guys laugh at them and ignore them, the little guys take things into their own hands. That's what's going to happen here."

Everett stalked to the desk, stuffed the pictures back into their envelope. "We're wasting our time with this jerk, London." He held the envelope under Mal's nose. "You'll see these on the front pages tomorrow, Waters. Then we'll see how your little guys stand up for you."

"One minute, Ev. Mal, change your mind. Before it's too late."

The man behind the desk stared at him wordlessly.

Everett stiff-legged it to the door, held it open. "You coming, London?"

The fat man sighed, nodded. He pulled himself to his feet. He looked sick as he walked to the door. Everett stood with his hand on the knob, sneered at Waters. "A goddam boy scout." He slammed the door behind him.

Mal Waters sat in his chair for a long time, watching the closed door.

Chapter 14

Lou Stewart sat behind his cluttered desk in the editorial office of the *Star* and stared at the front page of the rival *World* with stricken eyes.

A scare headline dominated a front page that was crowded with pictures:

D.A. IN DRUNKEN ACCIDENT; SHOWGIRL DIES IN CRASH

The pictures of the girl's body, the wrecked car, the apparently drunken Mal Waters and Captain Marcy Lewis escorting him into the patrol car took up the rest of the page alongside a two-column story of the accident. The story implied that responsible citizens of Jackson City, disgusted with their district attorney's antics, were preparing to demand his resignation.

Stewart pushed the button on the base of his phone.

"I know, I know," the voice on the other end told him before he had a chance to talk. "I'll be right in."

Stewart had his pipe going by the time Tom Harley walked in. The city editor's eyes fastened on the heavy black of the opposition's headline. "Quite a one to muff, chief."

"Yeah. Quite a one. Why?"

Harley shrugged. "He wasn't booked, his name wasn't on the blotter. Not when our man looked at it anyway."

"How'd the *World* get it?"

"I don't know. But I can guess." He walked over to where a water cooler was humming noisily, helped himself to a cup full of water. "Someone knew the D.A. was going to be in a wreck and that someone arranged for a *World* photographer to be on deck."

Stewart rattled the juice in his pipestem. "That would mean a deliberate frame." He watched the city editor drain the paper cup, crush it into a ball and throw it at the wastebasket. "I thought you were the guy who said Waters was in the mob up to his neck?"

"So I was wrong. The way things looked I had a right to call it that way. But then when he proved he was a stand-up guy I started to change my mind. This frame—"

"If it was a frame."

"It's a frame, chief. The reason the *World* got that story exclusively is because they wanted to give your boy Waters time to make a deal." He waved a hand at the headlines. "He didn't make the deal."

"Those boys really play rough." Stewart chewed on the stem of the briar thoughtfully. "Marcy Lewis was the cop who took the call to make sure there were no leaks." He thought about it, liked it. "I think you called it, Harley. But I don't know what we can do about it."

"We can scream frame, show that nobody but the *World* got a tip on it and—"

Stewart shook his head. "They can spike those guns fast enough. Tomorrow they'll be running a front-page editorial of how we tried to suppress the story and what a biased sheet we run." He lifted the phone off its hook. "See if you can get me the D.A. Try his office and his home both." He dropped the receiver back on its hook.

"Got something in mind?" the city editor asked curiously.

"Yeah. I want to ask the district attorney if he's made up his mind whether to resign or fight."

Mal Waters had made up his mind the minute the door closed behind the mayor and Max Everett. He had spent most of what had remained of the night writing his resignation. It contained an expression of his innocence, his determination to prove that innocence and a willingness to return to office only after he had proven it.

He had no way of knowing that the *Star* had been frozen out of the story completely, expected that as a newspaper it would publish the story in full. He completed his statement, sealed it in an envelope addressed to Mayor Ed London and left it on his desk. When he left his office toward morning, he left it for the last time, taking with him all of his personal effects. He went to his apartment, locked himself in for a badly needed twelve-hour sleep. By the time he saw the two Jackson City papers, a new edition was on the presses announcing his resignation "under fire."

Al Zito sat admiring the dimples that were his knuckles. A smug smile twisted the corners of his pouty lips upward. Finally he rolled his eyes upward, studied his visitors from under his heavily veined lids.

"I've already passed the word along to Barney Maurer and the other boys that they can open up as soon as they can get ready. See that there're no slipups."

Captain Marcy Lewis twisted uncomfortably on his chair, nodded. "Everything will be okay, Al."

"It better be," Zito told him. "It costs heavy to keep a place closed down." He rolled his eyes to the chair where Ed London sat, dabbing nervously at his forehead. "The guy you're appointing to sit out the D.A.'s term. He another son-in-law, Mr. Mayor?"

London shook his head. "He's a regular organization hack. You don't have to worry about him." He licked at his lips. "But don't you think it might be a little early to start operating again? I mean right after—"

The corners of the lips dropped. A bubble formed and burst in the center of Zito's lips. "Do you?"

"I don't know. The *Star* will probably point it up and people may start thinking—"

Zito snorted. "People don't think. They're told something, they believe it." The heavy lids veiled the disks of his eyes. "It cost us plenty to put you and your boys in and keep you in, London. Okay, so that's an investment. But we don't like people who threaten that investment. We expect to make money not shell out more. You know?"

"I know. But I just thought—"

"You don't hear good. I just said don't think. You're told something, do it." London licked at his lips, bobbed his head.

Marcy Lewis squirmed even more, looked uncomfortable. "Anything else on your mind, Al? I should be getting back to headquarters."

"Yeah. How's about this old guy, this Cleary?"

Lewis looked to the mayor, then at the fat man. "What about him?"

"He's trouble."

The homicide detective raised his hands, palms out. "Look, I don't like Cleary any better than you do. But he's been around a long time. Anything happens to him, it better be natural. He's got too many friends."

Zito scowled. "All right. So nothing happens to him. But keep him out of my hair. Or maybe something does."

Captain Matt Cleary had an inflexible routine. When he worked the twelve to eight, and these days that was his permanent shift, he never got out of bed before four. His daughter, Marta, who kept house for him, always placed the day's papers on the stand next to his bed. His first act, after a quick dash to the bathroom to splash cold water into his face, was to prop up the pillows, turn on the bed light and read the papers from the top of page one to the bottom of the last page—not excluding obituaries.

One of his most mournful duties these days was to check off one by one the old-timers whose names were making the columns for the last time.

Today he didn't get beyond the headline on page one of the *World*. He had just settled himself against the propped-up pillows, covered his thin legs with the blanket, when the headline hit him in the eye.

"Damn them," he roared at nobody in particular.

The door to the bedroom opened, Marta stuck her head in. "Father!" she chided him. Then, alarmed at the expression on his face, she hurried into the room. "Is anything wrong?"

Marta Cleary, at twenty-six, was anything but the popular conception of an old maid. The decision to stay home and care for her father was strictly her own, a decision half a dozen eligible men on the force would have liked to rule out.

Marta was tall for a girl, deep-breasted. She was Black Irish, her hair a curly jet cap that hugged her skull and matched the long, curling eyelashes that set the deep blue eyes off dramatically. Her mouth was full, even thick-lipped, always looked on the verge of a smile.

She had hedged against dependence on any man by graduating from the Jackson City Hospital School for Nurses. It was here that she had her first and only real romance. When the affair turned serious and the young intern asked her to set a date, she had told him that she wouldn't consider marriage until her father died. Whereupon the outraged young man had retorted, "That old goat will never die." The romance didn't survive.

She picked up the paper her father had dropped on the bed as he swung his skinny legs from under the covers and started to put on his pants. Her eyes skipped from the headlines to the pictures.

"I read it. Quite a mess," she said.

"It couldn't just be a coincidence," Cleary remarked. "They were out to get that boy—"

The girl stared at him. "You don't mean that somebody deliberately killed that girl? Just to get at him?"

Cleary jammed his arms into a shirt, headed for the hall. "He was giving them hell. Now they're hitting back."

Marta studied the face of the man in the picture with new interest. She wished there was better lighting, but even so it didn't look to her like the face of a hero.

She followed her father into the hall, watched him dial the phone clumsily with his splayed forefinger.

"Let me talk to Lou Stewart," he roared into the phone. He drummed nervously on the telephone stand while he waited. "Lou? Matt Cleary. What the hell's going on?"

He listened to the metallic voice on the other end for a moment.

"He what? Resigned?" Some of the anger drained from the old man's face, was replaced by disappointment. "I guess not. But I was beginning to think he had guts. The kind of guts that would help us break this thing wide open. Okay, thanks." He dropped the phone on its cradle, stared at it for a moment.

"Bad news, Dad?"

He looked up as though he had forgotten she was there, nodded. "The D.A. took a runout powder. He resigned and nobody seems to know where he is."

She held the headlines up where he could see them. "Do you blame him?"

Cleary growled deep in his throat. "He was our real hope. But they got to him."

"Got to him? You don't think—"

"There are more ways to get to a man than just with money. There's fear for himself, fear for his family, fear of exposure. There are lots of ways to blackmail a man into doing what you want."

She turned, dropped the paper on a hall stand. "Maybe you just imagine a lot of this, Dad. After all, you say the department is shot full of graft but you've never taken any."

"You don't have to bribe every cop to control the department. Just own a few key ones like Marcy Lewis, that's all you need. He can hand-pick the rest that have to be bought and you've got it made."

"But this could have been an accident. He might have had a couple of drinks, and—"

Cleary shook his head. "He was getting too hot, so they cooled him off. Permanently, from the looks of it."

"But how can you be sure?"

He looked at her soberly, squinted. "Because I was on duty last night between twelve and eight. And he wasn't booked nor was there any notation on the blotter."

Chapter 15

The wreck had been towed to Bryant's Garage on the outskirts of Jackson City. Mal Waters stood alongside it, eyed the damage and wondered how he had been able to walk away from it.

Ted Bryant came out of the shed where he'd been servicing a car, stopped alongside Waters. "Really wrapped that one up, Mr. Waters." He eyed the D.A. sympathetically. "Tough break about the girl."

Waters nodded. "Tough break." He nodded to the car. "Clean out the glove compartment? I had some papers and things in there."

The garage man shook his head. "Never touch the inside of a car until I get an okay. Got her locked up. Want the keys?"

Mal nodded, watched the other man head for the office, wiping the palms of his hands on his thighs. He walked around to the front of the car, examined the radiator and grill. It was a hopeless wreck.

Bryant stepped up behind him. "Ain't much you can do with that one, Mr. Waters. Ain't hardly worth towing away for junk." He held out a key case.

Mal unlocked the door nearest the wheel, found it had been sprung and resisted his best efforts to open it. The far door opened easily, accounting to some degree for his being alive. It was through that door the deputies had pulled him the night before. He used a key to open the glove compartment, started stowing the papers in his breast pocket.

He made a losing effort to keep his eyes away from the viscid dark brown stain on the upholstery near him. When he finally lost the battle and stared at it, he detected an odd shade of red in the stain. It seemed brighter than the rest. He bent over, studied it. Then, taking a pencil from his pocket, he fished it up, stuck it between two sheets of paper he was transferring from the glove compartment to his pocket.

"Find something?" Bryant asked him curiously.

"If I told you I found something that would prove I wasn't responsible for what happened last night, would you believe me?"

The garage man's expression was answer enough.

Waters turned his back on him, looked the car over carefully. There was nothing else to be found. He closed the car door, locked it and returned the keys to Bryant.

"Thanks."

He gave no sign of being conscious of the garage man's speculative stare as he walked to the rented car at the curb. Bryant was still staring as Mal Waters pulled away, headed for the heart of town. When the car was finally out of sight, the garage man unlocked the car, studied the spot from which he had seen the D.A. pick something red. But there was nothing there to indicate what it had been. Finally he shrugged and walked back toward the office.

Marta Cleary answered the door in response to the ringing. The man in the doorway was young, vaguely familiar. With a start she realized she had seen his picture on the front page of the paper a few hours before.

"Is Captain Cleary in?"

She nodded. "Yes, Mr. Waters. Come in."

Mal grinned mirthlessly. "My fame has preceded me."

The dark-haired girl merely stood aside until he had entered. "In the living room." She turned and led the way.

The living room was comfortable looking, lived in. A large-screen television stood in one corner, a well-worn leather chair facing it. The fireplace showed signs of having frequent use, flowers added color to the room. A large portrait of a woman who resembled the girl hung over the fireplace. The rug was soft colored, well cared for. Cleary sat on the end cushion of the oversized couch reading a book. He looked up as Mal entered, put the book aside.

"I've been reading about you," he grunted. "Lou Stewart's been trying to reach you."

"I've had things to do."

"Like running out?"

"Father!" Marta snapped at him. She turned to Mal, noticed for the first time how drawn and white he looked. "Don't pay any attention to Dad, Mr. Waters. He likes to impress people with his gruffness."

"It's something I'll have to get used to," Mal agreed. "I need his help."

Cleary peered at him, wrinkles digging white trenches in the leathery texture of his face. "What kind of help?"

"To clear myself. To finish what I started out to do. Smash Zito and his mob."

The old man tried to read the younger man's face. "Get him a chair, Marta." He continued to study Mal while the girl pushed a chair close to the couch. "You're not running away?"

Waters shook his head. He flashed a grateful grin at the girl, sat down.

"But you resigned."

"If I hadn't, would I stand much chance of not being run out of office?"

Cleary considered it, shook his head.

"The terms for not printing those pictures and not blasting the story were complete surrender. Would you have advised that?"

Matt Cleary pulled himself out of his chair, walked over to a cabinet, brought out a bottle and two glasses. He walked back, handed one to Waters, spilled some of the liquor into it.

"They gave you that choice and you didn't take it?"

"Now I know that's why Stewart's paper didn't get the story. It wasn't that they were being considerate of me. It was because in case I decided to play ball, they could control Everett."

The old man permitted himself a smile, spilled some liquor into his glass. "Drink up." He raised his glass in a silent salute to the woman in the picture on the wall, then drained the glass and set it down.

Mal smelled the glass, then took a deep swallow. "Real good."

The girl smiled at him. "That's Dad's private stock. You have to rate around here to get any of that."

"Now let's get down to cases," Cleary said. "You claim you were set up for that accident. Could you prove that?"

"Not to one of London's judges," Mal said. "I think I can prove it to you." He dug into his pocket, brought out the papers where he'd stuck the brown-red thing he'd found on the seat of the car. "What do you make of that?"

Cleary held it under the light, screwed up his face in concentration. The girl leaned over his shoulder.

"Looks like a petal to me. From a carnation, maybe?" she said.

Mal looked to Cleary. He nodded. "From a flower." He turned it over with his finger. "Blood on it."

Mal told them the details of how he found it.

The old man gave back the papers, leaned back and laced his big-knuckled hands across his chest. "That would mean it was under the body."

"Right where you'd expect it to be if it was knocked off someone who was carrying her when he dropped her on the front seat."

"You think she was dead when she was put in the car?" Marta asked. There was a faint blue color under her eyes that supplemented their deep blue.

"Dead or unconscious."

"Sounds reasonable," Cleary agreed. "But how can I help you?"

"You know Doc Denton, the medical examiner. He'll answer a question for you, won't he?"

"He won't stick his neck out, if that's what you're asking. Doc is too close to retirement to go looking for trouble."

"I don't want him to stick his neck out. I just want him to answer a perfectly fair question."

The old man scowled at him. "Such as?"

"What was the nature of her injuries. And were there any that might be incongruous to the way she received them."

Cleary considered it, nodded. "I can do that much. Not that it would stand up in court."

"Not yet, maybe. But a little piece here, a little piece there and maybe I can build a picture that will stand up."

"I wouldn't make book on it." The old man pulled himself up from the couch, walked to the phone in the hall.

"Are you sure what you're doing is the right thing, Mr. Waters?" Marta's blue eyes were clouded with concern. "Mightn't it be better to go some place else, make a new start and—"

"Turn my back on it?" Mal shook his head. "That's what I've been doing up 'til now—" He grinned at her self-consciously. "I don't know your name."

"Marta."

"Mine's Mal."

"I know." The half smile that started to wrinkle her nose faded. "Mal, you're one man. You can't go up against the organized vice in this town."

"Your father's done it."

"And what's it gotten him? What good has it done anybody? It's just been a waste of time. He would have been better off if he had done what you have a chance to do now. Go some place else, some place where there's decency."

Mal brought a pack of cigarettes from his pocket, offered one to the girl, drew a shake of her head. "That's just the trouble. There's no place to run. Sooner or later you've got to stand still and make a stand. This is my home town. I was born here and I grew up here. There'll never be a better place to make my stand. Win, lose or draw." He hung a cigarette in the corner of his mouth where it waggled when he talked. "I'm not trying to sound dramatic or heroic. If anything, I'm scared. But now that I know what's got to be done, I'm going to do it."

"I wish you luck. I have a feeling you're going to need it." She watched him smoke in short nervous puffs. "Can I ask you a question?"

"Sure."

"What's the significance of that carnation petal?" Waters took a deep drag from the cigarette, blew the smoke in twin streams from his nostrils. "It means I should have a talk with a man who wears carnations. A man Bonnie worked for."

"The paper said she worked for Barney Maurer."

The D.A. nodded. "That's right. She did."

Marta caught her full lower lip between her teeth, worried it. "You're not the district attorney any more, you know," she said finally. "You have no standing. Nobody in back of you. Be careful."

"I intend to be," he said.

Matt Cleary stamped back into the room. "Doc Denton wanted to know what I was driving at. In the beginning he didn't want to talk. Said it was all on his report." He grinned bleakly. "He finally admitted he's not satisfied with a depressed fracture on the back of the girl's skull. Injuries in an accident like that are usually frontal. That blood on the seat must have come from the wound in the back of her head.''

"Enough to kill her?''

The old man shrugged. "Eventually. But she was still alive when her head cracked against the windshield.''

Waters took a last drag on his cigarette, leaned forward and crushed it out in an ash tray. "She must have been sapped. From the rear.'' He straightened up, brushed a fleck of ash from his pants leg. "Thanks, Matt. As you say, it's nothing that would stand up in court. But it's another piece of the picture. The poor kid.''

"How can you say that? She's the one who set you up. She was as bad as any of them.'' Marta Cleary's eyes flashed indignation.

The D.A. shrugged. "Not exactly. There's two kinds of bad in my book. Bad you do voluntarily and bad that you do because you have no control over the circumstances. I don't think Bonnie could have refused to do what she did.''

"Why not?''

"I think she was telling me the truth when she told me Marcy Lewis was holding something over her head.''

"I won't buy that.'' Marta shook her head firmly. "Nothing he had on her could have been as bad as ruining a man's life.''

"Not even if it meant ruining the lives of people closer to her? Her father and mother are still alive. She got into trouble when she came into town and Lewis threatened to alert the police in her home town. Her parents would have had to know. It would have killed them.''

The girl's direct glance wavered, then fell. "I guess I have a nerve being indignant over it, if you're not.'' She looked up again, met his eyes. "You're a pretty generous person. Not many people would be that understanding.''

"Maybe I figure that whatever she did, she paid for it. They never had any intention of letting her live so she could tell the truth about what happened later.'' He held his hand out to Cleary, returned the firm grip. "I'll check with you as soon as anything happens.''

The old man nodded. "You do that.''

Waters turned to Marta. "It was nice meeting you. I hope I can do it again under pleasanter circumstances.''

"Come around any time. I'm sure Dad will be glad to help any way he can.''

Waters nodded, headed for the door. When it had closed behind him, Matt Cleary turned to his daughter. "Quite a guy?''

"Quite a guy.'' She didn't even apologize for the blush that crept up from her neck when he raised his eyebrows at her reaction.

Chapter 16

Barney Maurer's place looked different when it was closed. Mal Waters stopped the car at the entrance to the driveway that wound up to the house. A sign announced: *Closed For Alterations. Open on Monday, May 26.* He shook his head, muttered to no one in particular, "They sure don't waste much time getting things back to normal."

He doused the lights on the car, carefully felt his way up the driveway until he found a spot where he could park under the trees out of sight of the building. Then he got out of the car, melted into the shadows and covered the rest of the way on foot.

Without the flattery of the hidden battery of floodlights, the place was just a tired old frame building sprawling in the darkness. Tonight there were no cars in the parking lot; the amiable giant in the maroon uniform who presided over the door was gone; there was no bright light spilling from the windows on the ground, no feverish pitch of conversation. Just a tired old gray-white building, looking for all the world like an old lady relaxing with her make-up off.

Waters skirted the building to where he figured the French windows leading to the dinner room had been. The room itself was dark. He gently tapped out a small pane of glass above the knob, stuck his hand through, opened the door, and let himself in. He stood for a moment to let his eyes become accustomed to the darkness, then picked his way carefully through the tables to the bar. Here he stood for a minute to get his bearings, tried in his mind's eye to remember from which direction Barney Maurer had come the night he was summoned by the bartender.

Quietly he felt his way to the end of the bar, walked out into what he recognized as the entrance hall. He walked to the staircase at the end of the hall, looked around. The only sound in the place was that of heavy breathing. His own.

He decided to try the upper story. Slowly, testing every step before he put his weight on it, he ascended. Three doors opened off the small corridor at the head of the stairs. There was a thin thread of light under the center door. He walked up to it, put his ear against it. All he could hear was the blood pounding in his ears.

He reached down, slowly clamped his hand around the knob. Silently he cursed the haste that had caused him to come out here without first getting a gun some place. He tried the knob, it turned silently in his hand. He pushed the door open, stepped through.

Maurer was sitting in the chair behind a big desk. He was riffling through the drawer, only the top of his head showing. He looked up as he heard the door swing open.

Waters walked in, kicked the door shut with his heel. His right hand was sunk to the wrist in his pocket.

Maurer's startled eyes dropped from Waters' face to the hand in the pocket. "What's the idea?" he finally asked.

"I just dropped by to give you something that belongs to you." He dug his hand into his breast pocket, pulled out the paper to which the carnation petal adhered stiffly. "From your carnation."

Maurer's eyes dropped involuntarily to the carnation in his buttonhole. "I don't know what you're talking about," he growled. "But if you think you can bust in here and push me around—"

"You know when you lost it? When you carried Bonnie out and dumped her in the front seat of my car. That's where I found it."

A muscle jumped under Maurer's right eye, his lips went slack. "You gone completely crazy?"

"Who sapped her, Maurer? You? You hit too hard. The M.E. is going to be able to prove that's what killed her. The sap. Not an accident."

The big man licked at his lips, seemed to be getting the quiver under his eye under control. "Now I know you're crazy." He kept his eyes on the hand Waters kept in his pocket.

Suddenly he grabbed for a desk drawer, got it open and stuck his hand into it. Waters cleared the space between them, kicked the drawer shut on the hand. Maurer dropped the gun he was trying to grab, roared his pain. Waters pushed with all his strength, the desk chair up-ended, spilling the big man to the floor. He had the drawer open, the gun almost out when Maurer recovered, jumped on his back.

Maurer's big hand, clamped around Waters' wrist, kept him from raising the gun into firing position. Slowly, inexorably he twisted the wrist until the gun fell from Mal's nerveless fingers. Before he could scoop the gun up, Waters kicked it, sent it spinning across the room.

They wrestled soundlessly except for an occasional grunt or gasping for breath. Suddenly Mal lashed back with his heel, had the satisfaction of hearing Maurer growl with pain as it caught him in the shin. Maurer released his hold, Waters ducked away from him.

The big man turned and ran for the door. Mal caught him before he could get into the hallway. He spun him around, hit him in the stomach with his left. Maurer tried to raise his hands, but his reflexes were too slow to avoid the hard overhand that sent him reeling back.

Before he could get set, Waters was on top of him. Maurer tried to make his stand with the railing at his back, but it was too late. Waters' momentum carried him forward, gave added power to the right overhand. The low railing caught the big man's back, gave way with a screech and Maurer disappeared into the black well of the stairway.

Waters caught the banister, walked slowly and painfully down the stairs. He lit a match. Maurer was a tangle of arms and legs on the hallway floor. A thin stream of blood ran from the corner of his mouth. Waters felt for a pulse with no success.

He stared down at the dead man. He tried to feel some remorse, but it was like being carried back eight years to the day he had nailed his first Mig over Korea. He had always wondered what his first kill would feel like. And all he did feel was elation as he looked over the side at the plume of smoke the flaming plane left in its wake. He could only yell, "Compliments of Johnny Rizzo." Rizzo had gone out on patrol two days before and hadn't been heard from since. Now as he looked down at Maurer's body, he couldn't refrain from grunting, "Compliments of Bonnie."

Waters blew out the match, knelt next to the body. Quickly he went through its pockets, transferred a wallet, a small memo book and a key ring to his own. He felt his way to the staircase, climbed to the office on the second floor.

He closed the door behind him, wiped the film of perspiration from his upper lip with the back of his hand. The gun lay in the far corner where he'd kicked it. He walked over, picked it up. It was a .45, fully loaded. He stuck it in his waistband.

At the desk, he made a methodical search of the drawers, found nothing of any value. He dug Maurer's memo book, the wallet and the keys from his pocket, started to work on them.

In the wallet was $230 in cash, a number of courtesy cards for state and local police. One for the local police was signed by Marcy Lewis, another by the Mayor. Waters grunted, set them aside. Under the flap of the wallet was a small card bearing the notation: L6 2R18 2L 12. He studied it for a moment, laid it on one side.

The memo book was less enlightening. The numerous entries had been made in a makeshift code which would probably take weeks of working over without the key. He flipped to the back of the book, found a number of telephone numbers. One he had no difficulty in recognizing as the mayor's unlisted home number, another was just identified as "A. Z."

Waters leaned back in his chair, stared around the room. The construction of the walls made any sliding or secret panels improbable. Yet he was convinced there must be some place in the room where Maurer kept his more important papers. He pulled himself out of his chair, walked to the nearest picture, turned it aside. There was blank wall underneath. The wall safe was under the third picture.

He tried the keys on the ring he'd taken from the body, found one that fit. Then with a silent prayer, he tried the combination from the wallet. The heavy door to the safe swung open soundlessly, a small light went on in the interior.

Feverishly, Mal Waters pored through the neatly piled bundles of papers. For the most part they were disappointingly prosaic—insurance policies of various sorts, I.O.U.s, and periodic breakdowns of operating expenses against profit. An interesting item of operating expenses was listed as thirty per cent of gross to A. Z. Apparently the Syndicate, through its resident manager, was a third-interest partner in most of the spots operating.

Near the bottom of the pile, Waters found a single-spaced typewritten list. He opened it without much hope, caught his breath as his eyes ran down the columns. He shoved the rest of the papers back into the safe, closed it and re-placed the picture. Then he walked over to the wall, snapped off the light.

He opened the door, strained his eyes against the darkness, listened for any sound to betray another presence. He reached down, pulled the .45 from his belt. The heavy stock had a reassuring feel.

He felt his way down the stairs, through the bar into the supper room. The moonlight streaming in through the French windows gave the white-clothed tables an eerie look in the half light. Quickly he crossed to the door he had entered, slipped through.

His car was still under the big tree halfway down the lane. He slid under the wheel, kicked the motor to life.

Chapter 17

Al Zito stood in the bare light of the hallway, stared down at Barney Maurer's body. He sucked in and blew out his lips rhythmically. He looked up to where Joey stood watching him.

"How long ago would you say?"

Joey shrugged. "He was cold when I got here." A worried frown ridged his forehead. "Whoever chilled him went through his things. I found his wallet and his keys on his desk."

Zito nodded, waddled toward the stairs, looked at them with a sigh. Then grabbing the banister, he proceeded to pull himself up, step by step. At the top he stood panting, swearing under his breath at the necessity for the exertion. When he got to Maurer's office, he dropped into the desk chair, swabbed his jowls with the side of his hand.

Joey followed him into the room. "What about Maurer, Al?"

The fat man shrugged, scowled. "We got to get rid of him. Make sure he don't turn up." He picked up the wallet, dumped its contents on the desk top. "We can't afford any more publicity. These killings bring heat. There's too much already."

"But, Al—"

"You don't hear so good." The man behind the desk looked up, his eyes twin hooded menace. "I said we had too much killing already. Maybe before this Carter guy got hit we could laugh at them. But I hear things I don't like. Like a reform ticket this election. Maybe it gets in. You know what that means to us?"

Joey tried a placating smile. "I was just thinking—"

"Goddam it. All of a sudden everybody starts to think. Well, think of this. If that reform mob gets in, we're out. And then the big boys start asking questions. They ask why. You got an answer?"

The pleasant-faced gunman shook his head.

"Okay. Then do what I said. You and one of the boys get Maurer ready. I'll show you how we get rid of him with no heat." He watched with unfriendly eyes while Joey backed out of the room, headed for the stairs.

Captain Marcy Lewis was sitting in his shirtsleeves, finishing a glass of beer preparatory to retiring when the telephone rang. He swore at it softly, debated not answering it.

The querulous voice of his wife came from the bedroom. "Marcy! The phone is ringing."

"I can hear it, damn it. I'm not deaf."

"You don't have to swear."

The phone continued to peal. He sat staring at it, a vague apprehension gnawing at him. His wife appeared in the doorway to the bedroom. In her thin nightgown she was even skinnier and less appetizing than usual. Thin wisps of graying hair stuck at ridiculous angles from her head.

"If you won't answer it, I will. It'll be waking the kids."

She started to shuffle across the floor in her bare feet.

"Go back to bed. I'll answer it." He walked over to the phone, lifted it, held it to his ear. "Yeah?"

"Lewis? Al Zito."

The homicide detective turned to his wife. "It's for me."

She sniffed audibly. "Another one of your late assignments?" She turned, headed back to her room.

Lewis took his hand off the mouthpiece. "What's up?"

"Get out to Barney Maurer's place right away."

Marcy Lewis checked his watch. "You got any idea what time it is, Zito? Hell, I was just—"

"Look, Lewis. I want the time, I'll buy a clock. I want you. Now."

"But, Al—"

The voice on the other end of the phone cut him off. "Maurer's dead. He had the ice list. This time it's gone. Whoever killed him has it."

"Maurer dead?"

"Don't talk so much. Just get here. We got troubles." The receiver was dropped on the hook at the other end, the line went dead. Marcy Lewis replaced his receiver on its hammock, rubbed the heel of his hand across the stubble on his chin. He was uncomfortably aware that the vague feeling of apprehension that had dogged him all night had just given birth to a full-fledged emergency.

He walked into the bedroom, switched on the light. The thin woman lay in one of twin beds, the covers pulled up around her neck. She watched him slip into his holster, cover it with a jacket.

"You're going out?" she asked dully.

"You heard. There's trouble. I've got to be on deck."

She reached from under the covers, tucked a stray wisp of hair behind her ear. "You're not on duty, Marcy. You're not—"

"Goddam it, can't you understand? I'm always on duty." He reached into the top drawer of his bureau, brought out a box of cartridges, dumped a handful into his side pocket. "I don't know when I'll be back."

The thin woman watched him stride toward the door, snap off the light. A few seconds later the front door slammed. She lay there for a moment, straining her eyes against the darkness, then she put her face in the pillow and cried.

It might be true that he was on duty, it might be that girl that everyone knew he was keeping. It could even be that one night he would go out and not come back. But outside of inconvenience of the loss of his income it wouldn't mean too much to Elsie Lewis. The Marcy Lewis she had known and married had died many years ago. Even crying when he walked out on her night after night was more habit than emotion.

Al Zito sat in the chair behind the desk, glowering at Captain Marcy Lewis. "I'm not asking you, copper, I'm telling you. Maurer's going out of here. He's going out in your car. We can't take any chances of Mike or Joey being stopped."

A dull flush crept up from Marcy Lewis's neck, staining his face. "It's crazy, I tell you. Why don't you do it smart? I can get a panel truck tomorrow, we can roll him up in a rug, take him out—"

"Tomorrow is too late. He goes out tonight." The fat man's voice was flat, final. "Joey'll go with you. That quarry out near the state road might be the place. Just make sure he don't come up."

The homicide man started to argue, shrugged. "I think it's crazy."

"Crazy like a fox. Who's going to stop a department sedan with its red light on?" Zito smiled. "Sit down. Calm your nerves. The boys are putting him in your trunk now."

Lewis dropped into a chair, shook his head. "You said something about the ice list?"

Zito nodded. "Barney was taking care of the payoffs. He had it all broken down. Whoever killed him has it now."

"You got an idea?"

The fat man pursed his lips thoughtfully. "Waters, maybe."

The homicide man considered it, shook his head. "He's not the killer type. He—"

"What is the killer type, Lewis? You're an expert."

"What I meant was—"

Zito waved the objection aside. "There's no killer type. Anybody is a killer under the right circumstances. They take a kid out of college, they give him a uniform and a gun. It's the same kid, only now he's a killer. You take this jerk, Waters. He's an Ivy League softy who wouldn't hurt a fly. All of a sudden you give him a reason and he's a killer." He leaned forward. "You don't think so? Then how come he's a war hero? You think he got those medals from kissing the Reds?"

"That's different. During the war—"

"With him maybe this is war. You ever thought of that? Our trouble's been thinking like you. That this was a jerk, that we could put him out of commission just by threatening him with bad publicity. We were wrong. "

Lewis half rose from his chair. "Now, wait a minute, Zito. A guy like Barney Maurer can disappear and maybe nobody will care. But you kill Waters and the trouble we've got now is nothing compared to what we're going to have on our hands."

"Who said anything about killing him? I'm the guy who told you we can't have any more killing," Zito said.

"So how do we handle him?"

Zito pasted a smirk on his lips. "Leave that to me." There was a soft tap on the door. "Yeah?"

Joey stuck his head in, nodded to Lewis. "We're ready to go."

"You go with the captain, Joey. He'll need help." He rolled his eyes back to Lewis. "Remember, Lewis, he don't come up."

The homicide man pulled himself out of his chair, headed for the door. He turned. "What about the opening here? They've been notifying everybody they start running again on Monday."

"We open."

"But won't Maurer's absence—"

The fat man shook his head. "Word gets out that Maurer has taken a little trip. Maybe even to report to the Syndicate on what's been going on. Pretty soon everybody gets used to the idea he's not around. Maybe a few of the boys get the idea he took a powder because the heat was on. Pretty soon nobody cares and nobody asks questions."

"And that broad of his?"

Zito grinned. "The police department gives her an idea of what happens to her if she hangs around town. Maurer gets word to her that he's going under-cover for a while and sends enough loot to keep her happy."

"And quiet."

The fat man shrugged, raised his pudgy hands, palms up. "So where's the problem?"

Chapter 18

Mal Waters sat on the couch in his apartment, ran through the list of names on the ice list for the sixth time. He knew exactly what he should be doing. He should be meeting with Lou Stewart of the *Star* and Captain Matt Cleary and laying the groundwork for the cleaning up of Jackson City.

He stuck a cigarette between his lips, lit it and walked to the window. He was aware that what he was considering could blow up in his face, could conceivably undo all they had been able to do. Yet the fact of the matter was that Mayor Ed London's name was not on the ice list. Marcy Lewis's name was there, so were the names of dozens of important officers in the police department. But Ed London's name was not on that list.

He smoked in short, nervous puffs, stared unseeingly into the street below. Common sense told him there could be a dozen reasons why London's name wasn't on the list. He might not be getting graft directly, might be cut into some of the firms getting the juicy contracts. He might be on a direct payroll from Zito or his superiors. There were plenty of logical explanations.

But it wasn't logic dictating his actions, it was emotion. He couldn't bring himself to believe that the father of the girl he still loved could be so deeply involved that he would stand by and permit murder to be committed. Mal wanted desperately to prove to himself that London, like Mal himself, was guilty only of nonfeasance not malfeasance. He took a last drag on the cigarette, jammed it coal-down into the ash tray, started for the door.

There was only one way to find out.

He piloted the rented car across town in record time, swung it under the carport, walked around to the front of the big house and pressed the bell. After a moment, the door opened, Rita London stood in the doorway. Her eyes widened as she recognized Mal. She sucked her breath in softly.

"Mal! What are you doing here?"

"I want to see your father, Rita. Is he here?"

She looked undecided for a moment, then nodded. She stepped aside and as he brushed past her. "You've changed your mind, Mal? You're not going to dredge up a lot of mud?"

He turned. Her lips were half parted, he felt the full power of the slanted green eyes. He put his hand on her arm. "Honey, can't you understand—"

She shook his hand off her arm angrily. "I can only understand that you're being bullheaded. Trying to be a hero. At the expense of people who gave you everything you have."

He dropped his hand to his side. "Maybe some day you will understand."

The redhead shook her head. "That'll be too late. For us." She dropped her eyes. "After the usual decent interval, I'm announcing my engagement to

Max Everett." She rolled her eyes up to his. "I hope you'll wish us good luck, Mal."

He worked at a smile which didn't reach his eyes. "Of course, Rita. All the best."

"Dad's in his study." She walked past him, headed for the stairs. His eyes followed her until she disappeared on the floor above.

Ed London looked up from his desk with no show of enthusiasm as his former aide walked into his study. There was a bagginess under his eyes that was no part of his usual expression. He tossed the pen he had been using to the desk. "You want to see me, Mal?"

"Yes." Mal pulled his chair close to his desk. "As a friend, Mr. Mayor. After I tell you my story, you can decide what side you're on and what you intend to do about it."

A flash of annoyance clouded the mayor's brow. "Now, Mal, we've gone all through this. You know where I stand—"

"On the side of the angels. Well, maybe it's about time you knew which side that is." Waters dropped into the chair. "Suppose I tell you I can now prove that Tim Benson did not murder Judge Carter. Prove it well enough to stand up even in a court owned body and soul by Al Zito?"

"That's ridiculous."

Mal dug a cigarette from his pocket, stuck it in the corner of his mouth. "Is it?" He touched a match to it, drew a mouth full of smoke. "Let me try it on you for size. Then tell me if it's ridiculous." He leaned back, marshaled his thoughts. "Tim Benson was supposed to have killed Carter because the judge had evidence he was taking graft. Right?"

"Proven."

The ex-D.A. shook his head. "Implied." He paused for effect. "Suppose I tell you that I have that ice list in my possession and that Tim Benson's name is not on it?" He watched the small beads of perspiration glisten on the older man's face. "If he had been a grafter, his name would be on the list."

London stared at the younger man. "Why do you tell me this?"

"Maybe I'm crazy. Maybe because your name isn't on the list. Maybe that doesn't mean anything. Maybe you get your pay-off directly from the Syndicate and it wouldn't be on this list. But I'm willing to give you the benefit of the doubt. I'm hoping that you're not in so deep that once your eyes are opened you can't help me clean up this mess."

The mayor drummed on the edge of his desk with nervous fingers. "You're basing all this on the fact that Benson's name isn't on the list. Are you forgetting that he was identified by the judge's wife on her deathbed?"

"It was a faked identification."

"Ridiculous. Captain Lewis got it himself. The doctor verified her signature on the picture and—"

"The identification was framed. Marcy Lewis pasted two pictures together,

Benson's on the bottom. She identified the front picture but signed her name on the back of the bottom one."

"But why should Lewis—"

Mal smiled grimly. "Benson's name wasn't on that ice list. But Marcy Lewis's name is. He's on the Syndicate payroll."

"I don't believe you. Nobody else will believe you. Benson's guilt was so obvious—"

"Suppose I tell you that there's a plastic mold of the real killer's footprint. And Benson's shoe never could have fitted into it." He watched the expression on the mayor's face. "How about that?"

London reached into the humidor on his desk, selected a cigar. He tested its firmness by rolling it between thumb and forefinger. "Why hasn't this footprint shown up before now?" He bit the end off the cigar and spat it at the wastebasket.

"They got a little too sure of themselves. The razzle-dazzle of that deathbed identification had them hypnotized."

"What else?"

Waters grinned bleakly. "Isn't that enough for a starter?"

The man behind the desk wet the end of the cigar between his lips. "This is all your say-so." He stuck the cigar between his teeth, chewed on it. "A lot of it will be discounted because of your unfortunate experience the other night—"

"I was framed."

London raised his eyebrows patiently. "Of course."

"Bonnie Peters was dead before she was ever placed in the car with me."

"How can you know that?"

"The medical examiner found a severe fracture in the back of her head. It couldn't have been caused in the wreck. Only frontal injuries are caused by slamming against the windshield."

The mayor snapped a gold-plated lighter into flame, held it to the cigar. After a moment, he blew out a cloud of gray-white smoke. "You can understand that it will be hard for the average person to swallow, Mal." He leaned back. "Can I give you some advice?"

A grim tight look came into the younger man's eyes. "What's the advice?"

London took the cigar from between his teeth, studied the fine collar of ash that was beginning to form. "You had a good career here in Jackson City. You threw it away." He looked up. "Rita has told you about her plans?"

"That she's going to marry Everett?" Mal nodded. "I hope she's very happy."

"She will be," London told him. "Ev can give Rita what she wants—stability, position, acceptance." He stuck the cigar back between his teeth, chewed on it. "You could have given her that, too, Mal. But you chose to throw it away. Don't make another mistake."

"You mean by proving these facts?"

"If they are facts." London closed his eyes for a minute, seemed to be selecting his words. "You're finished in this town, Mal. Nobody can afford to touch you. Anybody who tries to help you, you'll drag down with you. Believe me. I know."

Mal started to get up. "I guess I was wasting my time. But I wanted to give you a chance to get out from under before the whole rotten structure came down on your head." He started for the door. "You see, I wasn't marrying Rita because she could give me position or security or prestige. I was marrying her for a reason maybe you can't understand. Because I loved her."

"Then if you love her, for her sake—"

Mal shook his head angrily. "I love her, all right. Maybe I always will. But now that I've had my eyes opened, I wouldn't want to bring kids into a town like this. I wouldn't want to live here. I couldn't live with myself if I closed my eyes now."

"You think it's different any place else? Any place you go, Mal, there'll be two kinds of people—the ones who give the orders and the ones who take them. Be smart—play with the ones who give them. That's where the percentage is."

Waters grinned grimly. "I never was a percentage player, Mr. Mayor. It's more fun to buck the house."

London shrugged. "I can't talk you out of destroying whatever future you have left. If you'd only take my advice—go some place else. You're a good lawyer, you can get started and—"

"I guess this will be the last time I'll be dropping by." Mal looked around the familiar room. "It doesn't seem so long ago it was the first time I came here. Rita brought me back to meet you after the country club dance where I met her. You never know, do you? Who'd figure it would be ending like this? Say good by for me." He turned, walked down the hall to the door, closed it softly behind him.

Ed London sat in his chair chewing on the end of the cigar. The side door to the study opened, Rita walked in.

"Is he right, Daddy? Is it true that Tim didn't kill the judge?"

The mayor pulled the cigar from between his teeth, studied the macerated end with annoyance. "What's the difference? Right or wrong, Mal's story is bound to stir up an unholy mess."

"But if all those things are true—"

London looked at his daughter. The annoyance drained out of his face leaving a look of concern. "Don't worry yourself about it, dear. You start packing. Monday you're off on a trip to Europe."

The girl walked over to the china cigarette box on a small leather-topped table, helped herself to a cigarette. She placed it between her lips. "There could be real trouble? For you?"

"There won't be."

Rita swung around, studied her father's face. She realized for the first time the lines of strain that had been added in the past few days. "You won't be able to stop him, Dad." There was a reluctant note of admiration in her voice. "He's stubborn when he wants to be."

"Leave that to us."

She stopped with the match halfway to her lips. "Us?"

"The organization. They'll know how to handle him."

"But you told him they'd laugh at him."

London knocked the collar of ash from the end of the cigarette. "I'm not so sure any more. There was a time when we had everything sewed up. We could stamp anybody flat who stood in our way." He shook his head wearily. "Things are changing. People are beginning to ask questions. A fanatic like Waters could stir up a lot of headaches. And he's got that Lou Stewart behind him."

"But nobody pays any attention to Stewart any more. Max Everett can shout him under the table any day. You said so yourself."

"And I believed it. But I didn't realize how deep we were getting in. It's one thing to swing a few contracts for friends, to sell suspended sentences on gambling raps, to give preference on tax rates. But murder's another thing."

"Why are you telling me this, Dad?"

London looked at her for a long while. His eyes were watery. "Because I don't know how the ball is going to bounce. And if things go against us, I don't want you to get the wrong picture of what I've done—"

Concern ridged the girl's forehead. "You are worried, aren't you?"

The mayor nodded. He put his cigar down in an ash tray, reached for the phone.

"What are you going to do, Dad?"

His eyes were sick. "I've got to pass along the information about what Mal Waters has on us." He looked up pleadingly. "You understand that."

"But they'll kill him."

"They won't kill him. There's been too much killing already." He started to dial.

Chapter 19

Captain Marcy Lewis stood at the window in his office, looked out into the park across the way. He was conscious of the burning sensation in the pit of his stomach, wondered why the bicarb tablet hadn't had its usual effect. He was trying to forget the events of the night before.

There was a knock at the door.

"Come in." He turned to see Paul Harris, the tech man, walk in.

"You wanted to see me, skipper?" Harris asked.

Lewis nodded, indicated the chair on the opposite side of the desk. He walked ponderously to his own chair, sank into it. From the bottle on the desk, he dumped another bicarb tablet into his palm, swallowed it.

"How long you been with the department, Harris?"

A worried frown creased Harris's brow. "Almost have my twenty-five in." He licked at his lips. "Anything wrong?"

"Yeah. Plenty." Lewis paused for a moment, let the other man worry. "I got word they're thinking of bringing you up on charges."

"Me? Why?"

"Negligence." He raised his hand, cut off a protest. "You were in charge of the detail the night Carter was killed. Right?"

"Sure, skipper. You saw me there."

"You made a moulage of the killer's footprint. It's missing."

The tech man's face turned gray. "But, skipper—"

"Let me finish." Lewis got up, walked to the water cooler, helped himself to a drink. "I know you weren't negligent. I saw the job you were doing that night. But there are some people trying to embarrass me. They're going to hit at me through you." He tossed his cup at the wastebasket. "At least they think they are."

Harris watched his superior anxiously. His Adam's apple bobbed, he cleared his throat with sharp barks. "Somebody removed that moulage. We're going to put it back."

"But how?"

Lewis walked back to his desk, dropped into the chair. "I have a shoe belonging to the killer. Can you make a substitute moulage from it?"

The tech man cleared his throat. "But, skipper—"

"Now let's get something straight, Harris. The disappearance of that moulage is going to embarrass me. But it's going to put you out of the department. If you don't want to do it, okay. But—"

"You've got me wrong, skipper. I'll do it. Sure."

Lewis exhaled slowly. "How soon can you have it?"

"A couple of hours," Harris said nervously. "I don't think it would be a good idea to do it here. I'd have to go home."

"Sign out sick. I'll okay it."

"Anything you say, skipper. But the shoe—"

"That's all taken care of." Lewis reached into his bottom drawer, brought out a brown-paper-wrapped parcel, laid it on the desk. "Was there any identifying mark put on the cast at the time you made it?"

"Just initials and a date. I can handle that."

"Good." Lewis leaned back, studied the nervous expression on the other man's face. "You do a good job, Harris. I wouldn't be surprised if you came up for retirement a sergeant."

The worry drained from the thin man's face. "Gee, thanks, skipper."

"Just see to it that the new cast gets into this office by this afternoon."

"Don't worry about it, skipper. It's as good as there."

When he left, Harris was carrying the brown-paper parcel.

Marcy Lewis sprawled in his chair exhausted. He had only started. Zito's early morning instructions to him had been explicit. There was evidence around that had been overlooked. Find it, destroy it and substitute new evidence that would stand up.

All that was left was to find the original moulage and destroy it. As he sat in his chair, massaging his tender midsection, he had a pretty good idea of where to start looking. Fervently he cursed Matt Cleary as a stubborn old fool. He realized that he hated the old man, not only because he had almost thrown this monkey wrench into the works, but because he was always there, uncompromising, as a reminder of the kind of cop Lewis had started out to be. But never became. Honesty and integrity made him nervous these days—and Matt Cleary smelled too much of both.

He debated the advisability of taking another bicarb tablet, decided a shot of bourbon might be more efficacious. From the bottom drawer of the desk, he brought a half full bottle. He filled a paper cup half full, washed it down with water from the cooler. He winced as it burned into the tender area, decided it made him feel better.

The door to Captain Cleary's office was open. Marcy Lewis walked in, looked around. The logical place to keep an item the size of a footprint moulage was either the filing cabinet or the small closet on the far side of the room.

Lewis settled for the filing cabinet, opened drawer after drawer, to find them filled with papers and reports. The door to the closet was locked, yielded easily to a thin strip of celluloid he carried in his wallet. On the top shelf of the closet was a cloth-wrapped object and a shoe. He took the shoe down. Pasted to the sole was a label that read: *Shoe taken from apartment of Tim Benson, March 8, 1958, in our presence.* It was signed by Matt Cleary, Sergeant Ed Rohan, Sergeant Pat McManus.

Lewis nodded his satisfaction. This would make the cheese even more binding. He made a mental note to arrange for Sergeants Rohan and McManus to be taken care of as soon as the heat was off. It was about time to break the back of the little core of old-timers Matt Cleary had been carefully licking into an organization.

He reached up, lifted the cloth-covered object down, uncovered it. It was the footprint moulage he had seen Harris make at the Carter house the night of the murder. His instructions had been to destroy it. But now his instincts told him that in his possession it might become an important bargaining point.

He closed the closet door behind him, walked to the door. The corridor leading to his office was empty. He carried the moulage to his office, stuck it in the oversized bottom drawer. He reread the label on the shoe, dropped it in on top of the moulage.

The trap had been set. And as soon as Harris delivered the new moulage, it could be sprung. Without thinking, he dumped a bicarb tablet into his hand, swallowed it.

The morgue in Jackson City is at the end of a long, silent corridor in the basement of the City Hospital. There are two doors at the far end, one lettered *Medical Examiner* on frosted glass, the other opening into a brightly lighted room, painted a sterile white.

Mayor Ed London walked gingerly down the hall, wrinkled his nose at the dank smell that permeated the corridor, turned in at the door marked *Medical Examiner*. A young woman sitting behind a white enameled desk looked up, did a double take as she recognized the mayor.

"Is Dr. Denton in?" London asked.

"Yes, Your Honor." She was visibly impressed by the visit. She pushed a key on the intercom, breathed heavily into it. "The mayor's here to see you, Doctor. Yes, I said the mayor." There was a metallic sound from the intercom. She snapped off the key.

Before she could get to the inner door, it was opened from the inside. Dr. Denton stood in the doorway, dry-washing bloodless hands, twisting his face into what was obviously an unfamiliar smile.

"Come in, come in." He held a clammy hand out, gave the mayor's hand a weak shake and dropped it. He watched London walk into his office with a slight apprehension, closed the door behind him. Then, rubbing his hands together, he hustled toward his desk. "We don't get to see much of you down here." He showed yellowing teeth in a smile.

"I like to get around once in a while. Visit all the departments in the city. We get complaints now and then. Unjustified, I'm sure. I like to see for myself." London looked around the office. It was simply furnished—a large desk, a row of filing cabinets, a bookcase full of technical volumes, a row of framed diplomas on the wall.

Dr. Denton watched his superior apprehensively. "Complaints, you say? Not of my department surely?" He tried for a weak laugh. "There's an old saying the coroner's customers never complain."

London brought his eyes back from a survey of the room to the medical examiner's face. He gauged the degree of apprehension. "I'm sure it's nothing we can't straighten out."

Denton's hand-twisting was more frenzied. "But what could it be?" He shook his head bewilderedly. "We do our best, and—"

"Perhaps sometimes we overdo it." London brought two cigars out of his pocket, offered one to the medical examiner. Denton shook his head. "Complicate things. You know?"

"But how, Your Honor?"

London made a production of biting off the end of his cigar. "Well, let's say that if a man has a bullet hole in his head, it's a waste of the taxpayers' money to do extensive tests for poison. Wouldn't you agree?"

"Why—why, yes."

The mayor stuck the cigar in his mouth, chewed it. "And if a girl is killed in an automobile accident, it's a waste of time speculating about which injuries killed her and which didn't." He looked up at the medical examiner. "The cause of death was the accident."

Denton licked at his lips. "But I didn't mean—"

London ignored the interruption. "Unfortunately, in a recent case, a young man for whom I have tremendous affection was involved. Because he is close to me, people who would turn this unfortunate occurrence to their own advantage, would like to make it seem something that it isn't. Do you follow me?"

"I—I think so."

"I hope you do. For your sake. Because unless the medical examiner's report on Bonnie Peters specifically shows her death was due to injuries sustained in that accident, I might get the idea that you've sold out to those other people." His gaze held that of the medical examiner.

"But all I said was—"

London got up. "I think we understand each other. This afternoon, I want your formal report on the Bonnie Peters case on my desk. Just in the event that I need it, I'd also like an undated letter of resignation." There was a stricken look on the medical examiner's face. He swayed, caught the desk for support. "But, Your Honor, I've served this department most of my life. There's never been any question of—"

"There's never been any question of your loyalty. If I find that the rumors I've heard about your taking part in a conspiracy to embarrass me are groundless"— he permitted the old campaign smile to light up his face—"your resignation will be returned to you with my refusal to accept it."

"Thank you, Your Honor. Thank you very much," Denton said shakily.

London nodded expansively, headed for the door. "By the way," he added without turning around. "Sign a release for the girl's body. It is being picked up today for cremation. I've had a wire from her people asking that this be done."

After London had left, Dr. Denton rushed to his files, brought out the folder marked Bonnie Peters. Hastily he removed a typewritten report, tore it and the three copies of it into small pieces. He punched the key on the intercom.

"Sally. Come in right away. I have a rush report to get out. A copy has to be on the mayor's desk in an hour."

Chapter 20

Mal Waters straightened up, looked at the other three people in the room. "Well, what do you think?"

Lou Stewart sucked on a long-dead pipe. "Dynamite." He looked at Matt Cleary for corroboration. The white-haired man nodded.

"But can you use it?" Marta Cleary wanted to know. "You have no proof beyond just a list of names. What's to prevent you from just writing up a list and leaving Benson's name off? Or even putting Dad's in?"

"That's where Lou and his paper come in." He tapped the list. "We know where to look now, and he has the manpower to dig up the proof."

"How?" the girl wanted to know.

"Here's a breakdown of what every joint below the Line pays to operate. Who the bag men are, how much is earmarked for the sergeant, how much for the lieutenant, how much for the captain." He tapped a cigarette on the edge of the table, stuck it in the corner of his mouth. "The *Star* has district men who know the inside of headquarters and the various precinct houses like the backs of their hands. Not much gets by them. Once they know what they're looking for, they'll find it."

Stewart nodded. "And we've got men who cover the tax office, and the courts."

"Right. Here's a list of the judges on the Syndicate payroll. We start checking back. How many suspended sentences, how many continuances that never came up for sentence. And we start to ask why. You see?"

"The boy's right, Marta," Matt Cleary said. "We save a lot of time we'd be wasting checking. We know who to watch and sooner or later we'll get what we want." He squinted at Waters thoughtfully. "You never told us exactly how you got that list, Mal."

"You wouldn't believe me if I did." He took a deep drag on the cigarette, exhaled twin streams from his nostrils. "What do you hear about Barney Maurer?"

"Nothing. Should I?"

Waters shrugged. "Just wondering." He turned to Stewart. "How fast can we get started on this, Lou?"

The newspaperman started to answer, broke off when the telephone in the hall started pealing. Marta left to answer it.

"For you, Dad," she called from the hall.

Cleary frowned his annoyance, stamped off to answer it. They could hear the rumble of his voice, then the sound of the phone being slammed into place. When he walked back in to the room, his face was black with anger.

"They're starting to hit back," he growled. "That was the mayor's office. I'm on indefinite suspension pending a departmental trial."

"What? They can't do that, Dad."

"They've done it."

Stewart knocked the dottle from his pipe. "What charges?"

"Removing evidence from the files. They found the moulage in my closet."

"Say, maybe that's a break," Waters pointed out. "We get off on the right foot. They'll probably try to play this down, but Lou can blow the lid right off it." He looked around. "Don't you see? It gives us a legitimate reason to ask whose footprint it was."

"They won't produce the moulage," Cleary argued.

"We'll make them. We'll ride them from now to hell and gone until they do."

Stewart nodded. "Mal's right, Matt. It could be a break in disguise. That's the way it is with these over-smart guys. You put the pressure on and sometimes they try so hard to cover up they start making mistakes. I think maybe Ed London has made his first big one."

"When is the hearing?"

"This afternoon. In the mayor's office. At four."

"We'll be there with you, Matt," Stewart promised. "This time it'll be the *Star* that's on deck with a photographer. It's about time our side came to bat." He got up. "I'm going back to the office. I've got a lot of work to do. It takes time to put out an extra." He picked up his hat from the table near the hall, stuck it jauntily on the back of his head and headed for the door.

Marta watched her father's face with concern. "Dad, you don't think—"

The old man worked at a smile, walked over, patted her arm. "Don't worry, Marta. They've tried to get the old man before. They'll try again. It's a pretty tough old goat they're after. You should know that." He picked up the ice list. "With this in our hands we can really give them a tussle."

"That's our big ace in the hole," Mal said. "Maybe we ought to have some copies made. Just in case."

The old man nodded. "Good idea."

"I can type. One-finger style," Marta told them. "I may take a little longer than a professional typist, but I don't imagine you'd want that thing floating around."

"Would you? It would be a big help."

The girl nodded. She picked the list out of her father's hand, started for the other room. She stopped, turned to Mal. "I hope you can finish what you've started, Mal. A lot of people can be hurt if you can't." She dropped her eyes, turned, walked into her room and shut the door behind her.

Matt Cleary stared at the closed door for a moment, then shrugged. He turned to Mal, put his hand on the younger man's shoulder. "Win, lose or draw, they're going to know they were in a fight, boy. Don't go blaming yourself no matter what happens. Sooner or later there had to be a showdown. All you did was make it sooner."

Mal Waters dropped the cab outside his apartment. The Matson Apartments was one of Jackson City's newer buildings—a pseudo-modern pile of brick and plate glass that looked like a waffle standing on end. Each room had its own wall-sized picture window and a small balcony made completely private by being indented into the grill of the waffle.

He rode the elevator to the fifth floor, followed a thick-napped carpet to 506, used his key. He stopped at the open door, stared in at the wreckage of his apartment. The desk drawers had been pulled out, their contents spilled on the floor.

The pillows had been pulled off the sofa and chairs and slashed open, the contents of his closets were piled on the floor.

"Come in. Join the party." A pleasant-faced man stood behind the door, walked around, showed Waters the gun he held in his fist. "Close the door."

Waters walked in, became aware of a second man in the room. The second man was thin almost to the point of wispiness. He had blond wavy hair that had started to recede from the temples.

"You've given us a lot of trouble, mister," the man with the gun told him pleasantly.

"What are you doing here?" Mal wanted to know.

"We're just returning a call you made on a friend of ours," Wavy Hair told him. His voice held the faintest trace of a lisp, was low, intimate as though he were whispering. "You were pretty rough on our friend. We don't like people to be rough on our friends, do we, Joey?"

Joey smiled. "No, Mike, we don't like it at all." He looked Mal over with interest. "You know, you shape up a pretty lucky guy. You get to walk away from a kill. You know why? The boss don't want any heat until after election. How soon is that, Mike?"

The wavy-haired man pursed his too-red lips, rolled his eyes up. "Maybe six months."

"After election, things may be different. Maybe then his friends get a chance to square things for Barney. You know?"

"You still haven't told me what you want."

Joey raised his eyebrows. "That's right. We haven't told you what we want. This friend of ours—the guy you got rough with—you've got something belonging to him. We dropped by to pick it up." He waved the gun at the wreckage of the apartment. "It wasn't here, so we waited for you to get back."

"I don't know what you're talking about. I don't have anything that belongs to anybody. You're making a mistake."

"Not us, Waters," Wavy Hair told him. "You're making the mistake."

He lashed out with the flat of his hand, knocked Mal's face to the side, then he backslapped it into position. Waters wiped his mouth with the side of his hand, stared at the smear of blood.

"It won't do you any good. Anything you can dish out, I can take."

Mike grinned bleakly, brought his right up, buried it in Waters' midsection. The air whooshed from his lungs and his body slammed back against the door where he slid to a sitting position.

"We've got all day," Joey told him pleasantly.

Mal gasped some air into his lungs. There was a dull ringing in his ears; the floor seemed to be tilting crazily as he struggled to his feet.

"He must like it," Mike grunted. He brought his fist back, prepared to smash it into Waters' face. "Hold it, Mike," Joey cautioned. "How can he talk without teeth?"

Joey walked over to Waters, steadied him against the door. "You ought to get smart, mister. Mike'll leave you as toothless as the day you were born. Where's the list?"

Mal shook his head.

Mike started for him, Joey shouldered him aside. "You just think you won't tell us. You have no idea how persuasive Mike can be." He stepped aside. "See if he has it on him, Mike."

Waters put up a token resistance as the wavy-haired man fumbled through his pockets, finally shook his head. "It's not on him. It's not in the apartment." He tossed the contents of Mal's pockets to the floor. "He left it some place." He caught the front of Mal's jacket, pulled him off balance. "Where?"

Mal continued to shake his head.

"It wouldn't be the newspaper guy. He wasn't at his office. He must have been with this joker." He squinted at Waters thoughtfully. "The cop. Cleary. That where you left it, mister?"

Mal licked at his lips. "No, I—"

Joey nodded. "That's it." He studied Mal carefully. "That daughter of his. Quite a dish, eh, mister?"

"She doesn't know anything about it," Mal croaked.

"Maybe we ought to find out." He turned to the wavy-haired man. "We'll let Mike have a talk with her. He doesn't like women. Especially pretty ones."

"Leave her alone, I tell you."

Joey nodded his satisfaction. "That's where it is. Run over there, Mike. Pick it up. She might take a little persuading—"

"She hasn't got it. I tell you she hasn't got it."

"Where is it?"

Mal licked at his lips. "In a safe place. A place where you'll never find it if—"

Mike lashed out with the flat of his hand, sent Waters staggering. "Stop lying."

The ex-D.A.'s eyes were watery. "Where you'll never find it."

"In that case it won't hurt to have Mike have a talk with the girl anyway. He can call us here and let you hear some of his methods with the girl. You'll be surprised how—"

"Don't." Mal leaned wearily against the wall. "I'll get you the list. Don't hurt the girl."

Joey nodded. "But there hadn't better be any tricks."

"No tricks." Mal staggered to the phone, picked it up, dialed a number. Joey moved up behind him, jabbed the snout of his gun into Mal's kidney. He stuck his ear next to Mal's at the earpiece.

After a moment, a voice answered. "Yes?"

Mal took a deep breath, tried to make his voice sound natural. "Marta? Mal. Have you started copying the list?"

"Not yet, Mal. I was planning to start later and—"

"That's all right. I have to borrow the list back for a few hours. I have some people I want to check it over."

There was a slight pause. "How can I get it to you?"

Mal looked around at the faces of the two men watching him closely. "I'll send a man for it. Give it to him."

"If you say so."

"Thanks, Marta." He dropped the receiver back on its hook. "You can pick it up at Cleary's house."

The wavy-haired man looked at Joey who nodded. "She was supposed to make copies. Hasn't started yet."

"Good."

Joey stepped away from Mal, said to Mike, "We'll go on over and pick it up."

Mike grinned. "Don't you think we ought to make sure our friend here doesn't get telephone happy?"

"He's all yours."

Mal saw the other man coming, tried to get out of his way. Mike cut off his retreat, chopped at Mal's neck. His head rolled forward helplessly. When Mike chopped again, Waters went to his knees. He managed to wrap his arms around the other man's legs, but he had no power to hold them.

Mike brought his knee back, knocked Waters over on his back. He tried to turn over, the floor tilted sickeningly and he slid into a merciful black void which erased the white-hot flashes and the searing pain from his skull.

Joey stared down at him without expression. "I don't think he's likely to get telephonitis in the next hour." He put his gun away, started for the door. As an afterthought, he walked over to the wreckage of a portable bar, found a bottle of bourbon. He walked back, spilled it over the unconscious man.

"Looks like every time we meet this sucker, we buy him a drink." He emptied the bottle, tossed it aside. "Trouble is, he doesn't know it."

Chapter 21

The cool-looking blonde in the outer office of the mayor's suite stood up at the sound of the buzzer. She nodded to Matt Cleary.

"You may go in now, Captain."

She watched the old man with expressionless eyes as he pulled himself out of the chair, crossed the wheat-colored rug to the door she held open. Cleary walked into the office, waited until the girl closed the door behind him.

Ed London sat behind the big desk, a serious expression on his face. "Hello, Cleary. Would you sit over there, please?" He indicated a big leather chair to the left of the desk.

Cleary nodded, looked around. Lou Stewart of the *Star* sat with his photographer facing the mayor's desk. Surprisingly Max Everett and his photographer were also present. To the right of the mayor's desk, Marcy Lewis sat examining his knuckles. He glanced up briefly as Cleary crossed to his chair, resumed the examination of his knuckles.

The mayor addressed himself to the press. "Gentlemen, I notified you of this hearing because, in view of Captain Cleary's long service with the department, I want to lean over backward to see that he gets every chance to clear himself." He looked over to the white-haired man. "I've already told the captain the nature of the charge against him. Unauthorized removal of evidence. I wanted you gentlemen to hear his explanation." He dropped his eyes to his desk, studied some notes he had penciled on a pad. "It could be a mistaken sense of loyalty to a fellow officer. Understandable, perhaps, but none the less a violation of his oath." He looked up. "This evidence, a vital clue in a murder case, was removed from department files and concealed in the captain's office."

"What's the nature of this evidence, Your Honor?" Stewart wanted to know.

The mayor said, "It was a moulage of the footprint of Sergeant Tim Benson, left on Judge Carter's lawn the night Benson shot him."

"Can we see it?" Stewart persisted.

"Of course, Stewart, you understand that your being here is a courtesy that—" He broke off, shrugged. He pushed down the lever of the intercom. "Call down to Captain Lewis's office. Have the moulage and shoe found in Cleary's office brought up." He depressed the lever. "In the meantime, would you care to give any explanation for your action, Cleary?"

The white-haired man shifted uncomfortably on his chair. "I removed that moulage from the department files because I was afraid it might be deliberately destroyed." His eyes met those of the man behind the desk. "I thought in the interests of justice, somebody should make sure it wasn't."

"The interests of justice?"

Cleary nodded. "That moulage is the footprint of the actual killer of Judge Carter."

The mayor cleared his throat. "Benson."

Cleary shook his head. "Benson did not kill Judge Carter. That's what I intend to prove with that footprint."

Max Everett smirked. "Maybe we ought to move up the retirement age of our police department. If you'll pardon my saying it, I think the captain's talking sheer nonsense. We all know who killed Carter." He looked over to where Stewart was busily making notes. "It's one thing to make up the news to try to sell papers, but facts are facts."

London turned to Marcy Lewis. "Have you ever discussed this with Cleary?"

"He's one of the old-timers. To him a man who wears tin can do no wrong. If he does, cover him." Lewis shook his head. "I don't operate that way, Your Honor. Nobody in my department uses his badge to bail him out for murder. There are rotten apples in every barrel. The sooner we get rid of them the better.''

"I say amen to that, Lewis," the white-haired man told him. "The sooner the better."

London hit the top of his desk with the flat of his hand. "Gentlemen! I don't want any personalities injected into this. This hearing is being conducted on a question of fact. Either Captain Cleary attempted to remove important evidence or he didn't." He glanced toward the door at the sound of a light tapping. "Come in."

The door opened, a uniformed patrolman walked in. He carried a familiar looking cloth-wrapped object and a shoe. Cleary and Lou Stewart exchanged glances, watched the officer cross the room, deposit the two objects on the mayor's desk.

London dismissed the officer with a nod, waited until he had left the room. He reached over, picked up the shoe, turned it over, read aloud the label pasted on the sole.

"You recognize your handwriting, Cleary?" He held the shoe out to the white-haired man. Cleary nodded. The mayor unrolled the cloth-covered object, exposing the moulage. He examined it, read the initials and the date scratched in for identification.

Cleary frowned, started to say something, but it was too late. The mayor had taken the shoe, placed it in the moulage. It was a perfect fit!

Max Everett nudged his photographer who was on his feet in a second. The explosion of a flash bulb brightened the room.

Lou Stewart sat staring stupidly at the shoe resting snugly in the moulage. He tore his eyes away, looked over at the stricken face of Matt Cleary. He nodded to a question from his photographer without taking his eyes away from the white-haired man. His photographer stood up, aimed his camera at the evidence on the desk, shot the picture.

Ed London rapped for attention. "This action of Captain Cleary's is doubly important at this time. Despite the overwhelming evidence that Sergeant Benson shot and killed Judge Carter there is an organized attempt being made to whitewash him." He looked sternly in the direction of Lou Stewart. "I can only be charitable in believing that Captain Cleary removed this evidence of Benson's guilt in a misguided loyalty to an unworthy member of his department. However, regardless of the motive, I am constrained to suspend Captain Cleary from active duty in the department indefinitely." He turned to Cleary. "I'm sorry. There is nothing else I can do."

Max Everett was the first on his feet. "Thank you, Your Honor. My paper will thank you editorially. As Cleary himself agreed, the sooner we get rid of men in the department who think they're above the law, the better." He motioned to his photographer. "If there's nothing else—"

London hesitated. "Well, as long as I have you gentlemen of the press here, I could give you another item." He riffled through his papers, came up with an official-looking document. "I have here the medical examiner's report on Bonnie Peters—" He looked up, explained, "The girl who was killed in Mal Waters' car."

"Well?"

The mayor glanced through the document. "Dr. Denton ascribes death to frontal fractures of the skull. The alcoholic content of the girl's blood indicated there had been considerable drinking—"

"All anybody would have to do was to get a look at Waters that night. Or smell him," the *World's* photographer grunted. "I was there. He smelled like he'd been swimming in it."

London nodded. "So I understand. I intend to turn this over to the district attorney to see whether or not there are grounds for prosecution of Mr. Waters on charges of criminal negligence leading to vehicular homicide. This might quiet some rumors that I've been bending over backward to be lenient with a man I once considered my protégé."

"What about the depressed fracture in the rear of the girl's skull?" Cleary demanded. "Denton told me himself—"

London peered at the report, shook his head. "There's no mention here of a fracture on the rear of the girl's skull. Of course, if you question the report, Dr. Denton would probably—"

"I wouldn't take that old quack's word for anything. I demand that an independent doctor be brought in for an autopsy to—"

"That would be impossible," London told him blandly. "At the request of her next in kin, Bonnie Peters' body was cremated this afternoon."

Chapter 22

Mal Waters sat on the edge of a chair, his face buried in his hands. The room reeked of whisky. He didn't even look up when the door opened and closed.

Matt Cleary stood at the door, shook his head pityingly. "They got you too, huh?" He wrinkled his nose at the smell of whisky, walked over to the window and opened it.

Slowly, painfully Waters lifted his face out of his hands. The side of his jaw was swollen and discolored. He seemed to have difficulty in focusing his eyes or recognizing the white-haired man.

Cleary squinted at him, walked over to where Mal sat. "You all right, boy?"

"They got the list," Mal told him thickly. "They got the list." He appeared to be struggling to make his eyes focus. "I couldn't stop them."

Cleary nodded his understanding. "None of us could, boy. We were crazy to try. Amateurs like us never had a chance with a bunch of pros like them." He walked to the phone, dialed a number, tapped his impatience with splayed fingers. "Marta? I'm at Mal Waters' place. Can you get over?"

"What's the matter, Dad? More trouble?"

"Somebody worked the boy over. He's in bad shape."

"Where's his place?"

"Matson Apartments. 506."

"I'll be right there."

The old man nodded, hung up. He walked back to where Mal sat weaving on the edge of the chair. He caught him under the arms, helped him to his feet. Then he half dragged, half carried him to the bathroom.

A cold shower had shocked Waters into some semblance of normalcy by the time the knock came on the door. Cleary left him leaning against the sink while he went to answer the door.

Marta made no effort to mask her concern. "Is he hurt badly, Dad?"

"He's had a bad time. Physically and emotionally."

"The list! Those men he sent for the list—"

"Zito's men," Cleary explained.

The girl looked past her father at the man leaning weakly against the sink. "They slapped him around a little. So he gave up the list." Her full lip curled contemptuously. "He knew what it meant to all of you—"

The old man shook his head. "They could have killed him and he wouldn't have given it to them."

"Then why?"

Cleary put his hand on her arm. "They told him they knew he'd left it with you. He couldn't be sure they were bluffing. He wouldn't take the chance."

The anger slowly left the girl's face. She caught her lower lip between her teeth. "I should have guessed. I'm sorry, Dad."

Cleary nodded. "See if you can get the bed into shape for him. I'll get him into the bedroom."

Marta crossed to the bedroom wordlessly. The same degree of wreckage greeted her there. She wrestled the mattress back onto the bed, managed to salvage some clean linen, and made the bed. By the time her father half carried, half dragged Waters to the bed, there was some semblance of order.

Mal offered no resistance and no help as they slid him under the sheet. Marta tucked him in efficiently, ran the tips of her fingers along the swollen side of his jaw.

"Think he should have a doctor?" the old man wanted to know.

The girl shook her head. "He'll be all right. Leave him to me." She took her father by the arm, led him from the room. "How about you, Dad?" She tried to read the answer in his face. "You didn't call after the hearing. I was worried."

"They've beaten us, Marta. I'm on suspension. Indefinitely."

"But the moulage! Couldn't you prove that it wasn't Benson that—"

Cleary shook his head. "I should have expected it. But I've known Harris for so many years. I always trusted him and—" He broke off. "They switched the moulage. Harris made a new one using a shoe of Benson's. It fit perfectly."

"Oh, Dad!"

He patted the girl's arm. "It's not that bad, Marta, I was due to sign myself out in a few years anyhow."

"But to go out this way—"

Cleary smiled wryly. "It doesn't matter much how you go out as long as you go out fighting for what you believe." He looked into the bedroom, the smile faded. "Besides, I don't have an awful lot of time left. Mal does. And what they're planning for him is a lot worse than what they did to me."

"What more can they do to him?"

Cleary ran the tips of his fingers along the stubble of his beard. "They're going to indict him for criminal negligence in the death of the cigarette girl. They'll pin it on him, too."

"You mean he could go to jail?"

"Probably. Even worse, chances are he'll be disbarred. They're out to teach him and anyone else who tries to go up against them a lesson they'll never forget." The old man shook his head. "And it's my fault. I couldn't let the dead stay dead. I kept fighting to get the whole thing reopened. Why, I don't know. Tim Benson was dead. They couldn't hurt him any more. Maybe it would have been better to leave things alone."

"You don't believe that. In every war, there have to be some casualties. You knew the chances you were taking when you started this. So did he. You're not crying. And I don't think he will."

Cleary massaged the tip of his jaw with his fingertips. "It was all so useless. We never really had a chance." He turned, walked out of the bedroom into the living room. After a moment she could hear him righting the furniture, putting the drawers back into the desk.

She looked down at the face of the man on the pillow. She wondered now why she had thought he looked weak the first time she had seen his picture in the paper. It wasn't the face of a hero, she remembered thinking then. Which showed how wrong you could be.

It was dark in the room when Mal Waters awakened. He stared at the gray-white patch of ceiling above his bed, tried to remember what had happened. He turned toward the window, winced with the pain. A dark-haired girl was curled up in a chair sleeping. He tried to get up on his elbow, fell back on the pillow with a grunt.

Marta opened her eyes, saw her patient was awake. She reached up, pulled on a light, got up and walked over to him with a smile.

"Sleeping Beauty had nothing on you. How do you feel?"

"I'm still alive."

"That's encouraging." She lifted him expertly, arranged the pillow under his head. "You're a pretty lucky boy. No bones broken." She looked around the room. "You did better than your furniture. Some of it'll never be the same."

He closed his eyes for a moment. "The list. They got the list?"

She placed her hand on his forehead, brushed the hair out of his face. "Don't think about it."

He opened his eyes, stared up at her. "Your father? What happened?"

"We'll talk about that in the morning."

He groaned. "They framed him, didn't they?" He didn't wait for an answer. "It's my fault. All my fault."

"Don't be silly. You couldn't do any more than—"

"It's my fault," he repeated. "I—I went to Ed London. I told him everything we had on him. I—I wanted to give him a chance to get out. I wanted to believe that he didn't know what was going on."

"But why?"

"Rita. I still love her, Marta. Sounds stupid, I know. But I didn't want to be the one who hurt her father."

The girl stared at him wide-eyed. "But it was all right for my father to be hurt. And for you to almost get your fool neck broken, and—" She broke off, caught her lower lip between her teeth. "I'm sorry. You're in no condition to think about it now. What's done is done, I guess." She turned, walked to the window. "Get some rest. We'll talk about it in the morning." She didn't turn away from the window. Outside it was still dark. Soon the first signs of day would lighten the sky, exposing all the filth that night had mercifully masked.

She heard a muffled sob from the bed, turned, walked back. Mal Waters lay on his back, staring at the ceiling, tears running down his cheeks.

Marta sat on the side of the bed. "Don't cry like that, Mal. I—I don't think any girl is worth that."

He shook his head. "I spoiled everything. For you. For your father. For everybody." He turned his head painfully. "I give you my word, Marta. They'll pay for it. Every one of them will pay for it. I'll make sure they do."

She nodded. "Well, you're going to need your strength for that. So how about getting some rest now?"

He closed his eyes, but she knew by the rigidity of his body that he wasn't sleeping. She turned the light out over her chair, tiptoed out of the room. Matt Cleary sprawled in a chair, legs extended in front of him, mouth hanging open. On the table at his elbow, his service revolver was ready.

"He's awake, Dad." Marta shook the old man. "I'm frightened. He sounds crazy. You want to talk to him?"

"Shouldn't he sleep?"

"Yes, but he won't. He's lying in there with his eyes closed. But I know he isn't sleeping. He's just lying there, hating. I can feel it."

The white-haired man pursed his lips thoughtfully, picked up the service revolver, stuck it in his belt. He followed the girl into the bedroom, waited until she turned on the light.

Mal Waters hadn't moved. He lay there, breathing shallowly, his eyes closed, his mouth an angry thin line.

"Hello, boy. How do you feel?" Cleary leaned over the bed, watched the eyes open. The tight expression at the mouth didn't soften.

"All right. Sorry, Cleary. It was all my fault. I tipped my hand to Ed London."

"Forget it. We were a bunch of amateurs going up against the pros. It had to turn out this way. Nobody's to blame."

"I'll get them, Cleary. Every last one of them."

The old man patted his shoulder. "Forget it. Nobody can go up against that mob and walk away. We did our best. We have nothing to be ashamed of."

"You don't understand. I sold you all out. I warned them about what we had. Gave them a chance to turn it against us." He studied the old man's face. "I'm through worrying about doing it the legal way."

"Now you're talking crazy. If you could go up against that crowd, which you can't, you know where you'd end up? In the chair. The courts don't differentiate between killing a man and a mad dog like Zito. They call them both murder."

"It doesn't matter about me. I'm finished. From now on all that matters is to see how many of them I can take with me when I go."

"That slugging you got must have affected your mind," Cleary roared at him. "You're not going any place. And you're not taking anybody with you."

Mal rolled over on his side, turned his back to the white-haired man. "I'm sorry about what happened to you, Cleary. And Lou Stewart. And the cigarette girl. All I've done is hurt everybody I've touched. From now on I start touching the kind of people where my jinx will do the most good."

Cleary looked at his daughter, shrugged. She shook her head, motioned for him to leave the room. After he had gone, Waters lay motionless. He was still lying there wide-eyed when day arrived outside.

Chapter 23

For the next three days, the *World* trumpeted to the people of Jackson City the story of how Captain Matt Cleary tried to tamper with evidence proving the guilt of Sergeant Tim Benson in the murder of Judge Carter. It dug into its files, reminded the citizens of the deathbed identification of Benson and his "confession" in destroying himself when the ring started to tighten around him. Editorially it inveighed against police officials who considered themselves above the law and who used their authority to shield murderers. At the end of the fourth day, the wide and popular support Matt Cleary had always enjoyed was smashed.

There was another item of interest in the *World* on that fourth day. It announced that Miss Rita London, "daughter of Jackson City's popular Mayor Ed London," was leaving for a tour of Europe and upon her return was expected to announce her engagement to Max Everett, publisher of the *World*.

Lou Stewart's *Star* had a bad four days. It's feeble efforts to protect Matt Cleary against the attacks of its more powerful competitor accelerated the waning of its influence. Even the hard core of conservatives who steadfastly refused to lose their faith in its guidance found their confidence in its editorial integrity shaken. Advertisers who had withstood the pressure on them to drop out of its columns for years suddenly found themselves canceling reserved space and copies of returns started to mount heavily.

It was easily an overwhelming victory for the administration. It had been vindicated at the time it counted most—six months before election. Any chance that the *Star* had of needling the electorate to take a closer look at the machinations of the party in power was gone. Its weak protests that a party in power too long abused that power fell on deaf ears.

The district attorney found little difficulty in persuading a captive Grand Jury that Malcolm Waters, former district attorney of Jackson City, should be indicted for criminal negligence contributing to the vehicular homicide of Bonnie Peters. Plans were announced to try the ex-D.A. upon his recovery from a "mysterious illness." The illness was no mystery to those citizens of Jackson City who listened to the word spread by the temporary maid who showed up the second day—and was sent packing by Marta Cleary—that the place "smelled like a barroom."

Rita London heard of Marta's moving into Mal's apartment through a transient cleaning woman who was a close friend of Mal's maid. By the time the story had reached her, it had assumed the proportions of a first class shack-up. So, when her father pressured her to make some form of announcement of her plans with Max, she had agreed to set the date for their marriage upon her return.

Al Zito had spent most of the four days in his office getting his operation back to normal. True, Barney Maurer hadn't returned to take over operation of his place, but a suitable substitute was standing in for him until such time as he did return. The other spots were open and in full operation. Zito found Mal's successor in the D.A.'s office far more amenable and co-operative and things had begun to run more smoothly. The only fly in his ointment was Mal Waters' refusal to be run out of town; he was already making plans to take care of that.

For Mal they were four bitter days. He had withdrawn into himself, refused to be drawn into conversation or to leave his room unless it was absolutely unavoidable. He watched the collapse of the revolt against the ins, knew that now the outs had no chance of taking over control of Jackson City. The systematic looting of the town treasury, the growth of hoodlum control, the inequities and vice that had characterized the past would be even accelerated in the future. He refused to be consoled by Matt Cleary or Lou Stewart, avoided Marta as much as possible.

Mayor Ed London, after a few bad hours, had begun to regain his confidence. The thing had gone off as smoothly as Zito had predicted in spite of London's misgivings. Rita had agreed to the European trip and was set to marry Max Everett when she returned. The dreaded appearance of Mal Waters to accuse him of betrayal didn't materialize and for the first time in too long he was beginning to breathe easier.

Marta Cleary had watched Mal's withdrawal into himself with sadness. At first she had been hurt when she realized that he still loved Rita London, that her growing affection for him was not reciprocated. Then, as the days passed, she realized there was something different about him, something that frightened her a little, even repelled her. She realized it most when she would come upon him unexpectedly. He would be staring at the blank wall with a cold, frightening expression. She was no stranger to violence of temper. Her father had an explosive reaction to things that annoyed him. This was nothing like that. It was cold, brooding, deadly. She shivered a little every time she recalled the tight, lethal look around Mal's eyes.

It was on the morning of the fifth day that Mal walked out of the bedroom without prodding. Matt Cleary had steadfastly maintained a vigil in the living room since the first day. He was sitting with Marta drinking a cup of tea when the bedroom door opened and Mal walked through.

"Well, he's rejoining the human race." Cleary grinned. He studied Mal's face, found it impenetrable. "Good to see you up and around."

"I've dogged it long enough," Mal said. He directed a tight smile to Marta. "I can't keep you folks from your home forever." He pulled up a chair, turned it around, straddled it. "Besides I've got work to do."

"You're not going to start that again?" The grin faded from the white-haired man's face. "Sit tight, maybe they'll leave the indictment hang. It's been done. Start something and they'll push it through."

"Mal, why don't you forget the whole thing?" Marta urged. "It's over and done with. Why don't you leave it that way?"

"Isn't it too late for that, Marta?" Mal asked mildly. "I've got nothing more to lose. They have everything. Why should I quit now when the odds are in my favor for the first time?"

"But you don't understand—"

"Maybe I do. For the first time. You see, they make a mistake when they leave a man with nothing to lose." He reached over to the table, snagged a pack of cigarettes. "They say even a rat will fight when it's cornered. At least let me have the dignity of a rat."

"But the odds are so stacked against you, Mal. If you keep it up, they'll strip you of everything you have to fight with. They can even have you disbarred." Marta got up, put her hand on his arm. "Don't think that we don't know what you've been through. Nobody blames you for what happened. It was just that we never had a chance."

Mal lit the cigarette, took a deep drag. "Nobody will ever have a chance against them. They perpetuate themselves in control. Things keep getting worse but nobody does anything about it. Because everybody agrees that you don't stand a chance. Pretty soon, they're right. Nobody can do anything about it." He puffed on the cigarette. "Nobody, that is, except a guy who's got nothing to lose. That's me."

"What do you think you can do?" Cleary wanted to know.

"I don't know. But I intend to find out." He looked at the teapot. "Do you have an extra cup?"

Marta jumped to her feet. "Of course, Mal. I'm sorry." She bustled about preparing a cup of tea for him, looking from him to her father and back. "How do you intend to find out?"

"I'm going to pay a visit to Al Zito today."

The cup fell from Marta's fingers, smashed on the floor. "You're crazy. They'll kill you."

Waters shook his head. "I wish they would. That would make it easy. They can't afford to do that. Not now, anyhow."

"But what do you expect to accomplish?" Cleary wanted to know.

The former D.A. shook his head. "I'm not sure. But I think one thing it will accomplish. It might goose them into doing something they'll be sorry for."

"I'm just hoping you don't goose them into something you'll be sorry for," the white-haired man said.

Chapter 24

Al Zito laid the red ten on the black jack, looked up with a scowl of annoyance as the door opened and Joey walked in. The pleasant face of the gunman was marred by a puzzled expression.

"Al, he's here. Wants to see you."

"Who's here?"

"That Waters character." He shook his head. "He acts kind of crazy. Says he's seeing you before he leaves. One way or the other."

"He heavy?"

Joey shook his head. "I frisked him. Not even a penknife."

The fat man leaned back, puffed his lips in and out thoughtfully. "Get Mike. I want you both in here. Then let him in." The heavily veined lids half masked his eyes. "He's got something up his sleeve."

Joey nodded, withdrew. Zito stared at the closed door thoughtfully, making and breaking bubbles in the center of his lips.

The door swung open. Mal Waters walked in, started for the desk. Joey walked up behind him, caught him by the arm. "That's far enough."

Waters shook the hand off his arm. "Don't worry. I'm not going to do anything—now."

Mike walked into the room, closed the door behind him, leaned against it, his hand dug into his jacket pocket. He watched Waters warily.

"Nice of you to come see me, Mr. Waters," the fat man told him in low, gurgling tones. "Too bad you didn't come before now. Maybe we could have worked some things out."

"This isn't a social call, Zito—"

"Mr. Zito," Joey snapped at him.

Waters ignored the interruption. "I just dropped by to tell you I'm going to kill you."

There was no change of expression on the fat man's face. "You should live so long."

"I will. Because you can't afford to kill me. And I have nothing to lose by killing you." He turned, cast contemptuous glances at the two bodyguards. "And I wouldn't put too much stock in their ability to stop me."

"Joey and Mike are real efficient, Waters. They know their business, and—"

Waters swung back to him. "And maybe they're getting tired of being number-two men. Maybe they won't try too hard."

"What's that mean?" For the first time there was a flicker of expression in Zito's eyes.

"No ambitious young fellow likes to stay number-two man all his life, does he, Joey?"

"Shut up," the gunman growled.

"You were number-two man once, Zito. What happened to your boss? His tough luck was your good luck."

Joey lashed out with the side of his hand, knocked Waters to his knees. Mal shook his head to clear it.

"That won't stop me. I'm still going to kill you, Zito. One way or another. That's the interesting part about it. You're never going to know when it's going to be or how."

Joey moved toward him menacingly.

"Cut it out, Joey." There was a hard note in Zito's voice. The expressionless eyes studied his number-two man in a new light. They dropped to the man on the floor massaging the back of his neck. "Maybe we can do some business, Waters. There's no need for more trouble."

"What kind of business?"

"You're a lawyer, right? They're getting ready to kick you out. Suppose I stop them?"

"Why should you?"

The fat man shrugged. "Maybe I need a good lawyer." He waved off an interruption. "Not in this town necessarily. I got interests lots of places." He nodded for Joey to help Waters into a chair. "Like maybe Arizona or Montana or one of those places." He lifted two cigars from a humidor, held one up. Waters shook his head. "Might take a long time. A year, maybe."

"And the girl? The one who was found dead in my car?"

Zito stripped the cellophane wrap from a cigar, shrugged. "An accident. Accidents happen." He looked up. "Too bad, but that's the way it goes."

"And Barney Maurer?"

The fat man's eyes narrowed. "Barney took a trip. If I'm satisfied with that, you ought to be."

Waters shook his head. "No dice, Zito."

"You know, you remind me of a guy named Benson. Quite a bit on your type."

"I know."

"He was stupid, mister. Stubborn and stupid. We tried to reason with him." He shrugged. "He wouldn't listen to reason." He stuck the cigar in his mouth, snapped a lighter into flame, touched it to the end of the cigar. "We don't want any more trouble if we can avoid it. But if we can't we have ways of handling it. That's why I hope you'll accept this assignment."

"And if I don't?"

Zito blew a stream of gray-white smoke across the desk. "Then that would put us both to a certain amount of discomfort. Yours would be very brief."

Waters shook his head. "Sorry. I'm not buying. I didn't come here to listen to propositions. I came here to tell you I was going to kill you. That still goes."

The man behind the desk clenched his teeth on the cigar. His eyes were little more than slits behind the discolored sacs that buttressed them. "Get him out of here."

Joey reached down, grabbed the front of Waters' shirt, pulled him to his feet. At the door, Mike had withdrawn the hand sunk in his pocket, bared a .38. The hand that held it had a heavy gold chain dangling at the wrist. Even that failed to make the muzzle of the .38 any less menacing.

Joey shoved hard, sent Waters staggering toward the door.

"Nothing happens to him while he's in here," Zito told them coldly. "Just get him out of here. And see that he doesn't come back."

"You're making a mistake, Al. Let us handle this guy our way and—"

The dull, heavy-lidded eyes settled on Joey speculatively. "Since when did you start telling me how to operate?" He pursed his lips. "I'm still number-one man. Remember?"

Joey's jaw dropped. "Hell, Al. You ought to know I'm smart enough to know that—"

There was no mistaking the menace in the fat man's voice. "Maybe that's the trouble. Maybe you're too smart. I heard of a case where a guy's head got so big they had to put a few holes in it to let the air out. That's a pretty funny joke, ain't it?"

"Yeah. Real funny."

"So funny a guy could die laughing," Zito told him.

Joey looked from Zito to Mike, got no encouragement, looked back. He licked at his lips. "I'll take care of this monkey, boss."

Mike opened the door, Joey pushed Waters out in front of him. Mike started to close the door, looked in on Zito who nodded slightly, closed the door softly after him.

Zito sat motionless for minutes, his eyes half veiled, his jaws working methodically on the cigar. He pulled it from between his teeth, scowled at the macerated end, slammed it angrily into the wastebasket. He pulled the top drawer of his desk open, brought out a small address book, riffled through the pages. When he found the number he wanted, he lifted the phone, gave long distance an unlisted number in New York.

Mary Lister stretched out lazily on the divan of the penthouse's sundeck, watching Murph make the drinks. He walked over, handed one to her, sat on the edge of the divan. Beyond the small hedge that lined the sundeck, New York dozed in the haze of a prematurely hot May day.

Murph was Sylvan Murphy, top brains in the Syndicate. It was he who first saw the opportunities and advantages of organizing crime on a businesslike basis throughout the country. He decried the system whereby bookmaking, narcotics and prostitution were unorganized, run in a haphazard manner with local mobs directing and getting peanuts for their troubles. The money was there, and loose. And nobody was doing an organized job of scooping it up. That's when Sylvan Murphy first called together a meeting of the board of directors of the Syndicate.

At first they were suspicious of each other, demanded to be shown. The boys who were growing rich with the slots in Louisiana and Florida, the mob who had a gold mine in numbers and narcotics in New York, the hoods who had the labor shakedowns in the palms of their hands—they all wanted to know why they should cut anybody else in. Even for a possible share of somebody else's golden take.

Murphy persuaded them they didn't have to throw everything into one pot. Every man was to keep what he had, but all were to work together.

"It's suicide," he warned. "One of your boys gets hit, you have to hit somebody else. That costs manpower you can't afford and it brings heat. The most important thing to avoid is heat. Maybe once the public didn't know what goes on. Kefauver fixed that for good. Now your best chance is to lay low."

At that first meeting, the directors grudgingly agreed to go along on one provision. Each boss remained boss of his own territory. No one got hit in his territory without his okay, and he would have the right to import talent to do the job by calling the Syndicate for the necessary specialists.

The program outlined by Sylvan Murphy had been an outstanding success from the start and today he sat as referee, the Syndicate's only contact with all members of the board of directors.

It was he, in turn, who drafted Mary Lister as bag man to carry messages and money from the various directors to the various troops who had been imported to do their missions. These messages and payments were considered far too confidential to be trusted to the more public carriers.

Mary sipped at her drink, stared up at the clear blue of the sky. "How about us knocking off for a while, Murph? Take a cruise. Just the two of us?" She got up on her elbow, studied his face. "Things are pretty quiet, and it's been a long time since we were away alone."

Murph grinned at her. He had the well-tanned face of a man who kept in trim, fancied his thick shock of wavy white hair. When he smiled, he exposed a mouth full of expertly capped teeth. The smile failed to defrost the icy blue of his eyes.

"Things are too quiet." He sipped at his glass, stared out over the haze. "But you're right. It's been a long time. Too long. I'm thinking of getting out, Mary. Soon."

"Will they let you?"

Murphy shrugged. "Everything is organized so it can run like clockwork without me. They don't need me any more. I sold them a program, contracted to prove that it could operate. That's all they bought."

"Sometimes the boys get unreasonable." She dropped on her back, stared up at the sky.

"I've taken out insurance," Murph growled. "The same kind you have. Nothing better happen to me."

The girl grinned lazily.

Somewhere a telephone pealed. Murph sighed, set the glass down, walked into the cool, dim living room. He crossed to a large walnut desk, opened the bottom drawer, lifted out a phone.

"Yeah?"

"This is Zito, Murph." The fat man's voice was blubbery, low. "In Jackson City."

"I know, I know. What's the emergency this time?"

There was a short pause, the heavy breathing of the fat man came through. "Same thing."

The frosty blue eyes were fixed on a point on the ceiling of the living room. "Sounds like things are getting out of hand down there."

"No, no. Not that," Zito said. "It's just that something's come up. I can use a little help. Sort of the feminine touch. You know?"

Murph scowled, wrinkles dug white trenches around his eyes. "You sure you're not overdoing that female touch, Zito? Suppose someone—"

"Everything is under control. There's just one guy's gone crazy. I can handle everything. But I could use Mary's help."

The white-haired man nodded. "All right. But remember, there's been too much heat down there already. We don't want any more."

"There won't be any," the fat man promised.

Murph dropped the receiver back on its hook, replaced the phone in the drawer. He sat for a moment in the dimness of the room, then walked out to the glaring brightness of the sundeck. The girl rolled over, studied his expression.

"Zito. In Jackson City," he said in answer to her unspoken question. "He's got a job for you."

Mary pouted. "I just did a job for him. Besides, I don't like Zito. I don't like those eyes of his. They look like a snake's."

"You won't be going there to look into his eyes." Murph's tone was clipped, cold. "I don't know what's cooking there, but there mustn't be any heat from this job. I want you to see to it."

She nodded sulkily. "When do I go?"

"As soon as you can get ready."

She rolled over on her back. "You can't come with me?"

"You know better than that." He walked over, picked up his glass from the floor alongside the divan, sat down beside her.

"I can leave on the plane tonight," she said tentatively.

He grinned at her. "Tomorrow night will do. There's not that much hurry."

Chapter 25

Lou Stewart sat in the *Star's* editorial office, shook his head. "You really pulled the cork this time, Mal," he told Waters. "He won't let you walk away from this one."

"That's what I'm hoping," Mal told him. "I want him to try for me." He stuck a cigarette in his mouth. "He's got to get fancy when he does. That's when they make their mistakes. When they get fancy."

"They haven't made many mistakes," Stewart reminded him. "We've had a corner on that market. We've pulled some dillies."

"I have, you mean."

"You sure this isn't another one?"

Mal got up, paced the office. "I don't think so." He smoked thoughtfully for a moment. "I think that by using myself as bait—"

"Which is no way to break ninety."

Waters shrugged, stopped at the desk, leaned over it. "You don't use minnows when you're fishing for sharks." He squinted through the smoke that curled up into his eyes. "You still buy the theory that Zito had Benson killed and framed it to look like a suicide?"

"Sure."

Waters nodded, pulled his chair close to the editor's desk, sat down. "I was there right after the body was discovered. There was no sign of a struggle, nothing. Just a body in the bed, a hole in its head and its hand hanging down next to the gun. It looked real good."

"These boys are no amateurs," Stewart said.

"Neither was Tim Benson."

"No." The editor dug his pipe out of his pocket, started filling it with tobacco. "So?"

"So how do you account for the fact that a smart cop like Benson was caught flatfooted? So much so that they could blast him, leave no signs of a struggle?" Waters shifted to the edge of his chair, his cigarette forgotten in the corner of his mouth, a quarter inch of ash on its end. The movement dislodged the ash which floated to his lap unnoticed. "Another thing. Benson was in his undershirt. His pants and his gun were on a chair halfway across the room. What's it sound like to you?—bearing in mind Benson is aware that Judge Carter has just been knocked off by the boys."

"Sounds like he should have taken his gun to bed."

"Right. So maybe there was a woman. And when they tried to frame me, what did they use? Bonnie Peters. Same M.O."

The editor took a deep drag on his pipe, formed a blue cloud of smoke with pursed lips. "You think Bonnie put Benson on the spot?" He shook his head. "I don't buy it."

"Neither do I. It had to be somebody a lot more important. Somebody who had more than the ice list. Because Carter already had that." Waters removed the stub from between his lips, and lighted a fresh cigarette from the butt, which he crushed out. "Who would that be?"

Stewart shook his head. "Rumor is that Marcy Lewis had himself a girl. A lot of woman from the neck down, but—" He tapped his forehead, shook his head.

"The stripper?" Waters considered it, shook his head. "Benson wouldn't waste time with her. How about Zito? He got a girl?"

Stewart shook his head slowly, positively. "Zito isn't the romantic type. Even Mary Lister—" He broke off, squinted at Waters. "Spell it out for me again. Your idea, I mean."

"Benson was a pro. He had the ice list, but he wanted more. He was playing house with somebody who was able to get him far enough away from his gun so a couple of Zito's killers could get at him without a struggle—" He broke off. "That give you an idea?"

The editor leaned forward, pressed the intercom button. "Harley, dig me up the clips on Mary Lister. Yeah, that's the one." He snapped the button off. "You ever heard of Mary Lister, Mal?"

The former D.A. shrugged. "Sure. There's certainly been enough about her and her gang connections in the papers. But my office never had anything on her"—he broke off with a rueful grin—"at least that I ever heard of." He studied Stewart's face. "I had her pointed out to me one time. She was with Zito. She wouldn't be his girl?"

"That hot pepper would burn the fat boy to a crisp," Stewart said. "She's not his girl and she doesn't work for him. She's supposed to work for the Syndicate. Chances are she was bringing him some orders. The big boys don't like to put them in writing."

There was a knock on the door, Harley walked in with a folder. "Here's the package on Lister."

"Thanks, Tom," the editor told him. "Ask Bob to bring us some coffee. We're going to be here awhile." He turned to Mal. "How do you like yours?"

"Black."

"One black, one regular," he told the city editor. He waited until Harley had closed the door behind him, dumped the contents of the folder on the desk. They started to pore through the clippings.

"Quite a career," Mal said. "This gal is more lethal than the atom bomb."

Stewart nodded. "Makes a habit of turning up where one of the boys is about to check out."

"You think she sets them up?"

The door opened, a copy boy brought in two containers of coffee, set them on the desk, then withdrew.

Stewart snagged one of the containers, noted the scrawled B on the cover. "Yours," he grunted. "I don't know if she sets them up. But I think she does bring the word for the hit." He took the other container, dug the top off. "Before a guy can be hit in any territory, the Syndicate has to get an okay from the resident manager. Here it's Zito." He sipped at his coffee, burned his tongue and swore softly. "Or Zito can send for her to order some troops to do a job."

"You know these things. Why don't you blast them wide open?"

The editor took another cautious sip from his container. "Knowing and proving. That's two different things." He knocked the dottle out of the pipe bowl, stowed the pipe in his upper drawer. "All this makes for interesting conversation, Mal. But neither of us has a chance of going up against Zito. Believe me."

Mal indicated the pile of clippings on the desk. "One thing I'm curious about. As I told you, I had Mary Lister pointed out to me one time. She was with Zito. Would there be anything in there to give us an idea about the date she was in town?"

Stewart set his container down, fingered through the clippings, came up with one with an item circled with heavy pencil. "Here's one. She arrived in town on February sixteenth." He looked up, pursed his lips.

"Benson was killed when?"

The editor lifted the phone from its hook, muttered into it. He drummed on the table while he waited. Finally he nodded, replaced the phone. "Benson died on March 1."

"That's all I wanted to know." Waters gouged the top out of his container, took a deep swallow. "Now you know why Benson was so far from his gun when the killers walked in. It was no amateur chippy that put him on the spot. It was a girl who specializes in it."

The editor leaned back wearily. "Suppose it was. What do you propose to do about it?"

"A girl like that should know plenty."

"Maybe that's why she's still alive. She knows too much. They didn't make the same mistake with Bonnie Peters."

"What mistake?"

"Story is that if Mary Lister even catches cold, the big boys worry. She's supposed to have planted photostats and sworn statements naming names, dates and places in ten cities. Anything happens to her and they go to the F.B.I., states' attorneys—all the places where they'll do real good."

"Sounds like the kind of a girl I'd like to meet."

The editor grunted. "Maybe Benson got the same idea. Look what it got him. Why should she talk? She'd be pulling the whole thing down on her own head." Stewart shook his head. "Want some advice?"

"What?"

"Crawl back to Zito, if necessary. Tell him you've changed your mind about that assignment—"

Mal grinned wryly. "You sound like you're quitting."

"You mean I've got a choice?" Stewart leaned back wearily. "Mal, I'm an old man. I guess I didn't realize how old I was. I'm about through."

"I'm just starting."

The old man grinned at him. "I can almost remember when I felt like that. Come tell me about it ten years from now. Ten years of knocking your head against a stone wall can age you real fast." The grin faded, leaving a strained look. "If you live that long."

Chapter 26

Mary Lister arrived in Jackson City two days later. She was met at the airport by Joey, driven directly to Al Zito's office. The fat man sat propped behind his desk awaiting her. Mike, the wavy-haired gunman, sat in the chair at the end of the desk, the position formerly held by Joey. He sat admiring the high gloss on his fingernails, made no attempt to break in on the fat man's thoughts. He hadn't been far from Zito's elbow since the day Mal Waters had stalked into the office.

Lou Stewart knew of Mary Lister's arrival ten minutes after the limousine had whisked her away. A newspaper has a sensitive network that picks up reports of arrivals and departures as efficiently as it probes into the workings of the various departments and precincts of the city it covers. Little escapes it.

The police, too, maintain a careful check of incoming and outgoing personalities. So Marcy Lewis was also apprised of her arrival within minutes of the landing of the plane.

Both made hurried phone calls. Neither reached their party. Mal Waters wasn't at his apartment and Al Zito shook his head when Mike reached to answer the phone. He wasn't to be interrupted today.

Joey left the car in the basement garage of the building, brought the girl up in the private elevator. He preceded her to the door, rapped, pushed it open. His eyes narrowed imperceptibly at the sight of Mike in his chair, said nothing. He stepped aside as the girl floated by him, leaving a cloud of expensive perfume in her wake.

She stopped in front of the desk, her hand on her hip, looked down at Zito. "I'm beginning to feel like a commuter," she told him. "I thought you said when I blew town the last time things were under control?"

"Things happen," Zito grumbled.

She nodded. "Especially in Jackson City."

Zito waved her to a chair. "This won't take long," he promised. He waited until she was comfortable. "I want a guy set up for my boys. It's got to be good and clean." He shrugged expressively. "So who do I think of? Mary Lister?"

"Maybe you think of Mary Lister too often, Zito. The last one was only—"

He pasted a smile on his full lips. "Would I take any chances with you?" He shook his head sadly. "I still have a copy of that file you kept on my poor friend Eddie Ryan. I wouldn't want anything to happen to you."

"There's also a file on Benson and every other job I've done for you."

"I know. So unless this was watertight you think I'd ask you to handle it for me?"

"Who's the guy? Anyone I know?" she asked disinterestedly.

"Name's Waters. Used to be D.A. here. Hard man to do business with."

A frown marred the placidity of the girl's forehead. "Murph know who this guy is, Zito? Sounds like anything happens to him could cause heat. Murph says there's been too much heat here already."

The fat man bobbed his head sulkily. "I know, I know." He reached over, selected a cigar, denuded it of its wrapping. "There won't be any heat. Nobody's going to be surprised to find out this guy did the dutch." He rolled his eyes up from the cigar to the girl's face. "He was kicked out of office because of a drunk-driving accident where a girl was killed. They're fixing to indict him for death by auto and the bar association is getting ready to kick him out." He smiled. "Why wouldn't a guy like that knock himself off?"

The girl leaned back in her chair. "It doesn't sound like he has much of a future," she conceded. She opened her purse, brought out her cigarette holder, screwed a cigarette into it. "I guess it'll be all right."

The fat man turned his head to where Joey stood. "Anyone see you bring her in here?"

Joey shook his head. "I brought her in through the private entrance."

Zito gave him a curt nod, turned back to Mary Lister. "The faster we wrap this one up, the better."

Mary tilted the cigarette holder in the corner of her mouth. "Suits me. There's nothing in this town to make me want to stick around. That last one took too long." She smiled up at Joey as he held a lighter to her cigarette, took a deep drag. The smoke escaped through parted lips. "Long jobs make me nervous."

"That was a different thing. We had to wait for the hit on the judge before we could set Benson up. If anything went wrong on the judge's kill, it wouldn't have paid off. This is different. I just want a guy out of the way. But it's got to look like suicide."

"You got any ideas?"

Zito nodded. "Waters has gone crazy. He wants to get me so bad, he can't even see straight. He'll take any chances to get at me." He chewed on his cigar. "Any chances."

"Where do I get to meet this character?"

"I've got a funny feeling he won't wait for you to meet him. I think he'll be coming to meet you."

"You didn't tell me this guy was a swami with a crystal ball. I thought nobody was supposed to know I'm in town?"

The fat man's eyes were almost closed. "Nobody does. But I'll see to it he finds out." He looked past her to Joey. "Where's she staying?"

"Barkley Towers. I got her a rear suite. Nobody on either side."

"Barkley Towers?" The fat man puffed his lips in and out for a moment, "Charley Rodgers runs it, Right?"

Joey said yes.

Zito paused. "He can be trusted. How are you going to get her in and out?"

"Service elevator. Charley will handle it himself."

"Good. Get her over there and stay with her until you hear from me." Zito's eyes came back to the girl. "I'll get Waters up there. From there on, you know what to do."

"I know what to do. I just hope you know what you're doing." She got up from her chair, walked to the door, waited for Joey to open it, left without a backward glance.

Zito turned to Mike. "Get me the mayor on the phone."

Mike obediently trotted to the phone, dialed a number, waited until Ed London's secretary answered. "Put the mayor on," he told her in his low, intimate voice. "Mr. Zito wants to talk to him."

He handed the phone to the fat man, walked back to his chair.

Ed London's voice was disturbed. "Al, I don't like you calling here. There's always a chance—"

"I didn't ask you what you like. I got something that has to be done. I want it done right away."

The phone was silent for a moment. "What is it?"

"This daughter of yours. What's her name?"

"Rita?"

"She hasn't left for that trip yet, has she?"

"She leaves Monday."

"Good. I want her to arrange to see Waters before she goes."

The sharp intake of breath from the mayor's end was audible over the phone. "What for?"

"They're old sweethearts. Maybe she ought to say goodbye to him."

"Look, Al. I don't want my daughter involved in anything—"

The fat man snorted. "She's involved in everything. Right up to her neck. Where did the dough come from for that fancy school? For her clothes? For this trip? Maybe I figure it's about time she earned some of it."

"Al, I don't want to discuss this over the phone. I—"

"I told you I don't care what you want. It's what I want that counts. I want her to set up a meet with Waters." A hard note crept into his voice. "Tonight."

"If you say so."

"I goddam well do say so. And here's what she tells him. She's still got a soft spot for him even though she's marrying Max. She happened to overhear that a girl named Mary Lister is in town and that Zito wants her out of town because she knows something about Benson's suicide. You got that?"

"Al—"

"You got it?" the fat man snapped. "Or do I have to have that kid of yours brought in here and persuade her myself?"

"Let me do it. Leave the kid out of it, she—"

"Tonight. And you stay out of it. He wouldn't trust you as far as he can throw you. Her, he might." He slammed the phone down on its hook, glared at it. "What the hell's the matter with everybody? All I get is arguments."

"You ought to leave Waters to me," Mike told him. "There wouldn't be any complications."

"You'll get him," Zito growled. "But my way. It's too close to election for him to disappear or to get hit any way they can point a finger. But I'll tell you this. As soon as election's over, there are going to be a couple of things straightened out around here."

Mal Waters felt the old familiar tightening of the pit of his stomach when Rita London walked into the roadhouse. Ever since he had received her call, he was trying to imagine how she'd be dressed, what they'd say. She stopped and talked to a headwaiter who led her toward his booth.

She looked drawn, a faint blue tinged her eyes. The waiter stopped at the table. "Here's your party, sir." He stepped back discreetly as Mal stood, took the girl's hand.

"Bring us two rob-roys, please," he told the waiter.

Rita slid into the booth alongside him, gave no sign that she was aware he was still holding her hand. "I hope I didn't keep you waiting. I—I've never been here before and I made a wrong turn." She looked from his face down to the hand he still held, looked up into his face again when he released it.

"It's good to see you, Rita," he told her.

She dropped her eyes, long lashes veiled them. "I—I didn't want to go away without saying goodbye, Mal."

"You are going then?"

She couldn't look at him. "When I come back, Max and I are going to be married." She felt the hurt in his eyes, covered his hand with hers. "I'm sorry, Mal. Sorry that everything had to turn out like this."

He grinned wryly. "But not sorry enough to change it?"

She withdrew her hand. "It's too late for you and me now, Mal. Too many things have happened. Too many things have been said."

"I guess so. I guess I couldn't change things back to what they were even if I wanted to."

"And you don't?"

"I can't."

"I'll never understand you, Mal. We had everything we wanted. Now—" She looked around. "We can't even see each other without sneaking away to some place where nobody knows us."

"I guess I don't understand myself sometimes." He pulled out a pack of cigarettes, shook two loose. "It's just that—well, just that some day a situation arises where you have to take a stand." He held the pack out to the girl, noticed how her hand shook as she transferred a cigarette to her mouth. "I thought I was right—"

"You were wrong, Mal."

He held a light for her, lit his own cigarette. "No one has convinced me yet."

"But Mal—that footprint, all that proof you thought you had. It was nothing." She dropped her eyes. "Then that accident—"

He reached over, covered her hand with his. "I can't convince you. You can't convince me. I guess it's—"

"There's someone who can."

Mal studied her face. "Who?"

"There was a girl involved with Benson. I heard Dad and Max talking about her. Her name was Mary Lister."

"So?"

"Doesn't that prove that Benson was on the gang's payroll? You've read about her. She's a gang girl—"

Mal cut her short. "What'd they say about her?"

The redhead took a deep drag on her cigarette, let the smoke escape through half parted lips. "She's in town."

"Where?"

She looked startled at the vehemence of his question. "Mal, you're not going to—"

"Where is she?"

"Room 608 in the Barkley Towers. But you won't find her. I heard Max telling Dad that Zito wanted her out of town. He didn't want the Benson thing dragged out into the papers again."

Mal consulted his watch. "The next plane doesn't leave until nine. She can't leave before then. I can still make it."

She caught his sleeve. "Mal, don't—"

"I've got to, Rita." He signaled for a check, laid a bill on the table. The head-waiter came over, mystified. "But your drinks, sir."

"Something has come up. I've got to get back to town. This'll cover for taking up the table." He turned to Rita. "You have your car?"

The color drained from her face, leaving her lipstick a vivid gash in the pallor. "You go ahead, Mal—if you have to. I—I don't think we should leave together. Dad would be furious. Max mightn't understand."

He leaned over, kissed her cheek. "Goodbye, Rita." He got up, headed for the door. She watched him until he had pushed through to the sunshine outside.

"Goodbye," she told him. She sat for a moment, until the cigarette was smoked down to a small stub, crushed it out. Then she headed for the back of the room where a bank of phone booths lined the wall of an alcove.

Chapter 27

There was a knock on the door. Joey got up from the chair, walked to the door. Mary Lister appeared in the doorway to the bedroom beyond, waited.

"Yeah?"

Mike's low voice came through the door panel. "Let me in, Joey."

Joey opened the door, turned his back, walked back to his chair.

"Something?" Mary asked Mike.

The wavy-haired man nodded. "He took the bait. He'll be here sometime this evening." He looked over to where Joey was studying his fingernails. "Zito wants us to go back to his place. He don't want the pigeon to get scared." Joey looked up, nodded.

"Don't I get to know the score?" Mary complained. "What am I supposed to tell this character?"

Mike walked with small, mincing steps over to where she stood. "He thinks Zito has been trying to run you out of town because you know something about the Benson kill."

The girl snorted. "Who'd swallow that?"

"Waters. The way the boss has it rigged." He stopped in front of her. Suddenly, without warning, he brought back his fist, slammed it in her face. She staggered backward into the room. He followed her. There was a scream, the sound of two sharp slaps.

Joey stood up, stared at the open door. He debated the advisability of interfering, decided against it. Mike walked out of the room, nodded for Joey to follow him. As they walked out of the apartment, he could hear the girl cursing wildly in the bedroom.

"What was that all about?" he asked Mike in the hallway.

The wavy-haired man grinned. "Like she said, who'd believe Zito was trying to chase her out of town? Unless it looked like he was." He led the way to the rear stairs. "She looks like someone's been talking to her now."

"She'll scream to the boys in New York. I hear she has a hands off label signed personally by Murphy."

"It's not the first time she's been slapped around. Besides, she was sent here to do a job. It's all part of the job. She'll get over it."

Joey grinned pleasantly. "Maybe. Me, I'm just as glad it was you who did the slapping. Just in case she doesn't get over it."

Mal Waters followed the worn nap from the elevator to the door stenciled 608 in peeling gilt. He knocked, waited. On the second knock he heard signs of movement inside the apartment. The door opened an inch.

"Who are you looking for?" The voice was low, sultry.

"My name's Waters. I'm looking for Mary Lister?"

There was a slight pause. "What for?"

"It's about a mutual friend. A man named Benson. He's dead."

The door closed. There was the sound of a chain being removed, then it swung open. "Come in."

The sultriness of her voice through the half-opened door hadn't quite prepared him for what he saw. She was tall, full breasted. Her ash blonde hair was caught behind her ears, allowed to cascade down over her shoulders. Her right eye was swollen almost shut, beginning to discolor. There was a puffiness to her lips. "Who sent you here?"

"Nobody. I told you I'm a friend of Tim Benson's."

"So?"

"I know he wasn't mixed up in that graft mess. I want you to help me clear his name."

She ran the tips of her fingers along the swollen eye. "Why should I stick my neck out?"

He grinned wryly at the marks on her face. "Maybe you've got as much reason as I have to hate Zito."

"Maybe I have," she conceded. "But how do I know Zito didn't send you? How do I know this isn't a trap?"

Waters shook his head ruefully. "Zito and I don't see eye to eye. I used to be district attorney here. He set me up for a frame that cost me my job and my reputation."

"He's a rat." The girl turned, walked into the room, dropped onto the couch, stared up at him. "But this time he went too far. Nobody lays a hand on me and walks away from it."

"He did that? Himself?"

"He doesn't do his own dirty work. Two of his boys did it. He was trying to persuade me to get out of town."

"Why?"

She shrugged. "Why did he take the trouble to put you on the spot? Anybody who doesn't jump when he snaps his fingers, the fat pig tries to muscle." She touched the side of her face gently. "I have some friends, too."

"Why does he want you out of town?"

She picked a cigarette from the humidor on the coffee table, tapped it lightly. "You say you're a friend of Tim Benson's? Well, so was I. As a matter of fact, we were getting ready to go away together when they killed him." She held the cigarette for a light. "Zito had it figured that Tim was just using me to get the dope on Zito's operations. He killed him and ran me out of town."

"So?"

"So I'm crazy. I haven't been able to get Tim out of my mind. I ran when Zito put the heat on because I was scared—all I could think about was saving my own skin. But I found out that it wasn't that important without Tim. So I'm back. This time I'm not running."

"Maybe we're both after the same thing? To clear Benson's name?"

"Maybe. But I bury my own dead, mister. Sooner or later, I'm going to be able to prove that Zito had Benson killed. Nothing's going to stop me."

Waters grinned at her. "Zito can make a real college try. Alone, you haven't got a chance. But if we work together—"

"Who've you got behind you?"

The ex-D.A. shook his head. "Nobody."

"You're going up against Zito alone? Knowing there's nobody to back your play?" She studied his face. "You must know you can't count on the cops. Zito owns them body and—"

"I know. I'm not counting on anybody. Except me—and maybe you."

The girl turned the full power of her eyes on him. "You know you can't win."

"I know I can't lose. I've got nothing left to lose. Zito has everything. Even if I lose, I win."

Mary Lister licked at her full lower lip with the tip of her tongue. "You know? You're quite a guy. You might just do it." She got up, walked to the kitchenette, returned with a bottle and two glasses. "Let's drink to it."

"You'll tell me what you know?"

She set the glasses and the bottle on the coffee table. "I'd be crazy if I did if Zito has your number up." She lifted the bottle, tilted it over each of the glasses. "As soon as he found out—"

"He'll never find out. Besides look at the way he pushed you around. Next time he might decide to—"

Mary swirled the liquor around in the glass, shook her head. "He won't do anything if I keep my mouth shut. Knowing something and telling what you know are two different things." She held the glass up. "Let me think about it."

Waters picked up the second glass, clinked it against hers, drained it. The girl put hers to her lips, took a swallow. She coughed, the drink spilled down the front of her dress.

"Damn." She got up, brushed the wet front of the dress. "It won't take a second to get into something fresh." She smiled, headed for the bedroom.

Waters was on his second cigarette when she reappeared. She had changed into a tight-fitting dressing gown that clung revealingly to the well-rounded figure. "You don't mind?"

"I'm flattered."

She slid onto the couch at his side, he could feel her thigh against his, could smell the heavy perfume she wore.

"Will you pour this time?" She smiled at him.

He reached over, spilled two fingers of liquor into each of the glasses, handed her one of them. As he picked up his glass, he checked his wristwatch. She pouted at him. "I hope I'm not boring you."

"Not a bit." He held his glass up in a toast, drained it. "I'm just trying to figure how much time I have."

She frowned at him. "I don't get it."

"I figure it should take Zito's guns about fifteen minutes to get here from his place. So that only gives me ten minutes."

The girl pulled away from him, set her glass down. "What are you talking about?"

"This is the way you worked it with Benson, wasn't it? Gave him the sweet talk and kept him occupied until Zito could send his boys over. You think you've got a patent on that? It was done thousands of years ago when a dame named Delilah set up another sucker named Samson." He watched her face. "You should have read the end of that story, baby. Delilah got careless and Samson pulled the whole works down around her head."

She got up, stared down at him. "You're crazy."

"No, but you are if you thought you could work the exact same routine twice." He held up his hands to ward off an interruption. "Oh, I know the cops would play along with it and it would be neatly hushed up. But didn't you think I'd recognize it?" He pushed the coffee table away, stood up. He pulled a gun out of his waistband. "You managed to get Benson away from his gun—over onto the bed. I'll keep mine." He waved the gun. "Or I should say Barney Maurer's gun."

The girl's eyes jumped from his face to the muzzle of the gun and back.

"Wondering why I'd have Barney's gun?" He grinned bleakly. "Barney's dead. I killed him."

She opened her mouth, started to say something, caught her lower lip between her teeth.

"Zito knows all about it," Waters assured her. "He even got rid of the body for me. I took the gun as a souvenir."

Her voice was low, husky. "If you think this is some kind of a trap, why don't you get out of here?"

Waters shook his head. "I'm staying. Nobody can keep running forever. Sooner or later there's got to be a showdown. Tonight you and me—we're face to face with it."

"Look, you think you can lick Zito? Okay, so maybe you can. But you're not bucking Zito. You're bucking the Syndicate. No man ever did that and lived."

"There's always got to be a first time."

"They'll break you like they've broken anybody else who got in their way." She licked at her lips. "But if you're real smart, maybe I can help. Maybe I can—"

He shook his head. "Maybe they will smash me. But when I go, I'm taking all of you with me."

"Worm food, that's all you are. Talking big, but you're as dead right now as if you were lying at the bottom of a quarry. I've heard a lot of guys like you. Talk big, then scream when the big one has their name on it."

"You should know. You've fingered enough of them."

"Sure I've fingered them. Big men—ten times as big as you. I listened to them tell how big they were. They all look alike with a hole in their head."

"And you? How do you look the next morning when you look at yourself in the mirror, Mary? After you set up a guy like Benson who never did a thing to you?"

She shrugged. "That's what I get paid for. What's the difference if he got it a few years sooner or a few years later? Nobody ever gets out of this world alive."

"When you were in the bedroom, you called Zito. You told him you had me here. Right?"

She shrugged again. "It's like you said. You can't keep running. If it's not tonight, it's tomorrow." She ran the flat of her hand down the front of her gown, tightened it over her breasts, her flat stomach, along her thighs. "Why don't you stop running? You're not going to live forever. You've got ten minutes so why don't we—" She broke off as he pulled another gun from his pocket. "What are you going to do?"

He tossed the snub-nosed .38 across the floor to her.

"Take you all with me. Remember?"

She fought a losing battle to keep her eyes from the .38 on the floor. "You're talking crazy again."

"No. It makes real sense. You just finished saying you set up a lot of men for a killing. Big men, important men. Anybody who knows as much as you do—

the names of the gunmen, who ordered the kill, how it was done and why—they wouldn't ordinarily live long. They'd be sort of an unexploded bomb that could go off any time."

"So maybe I was just shooting my mouth off. Trying to sound important, trying to—" The color had drained from her face leaving her make-up garish patches against the pallor.

"But you weren't just talking. The reason you're still alive is because you not only know all these things, but you've planted that knowledge so that if anything ever happens to you, it'll get into the right hands."

She stared at him fearfully, realization dawning. "Now, wait a minute. You can't kill me. That would be cold-blooded murder."

"Not murder. Let's just say justifiable homicide. Maybe even self-defense." He indicated the gun on the floor. "That's fully loaded. You might get lucky and make the first one count. In that case you walk away from it. Or maybe you wouldn't be lucky. I'd consider that self-defense." He could feel the drops of perspiration on his upper lip, along his hairline. "Or maybe you'll try to keep me here until the guns get here. Then I'd have to shoot you whether you went for the gun or not. That would be justifiable homicide."

She licked at her lips, shook her head. "Please, Waters. Give me a break. I swear I—"

"I am giving you a break. A better one than you gave Benson. I'm letting you get to a gun. You made sure he couldn't."

"I didn't kill him. If you think I did, turn me in and—"

"And have Zito spring you before the ink was dry? Believe me, if I could swing this without having you on my conscience—"

"Don't do it. You'll never be able to get the picture out of your mind. I should know. I've awakened in the middle of the night seeing their faces—" She watched his eyes. "I should know, Waters."

Waters licked at his lips. "Get the gun."

She shook her head. "You can't make me." Her eyes became glued to his finger whitening on the trigger. "You can't make me."

"You haven't got much time."

She backed away from him. "It won't work. You think those letters will be mailed?" She shook her head. "Only if I was double-crossed by the Syndicate. They'll know Zito didn't—"

Waters motioned with the gun. "I already told you. This is Maurer's gun. They'll be able to identify the slugs from slugs on file at headquarters. You think they'll believe Maurer's dead?" He shook his head. "The Syndicate's finished." He checked his watch.

As his eyes left her, the girl dove for the gun at her feet. She snatched it up, and its muzzle was spitting orange flame as she spun around.

Waters heard a lamp smash near his head, felt the tug as a slug touched his shoulder. He squeezed the trigger of Maurer's gun, felt it jump in his hand.

The blonde was thrown back by the impact of the heavy slug. She tried to raise the .38 into firing position but it had become too heavy. It pulled her arm down, then dropped from nerveless fingers. She clasped her hands across the red stain that was spreading across the front of her gown.

Mal dropped his gun, rushed over to her, eased her to the floor. She stared up at him through half-closed eyes.

"I never figured you'd do it. I thought you were soft—"

"I had to, Mary. Zito and the Syndicate have to be stopped, and this was the only way I could do it." Her eyes were glazing over fast, the lids starting to close.

Mal checked his watch. Time was beginning to run out. He crossed to the phone, dialed the number of the *Star* and asked to be connected with Lou Stewart.

"Stewart? This is Mal Waters. Now listen and don't interrupt. We don't have much time. Barney Maurer just shot and killed Mary Lister at the Barkley Arms."

He could hear the sharp intake of breath at the other end of the phone.

"Zito and his boys will try to conceal the evidence but they haven't got a chance. Have Cleary get a couple of cops he can trust over here as soon as he can."

"Mother of God," the receiver whispered at him. "This will blow the whole thing wide open. Lister has evidence planted that can put every top man in the Syndicate in the chair, and—"

"They know that, too. So as soon as this leaks out, the Syndicate will be taking care of Zito and his boys personally before the letters hit the F.B.I. and the state's attorneys' offices and—" He checked his watch. He was cutting it too thin. "I'll check you later."

He dropped the receiver on its hook, wiped his forehead with the back of his hand. He had barely started for the door when the phone rang. He stared at it for a moment, lifted it and held it to his ear.

The soft, insinuating voice of Zito's wavy-haired gunsel came through the receiver. "Mary, this is Mike. We're coming up the service elevator. Get him away from his gun."

There was a click as the receiver was tossed on its hook. Waters hung up. Without a backward glance at the sprawled body of the girl, he left the apartment, headed for the back stairs.

The indicator on the service elevator started to climb from "one" to "two" as Mal Waters disappeared down the stairwell and headed for the street.

THE END

Frank Kane Bibliography
(1912-1968)

NOVELS

JOHNNY LIDDELL SERIES
About Face (1947; reprinted as
   Death About Face, 1948; The
   Fatal Foursome, 1958)
Green Light for Death (1949)
Slay Ride (1950)
Bullet Proof (1951)
Dead Weight (1951)
Bare Trap (1952)
Poisons Unknown (1953)
Grave Danger (1954)
Red Hot Ice (1955)
Johnny Liddell's Morgue (1956;
   stories)
A Real Gone Guy (1956)
Trigger Mortis (1958)
A Short Bier (1960)
Time to Prey (1960)
Due or Die (1961)
The Mourning After (1961)
Stacked Deck (1961; stories)
Crime of Their Life (1962)
Dead Rite (1962)
Hearse Class Male (1963)
Johnny Come Lately (1963)
Ring-a-Ding-Ding (1963)
Barely Seen (1964)
Fatal Undertaking (1964)
Final Curtain (1964)
The Guilt-Edged Frame (1964)
Esprit de Corpse (1965)
Two to Tangle (1965)
Maid in Paris (1966)
Margin for Terror (1967)

NON-SERIES
Liz (1955)
Key Witness (1956)
The Living End (1957)
Syndicate Girl (1958)
Juke Box King (1959)
The Line-Up (TV tie-in, 1959)
The Conspirators (1962)

AS BY FRANK BOYD
The Flesh Peddlers (1959)
Johnny Stacccato (TV tie-in; 1960)

SHORT STORIES
(Alphabetical Listing)
10,000 Witnesses to Murder
   (*Smashing Detective Stories*, Mar
   1953)
Big Steal [Johnny Liddell]
   (*Manhunt*, Dec 25 1954; *The Saint
   Mystery Magazine* (UK), Feb
   1962; *The Saint Mystery
   Magazine*, May 1962)
Bullets, Back to Back [Johnny
   Liddell] (*The Saint Detective
   Magazine*, Mar 1954; *The Saint
   Detective Magazine* (UK), Mar
   1955)
Clean-Up (*Manhunt*, May 1965)
Compliments of the El Paso Kid
   (*Western Action*, Mar 1942)
Dead Drunk [Johnny Liddell] (*The
   Saint Detective Magazine*, Spr
   1953; Ed McBain's Mystery Book
   #3, 1961)

Dead End [Johnny Liddell] (*Mike Shayne Mystery Magazine*, Oct 1959)

Dead Pigeon (*Manhunt*, July 1957)

The Dead Stand-In [Johnny Liddell] (*Manhunt*, Jan 1956)

Deadly Error (*Web Detective Stories*, May 1961)

Evidence [Johnny Liddell] (*Manhunt*, July 1953; *Manhunt* (UK), Feb 1954)

Finish the Job (*Manhunt*, Jan 1954)

Frame [Johnny Liddell] (*Manhunt*, Aug 1954)

The Frozen Grin [Johnny Liddell] (*Manhunt*, Jan 1953; *Giant Manhunt #1*, 1953)

Get-Away Deluxe (*Famous Detective Stories*, Feb 1953)

A Grave Matter [Johnny Liddell] (*Web Detective Stories*, Aug 1960; *Argosy*, May 1964)

The Great Pretender (*Mike Shayne Mystery Magazine*, July 1960)

The Icepick Artists [Johnny Liddell] (*Manhunt*, Dec 1953; *Tough Stories Magazine*, Feb 1956)

Insurance (*Accused*, Mar 1956)

It's Murder (*Verdict*, June/July, 1954)

Keeper of the Killed [Johnny Liddell] (*Verdict*, Sep 1953)

Key Witness (*Manhunt*, Aug 1956)

Lead Ache [Johnny Liddell] (*Manhunt*, May 1954)

Live Blonde—Dead Millionaire [Johnny Liddell] (*Trapped Detective Story Magazine*, Aug 1957)

Louis or Schmeling? [with Ben Feingold] (*Champion Sports Magazine*, July 1938)

Make it Neat (*Manhunt*, Aug 1955)

Morgue-Star Final [Johnny Liddell] (*Crack Detective Stories*, July 1945)

Murder Feeds the Flames (*Crack Detective Stories*, Sep 1946)

Music to Die By [Johnny Liddell] (*Argosy*, Apr 1962)

A Package for Mr. Big [Johnny Liddell] (*The Saint Detective Magazine*, Sep 1954; *The Saint Detective Magazine* (UK), Oct 1955)

Pass the Word Along (*Manhunt*, Apr 1960)

The Patsy (*Mike Shayne Mystery Magazine*, Aug 1957; *Mike Shayne Mystery Magazine* (Australia), Sep 1957)

Payoff [Johnny Liddell] (*Manhunt*, Mar 1953; *Giant Manhunt #1*, 1953)

Play-and-Slay Girl (*Double-Action Detective Stories*, 1954)

Play Tough [Johnny Liddell] (*Manhunt*, Mar 1965)

Putt it There! (*Complete Sports*, Jan 1950)

Red, Hot and Dead (*Suspect Detective Stories*, Oct 1956)

Return Engagement [Johnny Liddell] (*Manhunt*, Feb 1955; *The Saint Mystery Magazine* (UK), July 1962)

The Rumble (*Mike Shayne Mystery Magazine*, Feb 1957; *Mike Shayne Mystery Magazine* (Australia), Mar 1957; *Mike Shayne Mystery Magazine* (UK), July 1957)

Slay Belle (*Manhunt*, Aug 1953)

Slay Upon Delivery [Johnny Liddell] (*Crack Detective Stories*, Jan 1946)

Sleep Without Dreams (*Dames,
    Danger, and Death* ed. Leo
    Margulies, Pyramid, 1960)
Suicide (*Rue Morgue, I*, ed. Rex
    Stout & Louis Greenfield,
    Creative Age, 1946)
Thirty Pieces of Lead (*Crack
    Detective Stories*, Sep 1945)
The Uncertain Corpse (*Scarab*, Nov
    1950)
With Frame to Match (*Come
    Seven, Come Death*, ed. Henry
    Morrison, Pocket 1965; *Edgar
    Wallace Mystery Magazine* (US),
    Mar 1966)

NON-FICTION
Anatomy of the Whiskey Business
    (1965)
Travel is for the Birds (1966; travel)
Louis S. Rosenstiel: Industry
    Statesman (2 vols, 1966)

www.ingramcontent.com/pod-product-compliance
Lightning Source LLC
Chambersburg PA
CBHW071746190726
48292CB00003B/884